"I begin to think you are my soul..."

Was that true? Caleb wondered. It was what Flora wanted to hear. The extravagant words came so naturally to his lips that he found it impossible to qualify them in his mind. This woman was so alive, so vulnerable, she blurred the boundary between truth and deception.

"Let's have a late supper," she said. "I'll tell Cato to light the fire in my bedroom."

"I—yes. That sounds lovely."

He dangled between opposing wishes, between desire and conscience. On the road, he had vowed to avoid another visit to her bedroom, where the boundary between truth and deception was certain to vanish. He had hoped for a chance to resume the talk they had been having when Major Beckford's emissaries had interrupted them two weeks ago.

But Flora only wanted to talk about, think about love...

By Thomas Fleming

FICTION

*Dreams of Glory
*The Officers' Wives
*Promises to Keep
*Rulers of the City
*Liberty Tavern
The Good Shepherd
The Sandbox Tree
Romans Countrymen Lovers
A Cry of Whiteness
King of the Hill
The God of Love
All Good Men

NONFICTION

1775: Year of Illusions
The Forgotten Victory
The Man Who Dared the Lightning
The Man from Monticello
West Point
One Small Candle
Beat the Last Drum
Now We Are Enemies

*Published by
WARNER BOOKS

DREAMS OF GLORY

OF GLORY

Thomas Fleming

WARNER BOOKS

A Warner Communications Company

WARNER BOOKS EDITION

Copyright © 1983 by Thomas Fleming
All rights reserved.

Cover art by Jim Dietz

Warner Books, Inc.,
666 Fifth Avenue,
New York, N.Y. 10103

 A Warner Communications Company

Printed in the United States of America

First Printing: May, 1983

10 9 8 7 6 5 4 3 2 1

Here sometimes the Great God makes Darkness His Pavillion; His footsteps are in the great Deep, and we cannot sound the Depths of His providential Actings. . . .

—GILBERT TENNENT

DREAMS OF GLORY

one

It was almost midnight on the thirtieth day of January in the year 1780. Flora Kuyper shivered in her canopy bed, on the icy second floor of her gambrel roofed farmhouse in the town of Bergen, just across the river from New York. Outside the diamond-paned window, the frozen earth cracked, echoing like a musket shot across the eerie white-dark landscape. The house heaved and groaned in the grip of the northeast wind. *Crack* went the earth again. Flora shuddered, wondering if it were an omen. She seized the playing cards from the mahogany table by her bed and quickly dealt thirteen of them, facedown. Holding her breath, she turned up the thirteenth card. It was the Queen of Spades.

Death. In Louisiana, that green hot world south of winter where she had been born, Flora had seen the

9

women sit in their shuttered parlors, laying out the cards while a fever victim struggled for breath in the next room. Mother Levesque, the juju woman, her immense black face a sweating parody of the moon, would turn up the thirteenth card. Flora remembered the groans and cries when the Queen of Spades cast her baleful eye at the dim ceiling.

Flora drew another card from the pack, remembering that the Queen of Hearts could break the spell. She turned it over. The Jack of Spades, the black Queen's leering accomplice, confronted her.

There was no Mother Levesque in Bergen, New Jersey, to curse the cards, to summon the spirits of Africa to fight the evil jinn of America. Flora was alone in this frozen world, where winter had become perpetual. The Great Cold, the Americans were calling it. Old men and women, people like Jacob and Mary DeGroot, her nearest neighbors, said they had never seen anything like it in their lives. For thirty consecutive days now, the temperature had not risen above zero. For a week at a time, stupendous blizzards had howled out of the north; huge drifts had blocked the roads. More than once, desperate men knocked at Flora's back door to beg food and shelter. They were deserters fleeing the American army camp in Morristown, forty miles away. They told stories of men being buried in their tents by the storms and dug out days later, frozen, dead.

Footsteps on the first floor. A door slammed. Angry African voices quarreling. Flora reached for a green bottle on her night table. She poured its viscous contents onto a spoon and let five drops fall into a glass of water. She drank it quickly as a man's booted feet mounted the stairs. A sweet calm enveloped her. She thanked God—or the devil—for laudanum.

The bedroom door opened; Caesar stood there in his blue-and-buff uniform. Firelight and candle glow mingled on the intense blackness of his face, with its wide flat nose and proud thick-lipped mouth. Flora had seldom seen a Negro as black as Caesar. Perhaps that was where her love for him had begun—with a wish to be devoured, consumed by his blackness, to escape her lying white skin.

Flora sensed his unease, his dislike of her bedroom. He was so big. The enormous head, the massive neck and shoulders, belonged to nature, Africa. She told herself that he had a right to feel out of place in this feminine room, with its royal-yellow wallpaper, its glazed-chintz curtains, the four-poster bed with its camlet hangings and parti-colored quilts. She regretted the contempt with which Caesar regarded these luxuries. She remained confident that she could persuade him to admire beautiful furniture, clothes, paintings, even if they were made by white people.

Was she right? Could she ever change this huge, willful creature? Flora suddenly remembered what her husband, Henry Kuyper, used to call Caesar: the brute. Henry had used the term affectionately, even admiringly, as he always spoke of Caesar. But a cruel meaning had lurked within the word. Too often lately, it had become the only meaning.

"I've decided to go," Caesar said.

"Why, *why*?" Flora said.

"I told you why—for the ten guineas."

"We have enough money."

"No one ever has enough money."

Those last words reminded Flora of another man,

with a similar attitude toward money. Caesar thought she was still thinking of the risk he was taking to return to the American camp in Morristown.

He smiled and sat down on the bed, shoving the cards aside. Caesar was not superstitious. He believed in nothing but himself, his size, his strength. Luck, devils, God—they were all nonsense compared to the power of his body, his will, the shrewdness of his brain. Flora knew he was wrong about the devils and God; she had no doubt both existed; she feared the devils and despised God. Flora even knew that Caesar was not as shrewd as he wanted her—and himself—to believe. No man who spends the first twenty-two years of his life as a slave, forbidden to read, unable to write, could learn enough to outthink the treacherous white world he was determined to defy.

"I've come back every other time. Why do you still worry?"

"The cards are bad."

"The hell with the cards."

With a flick of his hand he swept the cards off the bed. "When are you going to realize that you finally have a man who's not going to disappoint you?"

"We should have gone in the fall. We'd be in New Orleans now. Safe—happy."

"We would have been poor. I don't believe the poor are ever happy."

"My father was poor. I never knew a happier man."

Caesar curled his lip. "I'm sick of hearing about this marvelous father of yours."

For a moment she was afraid of him. She stared at his hands, with their wide pink palms and thick black

12

fingers. She remembered what those hands had done in another bedroom only a few feet from this one. She remembered last night's dream, Henry Kuyper's contorted face on the pillow, the dream she had every time Caesar slept in the house.

She was glad she had taken the laudanum. It allowed her to think about the dream without weeping.

"You said you'd buy your discharge. Once you had that, you could stay here at the farm."

"I can buy that anytime I want it. I'm going back for the hundred guineas they offered me to find Twenty-six."

Bits of blowing snow scratched against the windowpane. For a moment Flora saw William Coleman, the man Caesar called Twenty-six, shivering in an icy tent somewhere in the American camp at Morristown. She simultaneously rejoiced in his agony—and pitied him. She was afraid to tell this to Caesar. He thought Twenty-six was a stranger to her, an impersonal number in their network.

"It's too dangerous. If Beckford even suspected what you're doing, he'd have you killed."

"Beckford worships me. He almost kissed me when I brought him word of the raid Washington was planning on Staten Island."

"The Americans would hang you for that."

Caesar shook his head contemptuously. "I'm their one hope of finding Twenty-six."

"You don't have time to find him," Flora said. "Beckford tells me they're ready to start the mutiny whenever he gives the signal."

Caesar's mouth curled skeptically. "Why hasn't he given it?"

"General Knyphausen doesn't approve of one part of the plan."

"I think maybe Beckford's mutiny is not as ready as he says it is. He still seems to be trying to stir up the troops. Last week a new chaplain preached a sermon that practically told the men to attack the officers. Has Beckford mentioned him? His name is Caleb Chandler. I'll bet twenty guineas he's working for the British."

Flora shook her head. The name Caleb Chandler meant nothing to her. "If the mutiny succeeds, the war will be over. I want to be in New Orleans before it ends. Before Beckford can stop me."

"How can he stop you? You're an independent woman. You own this farm now thanks to Caesar. You're not going to forget that part of it, are you? No matter how much money or power that red-coated pig gets?"

"No," Flora said.

She could not take her eyes off Caesar's hands. Doubled into a fist, one of them could smash her face. Together they could seize her throat and snuff out her life. She, too, would become a bloated face on a pillow.

For a moment Flora wanted to tell Caesar that it was not Major Walter Beckford, it was the other man, Twenty-six, who would stop her. Who would claim her. But it was impossible. If she told him the truth about Twenty-six, Caesar would never go to New Orleans with her. He might even let those hands turn her into that ugly face on the pillow. She did not want to die that way.

"Maybe I ought to have that certificate freeing me before we leave for New Orleans," Caesar said.

"I'll give it to you now."

"No. It'd make talk when you registered it. There's too much talk around here already. Cato and Nancy with their shit about sin and damnation. They're born slaves. I'd still like to sell them before we go."

"I'll sell no one," Flora said. "You'll never get that certificate if you mention such a thing again. I might even sell you—"

Caesar's right hand leaped like a snake toward her face. It stopped a fraction of an inch from her cheek. She could feel its heat, as if it had a mouth, a soul of its own. Then it fell back onto the bed. "You'll always own me," he said. "And I'll always own you. Come downstairs and sing me one last song."

He helped her into her night robe and led her through the cold dark house by the light of a single candle. He put the candle on the harpsichord and stood beside her while her fingers found the familiar keys and her voice repeated the words she had whispered to him after their first time together.

> *Plaire à celui que j'aime*
> *Est ma seule victoire*
> *Et mes talents pour lui*
> *Sont des noveaux tributs.*

On that blazing July day, two and a half years ago, Caesar had believed her when she told him that she had never spoken or sung those words to the man he hated, the man who owned him, Flora's husband, Henry Kuyper. She did not know then that the loving words were Henry Kuyper's death sentence. She did not know they would echo through the house as she looked down on her husband's dead face.

15

As Flora sang the last line in her delicate contralto and the final notes dwindled inside the harpsichord's mahogany frame, Caesar put on the black woolen watch coat that had once belonged to Henry Kuyper. "Sing it again," he said. He wrapped a scarf around his face, covering his nose and mouth. "Keep singing it until you're sure I can't hear it anymore."

Tears streamed down Flora's cheeks. She sat there, playing and singing the song long after the front door closed and Caesar began his frigid forty-mile journey to rejoin the American army in Morristown.

two

"Chaplain, do you think I'm damned?"

The feverish eyes pleaded for hope. Caleb Chandler knelt beside eighteen-year-old Private Stephen Sprague of the 4th Connecticut Regiment and struggled to supply it.

"None of us can know the answer to that question," he said. "All we can do is strive to merit the reward God has promised those whose faith in Him is pure."

The northeast wind moaned through the surrounding woods. To Caleb Chandler it was a gloating, almost malicious sound.

"But you said—you said in your sermon last week— that maybe the Lord God had turned his face from America. We—wasn't worthy of salvation. Don't that mean we're all damned?"

"No—no. I wasn't speaking of men like you—good soldiers. You're too sick to wrestle with the mystery of God's intentions. Trust Him. Place yourself in His hands and ask Him to restore your health."

The young eyes searched Caleb Chandler's face for another moment. The chaplain tried to meet their challenge, but his mind was elsewhere, searching a face that was totally different from this innocent boy's—a man's face, craggy, aristocratic, commanding, with hollowed, haggard eyes and a deep-cleft chin, the face, Caleb had always thought, of a heroic archangel. But those wise, resourceful eyes did not respond to his stare; the proud, knowing mouth did not curve into a welcoming smile. Instead the mouth gaped; the glazed eyes saw nothing. Blood oozed from the slashed throat of the Reverend Joel Lockwood.

"Could you get me a drink of water, Chaplain?"

Private Sprague had closed his eyes, as if he did not like what he had seen on Caleb Chandler's face. Caleb filled a tin cup that dangled from the side of the nearby water barrel and held it to the soldier's parched, swollen lips. His eyes remained closed. Was it a reproach?

Caleb tried to pray for the dying boy. He tried to summon the memory of the sweet sense of God's mercy, the awesome awareness of His justice, that had filled his youthful soul when he listened to the Reverend Joel Lockwood's sermons in the white-walled church in Lebanon, Connecticut. But all the chaplain could see was Lockwood's dead face on the floor of the New Jersey tavern.

Liberty Tavern. That was the name of the place. The Reverend Joel Lockwood, who had confidently told Caleb Chandler that America could not lose the war because God had chosen her people to demonstrate the great truth, that liberty was the handmaid of grace; Joel Lockwood, who had declared that the war would prove for all time the power of grace, its ability to inspire the virtue of an entire people; Joel Lockwood, whose subtle mind used to imagine liberty and grace as dancers on a divine stage, so intimately, ecstatically joined that only God's eye could distinguish them, had cut his throat in Liberty Tavern, after three years as a chaplain in the Continental Army of the United States of America.

Private Sprague's breath grew shallow. The fever was devouring the last of his strength. Around him groaned and tossed at least fifty other men with the same disease. Camp fever, the army doctors called it. They did not know its cause or its cure. The sick men lay on straw pallets on the floor of the one-room log building that served as the hospital of the Continental Army in Morristown. As the flames dwindled in the huge stone hearth, winter crept into the room like an intimation of death.

Caleb threw more wood on the fire. He wrapped his cloak around him and prodded a fat orderly snoring in an anteroom. "I'm going now, Lodge. Watch that fire. Those men must be kept warm."

"Aye, Chaplain, aye," Lodge muttered sleepily. "Did y'hear the latest from Philadelphia? Stopped printin' money. They might's well. Nobody'll take the stuff. I can remember when you could tar and feather a man who wouldn't take Continental money. But them days is long gone, Chaplain. New days, new ways, some say. Sad days, bad ways, I say."

Lodge was from Massachusetts. He had been in the army since the Battle of Bunker Hill in 1775.

When Lodge talked about the glorious days of '75 and '76, he made it sound like the war had lasted fifty years. Soldiers of those good old times were all heroes and every civilian was a patriot. Vanished now, gone as totally as ancient Sparta, to hear Lodge tell it.

"Watch that fire," Caleb said. "Give some rum to Private Sprague. It may help."

"Ain't a drop of rum left in the camp, Chaplain. Mark my words, it's going to tear this army apart if they don't do somethin'. Not that the great man from Virginia gives a tarnation. He's sittin' there in his mansion, drinkin' his port wine."

Caleb nodded, tacitly agreeing with Lodge's criticism of George Washington. "When more rum arrives, give some to Sprague. I'm sure we'll get more in a day or two."

"Day or two will be judgment day for Sprague. You know that, too, Chaplain."

Lodge hoisted his squat frame erect. His foot struck something against the wall. *Clunk.* An empty bottle rolled out of the darkness.

"No rum for dying men but plenty for the hospital orderlies, is that it?" Caleb said.

"I bought that rum with my own money, Chaplain," Lodge said. "A man can't live at this work in this cold without rum. Why waste it on these pukers? They die just as fast with as without it."

For a moment Lodge's greedy whine personified everything that was wrong with Caleb Chandler's world. Although he was only half Lodge's weight, Caleb lifted the orderly off the floor and slammed him against the wall. "I said give Sprague rum!" he roared. "Or I'll come back here with a horsewhip and take the skin off you."

"Yes, sir, Chaplain. I'll give it to'm," Lodge gasped. "I'll give it to'm reglar."

Caleb Chandler flung open the door of the log hospital and strode into the darkness. The wind struck him as if it were a solid object, a slab of ice, battering his entire body. Maybe he deserved it, deserved punishment, for losing his temper again. There was no point in pounding underlings like Private Lodge against the walls. The orderly would only complain to the army's medical director and one more officer would be convinced that Caleb Chandler was either a fool or a madman. The chaplain stumbled down a path cut through the waist-high drifts and reached the road that led from Jockey Hollow, where the enlisted men and junior officers were encamped, to his own quarters near the Morristown green, two and a half miles away. It was hard for Caleb to believe that six short months ago he had stood before the president of Yale College, receiving his diploma, proud of having turned his back on a half-dozen lucrative pulpits to volunteer as a chaplain in the Continental Army.

He had been responding once more to the example of the Reverend Joel Lockwood, who had resigned as pastor of the church in Lebanon in 1776 and marched to war as chaplain of the 4th Connecticut Regiment. Lockwood had taught Caleb the Latin and Greek he had needed to pass his entrance examinations to Yale. He had persuaded Caleb's father and older brothers to pay his way for the honor of having a minister in the family. Even then it had been understood that Caleb would enter the church.

Now, after four months in Morristown, Joel Lockwood's suicide no longer seemed incomprehensible to Caleb Chandler. He understood why anyone, even a man whose faith had once been as vibrant as Joel Lockwood's, could slide into despair if he were a member of the Continental Army of the United States of America in the fifth year of the rebellion against King George III.

Instead of the band of brothers, committed to the defense of liberty, that Caleb had pictured, the army was closer to a pack of surly slaves, chained to their duty by their enlistment papers, the chains reinforced by rings of sentries with bayonets at the ready. Beyond the boundaries of the camp the people were indifferent, even hostile to the army. Farmers refused to accept the depreciated Continental currency. For whole days, sometimes longer, the army commissary had not a scrap of food to issue to the men. Ugly rumors drifted up from Philadelphia, where the Continental Congress, the army's legal masters, sat and debated and occasionally legislated. Scarcely a congressman was not in the pay of America's powerful but dubious ally, France, went one story. They were conniving to let the war remain a stalemate in America, pinning down half of England's army, while France carved off juicy chunks of the British Empire in the West Indies, Africa, India. Another story, which dovetailed neatly with the first one, portrayed the whole Congress as a pack of profiteers, busily making their fortunes, while the army starved. From the South came even worse rumors. Georgia had surrendered and South Carolina was planning to do the same. A British army was about to capture Charleston.

Then came a blow that seemed direct from God's hand. Early in December it had begun to snow. Caleb watched the soldiers, many of them shoeless, up to their knees in icy drifts, struggling to build log huts. On January 2, 1780, the intermittent storms became a blizzard that lasted four incredible days. By that time the army was a freezing, starving mob. The men swarmed into the countryside, robbing local farmers at gunpoint. Since that storm the temperature had not risen above zero. The northeast wind had never ceased its punishment. The men were on half, often one-third rations. Some said another blizzard or even another week of cold would be the end of the army.

Failure, defeat, was engulfing America. Why? There had to be a reason. Was the army—above all the enlisted men—the victim of a fundamental spiritual flaw? A moral inertia traceable to the character of America's leaders? Caleb Chandler had begun to think that was the answer.

By now the chaplain was well past the center of Morristown's long rectangular green; he was approaching the Ford mansion, George Washington's headquarters. Was this man, as rich as any English earl, the source of America's, the army's corruption? John Hancock of Boston was as wealthy as George Washington, but his money had come from trade. Washington's fortune was in land, worked by hundreds of black slaves. How could a slaveowner lead a revolution in the name of liberty?

When Caleb Chandler had raised the question at Yale, his classmates had laughed in his face. The best people in Connecticut owned slaves; there were thousands of them in neighboring New York and New

23

Jersey. Rome and Greece, the great civilizations of antiquity, sanctioned slavery. Caleb had dropped the subject. It did not seem important enough to argue about, in the warm comfort of his room on Chapel Street. He never dreamed the question would haunt him in the freezing hell of Morristown.

Caleb trudged into the wind, brooding on George Washington. His ownership of slaves was not the only reason the chaplain saw him as an evil influence on the army. More than once, in Lebanon, he had heard Joel Lockwood's best friend, William Williams, one of the Continental Congressmen for Connecticut, criticize Washington for his attempts to mold the army in his own aristocratic image, with extravagant pay and pensions for the officers. Worst of all, Williams had fumed, Washington, like most Southerners, despised New England men.

The Ford mansion's windows were still glowing. Often, on his way back from the hospital, Caleb had heard drifting from the house, the sort of hearty laughter created by port wine and a full belly. Now he saw an oblong of light appear in the front door. A man carrying a lantern. Caleb heard jovial goodnights. The lantern bobbed toward him.

A gust of wind burst under Caleb's cloak. He clutched at the flapping cloth. His toes, his fingers, were totally numb. He stopped and stamped his feet, hoping to restore a little circulation. The wind faltered for a moment and he heard something else: the groan of a human being. The wind whirled and died again. Caleb stood there, his heart pounding. *Uhhhhh*. There is was again. An unmistakable, separate sound. A death groan. It came from the deep snow in the

24

center of the green. But he could see nothing in the darkness.

"Sir," he called to the man with the lantern. "Sir, could you bring your light over here? I think there's someone hurt nearby."

The man approached. Muffled to his ears in a greatcoat of brown fur, he might have been a bear. They stood together for a moment while the wind gusted and died again. Once more it came: *Uhhhh-hhhhh*. The groan.

Caleb seized the lantern and plowed his way through the unpacked snow on the green. The man in the fur coat followed him, calling somewhat querulously, "Sir, that's my light—"

They both stopped. Caleb, holding the lantern at arm's length, looked down at the outline of a soldier almost covered by blowing snow. A bayonet protruded from the center of his chest.

Caleb dropped to his knees beside him. "Who did this to you?"

The man's lips worked. He gasped what sounded like numbers. "Forty—Twenty-six." He tried to say something else, but it was beyond his strength.

"Let's get him into the guard hut," Caleb said to his fur-clad companion.

"I think he's dead."

"A fire may revive him."

They picked up the possibly dead, certainly dying man and labored through the drifts to the hut in front of Washington's headquarters. "Halt," barked the sentry on duty. "Who goes there?"

"There's been a man stabbed," Caleb shouted.

"D'Estaing," growled the sentry.

That was the name of a French admiral. It was also

the sign for the night. What was the countersign? Caleb could not remember. "Lafayette," he guessed.

"Wrong," said the soldier. *Click* went the hammer as he cocked his gun.

"I'm Caleb Chandler, chaplain of the Second Connecticut Brigade."

"And I'm Hugh Stapleton, congressman from New Jersey," said the man in the fur greatcoat.

"You may be the Lord Almighty and the Archangel Gabriel," the sentry said. "But put your hands up or by Christ I'll make a lane through you."

They put up their hands. The corpse—by now Caleb was sure the man was dead—thudded to the snow. The sentry called for the officer in command. He and five other members of General George Washington's Life Guard came stumbling out of the hut, rubbing sleep from their eyes. Their half-awake state did not say much for the discipline of these picked troops, who were supposed to protect the commander in chief. Two of the soldiers carried the corpse into the hut. The officer ordered Caleb and Congressman Stapleton to follow them. "Keep your hands up," he said.

Inside, Stapleton began to seethe. "Damnation, sir, will you allow me to lower my hands? Or must I send one of your men to General Washington to identify me? I've just finished dining with him."

The soldiers paid no attention to the congressman. They were staring at the dead man on the floor before the fire. The sheen of snow that had covered his face was melting, revealing skin of deep, luminous black. He was huge. His shoulders were twice the width of any man's in the hut. He wore buff breeches and a dark blue coat with buff facings on the cuffs and lapels—the uniform of the New Jersey brigade.

"It's Caesar. Caesar Muzzey," one of the privates said.

"I was down to the old regiment yesterday," another private said. "They told me he'd gone over the chain."

"Gone over the chain?" Huge Stapleton said.

"Deserted," Caleb translated.

"Then what the hell was he doing on the green in his uniform?" the lieutenant asked.

The first private smirked, revealing several gaps in his teeth. "Caesar Muzzey came and went pretty much as he pleased."

"Like the rest of you damn Jerseymen," the lieutenant said. "Just because you're close to home, you think you can walk out of camp whenever you feel like it."

The first private stared somberly down at the dead man. "That wasn't it with Caesar. Most officers was scared of him. You can see why. Look at the size of the black bastard."

"Get him out of here," the lieutenant said. "He's making a mess."

Dark rivulets of melting snow, suggesting streams of blood, ran from the corpse across the raw wood floor. The two New Jersey privates picked up Caesar Muzzey and lugged him out the door of the hut.

"What will be done about this, Lieutenant?" Caleb asked.

The lieutenant shrugged. "What can be done? One of his own kind probably killed him. Down in Delaware, where I come from, they're always cutting each other up over wenches, gambling debts, and

27

the like. I lost one of my prime bucks in '77. Throat slit from ear to ear."

"You mean the army will make no investigation?" Caleb said.

"That's not for me to say," the lieutenant grunted. He was a heavyset, thick-bodied man, probably in his late twenties.

"Would you be more eager to find the murderer if Muzzey were white?" Caleb asked.

"Why, I don't know," the lieutenant said, scratching his head morosely. "My orders are to protect General Washington, not guard every square foot of Morristown. If some damned deserter gets himself stabbed in the dark, why should it be my affair, whether he's white or black?"

"I wonder if you really mean that, Lieutenant," Caleb said. "I'm afraid you're like most Americans. You look down on black men because so many of them are slaves."

The lieutenant stared at Caleb with growing astonishment.

"Caesar was a human being, Lieutenant," Caleb continued. "With the same right to life and liberty as the rest of us. I sometimes wonder if the troubles under which we're laboring are not being sent by God to awaken us to our indifference to our black countrymen."

"Go sing that song to General Washington," the lieutenant said. "I only own six slaves. He's got a good two hundred down in Virginia."

"There are men in America, even men in Congress, who don't think everything General Washington does is right. I wouldn't be surprised if Mr. Stapleton here is one of them."

Caleb knew that New Jersey usually voted with New England against the Southerners in the Continental Congress. He had heard William Williams tell Joel Lockwood that Jerseymen were "sound." But Chandler saw no welcoming agreement on Hugh Stapleton's handsome face.

"Chaplain," he said, "I own fifty slaves and the fact has never troubled my conscience for a single instant."

Everyone in the hut grinned his approval. Caleb heard an inner voice whisper, *Fool*. It was not the first time he had heard it. During his years at Yale the secret voice had often made him writhe and sweat. But he clung to his indignation. "I'm sorry to hear you say that, Congressman. I hope someday to have a chance to change your opinion. Meanwhile, a full report of this crime will be on its way to William Williams, member of Congress from Connecticut. He happens to be one of my neighbors in Lebanon. Mr. Williams not only feels as I do about Negro Americans, he concurs with my opinion that the officers of this army have much too callous an attitude toward the enlisted men. I wonder if you'd be so indifferent, Lieutenant, if an officer had just been found murdered?"

"You can bet your ass I wouldn't be, Chaplain," the officer snapped. "An officer murdered is mutiny. Which more than a few of us begin to think is the aim of those sermons you've been preaching."

"My aim is justice. An end to the soldiers' sufferings."

"Who do you think is responsible for starving this army? The officers? I ain't had a bite of fresh meat in two weeks. But I bet your friend Congressman Williams has had his share of prime beef in Philadelphia. You can report whatever you please to him, Chaplain. If you think anyone in this army's going to stand up and salute at the word 'Congress' your noodle's loose."

The lieutenant shifted his gaze from Caleb to Hugh Stapleton as he spoke. He meant his defiance for both of them.

"There are men in Congress who want to help the army," Stapleton said. "I'm one of them."

"Yeah, I know," the lieutenant said. "We all know what's happening in Philadelphia. Those goddamn cheapskate Yankees are the ones who're starving us. While they and their cronies get richer by the day."

The lieutenant glared at Caleb Chandler again. "If I were you, Chaplain, I'd warn your friend the congressman from Connecticut that after this war's over, maybe even before it ends, the rest of this continent is goin' to settle scores with you pious honkers. We'd all be better off if you started worryin' about that instead of who killed a runaway nigger."

The combination of the man's hatred of New England and his indifference to Caesar Muzzey's death coalesced with the disillusion in Caleb Chandler's soul. This was a test, he told himself. A test of America's integrity. Did the leaders of the nation's army believe those soaring words in the Declaration of Independence about liberty and happiness belonging by right to all men?

"I've changed my mind," the chaplain said. "Instead of appealing to Congressman Williams, I intend to bring this crime to the personal attention of General Washington. I will demand a thorough investigation of Caesar Muzzey's death and the apprehension and hanging of his murderer."

Again, the inner voice whispered, *Fool*. But Caleb refused to listen to it. He was more and more certain that God had led him to this confrontation in the January night. It was his destiny to find this dying black man, to hear him gasp those last mysterious words, to rebuke this sneering dismissal of his humanity. It was his chance to challenge the despair, the loss of faith in American and America's God, that had destroyed Joel Lockwood.

Congressman Stapleton yawned. "May I have my lantern, Chaplain? I'm going to bed."

three

*How happy the soldier who lives on his pay
And spends a half-crown out of sixpence a day
Yet fears neither justices, warrants, nor bums
But pays all his debts with a roll of his drums.*

A half-dozen British officers roared this favorite song into the frigid midnight on Jane Street in New York. They were on their way to the tangle of streets just east of Kings College, known as the Holy Ground. There, no fewer than five hundred willing ladies waited to relieve them of their cash and their frustrations.

In the comfortable study of his three-story town house on Jane Street sat a man who did not waste his time on carousing or whoring. Work was Major Walter Beckford's mistress, although a casual observer might have thought it was his stomach. He was one of those large, naturally bulky men who seem unbothered by—in fact seem almost proud of—growing fat. His red regimental coat, with the aiguillette of a general's aide on the right shoulder, only pretended to encompass his big belly. Youth—he was in his early thirties—gave his spherical pink cheeks and double chins a glow of health. Walter Beckford's soft white hand gripped a pen with the same determination that other soldiers grasped a sword or a gun.

On the table before him were a half-dozen books—dictionaries; Laurence Sterne's novel, *Tristram Shandy*; Blackstone's *Commentaries*. Beside them was a letter composed entirely of numbers. Each number told Beckford where to look in one of the books. Each line came from a different book. "I defy anyone to break this code," Beckford said to the burly man who sat opposite him, wearing the green coat and buff breeches of the Queen's Rangers, one of the better provincial regiments. With a flourish Beckford translated the last line and scanned the message.

We now have ten men in Washington's Life Guard. Within the week five of them will begin standing the same watch. This should lend itself to making the attempt on his life which we've discussed in previous letters. With him eliminated, the success of the mutiny is certain. As long as he remains alive, the possibility of his personal intervention threatens our plan. In spite of all our efforts, the majority of troops refuse to blame him for their daily misery.

"From one of my best men in Morristown," Beckford said. "He's built up a remarkable network inside the American army."

Skepticism was unmistakable on the burly man's face. Major Beckford gritted his teeth. He frequently tried to convince regimental commanders like his guest, Lieutenant Colonel John Graves Simcoe, of the importance of intelligence. Most of them remained indifferent or hostile.

On the whole, the message was not good news. Beckford thrust it into the top drawer of his desk and summoned from the hallway the two men who had brought it across the Hudson River. The older of the two was short and squat, with a weathered, crafty face. His companion was enormous, with the wide eyes and soft mouth of a trusting child. He wore his silken blond hair loose to his shoulders, completing the impression of overgrown innocence.

Beckford dropped ten guineas into the older man's grimy hand. "Here's your night's pay," he said. Turning to Simcoe, he casually added, "These two fellows are my jacks-of-all-trades. They carry messages, escort escaped prisoners through our safe houses in New Jersey, and, when the necessity arises, they'll burn down a rebel militia officer's house or cut a double agent's throat without a qualm. This one"—Beckford gestured to the squat man, who wore a tattered red British army coat—"Nelson, was a light-infantry sergeant in the Royal Welsh Fusiliers in the last French war. He retired to a farm in Bergen County. Tell the colonel what the rebels did to you in '75."

"Broke down my door and gave me a coat of red-hot tar," Nelson said. "Burned my house and barn and left me for dead. Which would have been the case if it weren't for this lad." He threw his arm around the young giant.

"Bogert is his name," Beckford said. "He carried Nelson on his back some forty miles to New York, where one of our doctors treated him."

"Claimed I was fairly cooked by that tar," Nelson said. "Roasted like a pig. Laid me in a tub of grease and kept me there for a whole month. Called it a bloody experiment. I tell you I was glad to get out of that damned tub."

In the lamplight, the skin on Nelson's neck still looked like underdone beef. It made Major Beckford anxious to get rid of him. He had ordered a jugged hare and some oysters sent up from Sam Francis's tavern for a late-night supper. Nelson was ruining his appetite.

"You are to proceed at once to Mount Hope, where you will find four escaped officers in a safe house. Escort them across New Jersey to the usual place, by the usual route. If you're intercepted, one man must be saved even if it entails the sacrifice of the rest. He's a major of the artillery named Whittlesey. With the officers, you'll find a man named Grey, a former captain in the American army. We have proof that he's a double agent. Kill him."

Nelson braced and saluted with some of his old Fusiliers style. "Yes, Major," he said, with a hint of mockery in his voice. "Glad to have met you, Colonel, though I didn't get your name."

"Simcoe."

"Of the Queen's Rangers? Now, I'm truly glad to have met you, sir. Always glad to meet a real soldier."

Major Beckford did not like the implied comparison. "I want you on your way by midnight, Nelson. Don't stop for a drink anywhere in the city. If I hear of you so much as loitering near a tavern, I'll cut your pay in half."

"I'll be as sober as a Methodist, Major. I promise you."

The two men clumped down the stairs into the night. Beckford again turned to Lieutenant Colonel Simcoe, a forced smile on his round pink face. "Twenty-six, our agent in Morristown, uses a courier who serves in one of the New Jersey regiments. He leaves the messages at a safe house in Bergen, where Bogert or Nelson picks them up. The Americans are notoriously lax about letting Jerseymen go home, with or without leave."

"So I hear," Lieutenant Colonel Simcoe said.

Was Simcoe telling him that there was nothing Beckford's spies brought in that was not common knowledge? Walter Beckford ordered himself to stop babbling like a schoolboy. He had said and done more than enough to impress Lieutenant Colonel Simcoe with the quality of his intelligence operations. Beckford reproached himself for letting this compact soldier, who had three wounds to prove his courage on the battlefield, intimidate him. Why did he read a mild contempt into Simcoe's opaque stare? Did the lieutenant colonel remind him of his hero father, Major General John Beckford? These warrior types all shared an unstated arrogance, a presumption of superiority. It was important to remember that they also shared a tendency to brainlessness.

Major General Beckford had refused to serve in America and had publicly denounced the war as a disgrace to England's honor. His simple mind had been seduced by the Americans' self-serving whimpers about taxation without representation and their rights as freeborn Englishmen. In his usual peremptory style, Major General Beckford had ordered his son to resign his commission and return to England when hostilities began in 1775. Walter Beckford had ignored him. By that time he was convinced that his father was an anachronism, hopelessly ignorant of the imperatives of running an empire.

Major General Beckford was not a reader. He was unacquainted with his son's favorite book, Edward Gibbon's *The History of the Decline and Fall of the Roman Empire*. The marvelous first volume, in which Gibbon described the opulence and happiness of Rome under the "good emperors," had illuminated the past, the present, and the future for Walter Beckford. He had read and reread it in 1776, often by candlelight in his tent, between scribbling dispatches and bearing messages and finding quarters and arranging meals for Lieutenant General Wilhelm von Knyphausen, the field commander of the twenty thousand troops that George III had hired from the Landgrave of Hesse and several other German princes.

Walter Beckford had been almost disconsolate, watching the royal army drive the Americans out of New York and hound them across New Jersey. The war seemed about to end and he had acquired only the merest scraps of glory. Now, four years later— four bitter, disheartening years for some generals and politicians—Walter Beckford had woven a web of influence and accomplishment that would qualify him to play a leading part in the new Rome that Britain was about to become.

Beckford had always thought that America would be difficult to subdue. Reading Gibbon had convinced him that this difficulty was a fortunate misfortune for England. The long war had required her to think seriously about her empire. When victory was finally won, she would accept her imperial destiny and govern along Roman lines the islands and continents she controlled. Freedom would be cherished at home, but in the provinces, British power, backed where necessary by bayonets, would prevail. Beyond question bayonets would be the policy for stiff-necked America. Walter Beckford wanted to rule one of these American provinces, eventually to rule all of them as the King's proconsul beyond the Atlantic.

From his wine rack Beckford took a bottle of Lisbon Particular, the world's finest port, and poured two glasses. "Now tell me more about this plan with which you tantalized me yesterday, at the Coffee House," he said to Lieutenant Colonel Simcoe.

Simcoe accepted his glass of port and drank half of it in a single soldierly gulp. "It's not the sort of thing we could discuss in a public place," he said. "I've been on the lookout for a capital stroke that the Queen's Rangers might perform before the rebellion collapses of its own inner rot. I want to remind His Majesty and the Parliament of the many thousands of their American subjects who've remained loyal."

"An admirable sentiment," Beckford said, refilling Simcoe's glass. "Everything I hear from England inclines me to believe that when this rebellion is over, Parliament will treat America with Roman severity. My father tells me the term has become popular with all ranks of people."

"How is the general?"

"Still the prisoner of his idiotic politics. I wouldn't mind so much if his opinions were his own. But politically he's a child. All he does is echo the opposition leaders."

"A shame," Simcoe said, demolishing another glass of port. "My older brother fought under him at Minden. He said John Beckford was the best general officer he'd ever seen in action. I've often wondered why you've been unable to convince him of the justice of this war."

Beckford almost laughed at the absurdity of the idea that he would convince his father of anything. The thickness of General Beckford's skull aside, he barely knew the man. During Beckford's boyhood, the general had spent most of his time on the Continent with a German mistress he had picked up in Hesse-Cassel after the Battle of Minden. Each year he made a ceremonial Christmas visit to Beckford and his brothers at the family's Surrey estate. His mother, as far as Beckford knew, never spoke to his father during these visits, although she joined them at the table each night for dinner.

Beckford slowly shook his head. "We must make him—and the opposition in Parliament—eat their words syllable by syllable, by winning without them."

"Let's drink to that," Simcoe said.

It was the first flicker of personal warmth Simcoe had displayed. As they drained their glasses, Beckford's batman, Private Oskar Kiphuth, announced that supper had arrived from Sam Francis's tavern. Beckford led Simcoe into the dining room. The jugged hare, which Kiphuth was reheating over the coals in the fireplace, filled the room with spicy odors. Pickled Long Island Sound oysters, a dozen on each plate, lay on beds of ice. A bottle of claret was open on the table. Beckford filled two glasses, spread a napkin over his big belly, and urged Simcoe to tell him about his capital stroke.

Simcoe glanced uneasily at Oskar Kiphuth. "Don't worry about him," Beckford said. "He doesn't understand ten words of English."

Simcoe nodded approvingly and began. "As you know, some picked men and myself struck deep into New Jersey last year to free a half-dozen poor loyalists who were being mistreated in the rebels' wretched jails."

"And you were most unfortunately wounded and almost captured on your return," Beckford said.

"A piece of bad luck," Simcoe said. "The thing is, we proved that a well-armed force on good horses can penetrate the state virtually at will. Their militia grow more and more timid and supine. What we have in mind is a prize infinitely more valuable than captive loyalists. Many of the Queen's Rangers are from New Jersey and they frequently get intelligence through smuggled letters or secret visits to their families. I dare say it's better stuff than you pick up from your high-priced spies."

"I only wish you and other commanders were more systematic about sending it to me."

Simcoe ignored the comment. Beckford found himself recalling a letter he had received from his father, last year, ordering him to transfer to a regiment and prove his courage on the battlefield, instead of wasting his time on "spies and politics."

"We've learned that Mr. Washington is quartered a considerable distance from his army," Simcoe continued. "Nearer to us in New York by several miles. I don't think it would be at all difficult for a well-chosen force to carry him off."

It was all so understated, it took Beckford a moment to grasp the full meaning of the words. Simcoe was proposing to capture George Washington. Decapitate the American army. Make their pretentious rebellion a laughing stock around the world by seizing their great man, the hero who had mesmerized half of Europe, including Major General John Beckford. That dunderhead had recently made a speech in Parliament comparing the Virginia tobacco farmer to Hannibal and the Duke of Marlborough. Capture George Washington! It was a simple, immensely daring idea—the sort of gamble that often succeeds in a war.

In the same offhand way, Simcoe began describing the force he would use to execute the coup. "It would require no more than eighty men. Every sixth man would be an officer. We would all wear the white woolen greatcoats issued to the army in Canada. They'll make us all but invisible in this perpetual snow. There's a wood near Morristown that my people know well. We would tie our horses there and debouch from this cover precisely at dawn. Two three-pounders on sleds should be enough to beat down the door of Washington's quarters while the men deal with his guard. In five minutes the general will be our prisoner, on the way to New York."

Lieutenant Colonel Simcoe munched a pickled oyster. "As for pursuit, I dare say it won't be a problem. My people tell me there's not a horse in the American camp. They've scattered their cavalry all over Morris County, as far west as Trenton, because they haven't the money for fodder."

Simcoe's intelligence was excellent. The horseless condition of the rebel army had already been reported to Beckford by agent Twenty-six. The major raised his glass of claret. "To you, my dear sir. To your daring and genius. I believe it will work. Rest assured I will bring it to General Knyphausen's attention immediately."

Knyphausen was the word, the name, that explained why Lieutenant Colonel Simcoe was dining with Major Beckford. On December 31, 1779, Sir Henry Clinton, the commander in chief of the British army in North America, had sailed south to attack Charleston, South Carolina, leaving Wilhelm von Knyphausen in command of His Majesty's forces in New York. General Knyphausen could be approached only through his aide-de-camp, Walter Beckford, for a very good but painful reason: the Hessian warrior spoke not a word of English. Beckford's father had insisted that he learn German as a boy because it was the language of England's chief ally in Europe. It had proven to be one of the few useful orders the general had given him.

As he toasted Simcoe's daring and genius, Beckford's agile mind was drawing a number of unspoken conclusions. One, the most obvious, was the probability that if Simcoe succeeded, his coup would totally overshadow the mutiny in the American army on which Beckford and his agent, Twenty-six, had lavished so much time and money over the past two years. For the present, Beckford saw it was vital to connect the two plans. Later it might become advisable, perhaps even necessary, to eliminate Lieutenant Colonel Simcoe from the combined operation. That would depend on how much of the credit Simcoe was willing to share with Walter Beckford. His present attitude was not promising.

"I see no difficulty in concerting this stroke with a mutiny we're planning in Morristown," Beckford said.

"In fact, the two dovetail so neatly I can only wonder why your idea didn't occur to me. Have you mentioned it to anyone else in New York?"

"Only to one of my officers in the Queen's Rangers. I trust him absolutely."

"I think we'd better adopt a code. Let's call our plan 'Inviting James to New York.'"

If Simcoe noticed that his plan had become "our plan," he said nothing. Beckford was about to pour another glass of claret and begin to discuss ways to coordinate the two master strokes when Oskar Kiphuth appeared in the doorway. "Sir," he said in German, "there is a woman downstairs. She tells me in French that she must see you immediately. She is most agitated. Her name is Kuyper."

"What's he saying?" Simcoe demanded.

"One of my female agents has come here, contrary to all orders. We have a safe house on Bowrie Lane."

"I've often wondered about the money spent on female spies. I can't imagine a man telling a woman anything of importance," Simcoe said. "But I might change my mind if they called on me of an evening. I didn't know you favored the ladies, Beckford. I thought you found boys more enticing."

"I've long since given up that youthful peccadillo, Colonel," Beckford said in his most frigid tone. "Moreover, I never mix business with pleasure. I'm afraid we must shorten our feast."

"Just as well," Simcoe said. "Hare always gives me a bellyache."

"Show the lady into the parlor," Beckford said to Kiphuth in German. He decided he was grateful for the interruption. Simcoe had told him all he needed to know. There was no point in giving him any more details about the mutiny or in revealing the part of his own plan that General Knyphausen had thus far vetoed—the attempt to assassinate George Washington.

Kiphuth returned to the dining room with Simcoe's cloak. The commander of the Queen's Rangers threw it around his solid shoulders and said, "Aren't you even going to give me a look at her, Beckford?"

"It's—somewhat irregular. Her identity is a secret. But . . ."

They went down the stairs to the second floor and Beckford pushed open the parlor door. Flora Kuyper was facing the fire. She turned to confront them. Her thick, dark hair was unpowdered and uncombed. She was not wearing rouge, but the cold air had added a faint flush to her oval cheeks, which were streaked with tears. Even in disarray, she was one of the most beautiful women Beckford had ever seen.

"Ah, Beckford, what hard duty you perform," Simcoe murmured. "Let me know the moment you have some word from Knyphausen."

With a brief, somewhat mocking bow to Flora Kuyper, Simcoe continued down the stairs to the street. Beckford strode into the parlor, slamming the door behind him. "What is the reason—what can justify—this extraordinary visit?" he demanded. "You've been told never to come here. This house is watched day and night. The Americans are well aware of my role in the army."

"Caesar is dead—murdered. I want to know who killed him—you—or William?"

"Dead? Are you sure?" Beckford said.

"Here's a letter from the man who says he discovered his body. A chaplain named Caleb Chandler. Is he one of your agents?"

Major Beckford was not used to interrogation from Flora Kuyper. He was not used to the way she was looking at him. The submission, the mixture of fear and gratitude he usually saw in her dark green eyes, with their exquisitely long lashes, had been replaced by a startling mixture of anger and hatred. He snatched the letter she had drawn from an inner pocket of her cloak, without answering her.

"It's addressed to my husband. They don't know about . . . his death," Flora said.

Beckford gestured to her to be silent and swiftly read the Reverend Chandler's neat, firm script. The first page described his discovery of Caesar's body in the snow; the second page dealt with the aftermath.

At first I was told by members of General Washington's staff that nothing could be done to solve the mystery of Muzzey's death. I considered this a double outrage—an example of the prejudice against the Negro race so prevalent in America, and the indifference with which the army's officers regard the death of an enlisted man. I immediately protested. Now we are to have an investigation of this murder. Whether the culprit will ever be found is another matter. The deed was done in the dark of night, and the drifting snow effectively covered the tracks of the killer. The motive could not have been robbery. Private Muzzey had in his pocket a dozen gold sovereigns (remarkable in itself) which had not been touched.

I write to you not only to communicate the melancholy news but also to inquire into the possibility of your shedding some light on this sad event. Perhaps you know the source of the uncommonly large amount of money that Private Muzzey had in his pocket. Perhaps you or some of your other slaves had heard from him since he entered the army. Any information

46

you can give me would be most gratefully received. I am determined to bring his murderer to justice in spite of the army's negligent attitude.

At the completion of the investigation, Congressman Hugh Stapleton has kindly agreed to take the body to your farm for burial. I gather Mr. Stapleton is an old schoolmate of yours. He recalled, when he heard your name, that Caesar was your personal servant for many years. I thought you and your other slaves would want to pay your last respects to him rather than have him tumbled into the common grave the army uses for enlisted soldiers.

With sincere sympathy for your loss, I am, dear Sir,

Your most obedient servant

CALEB CHANDLER
Chaplain, 2nd Connecticut Brigade

"This could not have come at a worse time," Beckford said.

"Did you kill him?" Flora asked again.

"Of course not. Why should I kill the best courier in my network—the only dependable one—when I've never been in worse need of communicating with Twenty-six?"

"Then it must have been William."

"Twenty-six. Call him Twenty-six. I want no one to know you have any connection with him. I very much doubt that he'd do such a thing without consulting me. However unpleasant Caesar probably was to him, as he was to me and everyone else who knew him, Twenty-six needed his services. He's always been a practical man—"

"Then it must have been the Americans."

"They seldom kill spies surreptitiously. They prefer to hang them. They're always trying to teach the faithful a lesson. I'm inclined to think the murderer

47

was someone with a personal grudge against Caesar. I'm sure he had enemies by the dozen in his regiment. They wouldn't dare attack him in daylight. But in the dark even a behemoth like him could be downed by a man who knew how to use a bayonet."

Flora began to weep—violent sobs that Beckford found intensely irritating. "My dear Flora," he said, "you're not helping matters with this excessive grief. He was only a slave, after all. What are you out—two or three hundred pounds? We'll pay you in full for him."

"Caesar was...a member of my family. I...I promised him his freedom. I...you—the two of us—led him into this business."

"No one led Caesar anywhere. He did only what pleased him. He was as arrogant a bastard as I've ever seen. And untrustworthy. I've thought for some time he might be a double agent."

"What if he was? He had no reason to love you. He only despised you less than the Americans."

"I hope such a sentiment doesn't inhabit your lovely breast, my dear."

The unspoken threat calmed Flora considerably. "I'm loyal," she said. "But am I safe now? Was Caesar carrying a message that implicated me?"

Beckford paced the parlor for a moment. He had long since learned that in intelligence work almost every reverse could be turned to some advantage if the director of the operation did not lose his head. An intelligence chief needed two things: good nerves and a comprehensive plan. Walter Beckford was confident that he had both. He picked up the Reverend Caleb Chandler's letter.

"This odd mixture of sympathy and indignation

that you've received from Chaplain Chandler is the best possible proof that the Americans don't suspect you. They're having a Continental Congressman deliver Caesar's body. They'd never put a man like that within our reach if they thought you were untrustworthy. If you behave well, we may gain more than we've lost from his misfortune."

"What do you mean?" Flora said, staring morosely into the fire.

"This congressman—Hugh Stapleton—is high on our list of disaffected Americans. We're quite certain he's a plum ripe for the plucking. He could be very useful to us in the aftermath of the mutiny. Why don't you charm him into confiding his private thoughts on politics to you, then keep him dangling until we're ready to draw him into our net?"

"I'm not interested."

"He's very rich, my dear. He made a half-million pounds in the West Indies running gunpowder and other goods for Congress during the first two years of the war."

"I'm still not interested."

Beckford took her arm and forced her to turn and face him. "My dear Flora, must I order you to be interested? I need to see a willing spirit in my agents. Otherwise I lose faith in them. The consequences can be very unpleasant."

Flora Kuyper reconsidered her distaste for Congressman Stapleton. "Is he old?"

"Not at all. He's about my age. I knew him slightly in London in the mid-sixties. He was quite a rake in those days. He's married since. Which dulls a man. But you must make some sacrifices for the cause. Tonight I heard something that virtually guarantees victory for us. I can't tell you what it is, but believe me, victory is very close."

Beckford had made this prediction so often in recent months, it had begun to make him uneasy. There was no doubt that the Americans were close to collapse. But only the men in headquarters knew that there were also signs of faltering determination in London. Every ship that arrived from England brought new rumors of secret peace negotiations. The latest gossip suggested that His Majesty's government, embroiled in a global war now that France and Spain had allied themselves with the rebel colonies, might abandon North America and concentrate its forces in the West Indies and India. Beckford had spent hours at his desk writing letters to members of Parliament, urging them to resist any suggestion of surrendering this immense continent, the part of the empire that would guarantee England's world supremacy for five hundred years. He had deluged his correspondents with details of the rebels' parlous morale, their desertion-riddled army, their feckless, quarrelsome Congress. He had enlisted his mother and her two brothers in this war within the war. One, Lord Thomas Lyttleton, the head of the family, had a seat on the Privy Council; the other was a Groom of the Bedchamber and a frequent hunting companion of the King.

Flora Kuyper intensified Beckford's unease by ignoring his prophecy. She freed her arm and turned away from him to stare into the fire again. For a moment an image flashed into Beckford's mind, as vivid as a scene from a play. He was in London, strolling through Pall Mall with Flora on his arm. Major General Beckford and his German mistress, her face a lurid mask of paint concealing the lines of age, approach. Beckford and Flora pass them without so much as a nod.

Absurd, Beckford told himself. Flora belonged by agreement to the man they called Twenty-six. She was replaceable in that Pall Mall scene by another woman, any woman of comparable beauty. But many things could happen to his old friend Twenty-six between today and the consummation of their intricate plan. Beckford had not seen any woman in America who came close to Flora Kuyper's exotic beauty. It was important that the woman in the Pall Mall scene be a trophy, a symbol of triumph, carried back to England as his father had brought his own mistress back from Germany, announcing his defiance of his pudgy English wife and the fortune for which he had married her. That kind of freedom belonged only to conquerers.

"Victory, Flora," Beckford said again, seeking a response that went beyond mere obedience.

She continued to ignore him. The firelight played on her mournful mouth, her downcast eyes. Walter Beckford struggled to control his exasperation. Women were as unknowable, as transient as the weather. Wayward personal emotions, such as sympathy for dead slaves, distracted them. Why was he allowing such a creature to make him doubt the certainty of that transcendent word, victory?

four

Idiocy, Congressman Hugh Stapleton thought as he watched the hospital orderlies lug the pine coffin out of the shed behind the army hospital. The Reverend Caleb Chandler walked beside the coffin, a model of morose Puritan piety. It was impossible to imagine him ever smiling, much less laughing or dancing. His worn wool stockings drooped, the wide buckram skirt and boot-sleeve cuffs of his coat had gone out of style in the 1760s, his cloak was a mass of patches, yet the fellow assumed that because he was a college graduate, a gentleman should treat him as an equal. As if a degree from Yale—or Harvard, for that matter—proved a man was anything but a canting Yankee hypocrite.

The wind came out of the northeast like a spear, piercing the beaver greatcoat that Stapleton's London tailor had guaranteed would keep him warm anywhere, even in Saint Petersburg. The slate-gray sky was unchanged from yesterday and showed no sign of changing tomorrow. The Yankees had not only exported their fanatic politics to the rest of America, Stapleton thought, they had also sent their abominable New England weather.

"It's good of you to do this, Congressman Stapleton," Caleb Chandler called as he and the equally ragged pallbearers approached the sleigh.

"I'm doing it as a favor to my old friend Henry Kuyper, Chaplain. For no other reason."

"I hope you can find time to question Mr. Kuyper about the money in Caesar's pocket and his whereabouts when he was absent without leave. General Washington's investigation made no attempt to explore those matters."

"General Washington has more important things on his mind, Chaplain."

"I wish I saw some proof of it," Chandler said. "He and his staff continue to live in luxury while their troops starve and freeze."

There it was again, that mindless Yankee hatred of Washington which Stapleton heard so often from the New Englanders in Congress. It was really a hatred of anyone who lived like a gentleman. They want to pull us all down to their patched-homespun grubbiness, Stapleton thought. To abandon all of life's pleasures and talk through our noses about salvation and righteousness. What perverse deity had gotten him— gotten America—involved with these creatures?

The orderlies heaved the coffin onto the floor of Hugh Stapleton's sleigh. "If I get any information— which I doubt—I will write to you, Chaplain," Congressman Stapleton said, wedging his fur-lined boots between the coffin and his seat and gathering a bearskin rug around his knees. He gave his Negro coachman, Pompey, a peremptory wave. Pompey cracked his whip over the heads of the two black Burlington geldings, which had won the admiration of that lover of good horseflesh, George Washington. The sleigh surged away from the army hospital and its attendant burial shed, away from the nearby rows of enlisted men's huts in Jockey Hollow, with their pervasive stench of urine and excrement. Congressman Stapleton took a small diamond-encrusted silver box from his pocket and tried to banish the stink with a corrosive snort of snuff.

This was more like it, he thought as the sleigh skimmed down the snow-packed road behind the powerful horses, jingling the first bar of one of his favorite songs, "The Good Fellow." He hummed the rest of it to himself as they raced along.

> *Good fortune attend*
> *Each merry man's friend*
> *That doth but the best he may;*
> *Forgetting old wrong*
> *With a cup and a song*
> *To drive cold winter away.*

Instead of cheering him up, the song made Hugh Stapleton melancholy. He thought of one of the last times he had sung it in his fine tenor voice, which had once set the fair sex sighing. Tom Barton of Philadelphia and Harry Brockholst of New York had been sitting beside him in this sleigh, with three of the prettiest girls in New Jersey around them, on the way to the old Three Pigeons Inn for a night of dancing and drinking and flirting and kissing. Only fifteen years ago. Where were they now? Tom Barton was a refugee in British New York, writing bitter ballads and essays ridiculing the American rebels. Harry Brockholst was dead, in a frozen grave outside Quebec.

They soon reached the center of Morristown, with its rectangular snow-heaped green surrounded by churches, taverns, stores, and private houses. "Stop at the general's headquarters," Hugh Stapleton called. Near the end of the green, Pompey reined in the geldings and the sleigh slithered to a halt in front of the fine Palladian doorway of the two-story hip-roofed house, the former home of Colonel Jacob Ford, Jr. Another old friend lying in a cold grave.

In the spacious center hall, Congressman Stapleton encountered Washington's diminutive young aide, Colonel Alexander Hamilton. "I only stopped to reassure the general that I have Muzzey's body and will deliver it as requested," the congressman said. "Mr. Chandler seems somewhat mollified."

"We're eternally grateful," Hamilton said. "I hope it won't take you too far out of your way."

"Far enough but I'm glad to do it. Let us hope it will keep your would-be Jeremiah quiet for a while."

"If it doesn't, we may resort to harsher methods," Hamilton said.

"Did you enjoy your evening with Miss Schuyler?"

Hamilton groaned. "Another one like it and I'll be a gone man. I hate to admit it, but she's everything I want in a wife. Religious, but not a saint."

"And beautiful and good-tempered and submissive but not doltishly dependent," the congressman added

56

with a laugh. "Sometimes I think we New Yorkers all want the same woman."

Hamilton shook his head. It was obvious that he was already a gone man. "I swore I wouldn't marry until I was thirty."

"I went through exactly the same experience."

"And you're still a happy man?"

"I'm sufficiently cynical to doubt that any husband of thirteen years is happy. But I wouldn't trade the first five or six years—"

"I'm afraid I know what you mean, Congressman."

"Give General Washington my regards. Tell him he can depend on my support in Congress, for whatever it's worth."

"It may be worth a great deal, Congressman. I'm convinced it's time for younger men like yourself to exert some influence. Otherwise—"

He spread his hands in a gesture that included the snowbound landscape and the starving men in Jockey Hollow.

Congressman Stapleton returned to his sleigh and resumed his journey to Henry Kuyper's farm in Bergen. Stapleton had come to Morristown as a committee of one, sent by the New Jersey congressional delegation to protest the Continental Army's supposed abuse of local civilians. He had volunteered for the job for only one reason—to escape Congress, with its interminable bickering and wrangling and windy speeches about nothing. Worse yet, the Delaware River was frozen, which meant there was no business worth doing in Philadelphia. Without business, that endlessly fascinating game of profit and loss, Hugh Stapleton tended to become restless. Only the chance to operate as a merchant for the past eighteen months in Philadelphia had made Congress endurable.

General Washington had been relieved to discover that Hugh Stapleton was the bearer of the congressional protest. "I can speak plainly to Malcolm Stapleton's son," he had said.

The words had irked Hugh Stapleton. He was tired of that designation, Malcolm Stapleton's son. He respected his father's memory. He had been one of the chief soldiers of New Jersey, the man who had outfitted an entire regiment at his own expense and led them against the French and Indians in Canada in 1758 and against the Spanish in distant Cuba in 1762. But Malcolm Stapleton was dead. His older son was a very different man. If you only knew how different, General, the congressman thought as he nodded acquiescently.

Hugh Stapleton had listened with apparent sympathy while Washington explained the situation in Morristown during the first week of the year 1780. After a four-day blizzard there had been no choice but to let the troops go into the countryside and take food where they found it. "Either that or the army would have disbanded," Washington said. "I suspect some in Congress would consider that a blessing in disguise. But I'm convinced that these men are America's only protection from defeat and disgrace. I'm sure your father told you what happened here in New Jersey in 1776, when we tried to rely on militia."

The old man had told him, with expletives that almost scorched the paper, that had still seared Hugh Stapleton's mind when he read them in the West Indies three months later. *I warned those Yankee sons of bitches in Philadelphia that they would ruin us with their prating about patriot militiamen. I told those goddamn cantankerous know-it-alls that nothing would stop the British but regular soldiers, well trained and well paid. Now it's come to pass.* New Jersey's militia, the part-time soldiers who were supposed to turn out in an emergency the way the Massachusetts farmers did at Lexington and Concord, had all stayed home and allowed the British to overrun the state, to almost turn it into a royal province again. Samuel Adams and his Yankee cohorts had denounced the Jerseymen as cowards, ignoring the difference between the tiny British army that had fought at Lexington and the immense host, backed by artillery and cavalry, that had invaded New Jersey.

Face to face with George Washington for the first time, Hugh Stapleton did not find him the pompous potential Cromwell described by his enemies in Congress. On the contrary, he seemed too soft-spoken and diffident to be the man who had led the slashing counteroffensive on Christmas night, 1776, that had rescued New Jersey—and the nation—from disaster. Stapleton wondered if Washington himself had begun to regard that three-year-old campaign as ancient history, as remote and meaningless as Malcolm Stapleton's heroics storming French and Spanish forts in the Seven Years' War.

General Washington had invited Hugh Stapleton to supper with the army's quartermaster general, Nathanael Greene, and ex-Major General Philip Schuyler, who was on his way to Philadelphia to become one of New York's congressmen. Schuyler had brought his daughter Elizabeth with him; Lieutenant Colonel Hamilton had been delegated to entertain her, with catastrophic impact on his emotions. There was a lot of joking about her capture of Hamilton, who had often boasted of his immunity to matrimony.

The talk soon turned serious. As they ate well-cooked mutton and a veal pie, Washington had poured the wine generously and explained what was wrong with Congress's solution to America's greatest problem—the rapid depreciation of the Continental dollar.

"When it takes a wagonload of money to buy a wagonload of hay, I can see why Congress thought it a waste of time to print any more of it. But money that must be spent by the wagonload is still better than no money at all. We are told that the states will now supply the army with goods in kind. New Hampshire, for instance, will ship us thirty thousand gallons of rum, Connecticut a thousand tons of wheat. But how can we get any of this to camp without money to hire wagons and wagonmen?"

"We have, at this moment, not a dollar in the army's treasury," Nathanael Greene reported. He was about Stapleton's age, a cheerful man at first impression, until you looked into his cold gray eyes.

"We haven't heard a word about plans for this year's draft from any state except New Jersey," Washington said. "Last year ten states never filled their quotas."

"And the men you got, if those I saw in Albany were a sample," Philip Schuyler added, "were mostly neutrals and criminals, almost every one resolved to desert at the first opportunity."

"Can you blame any man for deserting?" said Greene, "when no one has been paid for over a year now?"

Philip Schuyler, portly, pink-cheeked, and vehement, the quintessential Dutchman, began telling horror stories of earlier years, when he had commanded an army in northern New York. The New Englanders in Congress had decided one of their favorite generals should have his job. Schuyler had spent half his time fending off attacks on his integrity and ability while trying to fight a war without men, money, or supplies, all of which Congress failed to send him. "I am going to Congress for only one reason," the former general said, puffing furiously on a long clay pipe, "to make those goddamned Yankees listen to reason."

Hugh Stapleton drank the excellent port and murmured sympathetically while he mentally dismissed Schuyler's hope of single-handedly reforming Congress. The Dutchman's blunt, irascible style and his possession of one of the great fortunes of America virtually guaranteed Yankee hostility. It was George Washington who stirred the congressman's sympathy. He glimpsed the desperation beneath the Virginian's weary calm. Should he bring it to the surface by telling him that nothing was going to change Congress's feckless ways? They would dither and drivel and go back to bemoaning the decline of patriotism and haggling over whose relatives should get the biggest slice of the inflation-fat army and navy supply contracts.

Hugh Stapleton found it easier to remain silent, to drift with the current and hope that someone or something would extricate him from this rudderless ship of state before it blundered into shoal water. He wished he had listened to his instincts when France entered the war in 1778 and the conflict had engulfed the West Indies, making it impossible to do business there. With his fluent Dutch, learned from his mother, Hugh Stapleton had wanted to retreat to Holland. If the choice had been his alone, he would be matching wits with the canny merchants of Amsterdam instead of posturing in Morristown, pretending enthusiasm for a revolution he had disliked from the start.

But the choice had not been his alone. His wife had bombarded him with letters that pleaded, wheedled, begged, and finally threatened him with the loss of her affection, of his sons' respect, if he did not return home immediately. She had made him into this pseudo-patriot and politician. Since his return she had continued to harry him with her opinions and exhortations. That was why he had almost welcomed being delayed by the investigation into Caesar Muzzey's death. He was in no hurry to get home for another round of lectures.

But the investigation had been a bore. The ragged members of Muzzey's regiment had all insisted they knew nothing about his death. The name of Caesar's master was the only interesting fact the congressman had learned. Henry Kuyper had been one of a half-dozen fellow New Jerseymen at Kings College in 1761. Unfortunately, English was a foreign language to him—as it was to most of the Dutch farmers who lived in the large, fertile section of northeastern New Jersey legally known as Bergen County. Henry had failed almost every subject and quit before the end of the first year. He had gone humbly home to his farm on the heights of Bergen, where he no doubt resumed speaking and reading Dutch, praying in it each Sunday, and each Monday counting the English money he made from selling his milk and cheese and poultry and grain to the hungry New Yorkers on the other side of the Hudson River. It was easy to understand why Henry Kuyper would send a husky slave like Caesar Muzzey to serve as his substitute in this quarrel between the American English and the European English. Most of Kuyper's sort of Dutchmen, the solid, prosperous farmer class, regarded the war as madness.

Hugh Stapleton found himself speculating about the kind of man the shy, quiet Dutch boy he had known in 1761 had become. Almost certainly Henry had gotten fat and had no doubt married a Dutch *huys vrouw* who had gotten even fatter. She probably ordered him around and kept the books on the farm, in the style of many Dutch women. Henry probably smoked his pipe, drank his beer, and let her get away with it.

The savage northeast wind slashed across Hugh Stapleton's sleigh as the powerful horses challenged the steep slopes of the Short Hills. Descending the other side of this mountain rampart, the congressman passed rapidly through the towns of Springfield and Connecticut Farms, each dominated by its whitespired Presbyterian church, and was soon on the road to Newark. He did not meet a single sleigh; not a living person was visible in the towns. The cold was like a giant's hand, crushing life out of the state.

As they rounded a bend in the road the charred ruins of a farmhouse and barns appeared on the right. The tumbled timbers were black against the snow; the smashed windows were like the blank eyes of a corpse. In the next five miles they saw two almost identical ruins, dispiriting evidence that rebel Jerseymen had little hope of defending themselves against British and loyalist vengeance. In the last two years these brutal tactics had forced more than one man to abandon the revolution and espouse a pallid neutrality.

"Bad business, Master Hugh," Pompey said as they passed still another charred farm, within sight of the town of Newark. "Lettin' these fellows come over from New York and burn and rob us this way. Takes the heart out of everybody, it surely do."

"Yes," Hugh Stapleton said.

"Can't understand why General Washington doesn't send some men to fight'm."

White-haired now, Pompey had once been a fighter himself. He had marched to Canada and sailed to Cuba with Hugh Stapleton's father and stood his ground in more than one pitched battle with Frenchmen and Spaniards. Although Pompey was a slave, Hugh Stapleton regarded him as a member of his family, a friend as well as a servant. For a moment he was tempted to tell Pompey what Washington had admitted to him at dinner the other night. He dared not send his men beyond the perimeter of their winter camp at Morristown because he feared most of them would never return.

No, Congressman Stapleton would continue the role of patriotic spokesman a while longer. "The army is too small to patrol every road or guard every foot of the shore along the Hudson," he said.

"Can't understand why the army's so small. Why don't the other states send some men to help us? Seems like we fightin' the British all by ourselves."

"I'm afraid everyone is looking out for his own skin. That goes double for our Yankee friends to the east. Most of them haven't seen a British soldier since 1775."

Pompey laughed heartily. "Master Hugh, when you start on the Yankees you sound just like your mama."

"She knew what she was talking about. She did business with them for thirty years."

Pompey nodded and grew solemn as he guided the horses down the deserted main street of Newark. Hugh Stapleton wondered if he was recalling the years when he had driven his mother, Catalyntie Van Vorst Stapleton, to Newark, where she would often persuade some enterprising merchants to join her in buying the cargo of a newly arrived London freighter. No matter what was in the hold—dry goods or tinware, spices or fine silver—if Catalyntie Van Vorst Stapleton advised them to buy, they knew there would be a profit in it. No merchant in New Jersey— or in New York, for that matter—could approach her talent for "improving some moneys," as she called it.

Beyond Newark, the sleigh skimmed down the new stagecoach road across the salt meadows of the frozen Hackensack River to the town of Bergen on its long narrow ridge overlooking New York. "Master Hugh," Pompey said as the horses toiled up the slope of the ridge, "what happens if the 'Mericans lose this war?"

"I'll have to run for my life," Hugh Stapleton said. "They'll confiscate everything I own."

"Includin' your slaves?"

"Yes."

"That'd be a sorrowin' time for us. They'd sell us to the West Indies, maybe."

"They might."

"Didn't like what you told me about a black man's life down there."

To make sure Pompey and his other blacks did not succumb to the British promise of freedom to runaways, Stapleton had told them horror stories about the short, unhappy lives of slaves on the sugar plantations of the British West Indies. He had convinced them that the British would renege on their promise and sell them to these Negro-devouring islands.

"We're far from beaten, Pompey, believe me. General Washington plans a vigorous campaign this spring. There's hope of more aid from France—"

"Yes, master. That be the Kuyper farm, I think."

It occurred to Hugh Stapleton, as his eyes followed Pompey's pointing finger, that he was really two people, one, the congressman who told official lies; the other, a man who had once prided himself on telling the truth, however unpleasant, in business, religion, politics—the important things in life.

Pompey was right. It was the Kuyper farm. Hugh Stapleton remembered stopping at the house almost two decades ago on his way home from Kings College for Easter recess. On that warm April day the house had seemed an island of coolness in the sunswept green meadow. Now icy drifts were piled against the cut-stone walls. The wide, slope-roofed front porch, where Henry Kuyper had served him a glass of chilled buttermilk and they had sat chatting in rush-bottomed rockers, was now bare and forlorn. Only the red Dutch door with its gleaming brass knocker bid defiance to winter's pervasive white and gray. On the right side of the house a huge old oak, stripped of its leaves, loomed like a spectral guardian. On the left, several hundred feet in the rear, stood two massive Dutch barns.

Hugh Stapleton looked around him. New York was in clear view across the Hudson, which was frozen so solid, according to the newspapers, that men on horseback and sleighs could cross it with ease. The sight of the mile-long cluster of buildings on the tip of Manhattan Island sent a twist of regret through Hugh Stapleton's chilled flesh. He had lived in a well-furnished house on Jane Street for seven years before the war—the seven happiest years of his life, he ruefully admitted to himself. He had had a beautiful wife who devoted herself to his comfort and pleasure and who barely spoke a word in company without consulting his opinion beforehand. His ships carried cargoes of wheat and corn from the expertly tilled farms of New Jersey and New York to the West Indies and Europe, and brought back English cloth and furniture and tea, which he sold for whacking profits. Now he had a woebegone wife who did nothing but preach political sermons to him. He was condemned to living in a noisy tavern in Philadelphia and in a drafty semifurnished farmhouse when he came home to New Jersey while his New York house was occupied by a British officer, perhaps some lout of a cavalryman who put his boots up on the yellow Chippendale couch and spilled wine on the rose-colored wing chairs.

Congressman Stapleton's eyes wandered from New York to the Jersey shore of the Hudson. On Paulus Hook, where he had debarked from the ferry hundreds of times in prewar days, stood a stockaded British fort. The Union Jack fluttered above it, a flare of red against the gray sky and white river. There were almost a thousand British troops in the fort, which was little more than two miles away across the riverside marshes. Bergen was not the safest place in the world for a Continental Congressman. Hugh Stapleton was sure his horses could outrun anything the British had in their stables. But it was almost four o'clock. Darkness came early in January. By night Bergen would be distinctly unsafe for him—or for any other civilian. General Washington had warned him that British and American patrols prowled the roads, ready to shoot on sight.

Pompey urged the horses up the narrow lane to the Kuyper house. It was evident from their sluggish gait that they were very tired. The congressman threw aside his bearskin robe and mounted the steps to rap the round brass knocker.

A tall, husky Negro in red-and-blue livery opened the door. "I'm Mr. Stapleton," the congressman said. "Is your master or mistress at home?"

"Come in, sir," the black said. "My mistress is expecting you."

He bowed Stapleton into the center hall, took his greatcoat, and led him to the door of the parlor. An exceptionally pretty, dark-haired young woman stood with her back to the fireplace. She was wearing a dark green brocade dress with a fashionably looped skirt that revealed a pale green petticoat. The room pulsed with welcome warmth. Oil lamps cast a soft glow on a Persian rug, rose wallpaper full of English pastoral scenes, Chippendale mirrors and paintings in fine gold frames, a sky-blue Chippendale couch and matching arm chairs. It was extraordinarily stylish for a Dutch farmhouse. For a moment Congressman Stapleton felt he had been transported back in time to prewar New York.

"Good evening," he said. "I thought your butler said Mrs. Kuyper was here."

"I'm Flora Kuyper," the young woman said in a voice that had an intriguing hint of a foreign accent.

"Henry Kuyper's wife?" Stapleton said, unable to conceal his surprise. This woman was as distant from the stout Dutch *vrouw* he had expected as his own sour spouse was from the tender glowing girl he had married.

"His widow," she said, dropping her eyes. "Henry has been dead over a year."

"I'm sorry. I—I didn't know."

"In times like these, death becomes commonplace. You have—Caesar's body with you?"

"Yes."

A shadow passed over her face. He thought for a moment she was going to start ranting at him about the loss of her slave. But she only nodded mournfully and called her butler, whose name was Cato, and told him to see that the coffin was put in the barn. Turning again to Hugh Stapleton, she said, "You must stay the night. The roads are too dangerous after dark. Tory thugs come across the Hudson at will. A member of the New Jersey legislature was ambushed only last week."

"I must take the chance. My wife was expecting me two days ago."

"Please. If you were waylaid on my account I would never forgive myself. We have our last and best goose waiting for you in the oven. You must allow me to show my gratitude. Caesar was—was very dear to me. He had—a good heart."

Hugh Stapleton looked out at the gathering gloom of the winter twilight. He thought about his tired horses and the thirty miles of dangerous roads to Great Rock Farm. For a moment he envisioned the welcome he would receive there—his wife's wan face, his noisy younger son climbing on him. Then a blizzard of woes, worries, complaints. Perhaps he should heed this plea, in which he sensed—or was it hoped?—that there was more than mere patriotism. Besides, he was supposed to be helping to solve the mystery of Caesar's death. To this task he could easily add the mystery of how and where that shy Dutchman, Henry Kuyper, had found such an attractive wife.

"Please," Flora Kuyper said once more.

"Very well," Congressman Stapleton said.

five

So this was a congressman, Flora thought. He looked and acted like a spoiled English scion. He dressed like one, too. His apple-green frock coat was in the latest Pall Mall style, with a broad, contrasting collar and deep cuffs of darker green velvet. He wore a frilled jabot of fine batiste at his neck, and from beneath his fashionably long embroidered blue waistcoat dangled the requisite two watch fobs. His buff breeches were skintight in the London mode.

Hugh Stapleton called in his coachman and told him to complete the journey to his home near Hackensack, inform his wife of the reason for his delay, and return for him tomorrow. He retained his trunk and from it changed out of his traveling boots to elegant blue shoes with expensive silver buckles. He eyed his hostess's dress appreciatively. "You must have friends in New York, madam," he said. "I believe that gown is identical to one worn by Mrs. Robinson at a ball given by the Prince of Wales less than a year ago."

Was he being sarcastic? Flora wondered uneasily. "London trading"—buying English goods, above all expensive dresses—was strictly forbidden by Congress. Then she saw the smile in his eyes and realized he was paying her a compliment.

"What an unexpected pleasure, to find an American congressman approving what a woman has broken the law to wear—even when she imitates the Prince of Wales's mistress."

He laughed. "You expected one of our snarling Yankee saints, who think that any man or woman who dresses well is a traitor to our glorious revolution? Let me assure you, madam, I have no use for those hypocrites."

Flora smiled. "I'm so glad," she said. "I must confess I was a little afraid that your opinions might be extreme. I understand some of the patriots of New Jersey lean in that direction—although I don't really keep track of their views. I try to live quietly, and avoid politics."

"That's decidedly in your favor," Stapleton said. "Women and politics don't mix. My wife has taken up politics. It has soured her temper and ruined her sensibility."

"I find it hard to believe that mere politics could wreak such havoc," Flora replied. "I feel impelled, as a woman, to defend her. Have you been neglecting her?"

"I suppose so," the congressman admitted, taking a steaming glass of mulled Madeira from a tray proffered by Cato. "We've been married thirteen years. Do you really think love—I mean, the sentiment that blinds us to the faults of a spouse—can last so long?"

"I wouldn't know. I've never felt it."

Flora took her wine and sipped it, her eyes cast down. That was well done, she decided, spoken at just the right moment. When she looked up she saw bemused, erotic interest playing across her visitor's handsome face.

"But that's extraordinary, madam," he said.

"Did you know my husband well?"

"Moderately. I went to Kings College with him for a year. I saw little of him since. He was—"

"A good man, a kind man. But I didn't love him. It was a marriage of convenience. Does it disturb you to discover that a woman can do such a thing?"

"On the contrary, madam. I've never been one of those who feel a woman should find a man irresistible simply because he crooks his finger at her. Unless she takes fire, unless her sensibility is aroused, there can be no real affection."

Flora smiled. How glad she was that she had not trusted the advice she had gotten from Beckford, to discuss politics with this man. The congressman saw women as creatures apart. He thought they were intended to amuse, to soothe, to intrigue successful, powerful men, among whom he clearly numbered himself.

Flora sipped her wine and let Hugh Stapleton ask her the inevitable question—how had she come to marry Henry Kuyper? "He bought me," she said. "Just as you might buy my butler, Cato—though I would never sell him."

"You came out as a redemptioner?"

73

"Yes," Flora said, slipping smoothly from truth to fabrication. It was a plausible story, the tale of Henry Kuyper purchasing her from one of those English or German ships crowded with human cargo that docked regularly in American ports, where the passengers were "redeemed" for the cost of their voyage plus a profit for the shipowner. It was an easy way for the buyer to get a servant for six or seven years, the usual length of the contract the redemptioners signed to work off their passages. "Henry's mother disliked me from the moment I set foot on the property. Perhaps her woman's intuition warned her that Henry would disobey her for the first time in his life and marry me. I had to put up with her bad temper until she finally died, the year before the war began."

"You have my sympathy," Congressman Stapleton said. "I know what strong-willed Dutch women are like. My mother was one. I moved to New York to escape her."

"More Madeira?" Flora asked.

"Thank you. Is it Tinto?"

"From the southern vineyards. What a pleasure it is to serve it to an appreciative palate. My father was a Marseilles wine merchant who went bankrupt. The shock killed my mother. I was left alone, penniless. It was America or—sell myself in less attractive ways."

"How dreadful," the congressman said, with surprisingly genuine sympathy in his voice. "My dear madam, you have endured a great deal. I'm amazed that it has not in the least diminished your spirit, your—if I may say it—beauty."

Ah, Mr. Stapleton, Flora thought. If you only knew how much I have diminished my spirit, how much I am diminishing it at this very moment to preserve the beauty that you admire and I am beginning to hate. For a moment behind her smile she was virtually paralyzed by a spasm of grief. She could see Caesar in his coffin in the icy barn, his angry eyes closed, his proud mouth slack with death's nothingness. This American, who stood here paying her compliments, may have been one of his killers.

The congressman was admiring her furniture. "It makes me wish this damned war would end somehow and I could regain my house in New York. It was furnished much like this. I, too, am fond of Chippendale."

"Will the war ever end?" Flora asked.

"Some people think it could last another ten years, provided the British remain as inert as we are."

"What if the British roused themselves?"

"I prefer not to think about that, although circumstances seem to be forcing my mind in that direction. I've just spent four days in Morristown. Washington's army is a collection of half-starved scarecrows."

"The thought of a British victory fills me with horror," Flora said. "I know I have nothing to fear from it. I suppose it's my French blood."

"Allow me to disagree with that kind of national antagonism, madam," Hugh Stapleton said. "I'm inclined to think we have a perfect right to like or dislike individuals, but it makes no sense to dislike an entire nation. Such prejudices cut us off from a vast range of potential friendships. You think of yourself as French. Should I dislike you because my father fought your countrymen in the north woods twenty years ago?"

"I would hope not," Flora said, letting her voice surround the negative words with a positive invitation.

"Just so. We have idiots in Congress who think that way. But I am not one of them. I have friends in England whom I hope to see and love again, though I have opposed the greedy, aggrandizing policy of their government which gave our New England fanatics the excuse they wanted to start this stupid war."

"I'm amazed to find such detachment of mind in a politician," Flora said.

Hugh Stapleton liked that. He liked to think of himself as educating—perhaps even creating—a woman's mind in his image. She decided that she would have to appear naive without becoming stupid.

"It's a product of philosophy, Mrs. Kuyper. Without reflection, what are we? No better than beasts. Detachment enables us to find our way through life with a maximum of pleasure and a minimum of pain. To *enjoy* our liberty, madam, that's the important thing."

"I've never felt the exhilaration of such freedom," Flora said. "Perhaps because I'm a woman. Or because I've been unfortunate."

"But now your fortune has turned, madam. You sit here, sole heiress to the Kuyper estate, the finest three hundred acres in New Jersey. I'm surprised this parlor is not thronged with suitors all the day long."

Flora smiled, acknowledging the compliment. "I felt a year's mourning was required."

"So you've gone to church every Sunday, and let old Dominie Demarest put you to sleep?"

"Yes," she said.

"We have an even bigger bore in Hackensack, Dominie Freylinghuysen. My wife insists on my going, for the children's sake. But I'm not a believer."

"Nor am I."

"A woman after my own mind," Congressman Stapleton said, tossing down the last of his wine. "You're in danger of making me regret I married young. If I were free, madam, you might find me at the head of that throng of suitors you'll soon be facing. And I assure you that my interest would not be in your three hundred acres."

"If you insist on teasing me with these compliments, the regret will be more on my side," Flora said.

Cato summoned them to dinner. The dining room's cut-glass chandelier glistened in the candle glow from the wall sconces and the seven-branched silver candelabrum on the table. Cato served them goose in a dark gravy, flavored with preserved cherries. The wine was Château Margaux, 1769. The congressman said he had not tasted anything like it since he left London, four long years ago. For dessert Cato flamed a pair of his wife Nancy's crepes filled with sliced apples. With them came the rare French dessert wine, Vin de Rousillon, which also caused the congressman to exclaim with pleasure. They returned to the parlor to drink coffee laced with brandy.

By now the congressman's face was flushed. Winter had been banished from his mind and body. He cheerfully accepted a cigar. Flora studied the small brown tubes of tobacco in their mahogany box and said, "Will you consider me a loose woman if I join you?"

"I'll consider you a woman of fashion, which you

obviously could become—if you were willing to take the final step. You know the saying?"

"A lady can't become a woman of fashion until she loses her reputation?"

"Precisely."

The congressman took a tall candle from the mantel and lit her cigar. There was no question that she had him. But did she want him? Caesar dead in the barn, delivered to her like a piece of merchandise, the proud face crushed against the raw pine of the coffin lid. Could she betray him so soon?

"It may be necessary to lose one's reputation in London or Paris, Mr. Stapleton. But here in America we can be more discreet. We can have both pleasure and reputation. It's one of the things I like about your country."

"Servants talk," he said as Cato took away the coffee cups, then served more brandy.

"Not my servants," Flora said. "I permit only two in the house, Cato and his wife, Nancy. They are absolutely trustworthy."

Cato departed, carefully shutting the door behind him. "Then the question, madam," said the congressman, strolling around the room to look at the paintings, "comes down to those elemental principles that my father's old friend Ben Franklin so lucidly explained in his book on electricity—attraction and repulsion."

"Fascinating," Flora said. "What about scruples, Mr. Stapleton? Did Dr. Franklin write about those?"

Where did she find the will, the wit for this banter? She must be playing a part that Walter Beckford had written for her. Sometimes she thought he was Satan, and William Coleman one of his dark angels. They possessed her soul and body, and no one had the power to break their spell.

"Scruples are like buzzing flies, madam," Congressman Stapleton said. "If they blunder into the field of attraction, they flutter to the ground, knocked silly by its violence."

"You make it sound so fierce."

"It's like music, madam. Fierce, sweet, fierce again."

"As I told you, I've never—played the music you're suggesting. Never gone from fierceness to sweetness to—"

Liar, boomed Caesar from within his coffin. *Liar.* She saw his hands reaching out for her. Those murderous dark hands. Terrifying in their ferocity—and the sweetness they created. She saw them, black on her white breasts.

She sat down at the harpsichord in the corner of the living room. "Will you allow me to sing my favorite song for you?"

The words were on her lips: *Plaire à celui que j'aime.* It was a way of saying good-bye to Caesar, good-bye to the dream, however dubious, that he had given her of escaping the diminished woman she had become.

Liar, roared Caesar from his cold box, and the words froze on her lips. All right, she whispered to him. I will not sing it in French I will never sing it in French to anyone but you. *Not good enough,* roared Caesar, and she heard herself choosing another song.

The poor soul sat sighing by a sycamore tree,
Sing all a green willow;
Her hand on her bosom, her head on her knee,
Sing willow, willow, willow.

The fresh streams ran by her, and murmur'd her
  moans;
  Sing willow, willow, willow;
Her salt tears fell from her, and soft'ned the stones;
  Sing willow, willow, willow. . . .

That's better, whispered Caesar from the icy darkness.

"What a lovely voice," the congressman said. "I wish you preferred a happier song."

Congressman Stapleton sat down beside her on the harpsichord bench. "Is there nothing I can do to assuage that sadness?" he asked.

"I fear not," she said, her head bowed.

He turned her face to him and softly kissed her on the lips.

Kill him, Caesar said. *Tell Cato to kill him in my name.*

"No!" she cried, and fled across the room. She found herself face to face with the last thing she wanted to see, a portrait of Caesar and Henry Kuyper as boys. Each was dressed in an elaborate velvet suit, with lace cuffs and a ruffled collar. Caesar gazed up adoringly at his young white master, who sat on a pony. It was madness. Hugh Stapleton would be melting in her arms, if it were not for that dead voice out there in the winter night.

The congressman was baffled by her conduct. "Madam," he said, "I don't understand you. Have I said or done something that disturbs you?"

"No," she said. "You must take me—I can't offer myself. I'm not a woman of fashion. There are scruples, memories—"

It was very close to the truth and it penetrated his

rake's mask. He drew her to him with unexpected gentleness. "My dear, I'm not a mere cocksman. I feel a power, a hope of affection in you, beyond anything I've ever known."

"Show me," she said. "Rescue me—from the past."

He took a candle off the harpsichord and led her upstairs. Her bedroom fireplace was aglow with coals, banked by Cato with his usual skill. Before it was a tin tub, filled with water scented with attar of roses. "I must bathe," she said, "in spite of winter."

"Isn't it dangerous?" he said, amazed. Few Americans bathed between October and June.

"Everything is dangerous," she said. "Help me."

He undid the buttons on the back of her gown and she stepped out of it. Together they unlaced the stays that had added firmness to her soft, plump waist. She slipped the pannier belt that held the little half hoops on her hips and threw those fashionable encumbrances on a chair. Turning, she gave the Congressman a swift challenging kiss. She always felt freest when she escaped the confines of the feminine mode, free and wild, equal to the most confident man. She let him unbutton the petticoat and underpetticoat. They slid down her body to a soft heap at her ankles. Mounting the tiny three-step ladder beside the tub, she descended into the warm, scented water.

Memory flooded her. She saw Caesar beside the tub in the hot summer night, the black soap-flecked hands sliding down her flesh, his own body gleaming like oiled metal. *Bitch*, he roared at her from his cold coffin. But she had control of her fear now. You are dead, she whispered. I would do anything, give anything, to restore you to life. But it is not possible.

"I need—a little drink of that," she said, pointing to the laudanum on her night table. Faithful Cato had left a glass of fresh water beside it. She put five drops in the glass and drank it down. Soon Caesar's voice became more distant; she no longer felt any need to answer him. The congressman's hands were massaging her back, her breasts, exploring beneath the water the silken hair of love. She smiled and let his tongue probe her mouth. It was the best way to say good-bye to Caesar.

With no warning Caesar changed into another ghost, Henry Kuyper whispering in Dutch: *"Ah, myn Flora, myn Flora."* For a moment she relived the old struggle against indifference, remembering Henry panting above her while Caesar waited in the thick summer heat of the barn, ripe with hay and animal smells. One last time Caesar speared her like a triumphant hunter, taunting her, making her beg him for release, for breath, at last crooning softly, *Plaire à celui que j'aime.*

The congressman was inviting her to bed. He had removed his expensive clothes and found a purple robe in the big Dutch cupboard on the other side of the room. He was holding up a sky-blue dressing gown for her. She stepped into it and into his arms in one falling motion. "Take me, rescue me," she murmured, and he carried her to the bed.

He drew the curtains, and darkness consumed the ghosts around the fireplace. The blank, swift motions of desire dismissed memory. He was a man, the congressman. She savored the sinewy muscles of his arms and back as he drew her to him. She welcomed the first deep thrust of his sex, and his eager tongue in her lying mouth. At least this was not a lie, she wanted him now as much as she had ever wanted Caesar or any other man. She remembered his words downstairs: "a hope of affection in you." Even he, behind or beneath his boredom and self-satisfaction, sought a love that was strong enough to transform a mercenary world.

He began to stroke her slowly, deliberately, with the practiced skill of a man who knew how to extract maximum pleasure from this ancient ritual. Flora struggled to keep her will, her wish, focused on that promise of affection, to meet his rising excitement. But the knowledge that she was lying beneath this man on orders from Walter Beckford collided with this wish, with the possibility of affection. In the wreckage, Caesar's voice boomed out of the wintry night: *Never. Never love anyone but me*. Memories of other men, grinning peers and politicians for whom she had assumed this supine position, prowled in the distance like deserters in search of plunder. She should have sung the secret words, *Plaire à celui*. She should have dismissed hope, mocked love, once and for all.

"Ahhh," gasped the congressman. Flora felt his seed surge deep in her belly, a young man's coming, after many long, lonely nights. He lifted her against him and for a second they were together, his fists tangled in her hair, his lips against her throat. Then they were on the earth again, in Bergen, New Jersey, with Caesar in the cold barn growling *Never* and the British and their money and power a half-hour away across the frozen Hudson.

Congressman Stapleton cradled her in his arms. "My dear, my dearest Flora," he said. "You really are a goddess of nature, of spring. You transform winter—"

She had him. She had a congressman. She had a lover who thought he had rescued her from guilty dreads and lackluster widowhood, from the griefs and humiliations of her fictitious past. Flora wondered what Major Beckford planned to do with him.

six

Hugh Stapleton slept in Bergen, his arms around Flora Kuyper. Two dozen miles away in Elizabethtown, a saturnine man in a Continental Army uniform sat at a dining-room table reading a letter. It was addressed to one of the young ladies of the village and on first inspection appeared to be nothing more than a chatty note from a loyalist cousin in New York. The letter discussed fashions and balls and plays, handsome officers and their budding romances and foundering liaisons. The young lady was obviously fascinated by the British army's gallants. That was hardly unusual. Her cousin, who happened to be Susan Livingston, daughter of the rebel governor of New Jersey, had agreed in a recent letter that almost every female, rebel or loyal, was liable to contract a case of "scarlet fever" if she spent too much time with these red-coated gentlemen.

The man took from his pouch an hourglass-shaped mask and placed it over the chatty note. Almost all of the page was obscured, except parts of a half-dozen lines in the center. These communicated something far more important than affairs of the heart.

> *Some officers say the*
> *best way to finish the*
> *business is to kill a*
> *certain general or buy*
> *him off and claim they*
> *are indifferent as to*
> *which is done. They want*
> *to end the war this year.*

Muttering a curse, the man took another letter from a pouch on the chair beside him. This one was written in gibberish.

> byon nzitelnl tifeailr el uiltir mrtnelelf
> tpayr yh elkenl nrrnlc yl lyti ektuio

Beside the letter the man placed the key to this alphabet cipher. He soon had the message decoded: *First American Regiment in secret training. Rumor of Indian attack on Albany. Fearful mortality aboard the prison ship* Jersey. *Quantities of counterfeit money being sent to Connecticut.*

A knock. Instinctively, the man reached for the pistol on the table beside him. "Who is it?" he said.

"Usaph Grey, sir. I was hoping for a chance to speak with you."

"Just a moment."

The man swept everything off the table and into the pouch. Unlocking the door, he admitted a small, limping civilian with the darting, stricken eyes of a trapped rabbit.

"What happened to your leg?"

"I slipped on the ice coming across the Kill last night," Grey said. "Our sentries chased me. I never expected them out in this weather."

"We've improved the discipline in this place," the saturnine man growled. "Where have you been lately?"

"I got back from New England two nights ago. I carried a letter from Dr. Haliburton in Newport. He tells me that he has made a great catch. Metcalf Bowler, the chief justice of Rhode Island, has agreed to come over to them the moment affairs look promising for reconciliation."

"Did you copy Haliburton's letter?"

Grey shook his head. "Too dangerous. Anyway, it was in that same code. The one you couldn't break."

"God damn it," said the saturnine man, crashing his fist on the table. "If we get more than' one sample, we improve our chances a hundred percent."

"It's too dangerous, Major. They searched me at the ferry. Stripped me to my skin, in the damn ferry house, without even a fire. Let me stand there in below-zero cold while they went through every stitch. It was Beckford's orders. He's got a nose for double agents. I think he's wise to me."

"So you don't want to go back?"

Grey shifted from one foot to another. "I'd like to return to duty with my regiment, sir. My constitution is worn out from the strain."

The saturnine man pulled at his nose. He made an odd clicking sound with his back teeth. "How many other men do you think we have in your position, Grey? Trusted courier for His Majesty's secret agents, from here to Canada?"

"I don't know, sir."

"None."

"None," Grey said in a doleful echo.

"We'll double your money."

"It's not the money. It's—it's the consequences. I've got two boys. I don't want them to think of me dying at the end of a rope."

"Some good men have died that way."

"And who remembers them? Who remembers Captain Hale?"

"I do," snarled the saturnine man. "He was my best friend."

In spite of this warning, Grey sullenly persisted. "His own family scarcely mention him. They all feel the disgrace."

The saturnine man stared at the polished tabletop. He was back four years, in the fields outside the city of New York, watching Nathan Hale play football with the men of his regiment. Hale gave the ball one of his tremendous kicks, which had sent it soaring over the tops of some nearby trees while everyone watched, openmouthed. A trivial memory—the vanishing ball, the athlete's laughing face. But for a moment the man could think of nothing else.

"Captain Grey," he said, "when we caught you in treasonous correspondence with the enemy two years ago, we could have hanged you on the spot. We gave you a chance to repent of your crime and expiate the stain from your soul. But those charges could be revived at any time. Would you want your farm confiscated, your wife and boys turned into the road?

I can arrange to have it done—you hanged, them dispossessed—in a week's time."

"All right," Grey said with a sigh. "I'll go back for another run. They want me to meet some escaped officers in Mount Hope and cross New Jersey with them. In case they can't get through our lines around New York, I'm to take them through Connecticut and across the Sound. They seem uncommonly concerned about these gentlemen. Beckford offered me double the usual pay to meet them on time."

"Send me a careful list of their names, as well as the names of the houses in which you stay. Pay close attention to their conversations."

"How shall I get it to you?"

"Use the substitution cipher I gave you. Write it when you're safely out of New York. Leave it with the proper token at the Sign of the Elk in Stamford."

"I don't trust that innkeeper. He's drunk half the time. What's this month's token?"

The saturnine man handed him a six-dollar Continental bill. It was torn almost in half. "It'll buy you tuppence of brandy," he said, in bitter reference to the way inflation had made American currency laughable.

"I'll leave it with him for a tip," Grey said. "I want to be on the road when he finds the packet. He enjoys the business too much. The last time, he spent half the night winking at me, the rest of the time treating me as if I was a visiting general. Tell him I'm a peddler and should be treated like one."

"I'll tell him," the saturnine man said. "I must get on to Morristown with this pouch."

Usaph Grey limped from the room. Benjamin Stallworth sighed and rubbed his aching eyes. Had he sent Grey to his death? he wondered. Perhaps. But in a sense, Grey was already dead. Stallworth remembered the man's terror as he pleaded for his life in the Morristown jail two years ago. Grey had experienced death that night, sweating, trembling, puking. He, Stallworth, had chosen not to execute the sentence. Instead he had permitted him to survive as his creature; he had restored him to the half-life of the double agent.

Officially, Stallworth was a major in the 2nd Continental Dragoons. These horsemen served mostly as messengers, operating from small outposts dotted along the Connecticut shore, and across Westchester County into New Jersey. The major moved from outpost to outpost, ostensibly making sure that his men retained their military discipline on detached duty. Actually, he was like a patient spider, moving around the rim of New York, weaving webs of information and deception. Major Stallworth was the American army's chief of intelligence.

Another knock on the door. The man who entered the room this time was also an American spy—but that was where his resemblance to Usaph Grey ended. This second visitor was dressed in expensive, brilliantly colored clothes. He wore spots of rouge on his cheeks and Stallworth suspected he also tinted his lips. He walked like a woman; the movements of his hands, the tones of his voice, were effeminate. Paul Stapleton was a Williamite, the common term for men who were attracted to other men. The sin of Sodom had been popularized, almost legitimized, in England because King William the Third, hero of the Glorious Revolution of 1688, had practiced it. When Stallworth was a boy, his minister father had preached a sermon at the hanging of a Williamite, who had been caught corrupting the youth of Greenwich, Connecticut. Now the minister's son sat stonily at a table, concealing his revulsion, dealing with one of these perverts as a more or less trusted ally. The fact that Paul Stapleton was the younger brother of a Continental Congressman intensified Stallworth's distaste.

"Who have you seen on this visit?"

"I'm painting a portrait of General von Knyphausen. Beckford talks to him in German, which I don't know very well. I only got a smattering of it on my European tour. But I gather they're discussing some sort of coup. I hear variations on the verb *schlagen*. It must have something to do with politics. At one point Becky—I mean Beckford—referred to it as a *staatsmännischer Zug*—a stroke of statecraft."

Paul Stapleton was an artist by profession. He had been driven out of New York by the war. Late in 1777, he had unexpectedly asked General Washington for permission to return to the British-occupied city to paint portraits. Having spent several years in London, Stapleton had numerous friends among the British garrison. The officers, eager to see themselves on canvas, had already accepted his declaration of neutrality and guaranteed his safety. Only Washington—and now Stallworth—knew that this unlikely man had volunteered to serve as a spy and for two years had been bringing them information that he picked up while painting British and German officers and their mistresses.

"I hope you haven't finished your portrait of General Knyphausen."

"Not quite."

Stallworth rummaged in his saddlebag and came up with a tattered notebook. "Here's a dictionary of German phrases that I put together for my men, to help them question deserters. Take it with you and study it before your next visit."

Paul thumbed the pages. "I can't promise you much. Languages have never been my forte."

Paul Stapleton departed. Stallworth sat there, trying to measure the probability that he was telling the truth against the possibility that he was lying. Before the war Paul Stapleton had been Walter Beckford's lover. Had Beckford planted Stapleton and fed him information that was not significantly harmful to the British, while waiting to use him to mask a major operation? This possibility, coupled with his revulsion for Stapleton, always made Stallworth reluctant to act on anything the painter brought him.

An hour later, Stallworth said good-bye to his host, Colonel Elias Dayton, a large, solemn man noteworthy chiefly for his stupidity. From drops on enemy-held Staten Island, less than a mile away across the narrow Kill van Kull, and from carefully selected innkeepers and postmasters in New Jersey, Dayton collected the coded letters that Stallworth had just spent two hours deciphering. Dayton also had one or two spies with whom he worked personally. He was always convinced that their information was vital and infallibly true. By now Stallworth had learned to doubt every spy's report, to see behind it the frightened or boastful or greedy or reckless human being who wrote it.

Up the dark, frozen road to Springfield Major Stallworth rode on his careful Connecticut horse. The major's father had been a minister of the sternest of stern old New England school and the gloomy rigor of unrefined Calvinism was deep in Stallworth's bones. His world was inhabited by men and women with hearts corrupted by Adam's fall. How many times had he heard his father thunder from the pulpit: *We naturally as we come into the world are disaffected to God, are in league with Satan and in love with his cause and interest. Mankind are much worse than they are wont to imagine.*

Stallworth still concurred with that last sentiment, although five years of war had destroyed his faith in a supernatural explanation for it. Whatever or whoever presided over this frozen world, there was no question about mankind's capacity for treachery, seduction, and murder.

Through the neat village of Springfield, at the foot of the Short Hills, Major Stallworth rode, the bitter northeast wind at his back. At Bryant's Tavern in the hills above Chatham, he paused to pick up another coded message and some hot rum, then cautiously descended the steep slopes to the rolling country between Chatham and Morristown. An hour later he dismounted in front of General George Washington's headquarters.

The sentry before the guard hut across the road from the mansion challenged him and called out the sign for the night: "Lafayette."

"I don't know the countersign," snapped Stallworth, "but hold your fire. I'm Major Benjamin Stallworth of the Second Dragoons."

"Why sure, Major," said the sentry, lowering his gun. "Come right forward."

Stallworth strode up the path cut through the drifts to the door of the hut. As he reached the sentry he lunged at the soldier, tore the musket from his hand, and smashed the butt into his chest. The man toppled into the snow gasping with anguish.

"If I have anything to say about it, you'll be dismissed from His Excellency's Guard tomorrow," Stallworth snarled. "You have no right to recognize someone who doesn't know the countersign. He should only be recognized by the officer of the day. Where is he?"

The sentry staggered to his feet and fell through the door of the hut. An officer and the half-dozen other members of the guard sat sleepily around a small footstove.

"Lieutenant," the sentry gasped.

The lieutenant sprang to his feet, fumbling for his pistol. The other men lunged for their muskets, which were stacked against the opposite wall.

"Never mind," Stallworth roared. "If I were an assassin or part of an assassination squad, you'd all be dead men now. I've just taken the musket away from your sentry by the simple expedient of telling him my name. Where is your commander, Major Gibbs?"

Ten minutes later, while George Washington stood uneasily between them, Stallworth confronted Major Caleb Gibbs, commander of the Life Guard. A raw-boned Rhode Islander with a heavy country accent, Gibbs gestured at Stallworth, almost too angry to utter a coherent sentence. "Your Excellency, sir," he said. "I got to protest the unsoldierly, treacherous way this man tricked and assaulted one of my men a few minutes ago and possibly injured him."

"He deserved to be shot dead instead of just possibly injured," Stallworth said. "I recommend his immediate court-martial and dismissal from your Guard,

General—as an example to the rest of them. They've become dangerously lax."

"But the fellow did know you, Major Stallworth. He was a member of your troop of dragoons•in 1778," Washington said.

"The boy—he's only nineteen, General—tries to be polite to a former commander and gets his chest stove in," Gibbs fumed. "I say if anyone should be court-martialed or dismissed, it's Major Stallworth."

"I'd welcome a court-martial," Stallworth snapped. "It would give us an opportunity to investigate the conduct of Major Gibbs as commander of Your Excellency's Guard. Survival of your person and the survival of this country are synonymous, Your Excellency. There's nothing more important to which a court-martial board might give its attention."

"Gentlemen," Washington said, "I think you're both overwrought. Let's sleep on these charges and countercharges, and consider them in the calm light of morning."

Gibbs stamped out of the office. Stallworth dropped onto a straight-backed chair beside the General's desk and sat there drumming his fingers. Washington sighed and sat down behind the desk. He was wearing a dark blue night robe over his shirt, which was open at the neck. Most of the day's powder was gone from his reddish brown hair. A half-dozen already written letters lay on one side of the desk. He had been in the middle of another letter when Stallworth and Gibbs stormed into the office.

"Do you really think that was necessary?" Washington said.

"Your Excellency," Stallworth replied, "you'll recall when you chose this house for your quarters, I warned you that it was too far from the main army. My opinion was passed over. But you promised that you'd take extra pains to ensure the strictest discipline in your Guard. It hasn't been done. You're two miles from your troops, guarded by a pack of sleepwalkers!"

Washington nodded wearily. "A man can only do so much, Stallworth. Between the weather and no money and one hundred desertions a week, we've been on the stretch eighteen hours a day here."

Stallworth stared at Washington for a leaden moment, remembering the day that his taut nerves had snapped and he had marched into headquarters at Valley Forge to lecture the commander in chief on the carelessness with which civilians were allowed to go in and out of British-occupied Philadelphia. Instead of reprimanding him for impertinence, Washington had quietly explained that a fairly high percentage of these civilians were American secret agents.

Then, with an offhand humility that had astonished Stallworth, Washington admitted that security at the outposts was too lax. He was looking for a cavalry officer who might be interested in doing something more subtle than skirmishing with rival British patrols. Someone who could work with his secret agents. Was Stallworth interested? Stallworth's answer had been another lecture. He had given a great deal of thought to espionage since his friend Nathan Hale had died so needlessly in 1776. He would accept the responsibility only if he were given some authority over the agents with whom he worked. He did not want to be a mere spectator while brave men were given careless instructions, inadequate disguises, and suicidal missions.

Washington had merely nodded and begun telling Stallworth what some of the Philadelphia agents were doing. One apparent loyalist had access to the British commander in chief. He regularly carried letters Washington wrote, packed with false information about the growing strength of the American army, to this gentleman, who believed every word of them. Weren't they in Washington's own handwriting? Another spy, a sweet-faced Quaker lady, spent a great deal of time lying on the second floor of her house, her ear pressed to a crack in the floor, listening to the deliberations of British staff officers in her dining room.

"We've learned a few things about this business since we lost your friend Hale," Washington said.

That was the moment when Stallworth began changing his mind about George Washington. Over the next months, Stallworth realized that this man was prepared to accept almost any criticism, to tolerate the dislike of subordinates, the ineptitude of Congress, the hostility of New Englanders, in the name of victory. Stallworth had struggled to imitate his example. For the past year it had become more and more difficult as he watched Americans everywhere, even in New England, lose interest in the seemingly endless war. He had seen Connecticut troops working in the snow without shoes and stockings, and heard their officers damning Congress and the United States of America. For a year rage and disillusion had been building in Stallworth, intensified by the knowledge that the same thing was happening to everyone else in the army. Only this Virginian's uncanny calm, his refusal to lose his head, had enabled Stallworth to control himself.

"Maybe we're all half distracted with the way things are going," he said. "I'll apologize to Gibbs in the morning."

"Good. Would you like some port?"

"Grog would do better. I've been on the road for the better part of twenty hours."

Washington walked to the door of the office and called out, "Colonel Hamilton, would you ask Billy to bring some hot grog for Major Stallworth?"

In a few minutes, Billy Lee, the slave that everyone in the army called Washington's black shadow, appeared with a mug of steaming rum and water. Stallworth drank it greedily, leaned back in his chair for a moment, and closed his eyes. For another half-hour his tired brain could function. "Now let's get down to business," he said. "I want to hear exactly what happened."

Washington took a sheaf of papers from a drawer and studied them for a moment. "Caesar Muzzey was killed about two hundred yards from this front door. He spent the earlier part of the night at Red Peggy's, on the Vealtown Road, and left a message from Three-fifteen in the usual place there."

"What was the message?"

"Of little consequence, so far as I can see. A rumor that there's an expedition planned to the north for which they've imported winter clothing from Canada."

Stallworth clicked his teeth. "We'll soon hear they've imported skates to go up the Hudson on the ice."

"Muzzey left Red Peggy's about ten-thirty P.M. We know nothing of where he went or to whom he spoke between that time and twelve-thirty, when he was discovered with a bayonet in his chest."

"Was he dead?"

"No, he was able to say one or two words. They seemed to refer to a code about which we know nothing: forty twenty-six."

"Twenty-six," Stallworth said, all but leaping from his chair.

"The same thing occurred to me. Caesar was on his way to collect the hundred guineas we promised him for Twenty-six's identity. But I'm no longer so sure it's that simple."

"Excuse me for interrupting you. Please finish the story."

"By the time they got Muzzey into the duty hut he was dead."

"Who was the officer of the day?"

"One of our most dependable men, Lieutenant Conway of the Delaware line. He's been in the service for three years. Distinguished himself at the Brandywine."

"And the men he commanded?"

"Veterans, every one of them. No reason to doubt their loyalty."

"Nevertheless, I think we should learn all we can about them. As well as about Conway. I presume you made a thorough search of Caesar's body."

Washington nodded. "We opened the lining of every piece of clothing he wore. We found nothing but the ten guineas we paid him for the message from Three-fifteen."

"So we're left, for the time being, with the two people who found him, Congressman Stapleton and my fellow Yale graduate, the Reverend Caleb Chandler."

Washington nodded. "What have you found out about Chandler?"

"His family seems sound. Two older brothers who

served in one of the Connecticut militia regiments that pretended to fight for us in New York in '76."

"The Kips Bay sprinters?" Washington said, with a rueful smile. He could relax with Stallworth, who had long since outgrown his New England chauvinism. Most of it had vanished on that fall day in 1776 when he watched four thousand Connecticut militiamen stampede up the east side of Manhattan Island at the first glimpse of the British light infantry.

"The Chandlers are old New England stock. The father is an elder of the Lebanon church. The mother is related to Colonel Meigs of the Sixth Connecticut. But our friend Caleb was sponsored at Yale by the late Reverend Joel Lockwood."

"That's not in his favor."

"Agreed. But I could find no one who recalled Chandler making disloyal remarks at Yale. He has a tendency to extreme opinions. In his last year he became a violent foe of slavery. But that's not entirely surprising. The new president of the college is a strong critic of it."

"The president of Yale?" Washington said. He shook his head in his slow, reflective way. "You Yankees will drive me to distraction with your notions, yet, Stallworth. You want officers to fight a five-year war for paltry pay; you see military dictators sprouting like weeds every time a general makes a few demands. You expect men to be angels, Stallworth."

"Or devils," Stallworth said with a wry smile.

"To get back to Chandler. It hardly seems logical for a man who denounces slavery to murder a black, then demand an investigation of the crime."

"Unless we're dealing with a very subtle, very devilish mind, General. Remember what we caught the Reverend Lockwood telling Beckford: there were men in New England who were ready to make a separate peace. I got further confirmation of this trend tonight, from Grey. He says Bowler, the chief justice of Rhode Island, has begun crying quits. What if Chandler plans to use Caesar's murder to set the New England and New Jersey regiments at the throats of the rest of the army? Playing the idealistic parson could be the ultimate deception."

"If that was—or is—his plan, he should have chosen a more likable victim. From what you've told me, Muzzey was about as charming as a rattlesnake."

"The truth isn't important in such matters, General. Chandler may be planning to cry up Muzzey as the perfect example of the bondage of the enlisted men that he likes to talk about."

Washington shook his head, still unconvinced. "Could a Yale man have so little conscience?" he said, smiling.

"Anything is possible, from what I hear goes on at Yale these days. There aren't two students in the place who believe in God. When they're not writing plays or acting in them, they're drinking and whoring like Charleston rakes. Do we have men watching this fellow Chandler?"

"Day and night."

"Good. What about Congressman Stapleton?"

"We detained him in camp for a few days by asking him to help us in the pro forma inquiry we conducted into Muzzey's death. I had someone go through his baggage while the inquiry was in session but we found nothing."

"Do you know him well?"

"No. I met his father years ago, when I visited New York. A direct, outspoken man, with a very

101

distinguished record in the French wars. He was no enthusiast for independence. But, then, neither was I."

"We'll open a dossier on you immediately, General," Stallworth said with a flicker of a smile. "Stapleton's brother is one of our agents. That's in the congressman's favor."

"He's the portrait painter, who poses as a neutral?"

"Correct. But one patriot in a family guarantees nothing, these days. I sometimes think half the people in New Jersey have a relative living on the King's shilling in New York."

Washington nodded glumly. "I had my doubts about letting the congressman visit Mrs. Kuyper. But I wasn't prepared to take him into our confidence."

"Of course not," Stallworth said. "Let's see how he conducts himself with that charming lady. It may tell us a good deal about him."

"Did you pick up anything else in your travels that might shed some light on this mystery?"

"Something big is brewing, that's all we can find out. There's a lot of talk about a 'capital stroke' that will end the war. Muzzey's murder may have been connected to it. If Beckford found out he was a double agent, looking for information to sell us, he'd kill him without a qualm."

The General shook his head. "I'm afraid you've let the deaths of those other agents incline you to overestimate Beckford's bloodthirstiness. He's as likely as we are to let a double agent go on living, as long as he's useful. I suspect Muzzey was more useful to them than he was to us. The information he brought us from New York was trifling."

"I didn't trust him enough to let him anywhere

near a major network," Stallworth said. "All of which leads me to conclude that our resident son of a bitch Twenty-six sniffed out Caesar and killed him without consulting Beckford."

"Why did he leave the body in the snow two hundred yards from this house? It would have been far more sensible to bury it under a drift in the woods, where no one would find it until spring, if then. It's as if whoever killed him wanted us—or someone else—to know about it. Even to implicate us in the crime."

"I can't imagine who your someone else might be."

"If we knew more—if we knew anything—about Twenty-six, we might have the answer to that question. I can't see what he's gained by arousing us. If anything, it's increased his risks."

"All that makes admirable sense," Stallworth said. "There's only one way to find out if it's true. We must replace Muzzey. Find someone who'll become their courier as well as ours. Someone more loyal to us."

"Not an easy order."

"I have a candidate. This chaplain, Chandler."

"Chandler?" Washington looked dubious.

"We've got enough evidence to justify an arrest right now. Give me two or three days with him. I'll find out if he's one of theirs or just a fanatic. Either way, I'll turn him into one of ours."

"I'm not sure if I like this process you've developed," Washington said. "Tampering with a man's soul is a dangerous business. Remember what happened with the Reverend Lockwood."

"Lockwood was a drunkard."

"Chandler's awfully young."

"Is it any different, General, from ordering men his age to stand and die on a battlefield?"

"Yes," Washington said. "It is different. Don't forget that, Major."

Stallworth swallowed the rebuke. "I'll remember it, General. Do I have your permission to make the arrest?"

"Yes. Even if you don't succeed, it will at least put a stop to his sermons."

For a moment Benjamin Stallworth remembered the terror on Usaph Grey's face, the anguish in Joel Lockwood's eyes. It was not a pretty process; he was willing to admit that much. But a battlefield was not a pretty place, either. War, especially a war for national survival, was not a pretty business. "That much you can depend on, General," he said. "You'll hear no more noise from Caleb Chandler."

seven

Hisswrack! Hisswrack! Hisswrack! In the below-zero cold, Caleb Chandler watched a private from one of the regiments in his brigade being given thirty-nine lashes for striking an officer. The soldier clung to the whipping post, biting into a lead bullet to keep from screaming. The rest of the brigade stood in ranks, impassively watching his ordeal. In their ripped and patched uniforms, they looked like an assembly of beggars.

"Don't let up, Drum Major. Thirty-nine full strokes," growled the acting commander of the brigade, lean, imperious Colonel Jedediah Sumner, son of the richest man in Connecticut.

The drummer wielding the lash obeyed Colonel Sumner by redoubling the force of the next seven strokes. Caleb had seen at least a dozen men whipped since he arrived in Morristown in November. Each time the sight and sound had made him numb with revulsion. He had never dreamed that free men, fellow Americans, would have to be disciplined with such brutality.

After witnessing one particularly severe lashing—five hundred strokes for robbing chickens from a local farmer—Caleb Chandler had crossed frozen Primrose Brook to the camp of the 1st Connecticut Brigade and denounced the army's treatment of the enlisted men to his cousin Return Jonathan Meigs, colonel of the 3rd Connecticut Regiment. Meigs, already one of the most distinguished soldiers of the revolution, had regarded his clerical cousin with amazement. "Wait till you're in camp another month before you get so exercised," he said.

Chandler had now been in camp considerably longer than another month, and seeing soldiers lashed still incensed him. He had been almost as disturbed by the other punishments the army used to enforce discipline. Picketing dangled a culprit by his wrist from a hook on a tall post. The victim had the choice of enduring the pain in his arm or balancing his feet on a stake just sharp enough to cause agony if he placed his full weight on it. A man sentenced to the horse straddled a wooden plank, his hands tied behind him, a musket lashed to each leg. After a few minutes the pain in his private parts was exquisite.

Caleb could no longer complain to Colonel Meigs about the army's disciplinary methods. Relations between them had ceased to be cordial when Caleb preached to the two Connecticut brigades, and the New Jersey brigade early in the New Year. His text had been from Exodus. *Then the Lord said unto Moses: Go in unto Pharaoh and speak to him.*

Pharaoh, Caleb told the men, was authority, the officers and especially the generals of the army. Perhaps it was time that the enlisted men learned to speak to them. Perhaps it was time for Pharaoh to heed the complaints of those in bondage before the seven plagues devoured America, as they had devastated Egypt. The sufferings of the enlisted men cried out for justice and no one seemed willing to listen.

Some enlisted men had liked the sermon. But it had enraged the officers. Caleb's cousin Meigs had glared and shaken his head. Colonel Sumner had been more vocal. "These men haven't seen fresh meat for a month," he had roared. "If they go to Pharaoh, it will be with guns in their hands."

Caleb was tempted to ask Sumner how much fresh meat he had eaten lately. But that mocking inner voice had whispered *Fool* and he had swallowed the colonel's rebuke in silence.

Hisswrack, the last stroke fell. The lashed man, whose name was Twist, was untied from the whipping post and dragged into a nearby hut. Caleb followed him. Twist lay face down on the floor before the fire while his friends rubbed cold snow on his bleeding back. "Is there anything I can do?" Caleb asked from the doorway.

"Yeah, Chaplain," gasped Twist, "go tell Pharaoh to shit in your hat."

"I thought this might help," Caleb said, and held out a canteen filled with rum.

Twist took a long swallow. "Chaplain," he said, "maybe you ain't such a horse's ass as you seem like."

Outside on the frigid parade ground, the men

were being dismissed. Caleb stood there while they streamed past, not one even looking at him. He wanted desperately to let them know he was their friend, that he was still prepared to risk the abuse of the officers by speaking out for them. But it seemed more and more impossible to convince them of his commitment. They had turned bitterly inward, trusting neither officers nor chaplains.

With a sigh, Caleb Chandler set out for the camp of the New Jersey brigade. He was still trying to find out more about Caesar Muzzey. He had visited Muzzey's hutmates twice, and they had refused to talk to him, beyond growling that they did not know who killed Muzzey and cared less. Caleb had tried to assure them that he had no official connection with the court of inquiry General Washington had set up to investigate the murder. They had ignored him.

At headquarters, when Caleb asked about the investigation, aides turned him away with curt, vague assurances. General Washington was still very concerned about the matter. He had assigned an officer, Major Benjamin Stallworth of the 2nd Dragoons, to explore it fully. Exactly what was Major Stallworth doing? That was confidential. Nothing could be discussed until his work was completed.

Like the two Connecticut brigades, the three regiments that composed the New Jersey brigade lived in huts around a small parade ground in the long, shallow ravine called Jockey Hollow. The perpetual northeast wind lashed at Chandler as he trudged to the hut where Caesar Muzzey had been quartered. A half-dozen men were huddled around a small fire in the smoky interior. One man was wearing his blanket for breeches. Another was using his blanket as a shirt. Their stockings gaped with holes; their feet were wrapped in rags as substitutes for shoes. Their sooty, dirt-smeared faces had had no contact with soap and water for weeks.

"Hey, Chaplain, you back again?" asked Case, the hut's leader, a gaunt man with a face like a skull. He had been a tailor in civilian life and had kept his uniform fairly intact, except for his shoes. No one, not even a shoemaker, could rescue the shoddy shoes that Massachusetts contractors sold the army. Often they fell apart after a day's march.

"I'm back," Caleb said. "I'm still hoping you'll remember something that might help us find Caesar Muzzey's murderer."

"Chaplain, didn't I tell you last time we don't give a damn?" Case said.

"I brought some food and drink for you—and your brother soldiers," Caleb said, adopting the phrase that the enlisted men had begun to use when they spoke to each other.

Caleb held out the canteen of rum and drew a small ham from the pocket of his cloak. He had bought it from his landlady. Case swigged from the canteen and passed it to his brother soldiers. While they drank he whipped a knife from a sheath at his belt and sliced the ham into six pieces with almost miraculous speed. Each piece was only a mouthful but the meat and the rum transformed the men's attitude toward Caleb.

"Fire away, Chaplain," Case said. "We'll talk as long as the rum holds out."

"Who do you think killed Caesar?"

Case looked around the circle of dirt-smeared faces, each set of jaws working on the ham. "Just remember, you goddamn chompers, none of you ever heard me say this."

Everyone nodded vigorously and chewed away. Case nibbled on his slice of ham. "One of the officers done it for sure. Maybe our lieutenant. Name's Haldane. He went home on leave the day after they found Caesar's body."

"It wasn't one of us, Chaplain," said another soldier, with the face of a fourteen-year-old boy. "None of us *liked* old Caesar, mind you. But none of us hated him enough to go lookin' for him in the dark."

"Why did Lieutenant Haldane hate Caesar?"

"At Monmouth, Haldane hid behind a tree," Case said. "Caesar called him a cowardly bastard. Haldane didn't say a word. After that, Caesar went over the chain pretty much when he pleased."

"So Haldane and maybe a brother officer waited for Caesar in the dark," the boy said. "That's what we think."

"Did Muzzey ever talk about where he went when he left camp?"

Case grabbed the canteen of rum from a gray-haired man who was guzzling too much of it. "He had a wench," Case said bitterly. "Used to talk about layin' her. Drove the rest of us half crazy, the bastard."

"Did Caesar ever let on where this woman lived?"

Everyone shook his head. Caleb Chandler was baffled by what he was learning about Caesar Muzzey. It was becoming harder and harder to picture this black man as a martyr to prejudice. His hutmates apparently had good reason to dislike him.

"Caesar had ten guineas in his pocket when he died," Caleb said. "Where did he get the money?"

"Might have been from his sable lady fair," Case

said. "I suspect she was a free nigger. There's a lot of'm in this state."

"Used to tell us that he had the money to buy his discharge anytime he wanted it," the boy said. "Told us we was fools for bein' scared to try it. Said he could get us all discharges, for five guineas each, anytime."

"Discharges are for sale?"

"More than one way to skin Pharaoh, Chaplain," Case said, his skull face contorting into a laugh.

"Where? Who—who would do such a thing?" Caleb said.

Case smiled and drained the last of the rum from the canteen. "Don't he sound just like an officer, boys?" He handed Caleb the empty canteen. "We sort of think we know. But we ain't tellin' you, Chaplain."

Caleb groped for a response while *Fool* echoed ominously in his head. Case was right. He had sounded like an officer. Did becoming a brother soldier mean you stopped caring about victory? Was the cause poisoned beyond redemption?

The boy's eyes had a liquorish shine. He was enjoying this game of teasing the chaplain. "Might go down to Red Peggy's and ask her a few questions. Caesar spent a lot of time there."

"Shut your stupid mouth," Case snarled, and cuffed the boy on the side of his head.

It was not the first time Caleb Chandler had heard Red Peggy's mentioned. The place was a groggery about two miles from Jockey Hollow, on the Vealtown Road. There were several of these establishments on the outskirts of Morristown. Unlike taverns, groggeries

111

neither served food nor rented rooms; they specialized in cheap liquor.

Cowed by a warning glare from Case, Caesar Muzzey's former hutmates refused to say another word about Red Peggy. The goodwill created by the ham and the rum was vanishing into the murky air of the hut's interior. Caleb abandoned his pretensions to being a brother soldier and left the men with an exhortation. "I hope none of you will be craven enough to desert your country now, when your help is so badly needed."

"Seems more like the country's deserted us, Chaplain," Case said.

Half frozen, sinking into the snow with every step, Caleb trudged down the Vealtown Road to Red Peggy's groggery. He found himself yearning for his sturdy old farm horse, Horace, who had brought him to Morristown. Like the army's horses, Horace was being boarded at the stable of a nearby farmer. Even General Washington's mounts had been dispersed for the winter.

Only the emergence of a soldier in uniform enabled Caleb to find Red Peggy's place. It sat back from the road, an ordinary faded red Jersey farmhouse, without even the crude imitation of a tavern sign that most groggeries displayed. Inside, he found the parlor had been converted into a taproom. A welcome blaze crackled in a fieldstone fireplace. Behind a corner bar stood a buxom woman with a strong, not unpleasing face, topped by a mass of curly red hair. She needed no introduction.

Red Peggy looked vaguely disreputable at first glance. She wore too much makeup on her rounded cheeks and full lips. But her dress was as high-necked and modest as anything worn by the respectable ladies of Lebanon, Connecticut. Caleb allowed her the benefit of the doubt for the time being.

Perhaps a dozen drinkers sat at tables scattered about the room. They were being waited on by a squat man, not much taller than a dwarf, in a Continental army uniform. At the bar, Chandler asked for a rum toddy to banish the cold. The hot drink restored a semblance of life to his hands and feet. "Are you familiar with a New Jersey soldier, a Negro named Caesar Muzzey?" he asked.

Red Peggy looked at Chandler with uneasiness on her overrouged face. "What regiment be you from?" she said.

"I'm the chaplain of the Second Connecticut Brigade."

"Then what have you to do with Caesar Muzzey?"

"I'm trying to find out who killed him."

"I've told all I know of him to Major Stallworth," Red Peggy said. "Why all this fussing and fretting over a private soldier? You'd think it was a general we'd lost instead of a black private as wayward as Caesar Muzzey."

"Did he come here often?"

"Often enough. He was here the night he died. He was in great spirits. He sang us a love song in French."

"I've talked to some men who think Caesar came here to buy a forged discharge. Do you know anything about such a business?"

Red Peggy's blue-lidded eyes bulged; her powdered cheeks swelled. "What the devil are you talking about? Though I was born in Dublin, Ireland, I'm as much an American patriot as any man or woman on this continent. I saw my husband, Dan Walsh, die beside his cannon on Monmouth battlefield. If I even heard of anyone selling discharges in this house, I wouldn't wait to tell General Washington. I'd finish the traitor on the spot with this pistol."

She whipped a brass gun from beneath the bar and brandished it at Caleb.

"Madam, I'm not suggesting that you would tolerate such a thing. But you might have heard one of your customers talk about it," he said.

"Never!"

"Madam, please accept my apologies," Caleb said. "I came here without the slightest intention of accusing you. I was—I remain—concerned about the barbarous way Caesar Muzzey died. I regret the army's indifference to finding his killer."

"They're far from indifferent, I can tell you. Major Stallworth asked me enough questions to fill a book. I told him all I knew about Caesar Muzzey, which isn't much. Now I'll tell you. Many a night he got drunk here and damned the Americans. I called him for it more than once. With my poor husband lying dead in them Monmouth pine woods, I tolerate no Tory talk in this place."

"I'm sure you don't," Caleb said.

"Where would a black man get such ideas? A slave? In my opinion they could only have come from his owner, Mrs. Kuyper. The widow of the fellow who sent him into the army. Muzzey talked about her once in his cups. Said she taught him to read. Made her sound like a paragon. Who else could have stuffed his head with Tory opinions? I wouldn't be surprised if someone in his regiment killed Caesar for his disloyal talk. If you want to see justice done,

Chaplain, find out the truth about that woman. I suspect she's one of them secret Tories who should be run out of the state and her property confiscated."

"Did you tell that to Major Stallworth?"

"I didn't. It's none of the army's business. But a letter from someone like you, Chaplain, to the civil government of the state might make things uncomfortable for her."

"I'll have to give the matter some thought. I wouldn't want to accuse an innocent woman."

"Certainly, certainly. Have another toddy, now, before you go."

Red Peggy served Caleb his drink and turned to greet two customers from the Pennsylvania brigade. The chaplain gulped the rum while it was hot, hoping it would sustain him for the long, cold walk to his quarters. Within a mile, his body had totally forgotten the very idea of heat. Once more he lost all contact with his hands and nose and ears. The northeast wind whipped sadistically beneath his cloak. By the time he reached the Widow Clark's house on the Morristown green near Washington's headquarters, the chaplain's teeth were chattering and his bones were numb.

In Mrs. Clark's parlor Caleb found Lieutenant Charles Rutledge, a cousin of John Rutledge, the governor of South Carolina, sharing a bottle of Barbados rum with two friends. The swarthy, bull-necked lieutenant was boarding with Mrs. Clark while he recuperated from a leg wound that he had received storming the British fort at Stony Point the summer before. "Hey, Chaplain," Rutledge drawled, "you found out who killed your nigger yet?"

Lieutenant Rutledge already thought Caleb Chandler was peculiar, with his monologues on the misery of the enlisted men. Few Southerners were more instinctively aristocratic than the South Carolinians. When Rutledge learned that the chaplain was determined to find the murderer of a Nego deserter, he did not even try to conceal his contempt.

"I've discovered a good deal more about him than General Washington did in his inquiry," Caleb said, edging closer to the fire to restore his circulation.

"This is the Yankee parson I been tellin' you about, boys. Thinks we ought to free our niggers and give'm the vote," Rutledge said to his drinking companions. "Thinks it's a damn crime when one of them gets himself killed."

"How many niggers you got in Connecticut, Parson?" asked a burly young man with a jagged saber scar on his cheek.

"I don't know," Chandler said. "Perhaps a thousand or two."

"Wonder what you'd say if you had two hundred thousand, like we've got in South Carolina."

"The principle remains the same, no matter how many or how few," Caleb said. "Slavery is wrong and we must somehow find a way to get rid of it."

"Yeah?" said the third drinker, a thin redhead with an ominous choking cough. "You'd think twice if you saw one of'm run wild. Had one on our plantation—killed the overseer with an ax, then the overseer's wife and two kids. Run into the woods. We hunted him down like a bear."

"Who killed your nigger, Chandler?" Rutledge asked.

"It may have been one of his company's officers," Caleb said.

"Chandler," shouted Rutledge, "I warned you against

116

slandering the officers of this army. I've told you a dozen times that if you kept it up, I'd consider it a personal insult and ask you for satisfaction."

"And I told you that I consider dueling a criminal act, punishable—justly punishable—in New England by hanging."

"You Yankees," sneered the young man with the scar. "Always hidin' behind the law."

Fool, whispered the mocking voice. *You're a fool to think you can change the minds of these strange beings from the South. Maybe you're a fool to believe in this revolution that was supposed to create a United States of America. United for what, fool?*

A knock on the parlor door. The lined puffy face of the Widow Clark peered into the room. "Mr. Chandler?" she said. "There's a coachman here with a message for you."

Glad to escape the South Carolinians, Caleb hurried into the hall. A huge black man muffled to the nose in a watch coat, with a gray fur cap on his head, confronted him. "Good day, sir," he said with a brief bow. "My name is Cato. I have a letter for you from my mistress, Mrs. Kuyper."

Caleb Chandler opened the sealed envelope. The handwriting was delicate, very feminine, but clear.

Dear Sir:
    The minister of the Dutch church to which I belong refuses to conduct a funeral service for Caesar Muzzey, in whose death you became so unfortunately involved.

    He says Caesar was not a Christian and even doubts that he had a soul. Would you consider presiding at the burial? I would like to have some representative of the army, as well as a man of God, to bolster the

117

patriotism of my other slaves, all of whom admired Caesar and are distraught over his death. My servant Cato (who is Caesar's older brother), and my sleigh are at your disposal. You may detain him until it is convenient for you to come—if, as I hope, it is possible for you to do so. Rest assured I am prepared to pay whatever fee you see fit to charge for your services.

> Your most obedient svt.,
> FLORA KUYPER

Here was a chance for Caleb Chandler to demonstrate his concern for black men and women, a way to answer, without exchanging unchristian insults, those sneering Southerners in the parlor. It was also an opportunity to find out more about the enigmatic Caesar Muzzey, and his puzzling owner, who certainly sounded more like a patriot than the loyalist Red Peggy had labeled her. Caleb glanced past the black coachman at the winter world beyond the door. "Can we get there before dark?"

"No, sir," was the response. "But the roads are open."

"Let me pack my Bible and a change of clothes. We'll go at once."

eight

"Major Beckford, are you still with us?"

Face down, having just sprawled over a fallen branch in the predawn woods, Walter Beckford silently cursed Lieutenant Colonel John Graves Simcoe. The northeast wind drove icy granules of snow down his neck and up his sleeves. "I am most assuredly still with you, Colonel," the major said, scrambling to his feet. "March on."

Beckford ordered himself to defy the chills that were racing through his corpulent torso, to ignore the barbaric wind and cold. He would master the American weather, as well as the Americans. He fueled his determination by visualizing the immense estate, the magnificent house, the hundreds of slaves and servants that a proconsul of imperial Britain would command. Artists would fawn on him, wealthy provincials would shower him with gifts, beautiful women like Flora Kuyper would be at his disposal. What was the line from Gibbon? *The public authority was everywhere exercised by ministers of the Emperor and that authority was absolute*. There was the idea that fired the soul and warmed the body: absolute power.

Behind Beckford and Simcoe trudged a column of white-hooded soldiers. The lieutenant colonel raised his hand and the men halted. They were on the edge of a clearing in the woods. In its center stood a handsome two-story hip-roofed house, once the country seat of one of New York's wealthiest rebels. Behind it were a dozen huts. In front of the house was another hut, in which a fire glowed against the windows. A sentry stood beside the hut, stamping his feet against the cold.

"Attack plan A," whispered Simcoe to the loyalist American captain behind him. The captain passed the word in the same whisper and the column divided. Half followed the captain, circling the clearing to assault the house from behind. Simcoe began counting off the 120 seconds it would take them to get into position. At the same time, he waved a half-dozen other men forward. Inching across the clearing on their bellies, they vanished into the mixture of whiteness and semidarkness as Simcoe continued to count.

"One hundred and eighteen, one hundred and nineteen, one hundred and twenty. *Attack*."

Two artillery squads lunged forward, straining at ropes that towed three-pound cannon on sleds. Between them raced Simcoe and the remaining Queen's Rangers. The advanced crawlers leaped to their feet and charged the sentry. "Turn out," he cried, and fired his gun before they toppled him to the snow. Simcoe blew two shrill blasts on a silver whistle and his men unleashed howls that rivaled the war whoops of the Iroquois. From behind the house came an answering howl as the second half of the attack force burst from the trees to assail the huts. Men rushing from the huts were met with blasts of musketry.

Beckford watched from the edge of the woods as the survivors of these blasts ran toward the house. In sixty seconds muskets blazed from every window. The Queen's Rangers answered them with volleys of suppressing fire while the artillerymen maneuvered the cannon into position. In another sixty seconds the first gun boomed, followed instantly by the crash of the second one. Simcoe had promised a bottle of rum to the squad that fired first.

The door of the house hurtled from its hinges. Simcoe and six men plunged into the dark interior, muskets low, ready to fire from the hip. In thirty seconds they reemerged, still led by Simcoe. Behind him, two men half carried, half dragged a large figure across the clearing to the trees. The slack limbs and drooping legs suggested death. But Beckford knew it was a stuffed dummy wearing an American uniform. Simcoe blew three sharp blasts on his whistle and the gunfire around the huts abruptly died away. The rehearsal for the task of inviting James to New York was over.

"Four minutes and ten seconds," Simcoe said triumphantly.

"Remarkable," Beckford said.

A half-hour later, the stuffed figure sat on a sky-blue Queen Anne sofa in the elegant parlor of the Morris mansion, on the northern heights of Manhattan Island. Lieutenant Colonel Simcoe and Major Beckford stood before a huge blaze in the marble fireplace. The change of scene produced a subtle shift in their relationship. The snowy, wind-whipped woods, the marching men, the blazing muskets, were Simcoe's element. This parlor, this sumptuous house, was Beckford's element. He noted with satisfaction a pleading quality in Simcoe's voice.

"You must admit, Major, you've seldom seen men attack with such vigor, such enthusiasm."

"No question, Colonel," Beckford said, accepting a tankard of hot rum from a blue-coated German servant. "But it's easy to be enthusiastic when you know the enemy are only shooting blank cartridges."

"I've led these men. Let me assure you that the presence of the rebels will *increase* their enthusiasm. In the last three years they've killed, wounded, and taken six times as many men as they've lost."

"Everyone knows and admires the prowess of the Queen's Rangers, Colonel," Beckford said.

As he spoke he turned away from Simcoe, who had his back to the door, and stepped past him, a welcoming smile on his face. He had heard General von Knyphausen's martial steps on the stairs. In spite of the late hour, the short, sharp-featured Hessian was wearing his full uniform, the dark blue, black-cuffed coat and yellow waistcoat of the Regiment Knyphausen. A half-dozen decorations gleamed on his chest. The general felt ill at ease with his British compatriots and always needed the panoply of his rank to reassure him. Unfortunately, the uniform usually reminded the British of the surrender of the Regiment Knyphausen and two other German regiments in Washington's surprise attack on Trenton in 1776.

"Well, gentlemen, you have captured Mr. Washington for me?" Knyphausen asked in German.

Still smiling, Major Beckford translated the question into English.

"There he is, at your mercy, Your Excellency," Simcoe replied, pointing to the dummy on the sofa.

Beckford translated the words into German. Knyphausen laughed heavily and gave the dummy a formal bow. Then, uncomfortable as always because of his inability to speak English, he became the commander in chief. "Tell me how things went, Colonel," he said in German.

"The General awaits your report," Beckford translated for Simcoe. He added a slightly mocking sweep of his arm, as if he were introducing an actor on a stage.

"We used Plan A this morning," Colonel Simcoe said. "In which we assume Major Beckford's master spy is unable to work his miracle and corrupt Washington's guard. We made the best time yet, by five full minutes. I think we're ready to strike. All we need is Your Excellency's written order."

Beckford quickly translated the report into German. "No, no," said Knyphausen with a curt shake of his head. "First there must be a dress rehearsal against an American outpost. We must divert their attention from Morristown."

Beckford translated this negative decision with the same polite smile on his face. It did not produce an answering smile from Lieutenant Colonel Simcoe. "A dress rehearsal? That will take the better part of a month to plan," Simcoe said. "Some of my men may be captured. Or desert. Give away the whole game."

Again, Beckford translated. Knyphausen smiled

wryly. "I thought Colonel Simcoe had absolute confidence in his men," he said.

Now Beckford's smile contained an unmistakable edge of mockery, authorized by Knyphausen. His translation—and perhaps the smile—caused Simcoe to become even more defensive.

"I trust them in the mass," he said. "But they're still Americans. You can never be sure when a man's rebel relations will confuse his loyalty."

"What does Major Beckford think?" Knyphausen asked in German after he heard the translation of Simcoe's reply.

It was delicious, Beckford mused as he took a sip of his rum, how Knyphausen set up Simcoe like a decoy duck without the slightest intention of doing so maliciously. Beckford had carefully inserted in Knyphausen's mind, earlier in the week, the idea of first attacking an American outpost. After four years as an aide he had become expert at advancing, with just the right degree of vagueness and humility, ideas that the general soon adopted as his own.

"I was most impressed with the vigor, the rate of fire of Colonel Simcoe's men tonight," Beckford said in rapid German. "Their discipline, their timing, were excellent. But I must agree with Your Excellency. Admirable as these rehearsals have been in their planning and attention to detail, there is no substitute for the sound of real bullets in the dawn. By now I fear the men may have even grown used to hearing muskets fire, seeing them flash, without danger to themselves. An attack against an American outpost is just what they need. I request permission to join such an expedition."

"Permission refused," Knyphausen snapped. "I cannot risk my most valued subordinate on a scheme that I still view with misgiving."

"I assure Your Excellency that General Washington will be treated as a prisoner of war. I thought Your Excellency was pleased that we were presenting a plan with none of the disagreeable overtones of an assassination."

"I am, I am pleased," Knyphausen said. "But as a soldier, I still wish your king would send us enough men to give Washington and his army a sound thrashing."

The general was a fighter. Beckford could almost hear artillery rumbling in the German phrase for a sound thrashing: *tüchtige Prügeln*.

"I share your sentiment totally, Your Excellency," Beckford said. "But I assure you again that the King will be as grateful, perhaps even more grateful, to the man who ends this rebellion swiftly, no matter how he does it."

"I know, I know," Knyphausen said.

Simcoe could only stand between them like a deaf mute while all this guttural German flowed past him. He became more and more nonplussed. "Aren't you going to translate any of this, Beckford?" he asked.

"We were discussing the overall strategy, Colonel," Beckford said. "You must realize that your stroke has to be coordinated with political overtures to certain members of Congress."

"Yes, of course," Simcoe muttered.

"Tell Colonel Simcoe I give him the choice of the American posts at White Plains or Paramus," Knyphausen said. "When he decides, he may present his plans to me. Good day."

As Beckford translated this farewell Knyphausen

bowed stiffly to Simcoe and stalked from the room. Simcoe glared after him. "Tell me the God's honest truth, Beckford. Is he as stupid as he acts?"

"I prefer not to answer that question, Colonel," Beckford said. "Before you lose your temper, let me tell you with all due respect that I agree with the general, from an intelligence point of view. I'm quite certain that Washington's agents have already told him that you've issued winter uniforms to your picked force. There's a great deal to be said for using these men to beat up the American posts at Paramus or White Plains. Washington and his intelligence people will stop worrying about what we're going to do with those white uniforms and conclude that we've embarked on a program of such winter raids. They may even rush men to their outposts."

"I don't agree with you. I think they're just as likely to see it as a good reason to double the size of the general's Life Guard and revive their discipline."

"You're forgetting what I told you, Colonel, about our ability to corrupt the Life Guard. At the moment we're having some difficulty communicating with our chief agent in Morristown. A reason in itself for delay. Several days ago, our courier was murdered on the town green. We must assume it was on Washington's orders. We want to be very sure they haven't penetrated our network. There's a curious Yankee parson snooping about. I've arranged to eliminate him, to reassure Twenty-six."

"Reassure Twenty-six," snarled Simcoe. "Why? So he can sit snug in some farmhouse and send you moonshine about Washington's Guards? Damn me if I ever saw tuppence worth of value for the thousands of pounds you fellows spend on your precious intelligence. I never met a spy yet who wasn't a lying whoremaster, ready to sell you out to the other side for a piece of ass or a better offer."

"It is a devilish business," Beckford conceded. "But I still think it will pay handsomely if we can coordinate your attack with the night our men mount the guard."

"Pigshit," snarled Simcoe. "We don't need them."

"Then there's the problem of maneuvering your cannon if the snow melts. This major I have arriving imminently via our escape route will soon have an alternative—"

"This snow won't melt for a month—two months," Simcoe said.

"It may take that long to get General Knyphausen's approval of your plan to attack an outpost," Beckford said. "It's hard for a regimental commander to grasp the amount of paperwork that engulfs the commander of an army. Courts-martial, quartermaster returns, reports from the medical department, the provost marshal, the engineers—all compete for his attention. Now His Excellency has to report to two governments, Hesse-Cassel and London. And everything submitted to him in English must, of course, be translated first. He doesn't trust anyone to do it to his satisfaction except me."

Simcoe subsided. Was he beginning to understand that Walter Beckford was not going to let anyone walk away with the coup that ended the rebellion? Beckford hoped so. He was a reasonable man. All he wanted was his share of the glory.

"Give the general my deepest respects, Major," Simcoe said. "Assure him I'll have a plan of attack on your desk for translation in a week's time."

"Good."

At the door, Simcoe could not resist a parting shot. "I hope that spy who got killed was not your midnight beauty."

"No," Beckford said, "it was only a Negro."

nine

"The Yankee parson will get here tomorrow about noon?" John Nelson asked.

"If he comes," Flora Kuyper said.

"He'll come. Beckford says he's been sniffing around Morristown like a bloody hound in search of a scent. You're the bait, my pretty girl. We're the trap."

Beside Nelson stood his huge companion, Wiert Bogert, with his expressionless boy's face and blank blue eyes. "The bastard's close to his last sniff, by God, John," he said.

Flora never saw these two without a shudder of revulsion. The burned flesh on Nelson's neck, curling up his throat to the jawline, made him look like a rotting corpse, restored to mad, destructive life. Bogert was a murderous machine, empty of every feeling but hatred for the rebels.

The two had appeared out of the twilight that evening to inform her that they had four escaped British officers with them, badly in need of a good dinner. Flora had hosted similar dinners a half-dozen times in the previous six months. Her house was the last stop on the Liberty Turnpike, as the British called the escape route devised by Walter Beckford with the help of American loyalists. Traveling almost entirely by night, wearing their uniforms so they would not be shot as spies if recaptured, the escapees went from safe house to safe house in a month-long trek from prison camps in Lancaster, Pennsylvania, and Charlottesville, Virginia. The journey across New Jersey was the hardest because many roads were patrolled by Washington's troops. Hence Beckford's use of Bogert and Nelson as escorts.

Flora Kuyper's role as mistress of a safe house enabled her to maintain her wine cellar and keep her barnyard stocked with chickens, geese, and pigs. The British army had issued strict orders to loyalist marauders that the Kuyper farm was off limits to their thievery. There was nothing especially unusual about such directives. In the five years since the war had begun, hundreds of New Jerseyans had quietly made private truces with the enemy. The practice was called "taking a protection."

Nelson's question about the chaplain, Chandler, had taken Flora by surprise. Beckford had ordered her to invite him to preside at Caesar's funeral. She had obeyed, vaguely expecting some additional instructions. Did he expect her to seduce him, too? she wondered. Now she realized Beckford planned to kill the man.

"Is he an agent?" she asked Nelson.

"How the hell do we know? We just obey the major's orders, like you, my pretty."

"I hope you'll kill him—elsewhere."

Nelson grinned. "Don't you worry. We'll wait for the bastard a mile down the road at least. Take his money, which will be nothin' but filthy Congress paper, alas, to make it look like it was ordinary murder for profit. We got our orders from the major. Under no circumstances must Mrs. Kuyper be involved. The way Beckford moistens his lips and rolls his tongue around the inside of his mouth when he says your name. It's enough to make a man envious, Mrs. Kuyper. No matter how hard we try, we'll never quite render the major the kind of services you supply. Is it true what we hear, that you're the doxy who persuaded him to give up boys?"

"Shut your filthy mouth," Flora said. "Tell your officers that dinner will be served in an hour. I'll send something out to the barn for you and your friend."

What did one more death matter? Flora asked herself, hurrying out to the kitchen. Beckford could be right. In his letter the chaplain seemed no more than a naive enthusiast. But that kind of man might be more dangerous than a cynic like Congressman Stapleton.

In the kitchen, Flora told Nancy about their unexpected dinner guests. Her solemn black face betrayed no emotion. She simply raked up the fire in the big cooking hearth and went to the door to call her daughters, Sallie and Ruth, from the slave quarters beyond the barns. Nothing disturbed Nancy's equilibrium. She was a woman of faith. Watching her move briskly about the kitchen, laying out eggs and spices, flour and milk for a custard pie, deciding a shoulder of beef would satisfy four hungry soldiers, Flora found herself yearning for Nancy's serenity. But such simplicity was beyond her reach forever now. For a moment she stared at a carving knife on the bare oak table. A quick pass of that shining steel across her wrist and she would no longer see Caesar in the cold barn while she pressed her lying mouth against the lips of men like Hugh Stapleton. She would no longer dream of Henry Kuyper's contorted face. She would no longer have to fear a future in which Walter Beckford or William Coleman—Twenty-six—would own her.

Perhaps she would do it tonight, in the bath. Let her treacherous blood mingle with the warm water. Let the bewildered chaplain bury her beside Caesar. Perhaps, as a farewell gesture of defiance to Beckford and Twenty-six, she would leave a note, warning the chaplain that his life was in danger.

"Mistress, why don't you lie down?" Nancy said. "Take one or two drops of your laudanum. I'll rouse you in plenty of time for dinner."

"No," Flora said. "I must dress."

Nancy's shrewd eyes studied her. "You got to find forgiveness, mistress," she said while Sallie and Ruth bustled at the other end of the kitchen, out of earshot. "You got to find forgiveness for yourself and Caesar now. The Lord's punishment has fallen on him, justly, we both know. But I believe you have a right to His forgiveness, I truly do. I think you could find it if you had someone to help you lift your heart to the Lord. Maybe this preacher that's comin'..."

Flora shook her head. Nancy and Cato saw her with their slaves' eyes. They thought she was a kind mistress who had been seduced and corrupted by Caesar and his mad, murderous hunger for freedom. They only saw and pitied the Flora who paced the house in the night, silently weeping. They did not understand or question her obedience to Walter Beckford; that concerned politics, matters beyond their slave world. As Christians, they only grieved at its harm to her soul. They had no idea of the depth and breadth of Flora's mourning, how far it transcended Henry Kuyper's pathetic demise. They could not even imagine that she was about to become an accomplice in the murder of the man of God they hoped would comfort her.

Upstairs, Flora dressed with her usual care. She chose a gown of deep purple, its skirt and sleeves trimmed with gold braided silk. For a while she tried to read her favorite poet, François Villon, to compose her mind. But Villon was a world. What one found in him depended on the state of the reader's soul. His reckless mockery of all things sacred and respectable, which had once exhilarated her, was negated by his obsession with death. Suddenly she found herself reading again and again the *Ballade de la grosse Margot*, Villon's testament to a prostitute. She flung the book aside and paced the room, weeping.

A knock on the door—Sallie informing her mistress that dinner was served. Flora dried her eyes, took three drops of laudanum to steady her nerves, and descended to greet her guests. They had done their best to brush and clean their uniforms for the occasion, but their red coats and white breeches still showed the effects of a month of sleeping in barns and trudging through woods to escape American patrols. Three of them were young: a husky captain named Tracy with a hard, sensual mouth, and two lieutenants, an apple-cheeked baronet named Gore and a bulky, red-haired Scotsman named MacKenzie. The fourth man, Whittlesey, was a balding, gray-faced major with quizzical, kindly eyes. He reminded Flora of a priest she had known in New Orleans.

The younger officers were eager to talk about their adventures on the Liberty Turnpike, in particular the discovery that their American guide, a man named Grey, was a double agent. "Major Beckford's fellows, Nelson and Bogert, arrived just in time. The scoundrel would likely have turned us over to the first militiamen we met," Lord Gore said.

"What did you do with him?" Flora asked.

"We did nothing," Captain Tracy said. "Nelson and Bogert took him into the woods their first night with us and came back without him."

"How terrible," Flora said.

"Major Whittlesey rather agreed with you," Lord Gore said. "Personally, I would have been happy to cut the beggar's throat myself."

"And I," said MacKenzie. "In Scotland we know how to deal with traitors."

"I merely said I disliked killing a man so callously," Major Whittlesey said. "Then bragging about it."

"In war, Major, it's necessary to use crude instruments like Nelson," Lord Gore said.

Captain Tracy began telling Flora how eager he was to meet the Americans in battle again. "One good push, that's all it will take, and their Congress and committeemen and militia will come tumbling down. In Pennsylvania everyone's sick of the war."

Lord Gore and MacKenzie, who had escaped from Charlottesville, concurred. Gore had another idea to

134

hasten the American collapse. "The Negroes are their Achilles' heel. We should arm them to fight their rebel masters."

"And how do we get the guns back from them?" asked Major Whittlesey. "There's no point in winning the war by turning half this continent into Africa. In fact, there's no point in winning the war by burning as many houses as I've seen in ruins here in New Jersey. What have we won if we turn the country into a desert? No, my young sir, we must somehow break up Washington's army. That done, the war will be over without another house burned, another innocent family ruined. I'd never have undertaken this long march from Lancaster without Major Beckford's assurance that I could give essential service to accomplish this."

"Are you going to perfect your repeating rifle, Major?" Tracy said with a teasing grin. "So Beckford can march down to Morristown and scatter Washington's army with a corporal's guard?"

"Most of us dream of lasses," Lieutenant MacKenzie said. "The major dreams of machines."

Lord Gore, whose choirboy looks concealed a hunger for vengeance, pursued his argument with Whittlesey. "I dare say most of those burned houses didn't belong to innocent families. Taken in the mass, the Americans are the greatest villains on earth. Ten times worse than the Irish. I concede the wisdom of a swift stroke to behead the rebellion. But once that's accomplished, I think we should free the slaves and set up one or two colonies of loyal blacks here in their midst, as we planted the Scots Protestants in Ulster to make the Irish behave."

"I'll drink a toast to that," Flora said, raising her

wineglass. "Tonight you'll be sharing the barn with the body of a black man who would have welcomed such a plan. He was a spy for His Majesty, inside Washington's army. They found him out and murdered him in the most cowardly way."

"That makes me feel better about the way Beckford disposed of Mr. Grey," Major Whittlesey murmured.

"I think it's you who deserve the toast, madam," Captain Tracy said, raising his wineglass. "No doubt you set the fellow to the business and guided him in every step."

"Hear hear," said Lieutenant MacKenzie, seizing his glass. Flora had to sit there, smiling and modestly bowing her head before the salutes of His Majesty's officers.

Captain Tracy, a cavalry officer who had been captured in 1778, poured himself another glass of wine and began looking at Flora with eyes that suggested amorous ambitions. "I wish there were more women in America with your courage—and beauty, madam."

Flora ignored the compliment and turned to Major Whittlesey. "Do you think it possible that the King would create colonies of free blacks here in America?"

"Not likely," Whittlesey said. "They're property. Those who belong to rebels will be confiscated and sold to help pay the cost of this damned war. But we may settle the German troops and some of our officers and soldiers here on confiscated lands. They and their children will be a sword at the Americans' throats until they forget their rebel ways."

Captain Tracy, deciding Flora was beyond his charms, pursued this idea with gusto. "I can see myself now, sitting on my plantation house veranda, a black wench on either knee, as drunk as Sir Toby on his wedding day."

"And what will your wife be doing meanwhile?" Lieutenant MacKenzie said. "Selecting some black stallion from the slave quarters, like as not."

"He's right, Tracy," Lord Gore said. "From what I heard in Virginia, there's many a husband wearing black horns."

"I'll take my chances," Tracy said, draining his wineglass.

For a moment Flora was swept by blind, blazing hatred of their confidently smiling white faces. She wanted to kill them, to kill every white man in America, in Caesar's name. They were all the same, King's men or rebels, they saw black men and women as animals to be used for their convenience and pleasure.

A jingle of sleigh bells interrupted the exchange between the two officers. "Dear God," Flora whispered to herself, springing up and rushing into the hall. Opening the top half of the Dutch door, she saw the dark hulk of Cato's sleigh and horses outlined against the snowy landscape. With him was the Reverend Caleb Chandler, twelve hours ahead of schedule.

"Gentlemen," Flora said, having hurried back to the dining room, "I fear we must interrupt our feast. A chaplain from the American army is at the door. I invited him from Morristown at Major Beckford's orders. He was supposed to arrive tomorrow."

She rang the bell, which summoned Nancy from the kitchen. "Clear the table at once," Flora said.

Flora found herself enjoying the discomfiture of her uniformed guests. Captain Tracy grabbed a slice of beef he had intended to consume at leisure and stuffed it into his pocket. Lord Gore forgot he was a peer and imitated him. Lieutenant MacKenzie almost choked himself trying to finish his wine and simultaneously cram down a mouthful of Nancy's rabbit pie. As they fled through the kitchen and across the yard to the cold barn, Flora thought: *May Caesar's ghost haunt your filthy, slave-owning dreams.*

The front door opened; footsteps and voices echoed in the hall. Flora quickly mounted the back stairs to her bedroom and waited in her bedroom until Cato knocked on the door and informed her that the Reverend Chandler was in the parlor. "He's a fine young man, mistress," Cato said. He shared Nancy's hope that the minister could heal her troubled soul.

The word young surprised her. She had pictured the Reverend Caleb Chandler as a gray-haired, angry-eyed divine, not unlike the Reverend Jacobus Demarest, pastor of the Dutch Reformed Church in Bergen. Descending to the parlor, she found Cato's adjective an understatement. The man standing before the fire had a face that was better described as boyish. The blue eyes had an innocent shine to them. The forehead was high and noble. The rather long, delicate nose was matched by a wide, mobile mouth. It was an unfinished face, remarkably unblemished by vanity or vice. Flora could not help contrasting it to the stylish arrogance of Congressman Hugh Stapleton, the comfortable egotism of the just-departed British officers. Mr. Chandler's clothes were as unassuming as his face. His cloak was patched and threadbare, his tan breeches and blue coat devoid of decorations and lace, and in a style at least a decade old.

Then Flora remembered Wiert Bogert and John Nelson in the barn. She remembered that she had invited this boy-man to her house to become their victim.

"How do you do, Mr. Chandler," she said with a tremor in her voice that she quickly controlled. "You're just in time. I was about to sit down to supper."

"My stomach agrees that would be most timely, madam," the chaplain said with a smile.

"First a warm drink to thaw you out."

"I've seldom been so comfortable in a sleigh," Chandler said. "Your lap robes are worthy of royalty. I marvel that you haven't had such things looted by the enemy, living where you do."

"We keep them well hidden, along with the silver," Flora replied.

She rang for Cato and asked him to heat some Madeira. Chandler looked around the sitting room and remarked on the beautiful furniture.

"My late husband was very indulgent," Flora explained. "He bought these pieces in New York just as Congress banned such importations. He wanted to make me feel at home."

"You're English-born?" Chandler said in a suddenly harsh tone. His face relapsed into a disfiguring frown.

"No," she said. "I was born under the flag of France."

"Ah," he said, his smile returning. "I'm an admirer of the French language. I studied it at Yale College. I can't speak it, but I've read with rapture the poets of France."

"François Villon?" Flora said. "He's my favorite."

Chandler closed his eyes and recited with the most atrocious accent Flora had ever heard the first lines of Villon's famous "Ballad of the Ladies of Days Gone By":

> *Dites-moi où, n'en quel pays*
> *Est Flora la belle Romaine...*

She smiled and finished the verse in French, seeing and hearing her father reciting the words, with an accent that made her mother laugh. Now you must tell me what it means, her father would say with that sad smile, and she would eagerly translate it:

> *Tell me where or in what country*
> *Is Flora, the fair Roman girl?*
> *Archipiades or Thais?*
> *Who was her only equal?*
> *Or Echo, replying whenever sound is made*
> *Over river or pool?*
> *Echo who had more than human beauty.*
> *But where are the snows of yesteryear?*

Ah, yes, her father would sigh, where are the snows of yesteryear?

"Madam?"

Flora stared dazedly at Caleb Chandler. He was smiling at her, his face aglow with pleasure. "Oh— yes," she said.

"I asked—if you would please recite it again. Both verses."

She obeyed.

"It sounds so beautiful on your lips," he said. "In my mouth it's like the scrapings of a wretched violinist."

"Your accent does need improvement," Flora said. "But you overcome it, I think, with the sincerity of your sentiments."

"You're very kind," Chandler replied.

No, she thought, *I'm nothing of the sort. I'm your murderer.*

"You haven't told me where you were born. Was it Paris?"

"No another part of France, here on your continent. New Orleans."

Why not tell him the truth, or part of the truth? She was tired of ingenious lies.

"Ah," he said. "Was it there you learned to speak English so well?"

"Yes," she said. "My father was a merchant who did a great deal of business with England."

"But how did you reach this part of the world and marry Mr. Kuyper?"

"I came to New York with my father on a trading voyage. He fell sick and died there. Mr. Kuyper took pity on my distracted, penniless state."

"Indeed, madam, I would say, without knowing your late husband, that he was a very fortunate man."

"Now you are being too kind."

"By no means, madam. I'm now your admirer twice over."

"Why twice, sir?"

"I'm all but struck speechless by your beauty, now

141

that we're face to face. Before, I was an admirer of your goodness of heart."

The irony of these words almost made Flora blurt a denial. "I—I don't understand," she said.

"I had time for extensive conversation with your servant Cato as we rode here tonight. He's most extravagant in his praise of you, madam."

"I've tried to treat him—to treat all my slaves—well."

"He says you've promised to give them their freedom as soon as it's possible for you to do so."

"That's true. As long as the war lasts, I can borrow nothing on this property. It's too close to the British in New York. The state of New Jersey requires a bond of two hundred pounds to free a single slave. I have seven of them."

Caleb Chandler strolled over to the painting of Caesar and Henry Kuyper. "That's a picture of my husband and Caesar," Flora said. "He—Caesar—was born a slave here on the farm. They were raised together."

The chaplain shook his head and turned to face her with a rueful expression. "I'm almost ashamed of myself."

"Why, for goodness' sake?"

"For one of the motives that brought me here. Suspicion of you, madam."

"For what reason?"

"There are some people who think you're a British sympathizer. I see already the notion is ridiculous. A woman who despises slavery cannot possibly be serving the nation that wants to make slaves of us all."

How naive, how sincere he is, Flora thought. He believes the Americans' self-serving political slogans.

"Who's accusing me?"

"A person of no consequence. A grog seller who drew certain conclusions from Caesar's talk."

"Caesar's talk?"

"I'm not sure exactly what he said. Perhaps he admired you as much as Cato does. No doubt you promised him his freedom, too."

"Yes."

"Such is the perversity of some minds, you might be suspected or, more precisely, slandered simply to silence you. The Reverend Jacob Green of Hanover, not far from Morristown, was mobbed for preaching a sermon against slavery not long ago."

Flora hesitated, wondering whether to pursue a dangerous subject. The sincerity of Caleb Chandler's face proved irresistible. "You feel strongly about slavery yourself, I gather? Your comments in your letter—"

"The conviction grows on me with every passing day. I begin to see the very idea as monstrous—a crime."

He was either sincere or a superb actor. His face blazed with indignation. The boyishness vanished. He was a strong, angry young man.

"You're the first American I've met with such a delicate conscience," Flora said, letting sarcasm steady her voice.

He nodded mournfully. "Everyone I know considers it an oddity. Or, to be more precise, considers me an oddity. I come from Connecticut, you see. It's known as the land of steady habits. Odd notions are frowned upon severely."

"Where did you get this—odd notion?"

"It started with my dissatisfaction with the faith into which I was born—and am now licensed to

143

preach. I have—secretly, I assure you, because it would give my mother and father pain—explored other creeds. A Quaker friend gave me some books—among them a tract by a Friend from New Jersey—John Woolman—condemning Negro slavery. I thought his arguments were irresistible. What was it that led you to your convictions about the matter, madam?"

"I?" she said, dismayed by the perfectly natural question. "I . . ."

"I believe it is sanctioned by the French in New Orleans, as it is in their West Indies islands, is it not?"

"Yes, but . . ."

The truth. How blessed it would be to tell him the truth, as he had told it to her. But it was not possible. The truth would destroy her. But a lie would destroy him. A lie had brought him here. More lies would hold him here until Wiert Bogert and John Nelson delivered the British officers to New York and returned to kill him.

For a moment Flora remembered Nancy's words: "You got to find forgiveness for yourself and Caesar now."

No, it was not possible.

"In New Orleans it's not at all uncommon for kind masters to free their slaves in their wills. There are many free blacks—and mulattoes."

Cato appeared in his livery to serve the mulled wine. "I understand you and Mr. Chandler have been conversing about a good many things," Flora said.

"There were some points of doctrine I welcomed a chance to ask him about, mistress," Cato replied.

Dear Cato, Flora thought, your wish to save your

soul and mine will lead us both to destruction. "As Cato probably told you, he preaches on Sunday to our blacks and many from other farms. He's rather famous among his people."

"He knows his Old Testament," Caleb Chandler said.

The chaplain waited until Cato withdrew to take up another topic. "He seems reluctant to talk about Caesar."

"He—he wasn't—especially close to him. Cato is much older—at least ten years. Caesar was a field hand."

"Did Congressman Stapleton discuss Caesar's death with you when he returned his body?"

"No."

"I feared his interest in the matter was slight. He owns fifty slaves and apparently regards them as little more than cattle."

"I'm not surprised," Flora said. "The congressman strikes me as a man interested in little but his own pleasure."

"There are puzzling aspects to Caesar's death—the money in his pocket, for instance. Ten sovereigns. Where would a private soldier get those? Also, he was absent without leave for a week. Not the first such absence. Did he usually come here? When was the last time you saw him?"

Flora found herself suspecting Mr. Chandler's innocence. She did not know what Cato had told him but if she contradicted it, she was caught. "Caesar came here now and then," she said warily. "He was always welcome."

"You saw no reason to wonder at these appearances? Or to reproach him?"

145

"I knew—and still know—nothing of the army's regulations. I thought he had leave to come. He never stayed long."

"And the money? You have no idea where he might have gotten it?"

"None," she lied.

"Cato hinted that Caesar had irregular habits—wild opinions. Did you know him well enough to hear about these things?"

"I knew that he hated America and Americans. Can you blame him?"

And so do I, she wanted to add, triumphantly, recklessly, in Caesar's name.

Instead of shock and anger, Flora was surprised to see sadness, regret on the Reverend Chandler's face.

"Madam, America is my country. I can't justify such an opinion."

"Why not?" she said. "Believing as you do that slavery is wrong. There are a half-million slaves in America. Can a nation guilty of a half-million wrongs be worthy of admiration?"

She was talking like a madwoman. Did she *want* him to find out the truth about her? All she had to do was plead ignorance. Reiterate that Caesar was a field hand, that she had barely spoken ten words to him. But her uncertainty about what Cato had said on the road coalesced with a need to speak the truth or some semblance of it to this innocent, earnest young man.

Her frankness drew a troubled response from the Reverend Caleb Chandler. "Those are dangerous thoughts, madam. Not entirely unwarranted, I admit. I've drifted toward them more than once. But what's the alternative to fighting for America? Will our British enemies do any more for these poor people? It was their policy, their ships, that first brought the blacks among us in chains a hundred years ago."

This uneasy rationalizing obviously clashed with Caleb Chandler's sympathy for Caesar, for his race, for the poor and friendless of this world. Flora saw that the chaplain was a divided spirit, part scholar and part something deeper and finer than creeds and formulas. She could not let Wiert Bogert and John Nelson kill him. She could not bear his death on her conscience.

He would never know what she was risking for him. No matter. Perhaps there was such a thing as expiation. Perhaps a caring God, if He existed, would accept it as a part payment for her other sins.

"I'm sure you're right, Mr. Chandler," Flora said. "Now, as to the time of the funeral. I had planned it for the day after tomorrow. But since you're here so early, I see no reason why we can't have it tomorrow and permit you to speed back to your duties in Morristown."

"Whatever you say, madam. I'm at your service."

It was all so bland, so indifferent. For another moment Flora was again assailed by the wish to tell him the truth, or at least the terrible part of the truth—her need, Caesar's need, for prayers of forgiveness, for the mercy that she had once believed descended from heaven with the Blessed Virgin's smile. But she had become a stranger to the truth. Which meant that mercy must remain a stranger to her.

"Finish your wine, Mr. Chandler," she said. "It's time for supper."

ten

"Why do so many Americans dislike New England men?"

"What, madam?" murmured Caleb Chandler.

"This dislike of New England men. Are you not all Americans?"

It was a question that ordinarily would have aroused Caleb to a torrent of rebuttal. But he found it hard to think about New England while he was sitting at the dinner table with Flora Kuyper. Her gown, worn low in the fashion that no doubt prevailed in that outpost of Paris, New Orleans, exposed most of her firm, full breasts. His eyes traveled from these lovely curves to her bare shoulders and perfectly proportioned neck, her naked arms. Never in his life had he seen so much female flesh, but there was not the least hint of sin or obscenity in the experience. It was all *natural;* the word beat in him again and again as he watched this woman turn her head, pick up a glass. All her movements had an innate grace, a flow that made him feel as if he were watching an accomplished actress gesture, speak, smile.

She did not smile often. An undefinable sadness lay like a veil on her oval face, which was dominated by dark green eyes and a languorous mouth. Her skin had an incredibly smooth ivory luster. Her hair was undressed, in the country style, but it had no need of the hairdresser's art. It was black as a winter night, falling to her shoulders in luxurious curls.

"New England," Caleb said. "Ah, yes. We're much misunderstood, madam. The rest of America dislikes us because we persist in the faith of our fathers. We resist the luxuries of this world—with which the English are so eager to inundate and corrupt us."

"And you agree with this Puritan attitude?" Flora Kuyper said with a small smile. "Even when your favorite poet, Villon, writes so incomparably: *'Il n'est trésor que de vivre à son aise.'*"

He knew the verse: *There's no delight like living at your ease.*

"One may admire the poet, but not all his sentiments, madam."

Flora Kuyper pouted and sighed. "Does that mean you disapprove of all this?" she said, gesturing to the expensive china and silver, the succulent beef and rabbit pie they were enjoying.

Caleb felt humiliation and confusion infest him like a fever. He began trying to explain himself. "I

150

doubt if I would complain at bread and water if they were served with your presence, your conversation to enhance it, madam. It's not rich food or beautiful things in themselves that New England condemns. You'll find as much good eating and silver plate in Boston and New Haven as you will anywhere in America. It's what men and women do to possess the pleasures and treasures of this world that alarms us. We believe that people should be ready to forgo ease rather than compromise their principles."

"Ah, Mr. Chandler," Flora Kuyper replied with another unnerving sigh. "What if you're a person who admires such principles but you have given your love to someone whose spirit has already been corrupted by the pursuit of wealth?"

"Then you must seek by prayer and, if need be, by fasting to sunder yourself from such a love."

"Do you think we have the power? So often the heart becomes infested, controlled by another person, and there's little we can do about it."

"You sound as if you're speaking from experience, madam."

"I am."

There was a tremolo of sadness in her throaty voice. Caleb groped for words to express his sympathy. "The Bible tells us to judge not. I would be the last to condemn a divided heart. I, too, know—in another way—the pain it can cause."

"I am afraid I don't understand."

Now the sympathy flowed from her side of the table. Caleb felt his words responding to it; they seemed to be summoned from deep within his body by her puzzling combination of beauty and sadness.

"One can love not only a person but a calling, a creed, a faith. I came to Yale on fire with enthusiasm for the ministry. For the faith of our fathers. In six months I had a nickname—Tom Brainless."

"What does it mean?"

"He's a character in a poem written by one of the college's tutors, John Trumbull. A model of a country fool, madam. Yale, you see, is dominated by city-bred young men—sons of merchants and lawyers from New Haven, New London, Hartford. They regard it as their duty to mock farm boys from little towns like Lebanon, my home. As for religion, they laugh at it. They'd rather read a play or a poem than study the Bible. I tried to defend the old faith at first. But in the end—they taunted me into silence. That's why I began exploring other creeds. Now I begin to fear the ministry is wasted on me. My mind—and heart—are infested with doubt. I volunteered as a chaplain in the hope that service in a good cause would restore my faith. But what I've seen in the army has only deepened my doubts."

Caleb wondered why reproach, disapproval, was not visible on Flora Kuyper's lovely face. He had just made a confession to her that he had concealed from everyone—even, to some extent, from himself.

"I know some of what you're feeling," Flora Kuyper said. "I was educated by the Ursuline sisters in New Orleans. But I—I lost the sweet, simple faith they gave me."

"What, may I ask, was the cause of your disillusionment?"

Her eyes searched Caleb's face for a moment. She seemed disappointed—or at least unencouraged—by what she found. "The story is too complicated—and we're too strange to each other, Mr. Chandler," she said. "If you were a priest, your lips sealed by the secrecy of the confessional, I might kneel beside you and tell you a great deal. That's the one thing I miss from my childhood faith—the sacrament of confession. How marvelous it was to escape the burden of one's sins, even childish ones. Now that we know, as adults, what sin really is, the idea becomes even more precious. Why did you Protestants abandon it?"

"Because we believe God forgives the repentant sinner directly, without the agency of men."

Flora Kuyper shook her head. "Men and women need the words, the feeling of forgiveness, the *experience*, Mr. Chandler. Don't you feel better for having confessed—I don't believe there's a better word for it—your feelings about the ministry, even though I have no power to forgive you?"

An extraordinary surge of feeling swept Caleb. He wanted to say something extravagant, absurd. *Madam, you have more power than you realize*. A smiling Flora Kuyper pushed her chair from the table, apparently unaware of the violent emotion she was arousing. "We're growing too solemn. Let's have some music. Do you play an instrument, Mr. Chandler?"

"No," he said as they walked to the parlor. "But I've been to singing school every year of my life since the age of four. I went to Boston one summer and studied under the great Billings."

"I don't know him," Flora said.

"You should. He's our first American musician. The next time I visit—if you will permit me such a pleasure, madam—I'll bring my copy of the New England Psalm Singer. It's not all psalms, let me assure you."

"Sing one of Billings's songs for me. I'm sure I can pick it up on the harpsichord."

"No, it would be too awkward. I prefer them done rightly or not at all. Let's enjoy your favorites, which I am sure will please me infinitely."

"You flatter me. Here's one I set to music myself, from an old *chanson* by Charles d'Orléans, a contemporary of Villon. Do you know him?"

Caleb shook his head. She began to play a delicate, haunting melody, to which she added a soft, subtle contralto. The French words rhymed beautifully. Caleb was only able to translate them into prose.

> *I think nothing of those kisses*
> *Given by convention*
> *As a matter of politeness.*
> *Far too many people share them.*
>
> *Do you know the ones I value?*
> *Secret ones, bestowed in pleasure.*
> *All the rest are nothing*
> *But a way of greeting strangers.*
> *I think nothing of those kisses.*

Standing behind her at the harpsichord, Caleb breathed Flora Kuyper's perfume. Her dark, gleaming hair, her graceful neck, were only inches from his fingers. A kind of delirium consumed his mind. He did not know how long he stood there listening to her sing other songs. In the end he begged her to play "Secret Kisses" again. He joined her, hoping his vigorous baritone would compensate for his deplorable pronunciation.

"Now I must hear one of your New England songs," Flora said. "With such a voice, you don't need an accompanist."

"I'll sing you my favorite, 'Chester,'" Caleb said. "It's far superior to 'Yankee Doodle' in my opinion."

She sounded the key of G for him and Caleb began. He always felt confident, at ease, when he sang. William Billings himself had praised his voice.

> *Let tyrants shake their iron rod*
> *And Slav'ry clank her galling chains.*
> *We fear them not, we trust in God.*
> *New England's God forever reigns.*

On he sang, through the rolling, sonorous notes, the unflinching words, with their vivid testament of New England's fierce spirit of resistance, to the thunderous climax.

> *When God inspired us for the fight*
> *Their ranks were broke, their lines were forced,*
> *Their ships were shattered in our sight*
> *Or swiftly driven from our coast.*

> *What grateful offering shall we bring?*
> *What shall we render to the Lord?*
> *Loud hallelujahs let us sing*
> *And praise His name on every chord.*

Flora Kuyper sat at the harpsichord, gazing up at him, her eyes wide with amazement. Or was it dismay? Caleb could not tell.

"When it's sung by a full choir, it's very grand," he said.

"It's enough to hear you sing it, Mr. Chandler," Flora Kuyper said. "For the first time I begin to understand this war."

He was not sure what she meant. But the compliment pleased him.

"Is seven o'clock too early for the funeral service tomorrow?"

"I'm at your disposal, madam."

"Let us set it for that hour so you may get safely back to Morristown in time for your dinner. I'll tell Cato. He wants to invite some of Caesar's friends from nearby farms. Now let me show you to your room."

She led him up the red-carpeted stairs to the second floor and into a bedroom with a banked fire glowing in the grate. The wallpaper was a soft rose, full of classical shepherds and shepherdesses. The furniture was in the heavy Dutch style of the early part of the century.

"Here's your candle," she said, thrusting it at him without warning. His hand missed the lip of the pewter holder and it went clattering to the floor. "Forgive me," she said. "This was Mr. Kuyper's room. I never come in here without doing something clumsy."

He lit the candle on the coals and inserted it in the holder again. "No damage done," he said.

"Sleep well, Mr. Chandler."

Caleb found himself incapable of fulfilling this polite wish. He lay in the big tester bed for at least an hour thinking about Flora Kuyper—her grace, her composure—and that puzzling sadness lurking beneath the surface of her manner. He had never met a woman like her—a woman who had read François Villon, who spoke and sang flawless French, and wore fashionable clothes with such ease. He compared her to Deborah Hawley, the Lebanon girl he had been halfheartedly courting. Deborah of the lush figure and blooming country cheeks was moderately attractive at a distance. But she walked with a loping gait and her laugh was like the bellow of a calf. She thought novels and plays and most poetry, except the psalms, were sinful. Her dresses were all inherited from her mother and her aunts, and the vanity of lace on her friend Polly's cuff or the price her friend Susan paid for a muff could dominate her conversation for an entire afternoon.

Flora Kuyper was a woman of the world. The familiar phrase reverberated in Caleb's mind. His religion warned him to suspect such creatures, to guard against their corruption, their powers of seduction. But Mrs. Kuyper seemed to combine her worldliness with compassion and kindness and sympathy. There was nothing hard or acquisitive about her. On the contrary, he sensed a need, a wish, for protection.

Stop, Caleb told himself. Go to sleep. What could Tom Brainless, the country fool from Lebanon, offer such a woman? To her, he was a raw boy without money or *savoir faire*. Perhaps all this pondering was an attempt to evade the desire Flora Kuyper stirred in him. He wanted her, wanted her now, naked beside him in this bed, wanted his hands in that dark coiled hair, his lips on that mournful mouth.

Risking the winter chill that was creeping through the room as the fire died, Caleb took his Bible from his traveling bag. He laid the book on its spine and let it fall open. The first lines that struck his eyes were from Ecclesiastes 10:8. *He who digs a pit will fall into it; and a serpent will bite him who breaks through a wall.* No light there. He put the book on its spine and let it fall open again. This time it was Isaiah 45:15. *Verily thou art a God that hidest thyself.* Equally baffling.

Caleb finally went to sleep and dreamed he was in a garden full of curiously trimmed hedges, forming a maze. At the end of it he saw Flora Kuyper in a gown of glowing white. He kept glimpsing her and losing her as he wandered through the maze. He himself, he discovered to his confusion and dismay, was naked. Eventually he emerged to find not Flora, but a statue of her, a sculpture of pure white marble, its head bowed, a grieving nymph at the funeral of Dionysius. The statue was naked, revealing a body of stunning perfection. On her cheeks were frozen two or three lapidary tears. *I am too late,* flashed through Caleb's bemused brain. Forgetting his own nakedness, he flung his arms around the statue and pressed his lips to the cold stone mouth. But the marble figure did not, as in some classic fable, stir to joyous life. Instead the face shattered beneath his lips; the body crumbled in his arms.

A dark voice, which might well have belonged to God, began calling Caleb's name. He grappled with an overwhelming dread. The voice drew closer. Caleb opened his eyes and gazed up at Cato's black face. "Six by the morning clock, Mr. Chandler," he said. "I'll light your fire and the room should be ready for habitation in a few minutes."

"Thank you, Cato," he said.

"Ten below zero outside," Cato said. "The field boys been up since five hacking out Caesar's grave. They had to use axes and saws to cut through the topsoil. Frozen down almost two feet. Sure makes you think the Lord is angry with this nation, sending us such a cold."

"Yes," muttered Chandler.

"Mistress is waiting for you at breakfast. She was up when I come into the house at dawn. Some nights she doesn't sleep at all."

Caleb Chandler shaved, dressed, and descended to the dining room. Flora Kuyper sat at the table, on which bacon, eggs, ham, and fresh bread were arrayed in profusion. She was wearing a simple green dress, with a blue apron and matching blue shawl. Her mood was muted, somber.

"Did you sleep well, Mr. Chandler?" she asked.

"When regret finally allowed me to close my eyes," he replied.

"Regret?" she said in a startled voice. "What were you regretting?"

"That we couldn't continue our music. I wish we could have thrown prudence to the winds and sung till dawn, madam."

Flora Kuyper smiled forlornly. "Yes, I wish so, too. I heard your voice in my dreams."

"Does that justify my hope for another singing session?"

"No," she said, with what seemed to him unnecessary sharpness. "It wouldn't be wise—or safe. I'm too close to the British lines. It was rash of me to ask you to risk even this visit."

"Madam, although I wear a clergyman's collar, I

159

carry a gun. I have little fear of the kind of vagabonds that prey on travelers."

"These aren't vagabonds. They're in British pay. They prowl the roads around here, day and night."

Caleb heard rejection, impatience, in her sharp tone. He was disappointed but not entirely surprised. Hadn't he told himself last night that Tom Brainless had nothing to offer this woman? Their conversation at dinner, the music after it, had been mere politeness on her part; gratitude for his willingness to preach at Caesar's funeral.

"Is there anything you'd like me to say about Caesar? Any special characteristic that you want his family and friends to remember?"

Flora Kuyper literally trembled. He was puzzled by her agitation. "I—I leave that to you."

At 7 A.M. she wrapped herself in a fur-lined cape and followed Caleb out to the barn. It was a huge structure, in the style of many Dutch barns—as large as a church. About fifty blacks were assembled in the center. It was the first time Chandler had ever seen so many of their race together. He was surprised to discover that they were a very mixed assemblage of humankind. Some were brawny, others skeleton thin. He saw friendship on several faces, sullen distrust on a few. Intelligence and interest gleamed from some eyes, boredom from others.

Caesar's coffin sat on two trestles at the head of the congregation. In spite of the cold the air in the barn was redolent with the smell of animals and hay. Caleb mounted a small platform set up behind the coffin, so that Caesar rested at the level of his knees. Someone had removed the coffin's lid and prepared his body for burial. Caesar lay there in his uniform, his eyes closed, his thick-lipped mouth drooping at the edges, in a kind of silent resentment of death. The flat nose, the massive jaw, were quintessentially African, as was his intense blackness.

"My fellow Christians," Caleb said, "I am here from the American army to help you mourn the death of one of your brethren. I did not know Caesar Muzzey. Everything I've learned about him since his death has convinced me that he was a brave soldier. He risked death in the war America is fighting to throw off her oppressors. I hope that the memory of his service—and the service of other men of your race—will in the years to come persuade Americans to lift from your shoulders a greater oppression than most white men have ever known—the bonds of slavery. The Bible tells us that God sees all the oppressions that are practiced under the sun, and the tears of the oppressed who have no one to comfort them. Until the day of your freedom, remember that God is there in the person of His Son Jesus. Let Him be your comforter. Let Him give you the courage—the same courage that Caesar possessed—to bear your burden patiently till the time to strike off your chains is at hand.

"Now let us join in reciting a Psalm of David.

" 'Hear my voice, O God, in my prayer; preserve my life from fear of the enemy.

" 'Hide me from the secret counsel of the wicked; from the insurrection of the workers of iniquity.' "

The solemn black voices intoned the words with him. They were obviously familiar with the psalm. In

161

the front rank, Chandler saw Cato, reciting in a deep rumble, his eyes closed.

"I hope now you will join me in a song of mourning, a new song, written by a Boston composer, William Billings. The words are from the Bible. They were spoken by King David over the corpse of his son Absalom. I will sing it for you first, then ask you to join me."

He took his pitch pipe from his pocket, sounded the key of G, and sang "David's Lamentation."

> *David the king was grieved and moved.*
> *He went to his chamber and wept*
> *And as he went he wept and said:*
> *O my son*
> *O my son*
> *Would to God I had died*
> *Would to God I had died*
> *Would to God I had died for thee*
> *O Absalom*
> *My son*
> *My son.*

The slaves joined him in the reprise, Cato leading with a magnificent bass. The melody soared to the roof of the barn, the reiteration of the strong, simple phrases achieving a grandeur that the setting made doubly remarkable. Gazing down the ranks of black faces, Caleb's eyes found Flora Kuyper standing to one side at the rear. She was weeping. It struck him as odd. He noticed none of the blacks were shedding any tears for Caesar. From what he had learned about him, this was not surprising. Why was Flora

Kuyper so grief-stricken over a black field hand whom she could have known for only a few years?

As the last notes of "David's Lamentation" sounded from the lips of the singers, two young blacks placed the lid on Caesar's coffin. Joined by two others, they carried it out to the open grave beneath a huge, winter-stripped oak tree, on a hillside about a hundred yards from the Kuyper house. The moist earth beneath the frostline still smoked in the bitter air. Because of the cold, Caleb said only a brief final prayer for Caesar's soul. The blacks trudged off to their nearby farms and the pallbearers began shoveling dirt into Caesar's grave.

In the house, Flora Kuyper thanked Caleb for his assistance and offered to pay him whatever he suggested. "Madam," he said, "your hospitality last night has more than rewarded me for my journey."

She briskly ordered Cato to prepare the sleigh and horses for the trip back to Morristown. On the road, Cato was again eager to discuss theology. He had been impressed by the sight of Caesar's coffin descending into the smoking earth. He wanted to know if Caleb thought that salvation could be won by an unrepentant sinner if he sought it only at the moment of his death.

"You think Caesar was a sinner?"

"I'm afraid I do."

"May I ask the nature of his sin?"

"I—I don't feel free to say."

Caleb changed the subject by teaching Cato several Billings songs, including "When Jesus Wept" and "America." Cato especially liked "When Jesus Wept," which was a fugue to be sung by several voices, a new idea in church music.

Except for a dispatch rider and a farmer or two in sleighs, they met no one on the road. The great cold continued to paralyze New Jersey. The sky remained slate gray. The wind hurtled out of the north with the cutting edge of a Toledo sword. Flora Kuyper's two powerful horses swept the sleigh along at a rapid pace. By mid-afternoon, they were on the outskirts of Morristown. In a few more minutes, Cato said good-bye to Caleb at the Widow Clark's door.

Inside, the chaplain found Lieutenant Rutledge and a friend playing cards in the parlor. "Say, Chandler," Rutledge said, "they want to see you at headquarters right away. Told me not to let you leave again if you came back. You in some sort of trouble?"

"Not to my knowledge."

"You promise to go to headquarters direct? Now?"

"Of course."

"Good. I hate to take this bad leg out in the snow. The cold gets into the bone."

Caleb trudged down the road to the Ford house. In the center hall, he encountered General Washington's aide, Colonel Alexander Hamilton. "Well, Mr. Chandler," Hamilton said, "we thought you might have decamped to New York."

"What in the world are you talking about, sir?" Caleb replied.

"Go in there."

Hamilton pointed to an empty parlor on the west side of the hall. Caleb sat down in one of the straight-backed chairs, bewildered. A tall, lean man with a hard, hatchety face appeared in the doorway. He wore a Continental Army uniform.

"Mr. Chandler?" he said, in an accent that unmistakably identified him as a New Englander. "I'm Major Benjamin Stallworth. I've been ordered by General Washington to place you under arrest for the murder of Caesar Muzzey."

eleven

"I dell you, Coongressmun Stapleton, unless more is done and done soon, the peoples vill fall away from us like leaves from a rotten oak."

Cornelius Ten Eyck, corpulent chairman of the Bergen County Revolutionary Committee, added a puff from his clay pipe to underscore every third word of this doleful prophecy. The other seven members of the committee, each as Dutch and most of them as fat as Ten Eyck, puffed on identical pipes and nodded in ponderous agreement. Dressed in their sober Sunday black suits, the committeemen sat around the crude plank table in the dining room of the house at Great Rock Farm. On the walls hung several paintings of scenes from Greek mythology done by Congressman Stapleton's brother, Paul, in the style of the French court painter,

Boucher. The pink-cheeked cupids and golden-haired nymphs clashed violently with the rough, timbered walls and beamed ceiling of the old house. The elegant art only increased the congressman's irritation. It reminded him of his comfortable prewar life in New York. It also reminded him of his embarrassing brother.

"I wish I could assure you that something—anything—will be done," Hugh Stapleton told the committeemen. "But I can only report a general indifference to New Jersey's sufferings. New England, Pennsylvania, Virginia, Maryland, haven't seen a British soldier for so long they find it hard to believe Jerseymen are fighting for their lives."

Meetings with the local politicians who had sent him to Congress were an inevitable part of Hugh Stapleton's visits home. This one, like all the others, was a litany of complaints in a cloud of tobacco smoke. The congressman's constituents wanted Washington's army to protect them from British raiders; they wanted Congress to stop the army from seizing their grain in exchange for nothing but promissory notes; thcy wanted, above all, something done to stop their money from depreciating.

"On Thursday last, Coongressmun, ve haf an auction in Hackensack," Chairman Ten Eyck said. "Marinus Van der Donck died of a cancer and his goods go for sale. The prices, Coongressmun! An old mare, supposedly to be eleven years but probably fifteen, sold for eight hundred and five pounds. That's four thousand and twenty Coontinental dollars, Coongressmun! A frying pan sold for twenty-five pounds; three roosty knifes and forks for twenty-two pounds—"

"I know, I know," Hugh Stapleton said. "The prices in Philadelphia are no better."

"What's to be done, Coongressmun? How long can any peoples support such a government?"

Not a politician by nature, Hugh Stapleton did not know what to say to the lamentations of these earnest Dutchmen. They seemed to be implying that everything Congress did wrong was his fault.

Stapleton's wife, Hannah, and two black servants emerged from the kitchen and began refilling the committeemen's tankards with hot cider. By now each of them had consumed a gallon of the stuff, a country drink that Hugh Stapleton's city palate loathed. Watching his wife in her loose flannel gown, a soiled apron tied carelessly around her waist, her hair undressed and lank, waiting on these querulous Dutchmen, Hugh Stapleton's mind drifted to Flora Kuyper, only thirty miles away, in her tasteful parlor wearing modish silk and brocade.

The congressman had been barely civil to his wife since he arrived home. At dinner the first day she had pestered him with questions about their elder son, Charles, who was living with their Kemble relatives outside Morristown and getting excellent instruction from a local schoolteacher, Ashbel Green. The congressman had managed a brief visit with the boy during his three days at Morristown. Hannah asked the usual maternal questions: Had Charles lost weight? Was his color good? Were his spirits lively? Did he ask for her? "He did not so much as mention you," the congressman had snapped.

Hannah's eyes had filled with tears. His brother,

Paul, had glared at him. Succeeding conversations had been equally unpleasant. That night Hannah had descended on him with the accounts for the family's ironworks, Principia Forge, and for Great Rock Farm. She began demanding a host of decisions and opinions. She was sure the forge master, an oily German named Klock, was cheating them. She rattled on about ditching and crop rotation and other agricultural procedures about which Hugh Stapleton knew nothing. A glance at the accounts for the forge made it clear that Klock was cheating them. But the amounts were trifling compared to the money Hugh Stapleton was making as a merchant and privateer owner in Philadelphia. He could see no point in a trip into the Ramapo Mountains in this abominable winter weather to argue with Klock about how much he was paying ax men to keep the furnace stoked. The congressman had—curtly once more—told his wife that men of the world understood that a little thievery was inevitable. When she tried to argue with him—she had no idea how much money he was making in Philadelphia or how much he had made in the West Indies—he had slammed the books shut and told her to go to bed.

The committeemen finished their final round of cider and went home. Hannah and the servants collected the empty tankards and retreated to the kitchen. Hugh Stapleton sat in the smoky dining room, thinking about Flora Kuyper. It would not be easy to find a pretext for visiting her again. She lived too close to the British lines to make her house a sensible destination for a Continental Congressman.

"Mr. Stapleton? Hugh."

Through the haze left by the committeemen's pipes Hugh Stapleton saw his wife sitting at the opposite end of the dining-room table.

"Now what is it?"

"I have a need—a wish—to talk with you. Art thou—are you—angry with me?"

"No," he said. "Why should I be?"

"Thy—your manner of address to me, since you came home, is often so harsh. I've searched my conscience, thinking there must be some reason for it. But I can find none."

"I'm not aware of the least harshness in my address," the congressman snapped. "We're old married folks, my dear. We can speak bluntly to each other when the occasion calls for it."

"True enough, I suppose. But . . ."

She twisted a handkerchief in her hands. He saw tears in her eyes. "Why don't you think of me instead of your own sensitivity?" he said. "Twelve hours a day, I sit there in Philadelphia listening to fools argue about nothing. Don't you think that's enough to sour any man's temper? Must I play the smiling sunbeam when I come home for a few days? I'm not one of your Quaker kinfolk with a heart overflowing with universal love. What do I find when I get home? Nothing but your woeful face and my brother's silent reproaches when I give you a short answer. I really think he's half in love with you. If it were any other man, I'd worry about you misbehaving."

"That's cruel—and vicious," Hannah cried. "Paul can't help what he's become. He has a loving heart. I believe a loving God will forgive him."

"Oh? The sinner merits forgiveness but your husband is condemned for failing to treat you with perfect politeness?"

"Paul may have been a sinner once. But he's struggled against his—his weakness. You seem to take pleasure in your faults."

"Faults? What faults? I've tried to make it clear to you, madam, I'm not aware of any fault whatsoever in regard to you. If there is a problem between us, it's caused by your overheated imagination—and your ridiculous political ideas."

"I have no pretension to political ideas," Hannah said. "I only try to tell you what I see before my eyes. What you and every man in Congress should know. We're losing this war. The people are abandoning Congress—the cause. You heard what the committeemen said."

"Ah!" Hugh Stapleton dismissed the committeemen with a wave of his hand. "They've been saying the same thing ever since I went to Congress."

"And you've been giving them the same answer. If you care about the country, about your sons, you should be urging them to resist—resist to their last bullet—instead of feeding their prejudices, their self-pity, by telling them that New Jersey is the most put-upon of the states, doing more than its share, without a jot of appreciation from the rest of the continent."

"That's nothing less than the truth!" Hugh Stapleton roared. "But, madam, what right have you to eavesdrop on my political sentiments? What I said to the committee was in the utmost confidence, as their representative in Congress. They're entitled, as my constituents, to a frank report."

"They need your *leadership*, your moral guid-

172

ance," Hannah said. "They hear the same complaints you aired to them tonight from every coward of a militiaman who won't turn out to fight. Your father, sick as he was, with four times as many British soldiers in New York, and just as little help from the Continentals, never talked that way in '77."

"My father has nothing to do with this argument," thundered the congressman. "Will you stick to my main point, the impropriety of your eavesdropping?"

"I was not eavesdropping. I was in and out of the room serving food and drink, and could not help hearing what you said."

"Nevertheless, you have no business correcting my politics. As a woman you have no head for it, in the first place. In the second place, as my wife you're duty-bound to respect my opinions."

"I never heard such nonsense in my life," Hannah said.

"Madam," he said, "you will do me the greatest favor if you will leave me this instant. You've tried my temper to its breaking point."

She sat there like stone, then with no warning began to weep. "Husband," she said, "I didn't come in here to quarrel with thee."

"If so," he said, "you've beautifully disguised your intensions. Now please go."

Hannah fled upstairs, sobbing. The thought of sleeping in the same bed with her was so repugnant, Hugh Stapleton sat up for hours reading a report on the army that Washington's aide, Alexander Hamilton, had prepared. It did not improve his humor. Most regiments were at half strength. Officers were resigning by the score. The enlistments of two-thirds of the men in the ranks were expiring in May and there was little hope of reenlisting more than ten percent of them. While the congressman pondered these ominous facts his mind roved down the road to Bergen, where Flora Kuyper slept—he presumed—alone.

A door slammed. The congressman sprang up, shivering violently. He had let the fire go out. The parlor was as cold as an icehouse. "Who's that?" he called.

"Your brother," Paul said. He came into the parlor peeling away scarves and gloves.

"Where have you been?"

Paul smiled mockingly. Underneath his greatcoat he was wearing one of his best outfits, a vermilion coat with a pale green waistcoat and rose breeches. His white silk gold-clocked stockings descended into bright red shoes with enormous silver buckles. He was wearing his blond hair powdered and rolled around his ears in a sort of parody of an old-fashioned wig. Two patches of rouge shone on his powdered cheeks. He was a total anomaly in this country parlor, with its rundown furniture and unpainted wood walls—a New York macaroni in the middle of snowbound New Jersey.

"What have you done," Hugh Stapleton said, "brought one of your pretty boys from New York and hidden him in Hackensack to fool your poor sister-in-law?"

"That," Paul said with a toss of his head worthy of a leading lady on a London stage, "is nonsense. I've been playing chess with a friend."

"Does he also dress in the latest style? Or is he one of those who likes to prance about in skirts?"

"Brother, your manners are as dismal as your politics."

"I've made it clear a dozen times that I'm utterly indifferent to your morals. I shouldn't even mention them were it not for a lecture I just got from my wife about your goodness of heart and my failings in this department."

"If we're going to debate the merits to that remark, for God's sake put some wood on the fire."

Hugh Stapleton threw some brushwood and a fat log on the coals, and the room gradually regained a semblance of warmth. Paul stood with his delicate painter's hands held out to the blaze, the firelight playing on his brilliant clothes and handsome, brittle-featured face. From childhood Paul had been a thin, dreamy boy with no interest in wrestling or football, hunting or fishing—the despair of his soldier father, the pet of his merchant mother. Hugh Stapleton had long resented the way his mother had indulged and spoiled Paul, virtually ignoring her elder son. She had supported Paul until she died and left him enough money in her will to spend three years in Europe, improving his art and ruining his morals. These memories did not dispose the congressman to accept the sermon on benevolence that Paul began giving him.

"The truth is, brother, you've treated Hannah abominably since you came back from the West Indies. On this visit you've outdone yourself. You speak to her as if she were a servant, when you speak at all."

"Since you know absolutely nothing about living with a wife, I suggest you shut your mouth."

Paul became intensely agitated. For a moment the congressman thought he was going to burst into tears. "I've vowed to talk to you about this, no matter what you say to me. Hannah loves you with a violence that—to be frank—dismays me. I always thought you were like Mother, incapable of loving or being loved by anyone. I assumed you'd marry a mirror image of yourself, a woman of fashion who'd cherish some faint affection for you as long as you kept her well housed and gowned. But you surprised me completely with Hannah. Even more by—by winning her love. You can't ignore a fact like that, Hugh. It becomes a—responsibility."

"Responsibility!" the congressman snarled. "I'm sick to death of responsibility. First I have to apologize to eight blockheaded Dutchmen about the way Congress is losing the war and then I'm supposed to cringe because my saintly sodomite brother calls me a failed husband. To hell with all of you."

"We *are* losing the war."

"What do you mean, we? You have nothing to fear. Neuters like you can laugh at fools like me. I might have imitated your bad example if it weren't for my patriot wife. That alone is reason for me to snap at her. Without her exhortations I would have gone back to Holland in '78. But I had to come home and rescue the family honor. My country needed me. Dear God. I could be sitting in Amsterdam at this moment, with a plump trollop on either knee, singing an old-fashioned drinking song instead of arguing with you about responsibility."

"You came home because you loved her, Hugh. I saw you in New York, in those years. You were the happiest husband in America. I—I envied you that happiness."

"If I was happy, it was because I had a wife who tried to please me. Now it seems I'm supposed to please her—by prating about patriotism and lying about our glorious cause. I'll be damned if I'll do it any longer."

"Hugh, try to understand how we live here. In terror every night. Only when you come home does the place get any protection. Hannah's nerves are bad. You can't live in constant fear without having it depress your spirits."

"Fear of what? No one's going to attack this place. The British are gentlemen. They might enjoy catching me but they're not likely to abuse a congressman's wife."

"The people the British send into Bergen County by night are not gentlemen," Paul said. "Two women were raped within a mile of here in the last six months. They—they use our barns to hide escaped prisoners on the way to New York."

"Have you notified the militia?"

"No. I—I persuaded Hannah to say nothing. I was afraid it would compromise my neutral status."

"And she dares to lecture me about giving moral leadership? She'll hear from me about this tomorrow. I've half a mind to wake her up and confront her with it now."

"No! Hugh, please. That was stupid of me to even mention it. Promise me you'll say nothing. To her or the militia. They're useless. They can't protect us even if they thought it was worth the effort. I know the men who operate the escape route. Liberty

Turnpike they call it. They'd burn this place over our heads."

Congressman Stapleton went to a cupboard and poured himself a glass of Barbados rum. The winter cold, was settling in his chest. He would have a miserable cough and a running nose tomorrow. "What a mess," he said. "Perhaps we should imitate our hero father—get drunk and stay that way."

He took a long swallow of the dark brown liquid. Warmth flooded his body. It made him think of Flora Kuyper. Warmth there, too. Warmth and happiness such as he had not known for years.

"I think you'd do better to keep a clear head," Paul said. "If Congress really manages to lose this war, what are you going to do?"

"It depends on how we lose," Hugh Stapleton said. "As long as Washington holds an army together at Morristown, we can negotiate a fairly advantageous peace."

"What if Washington can't do it? What if the army collapses or mutinies? New York is full of rumors about some tremendously clever stroke that will finish the war overnight. It seems to have something to do with a British plot to stage a mutiny—and provoke Washington's assassination."

"If that happened," Hugh Stapleton said, "it would behoove a Continental Congressman to find asylum in another country for a while."

"No doubt you have a plan?"

Until that moment Congressman Stapleton had had no plan. He had not considered the possibility of an American collapse even after he saw Washington's surly, starving troops at Morristown. Now, for the first time, he thought seriously about flight from the faltering rebellion.

"Of course I have a plan," he said. "One of my privateers, *Common Sense*, can outrun anything on the ocean. I've got the money I made in the West Indies invested in Holland."

Paul nodded. He seemed depressed by his brother's assurance. "No doubt you'll get word to us in time to bring Hannah and the boys to Philadelphia."

"Yes—of course."

"Give me a swallow of that rum," Paul said. "This fire is fading fast."

Hugh Stapleton poured him half a glass. Paul stared into the flames. "The old man would stay and fight it out."

"Like a trapped bear. That's all he'd know how to do," Hugh Stapleton said. "I'm glad I inherited Mother's brains."

"He wasn't as stupid as she tried to make us think he was," Paul said. "He was a great soldier in his day."

"I'm surprised to hear you taking his side," Hugh said.

For a moment Paul glanced at the huge double-barreled musket over the fireplace—the gun Malcolm Stapleton had carried to his numerous wars. Pompey kept it polished and oiled as religiously as he had when the old man was alive. In the nearby corner was a glass-fronted cupboard with a half-dozen other muskets in it.

"We had a sort of reconciliation in the last six months before he died," Paul said. "I suppose it was an acceptance of the fact that neither of us was going to change. I painted his portrait. Would you like to see it?"

"Why not?"

Paul took the canvas from the drawer of a nearby chest and unrolled it on the floor. It was not a portrait of the bored, frequently drunk old man Hugh Stapleton had known. This was a figure from a whirlwind, a soldier poised on a parapet with enemy guns belching death in his face. He was looking back, one muscular arm raised, waving on men behind him. The massive face, with the thick fighter's jaw, was alive with battle fury.

"That's really rather good, Paul," Hugh Stapleton said.

"It's how the men around here remember him," Paul said. "The ones who followed him to Canada in '58 and down to Havana in '62."

"Not many of them came back, as I recall."

"No. He talked about that—those last months— when he was dying. He didn't regret the deaths. He said they won something important by fighting beside the British—honor. That's what he was afraid we'd lose in this war."

Hugh Stapleton finished his rum. "You know what Shakespeare wrote about honor. You can't eat it or drink it or spend it."

"Remember he put those words in the mouth of Falstaff—a buffoon."

"You're not sounding very neutral, brother. What's happened? Has the love affair you were having with that fat fop Walter Beckford gone poof?"

"That ended a long time ago," Paul said. "But it did give me—certain insights into the British mind. They've acquired a rather alarming attitude toward

Americans, Hugh. A mixture of contempt and hatred. I fear that any so-called peace terms—if they have the power to impose them—would be very harsh."

"For some people. Like those who've been idiotic enough to serve in the Continental Congress. If it weren't for the boys, I'd be tempted to leave my patriot wife behind to see what her kind of harebrained enthusiasm leads to."

"I hope you're not serious."

"Why not? I assure you I wouldn't miss her, in bed or out of it. Perhaps I'll leave her to you, brother. You can enjoy a union of the spirit if not of the flesh."

"You disgust me. You've always disgusted me."

Paul's voice went shrilling into the top of his throat. Hugh Stapleton laughed. He was being outrageous and he knew it. He had always played the brutal realist when confronted with Paul's ethereal idealism. Like too many brothers, they continued to inflict wounds in the cruel ways they had discovered as boys.

The tall case clock in the upper hall bonged 3 A.M. as Hugh Stapleton slipped into bed beside his sleeping wife. Without his brother to goad him, the congressman's cynicism rapidly subsided into barren depression. His life was turning into a disaster in front of his eyes. Was he really ready to run for cover like a hunted fox? He heard George Washington saying, *I know I can speak freely to Malcolm Stapleton's son*. Once he had been complacently proud of that designation. For all his faults the old man had been a famous soldier. But the memory, the fact, was becoming more and more meaningless. Malcolm Stapleton was dead. Hugh Stapleton was living in a world that his father could never have comprehended.

It was almost dawn before the congressman fell asleep. At 7:30 his five-year-old son, Malcolm, came scampering into the bedroom to pull on his arm and demand a ride in the sleigh. Hugh stumbled downstairs to breakfast and sat there glowering at his wife and brother. Paul was about to depart for New York, where he was making more money as a painter than he had ever made before. He also had a fair number of commissions from American officers in Morristown. But he talked, in his effeminate way, of dropping them because the Americans insisted on paying him in depreciated paper money.

"I told them I was *not* neutral about Continental currency," Paul said with a giggle. "Having gotten a glimpse of America's prospects from a *candid* talk with my dear brother last night, I may be even less neutral the next time I go to Morristown—if I even bother."

Hannah gave her husband one of her woebegone looks, as if she despaired not only of his patriotism but of his soul's salvation. The congressman finished his breakfast feeling even more disgruntled with his wife and with the war that had demolished his contentment. He sneezed violently as he retreated from the table and did not even reply when his wife murmured, "God bless you." In the parlor, his nose began to run. He was, as he had feared last night, getting a nasty cold. Logy from lack of sleep, he sat before the fire and tried to read the latest edition of the *New Jersey Journal*. The editor was an ex-artillery officer who had been mustered out of the army to launch the paper as an antidote to the loyalist newspapers published in New York. The *Journal* was full of gasconades about the resolute Americans and mockery toward the cowardly British.

About 10 o'clock, Maggie, Pompey's daughter, brought him a package. She said that it had been handed to her by a coachman driving a fine team of white mares. "There he goes now," Maggie said.

Hugh Stapleton peered out the window at the gray-and-white landscape and saw Cato, Flora Kuyper's servant, leaving the circular drive in front of the farmhouse, heading his team toward the main road. The congressman ripped open the package and discovered the blue shoes he had put on when he decided to stay for the night at Flora Kuyper's. His son Malcolm came bounding into the room and again begged him to take him for a sleigh ride. Seeing the shoes, Malcolm asked if he could wear them. The congressman chose the lesser of two evils (the other being the sleigh ride) and gave him the shoes. The boy slipped his small feet into them, then pulled out the right foot and peered into the toe. "There's something in here, Papa," he said.

Hugh Stapleton's fingers touched paper. He extracted a note.

My dear friend:

I cannot stop thinking of the pleasure your visit gave me. Cato found these shoes under your bed. Would that we could meet again! But I am loath to tempt you into such a dangerous neighborhood.

Regretfully,
FLORA KUYPER

183

"Who's the letter from, Papa?" Malcolm asked.

"From a lady. I stayed at her house the other night and forgot my shoes."

Malcolm found this hilarious. "How could you forget your shoes? Weren't they on your feet?"

"I had another pair on my feet." And I will soon have them on again, he thought.

By noon Hugh Stapleton was packed. Ignoring the dismay on his wife's face, he declared that politics made it imperative for him to return to Philadelphia immediately. He had messages from Washington to deliver to certain congressmen. "Surely you can't criticize me for doing my political duty, can you, my dear?" he said.

"You said you would stay at least two weeks."

"I believe you told me only last night that our nation's affairs were in crisis," he said.

Hannah looked so sad he felt momentarily ashamed. He soothed his conscience by telling himself that destiny was conspiring with desire to overwhelm his will. It was an easy thing for a willful man to believe when his world was writhing in history's grip.

Pompey was at the door with the Burlington geldings hitched to the sleigh. With masterful hypocrisy, the congressman told Pompey that he would endure the strain of driving to Philadelphia without him. "I want you here to guard the house against loyalist raiders. I hope it will calm Mrs. Stapleton's nerves to have someone nearby who can use a gun. Keep my father's old musket loaded at all times and show her you know how to use it."

Flattered by his master's trust, the burly old black promised to be ready to defend the house on a moment's notice. Hugh Stapleton seized the reins and headed for the main road. In two hours he was knocking on Flora Kuyper's door. She greeted him in her sitting room, looking as pale and disconsolate as the wife he had just abandoned.

"I got your note," he said. "I almost missed it."

"I—I merely wanted you to know my feelings," she said. "I—I didn't really expect you to risk another visit. So soon, at least."

"You seem unhappy."

"I—I've been assailed by a most melancholy humor all day."

"Why, madam?"

"I don't know. Perhaps the times. Perhaps—it has something to do with you. I found myself wishing to see you again—and telling myself it would be far better if you tore my note into a thousand pieces and dismissed our meeting as—a night's indiscretion."

"You must know it was much more than that."

"It was—for me. But you're a man of the world. No doubt you have had many such conquests."

"If there was a conquest, madam, it was on your part. Since I left here I haven't passed an hour, day or night, without thinking of you."

"I've had similar thoughts. But you're a married man, Mr. Stapleton. What can either of us hope to gain from continuing our friendship?"

"Happiness. Enough happiness to satisfy our souls for a lifetime."

"How? Even as you sit here my heart leaps at the risk you take to visit me again."

"I've thought of that," the congressman admitted.

185

"I must either resign my seat in Congress or persuade you to come to Philadelphia with me."

"Both are out of the question," Flora said. "I won't be responsible for your abandoning the cause of your country—which is also mine by adoption. I can't go to Philadelphia. I have seven slaves, a farm to protect. All I own in the world."

"What if I told you the truth, madam, that the cause of your adopted country is no longer worth defending? It may have been once, in those glorious days of 1776, when everyone was sure of America's virtue and patriotism. Now we know those qualities were chimeras, imaginary visions as fanciful as the nonsense in the Bible."

"Then, why should I go to Philadelphia and join you in defending this—this nonsense?"

That was the moment when memory and desire fused in Congressman Stapleton's mind. The memory of his conversation with his brother, Paul.

Of course I have a plan....

You'll get word to us in time to bring Hannah and the boys to Philadelphia....

Perhaps I'll leave her to you....

Here was the other half of his mind—or, better, his soul. The better half of his soul. Here was beauty and admiration and consolation for Catalyntie Stapleton's son, whose shrewd Dutch brain tells him it is time to run for cover.

"You wouldn't stay in Philadelphia very long, madam. I have a fast ship—and a half-million pounds waiting for us to enjoy in Amsterdam as soon as the ice melts in the Delaware."

"Amsterdam," Flora Kuyper said, a smile banishing her melancholy frown. "I've never been there. I've heard it's charming."

twelve

Major Benjamin Stallworth studied Caleb Chandler's haggard, sleepless face. It was the fourth day of his interrogation. From 6 A.M. until 6 P.M. Stallworth had paced the bare room in the unheated house off the Vealtown Road, snarling questions and accusations at his prisoner. Then Alexander Hamilton took charge of the verbal gauntlet, continuing it until midnight.

, For a moment Stallworth felt a tremor of remorse. It disturbed him, out of all proportion to its intensity. He had never felt a trace of such an emotion with other prisoners. Was he losing control of his nerves? Was he afraid of repeating the mistake he had made— if it had been a mistake—with the Reverend Joel Lockwood? No, Stallworth told himself, glaring coldly at Caleb Chandler until his stare matched the temperature in the room. The regret was not for Chandler. It was his own naive self he was mourning, the slogan-chanting college graduate, marching to war in the good cause. Caleb Chandler reminded him of that nincompoop, who believed the ministers in every pulpit, thundering confidence in America's virtue. Perhaps he still wished he could believe in that myth, and the larger myth behind it, the God of righteousness and His grace. But Stallworth was a servant of necessity now.

Besides, there was still the possibility that Caleb Chandler was a traitor. Stallworth had begun to doubt it. But the thought enabled him to begin the day's interrogation with the requisite contempt in his voice.

"Do you believe me now, Chandler? Are you prepared to admit that your hero, Joel Lockwood, was ready to turn his coat?"

Yesterday, Stallworth had read Chandler the letters that Lockwood had written to Major Walter Beckford. Letters that Caesar Muzzey had conveniently betrayed before carrying them to New York.

"Yes," Caleb said in a leaden voice. "But that doesn't mean I'm a traitor."

"Oh, no," Stallworth said. "Not at all. Just because your mentor—the man whom you called in one of your letters the captain of your soul—is a traitor, that doesn't mean you're one. It just raises the probability a little higher. When we add to it all the other probabilities—no one else had a better opportunity to murder Caesar Muzzey, no one else had a better motive, presuming, as we must, that you're in British pay. No one else has preached traitorous sermons to the troops. No one else arranged to send one of our congressmen to the house of a known British agent, where only good fortune prevented his capture. No one else proceeded to spend twenty-four hours with that same British agent, for Christ knows what hellish purpose. When we pile all those probabilities on top of one another, Chandler, they become a gallows high enough to hang you."

"I've told you a hundred times I knew nothing about Mrs. Kuyper being an agent. I knew nothing about Lockwood. I knew nothing about Caesar Muzzey. I only wanted to see justice done."

Stallworth shook his head. "Chandler, your feeble pleas won't convince a court-martial board. There are too many coincidences. Your one chance for life is to tell us the truth. Confess your guilt. Give us the names of the other people in your network. Who recruited you?"

"No one. Major, please believe me. I'm not a spy. I—I'm ready to die for the cause. I came here believing everyone—Joel Lockwood, the soldiers, the officers—felt the same way."

"Have you ever seen a man hanged, Chandler?"

"No! I told you—I—I never have."

"I saw General Putnam hang one of your royalist confederates, a Ridgefield man named Jones, about a year ago. It was a dismal scene. His parents and relatives wringing their hands, wailing. You can be sure we'll hang you back in Connecticut, as an example to others of your traitorous ilk."

Stallworth had said the same thing yesterday, and the day before. It was part of the process, to say something over and over, pretending it was for the first time. It made the prisoner wonder if his previous answers had been heard. It made him feel more and more trapped, desperate for a normal response.

"Tell me about your visit to Mrs. Kuyper, Chandler. How many times did you fuck her?"

"I told you—I never touched the woman."

"Horseshit, Chandler. You admitted yesterday you thought about it. You were almost ready to tell the truth. We know she fucks for the King, Chandler. She's probably fucking that Continental Congressman you sent to her, right now. I have to admit it, Chandler, that was a coup. Beckford must have paid you a hundred guineas for that one. Handing them a congressman that way. A sitting duck. Or, to be more exact, a fucking duck, that they can haul off to New York anytime they please."

"I told you I didn't *know*," Caleb Chandler shouted.

Stallworth pulled a chair across the room and sat down, only inches from Chandler, jamming his knees against his legs. "Come, now, tell me man to man. I like to hear these kinds of stories. I'm a connoisseur, Chandler. I used to command the military police when we had a garrison in New York, in '76. I used to go through the Holy Ground every morning, dragging out the drunks and an occasional corpse. I saw the ladies in their lacy nightclothes. That's when I stopped believing in *virtuous* Americans—the kind of horseshit you parsons shovel from pulpits. That's when I saw how this war would have to be won."

"I didn't touch her."

"Not even a finger on those juicy tits? Not even

190

a rub against that pussy? As dark and fine as angel's hair, I hear it is. Tell me what it was like, Chandler."

"I didn't touch her!"

Stallworth abandoned his chair and retreated to the other side of the room. "That gives me even worse apprehensions, Chandler. Is it possible that Yale has produced another Williamite? We had one there in my day. We drove him out of the place. From what I hear of the school's progress in corruption, you may have been the most popular scholar in Connecticut Hall. It would explain your seduction by Walter Beckford, the chief sodomist in the British army—a notable title, since they have so many. It would explain your indifference to Mrs. Kuyper."

"I am not indifferent to Mrs. Kuyper. I told you I thought she was the most beautiful woman I've ever met. I—"

Stallworth went to a table in the center of the room and wrote in a book, repeating each word as he inscribed it. "Prisoner—denies—being a sodomite in spite of—extensive evidence—to the contrary."

Stallworth shook his head. "That won't go down well at your court-martial, Chandler."

"I want to see General Washington," Caleb Chandler said. On previous days these words had been a demand. Now they were a whimper.

"To make a full confession? You can do that as well to me."

"To protest this—this outrageous slander. These accusations."

"General Washington doesn't see prisoners under arrest, Chandler. He appoints a court-martial board to hear the charges and then approves—in most cases—the board's findings. Let's talk about your family, Chandler. We've been investigating them. Your two brothers were among those glorious Connecticut heroes who ran for their lives at Kips Bay in 1776. They haven't lifted a finger for their country since."

"They're married men with families—"

"Maybe one of them," Stallworth continued, as if Caleb Chandler had not spoken, "is the evil genius behind your treason. We've found that the traitor and the coward often go together. Are you refusing to confess out of some misguided sense of nobility? Better for you, a bachelor, to hang? We're prepared to hang you both, Chandler. We will, too. Your silence will only delay your brother's execution. Your whole network is exposed, Chandler. There's no hope of protecting anyone. Only a full confession, a plea for mercy, can save you and your brothers."

"I will never plead for mercy from you—you son of a bitch!" Caleb Chandler shouted.

"Oh?"

Defiance at this point was a good sign. It usually preceded surrender. Stallworth paced the room, pretending distress.

"All right. I'll admit something, Chandler. I don't want to hang you. That clerical coat you're wearing may yet save your worthless, probably traitorous neck. I said the same thing to the Reverend Joel Lockwood. That bastard Rivington, the publisher of the *Royal Gazette*, would make too much capital out of the Americans hanging a man of the cloth. What better proof that the glorious cause is collapsing? I'm going to offer you the same chance we gave the

Reverend Lockwood. You can live—if you agree to become a spy for us. What we call in the espionage business a double agent."

"Joel Lockwood—agreed to that?"

"For the same reason you'll agree to it, Chandler. To save your worthless life!" Stallworth roared.

He paused to let the shock penetrate the prisoner's crumbling defenses. "I hope your nerves are better than Lockwood's. What I want from you is more difficult. All he had to do was go back to Connecticut and pretend to be a turncoat, then report to me everyone who nibbled at his bait. Perhaps my mistake was not offering him the consolation I'm giving you, Chandler."

"What's that?" Caleb Chandler asked.

"The opportunity, the necessity, to make love to Mrs. Kuyper. To plant yourself so deep in her affections, Chandler, that she invites you to become a spy for Beckford."

"Then what happens?"

"She'll send you to New York, where Beckford will put you through a gauntlet not much different from the one I'm administering to you. If you survive it, you'll become Muzzey's replacement."

"Muzzey's replacement," Chandler said. The idea seemed to bemuse him.

"Then you'll begin to think and live as a double agent. You'll begin to prove your patriotism, Chandler, always remembering that I assume you're a traitor. I'll accept as proof to the contrary nothing but facts—information that's useful to us. That moves us toward victory. Anything else, any facts that prove harmful, will move you a little closer to the gallows."

"You're telling me, in the name of the government of the United States, to lie to this woman, to pretend to love her, to seduce her if necessary?"

Stallworth clicked his teeth in exasperation. "Chandler, how many times do I have to tell you? Flora Kuyper's a whore. She fucks for the King. You won't seduce her. It'll be the other way around, to guarantee your enthusiasm for His Majesty. You won't be the first man to lift her skirts and you won't be the last. The important thing is the purpose, Chandler. To get you into the network run by their agent, Twenty-six."

Chandler barely listened to him. He shook his head, groping for another defiant answer. Stallworth sensed he was on the edge of collapse.

"Are you worried about your immortal soul, Chandler? As far as I'm concerned, the only thing you're risking is a case of the pox. We're not under the command of Jehovah any longer, Chandler. His name has become Necessity and His voice speaks through a cannon's mouth. And through your lying mouth. And mine. What happens to our souls doesn't matter, Chandler. Only one thing matters. Victory."

For a long moment the prisoner said nothing. He was staring at Benjamin Stallworth with the same bemused expression on his face. "Such faith I have not found in all of Israel," he said.

The voice, the eyes, did not belong to Caleb Chandler the naive Yale graduate. Those words, mocking the God of the New Testament, were spoken by a different creature, a numb, bitter cynic.

Washington was right. It was different from ordering a man to stand and die on the battlefield. But it was necessary, Stallworth told himself. Necessary. For victory.

thirteen

One minute we're up to our eyes in the bracken, these damn green fronds so thick in our faces a man couldn't see an inch ahead of him. Jesus, they were like hands, women's hands lulling us to sleep there in the twilight, the dry, dead hands of ghost women, who came back no matter how many times you pushed them away. Then I heard a chunk and I knew only one thing made such a sound, a tomahawk going into a man's skull. The Indians were all around us. I dropped flat and saw a pair of painted legs a step away from me. I gave him both barrels in the belly and yelled, "Down, down, for God's sake. Shoot for the belly and go for the balls with your knives. Cut off their goddamn red peckers."

The woods exploded with shots and shouts, whoops and screams. We slashed and fired, fired *and slashed, and the bracken fell around us like wheat sheaves scythed by our buck and ball. In five minutes it was as still in those woods as in a midnight church. Not an animal, not a bird, much less an Indian, breathed lest he die. I whistled the lads to me and we counted noses. All were sound except Gus Pearce. We found him not ten feet away from me with the tomahawk still in his skull. Near and around we found ten dead Indians, whom we scalped and gelded, so their friends would know we had their souls in our packs—the scalp knot, I mean—and their courage in our bellies. Yes, we ate their private parts, just as they ate ours. The only difference was we waited until they were dead to take them. They'd roast a man living and eat them in front of his eyes. The British regulars couldn't bear such fighting. A single war whoop turned their legs to jelly. Only born Americans could meet the Indians in their native woods.*

Hannah Cosway Stapleton lay in her bed at Great Rock Farm, listening to a dead man. She did not understand why or how Malcolm Stapleton's voice continued to echo in her skull. The stories he had told her from his warrior years fighting the Indians and French in the north woods were invariably gruesome and barbaric. One would almost think he had been going out of his way to revolt her Quaker soul, with its inherited disapproval of war. But she had abandoned Quakerism to marry Hugh Stapleton. She had listened to her father-in-law's tales of horror and heroism with a guilty fascination. Gradually she had begun to see them as a kind of initiation; the old man's way of telling her she was now a member of the family. The grisly details, the specific, sexual words that soldiers preferred, were also a kind of compliment, a way of telling her he believed—or at least hoped—she would be as brave, as steady in the face of war's brutality, as a man.

She had tried, she was trying, Hannah thought, turning on her back to stare into the cold darkness of her bedroom ceiling, thicker than the wind-swept darkness outside the window. She was trying—and failing. It was so hard to control her fear. It came in waves, like a flood engulfing the farm, the house, the bedroom; finally lapping up through her body, spuming into her throat. Nothing could stop it—will, wish, not even desperate, beseeching prayer. Hardly surprising, the last failure. Prayer depends on faith. In the world around her, in her own heart, God had become an absent stranger.

The Bible said that God was love. Perhaps when love died, God vanished with it. A kind of death. No. Hannah struggled to defend herself against that enormous conclusion. Love was not dead. It was wounded, perhaps in danger of expiring. But it was not dead.

More and more, as Hannah thought about her life through half and sometimes all of a sleepless night, it divided into two dreams, one good, one bad.

The good dream began at Peachfields, her father's estate near Burlington, on the Delaware. There she had been surrounded by love; the great house, its guardian trees, the very earth had seemed to abound in affection. As the oldest daughter, she had been her mother's favorite. Her father's double success as a merchant and farmer had made their lives affluent and easy. Visiting cousins, uncles, aunts from Philadelphia, all fellow Quakers, added zest to their country lives. On Sunday there was a quiet communion with a benevolent God at the meeting house in Burlington town.

That part of the good dream had ended like a novel, those delicious books that she and her sisters were forbidden to read but smuggled into their bedrooms anyway, to peruse by candlelight and compare with sighs and smiles. The handsome, well-born scion, who always solved everything by finally offering his hand to the virtuous maiden, had appeared in her own life at precisely the right moment, when she was nineteen. Hugh Stapleton had strolled up to her at the ball the town of Burlington gave for the annual meeting of New Jersey's legislature (his father was on the governor's council) and had boldly written his name on every line of her dance card.

He was not a Quaker, a fact that troubled her mother but no one else in the family. He candidly admitted that he was not religious but he wanted a wife who could give religion to his children. Her father was delighted at the prospect of an alliance with the Stapletons, one of the wealthiest families in East Jersey. So in 1767 Hannah had come to the mansion on Hackensack's green, a bride welcomed by her smiling in-laws. There the good dream temporarily faltered.

The Stapletons were not a happy family. The patriarch, Malcolm, the province's leading soldier, was a coarse, profane man who drank too much and plainly disliked his wife. It had been one of those arranged marriages, common in the early decades of the century, between wealthy New Yorkers and land-rich, cash-poor New Jerseyans. Elegant Catalyntie Van Vorst had apparently looked with disdain on the martial scion of the Stapletons, whom she had been consigned to marry. She refused to live in the seventeenth-century house on Great Rock Farm. Instead she had used her dowry to build an opulent town house in Hackensack. There she attempted to remodel her warrior husband into a city gentleman, with disastrous results. The frequent wars between England and France had rescued Malcolm Stapleton from her scathing tongue, but not before the marriage had become a sepulcher.

Catalyntie consoled herself by devoting her days and nights to the business she had inherited from her mother. Running their own businesses was a tradition among New York Dutch women, but few could match Catalyntie Van Vorst Stapleton's acumen. Transferring the company from New York to a store on the Hackensack River, she rapidly amassed a fortune selling furniture, cloth, silver, and china to the Dutch farmers of Bergen County, the most prosperous plowmen in America. She invested her money in a copper mine, an iron furnace, and several ships. She filled her Hackensack house with fine paintings, Oriental rugs, English silver, Chippendale furniture. If Catalyntie loved anything besides business, it was beauty.

She had a profound and—Hannah now realized—an unhealthy influence on her sons. She turned both against their father and then tried to dominate them. She was the most willful woman Hannah had ever met. To escape her, Hugh announced that he was going to take his share of the family business and transfer it to New York. Catalyntie had asked Hannah if she wanted to live in "that stinking city." Hannah had meekly replied that she was ready to live wherever her husband chose.

"You Quakers with your humility and love," the old lady had said. "You'll find respect is more important than love, in the end. In both ends, in fact." She added a gesture that left little doubt of what she meant. A year later she was dead of an apoplexy brought on by an argument with a Yankee ship captain who had tried to cheat her with a cargo of inferior cotton.

Life in New York had been a shock to a country girl from Burlington. To Hugh the city had long been a second home. He was untroubled by the violent contrast between rich and poor, the parading prostitutes, the drunken sailors. He loved the "ton," as he called the high life, with its round of dinner parties and balls. He insisted on an absolute end to his wife's Quaker inhibitions about expensive clothes and Hannah soon had one of the most dazzling wardrobes in the city. When her mother came to visit, she took one look at the array of silk dresses, lace petticoats, the dozens of bonnets, and the drawers full of silk stockings and gloves, and murmured, "Oh, my dear child, I fear for thy salvation."

How silly, how ridiculously old-fashioned those words had sounded in 1770, only ten years ago. Hugh's business was thriving, his ships were ranging the seven seas, she was about to give birth to their first son. For all his love of elegance and style, he was a devoted husband. He often confessed his amazement at the way he enjoyed married life—an oblique reference to his parents' unhappy marriage. He used to call her his country titmouse and joke about the way she had learned to live with the city titmouse. Sometimes he talked bawdy. It was both shocking and thrilling to her. "How's my favorite country tit?" he would say, catching her from behind to kiss her on the neck.

"Really, Mr. Stapleton," she would whisper, "where do you think you are—in the Holy Ground?"

"It's where I hope to be later tonight," he would say, slipping his hand over her breast. She would spring from his grasp, blushing and crying, "One blasphemy at a time is all I can stand."

She had totally forgotten the life of prayer that had been such a central part of her country days. Her husband had become her god, so violent was her love for him, so complete her desire to please him. *I want an amorous wife,* he had said, and she was soon as amorous as Madame de Pompadour. *I want a beautiful wife,* he had said, and she was ready to spend eight hours a day enduring the tortures of the hairdresser, lacing her whalebone stays to the point of anguish, prowling the shops in search of new skin creams and lotions. She saw herself as redeeming him from his faithlessness, his doubts about married love. When he chided her for being too shy, for acting like a bumpkin at their first dinner parties, and forbade her to use the Quaker "thee" and "thou" except in the intimacy of their bedroom, she had been as humble as a penitent under rebuke from the monthly meeting, indeed from all the monthly meetings of all the Quakers in the world. She had forced herself to become as forward, as blasé before the "hells" and "goddamns" and wenching talk that were the staple of New York parties, as the most loudly and proudly self-proclaimed women of fashion.

Then the bad dream, the war, had begun. It had been hard to believe its reality at first. It had gone so swiftly from rioting and mobbing to regiments of grim-eyed Yankees parading New York's streets with muskets on their shoulders while the King's ships-of-the-line loomed above the town, with their tiers of cannon. Hugh kept saying it was all madness begun by Boston fanatics. He and other merchants had tried to be voices of moderation, of peace, and were soon suspected and reviled by both sides.

She was pregnant with their second child when the trouble started. Hugh had sent her out to the family mansion in Hackensack, where old Malcolm Stapleton sat stupidly drunk most of each day, bemoaning the idea of opposing the King and destroying the British Empire he had helped to found by drubbing the Spanish and French and their Indians in previous wars. Yet he was ready enough to roar out defiance of Parliament at committee meetings. He was a born fighter and Hannah shuddered at the thought that her children might inherit his warrior blood.

With business at a standstill, Hugh decided to go to Amsterdam and set up a partnership with one of his Dutch relatives. He was his mother's son. Nothing, not even a war, was as important as "improving some moneys." No sooner had Hugh transferred his capital to Holland than war began in earnest in Massachusetts. Instead of coming home, Hugh became the unofficial representative of a half-dozen Dutch firms at St. Eustatius in the West Indies, where he was soon funneling tons of badly needed gunpowder, muskets, cannon, and uniforms to Washington's army. Hannah was left to cope with managing all the affairs of the Stapletons at home. Old Malcolm was a hopeless businessman. Paul Stapleton, driven out of New York by the war and living at Great Rock Farm to avoid his father, professed only irritated indifference to the family's finances. Like his father, he devoted most of each day to getting drunk. Hannah was left to preside at the Hackensack town house in Catalyntie's place and simultaneously supervise the operation of a 500-acre farm, an iron furnace, and a copper mine.

As she struggled with accounts and listened to the smiling lies of the foundry master, a fat, cunning German named Klock, somewhere Hannah could hear Catalyntie Stapleton laughing. *Tell me the good of your love and humility now, my little Quaker. Now you are learning how much the world values them. Humility gets stepped on. Love gets neglected. Hugh is like me. He knows the only thing worth loving: money.*

Then came not tales of war from distant Massachusetts, but war itself, sweeping over New Jersey like a giant wave from the depths of the Atlantic. First the sullen, beaten Americans, then the confident, pursuing British, then the mob.

Some of the mob were loyalists, who sincerely believed that the rebellion had been started by scheming malcontents who deserved to be punished. But most of them were farmhands, runaway slaves, indentured servants, hungry for a chance to vent their hatred of the rich, hungrier for loot. They gathered in front of the Stapleton house, howling for "the congressman." Malcolm Stapleton had been a member of the first Continental Congress in 1774 but had resigned rather than vote for the Declaration of Independence. Until Congress approved that document, he had denounced Yankee extremists as ferociously as British oligarchs. Thereafter he had swallowed his disapproval and stood with his country. Too old to join Washington's army, he had accepted command of the revolutionary militia in Bergen County. To the loyalist-led mob, this made him a traitor.

They dragged the old man out of the house and hustled him across the Hackensack green to the dank stone jail. Then they swarmed through the house, smashing the crystal chandeliers, hacking the Chippendale furniture, stuffing the silver forks and spoons, the silver bowls, the teapots and trays into sacks. Hannah had rushed into the street to find the British commander, a bored young captain who told her that as long as his soldiers were not looting, what the loyal Americans did to the disloyal Americans was none of his business.

So she went back to the wrecked house and told the black nurse, Maggie, to take her frightened little sons, Charles and Malcolm, to Great Rock Farm. She would stay in Hackensack; it was her duty. Her father-in-law would need food and drink and firewood in that vile jail. She would be safe enough, she assured Maggie. There was nothing left to steal. Besides, the mob had already turned its attention to the other houses on the green.

Two hours later, as the chaos outside subsided,

Hannah heard footsteps crunching through the broken glass on the first floor. She went to the head of the stairs. They looked up at her through the twilight—the huge Dutch boy with his floppy hat and the short, squat Englishman with the dirty red soldier's coat. She knew what they wanted. The obscenity was gleaming in their eyes, shining in their smiles. "No," she said. "No."

They did not say a word. They started up the stairs. She stood at the top, frozen with dread, disbelief. The Englishman had a shark's face, the same recessed jaw and gleaming upper teeth she had seen on one of those sea killers hanging on a Delaware River dock. The Dutch boy's smile was closer to a grimace, a scar. The fading light from a round window on the first landing touched their faces but left their bodies in darkness, converting their ascent into a vile parody of salvation. On they came, their boots striking each step in unison, each crash echoing through the empty house.

Suddenly there was a shadowy figure at the bottom of the stairs. "Stop," shrilled a voice that might have been a woman's. "If you touch her, I *guarantee* I will have you hanged. I am a *very* personal friend of Major Walter Beckford, aide-de-camp to General von Knyphausen."

It was Paul Stapleton.

The two faces ceased their ascent. The huge Dutch boy turned toward the speaker, who had neither gun nor sword. "I kill him, John?" he asked.

"No. No, lad," the Englishman said. "It never pays to kill an officer's personal friends. Even if we know what kind of personal friends Major Beckford is likely to have."

"I'll remember that, Nelson," Paul said. "Once this rebellion is suppressed, the first thing we'll do is put scum like you in your place. Now get out of here."

Slowly, sullenly the two monsters clumped down the stairs and out of the house. Paul joined Hannah on the second-floor landing. She wanted to thank him, to make some gesture of gratitude. But she could not move or speak. She felt separated from her body, outside it, watching herself stare blankly at Paul as if he were a total stranger. Terror had turned her into one of those wax figures of the famous and infamous that sculptors displayed in galleries. Terror and something worse, a fear, even the knowledge, that the world had been transformed, that God had turned his face away from it. Or worse, that He had never been here, warming her heart, her life.

Her hands still gripped the newel post, as if it were a stanchion on the deck of a careening ship. The darkness seemed to swirl from the stairwell to engulf her. Paul touched her cheek. "It's all right. They're gone," he said.

Hannah shook her head, trying to tell him that they would never be gone, that the terrible truth they signified had become part of her flesh. But there was no point in telling this to Paul Stapleton. He was a walking, talking mockery of the God of Love that Hannah Cosway had worshiped. She remembered her husband's words the first time his brother had come to dinner in New York, accompanied by a handsome young man. *He's a Williamite.* She had had to ask, in her country naiveté, what that meant. *The sin of Sodom. It's*

*very popular in London, which is where Paul ac-
quired the taste. We've got quite a tribe of them here
in New York. So far, no fire or brimstone has fallen
on either place.*

Gently, Paul pried Hannah's hands from the newel
post and held them for a moment. "They won't come
back," he said. Then, with the same deliberate gentleness, he embraced her. She was amazed to discover that this simple gesture made her feel human
again, in spite of the liquor on Paul's breath. A gust
of grief swept over her; tears—tears of mourning—
spilled from her eyes; something, someone, had died.
Was it God or Hannah Cosway, the trusting, loving
Quaker girl?

"In spite of its being late in the day—which means
I am thoroughly drunk," Paul said, "the moment I
heard you were staying alone, I rode here at a gallop.
I know these sort of swine travel on the fringes of the
army, looking for loot and anything else they can
find."

"Your father—he'll need—"

"He can manage on bread and water for a night.
Come out to the farm with me now."

Paul put Hannah on his horse and walked her to
Great Rock Farm. The next day he used his influence
with friends in the British army to free his father
from the county jail. The old man joined them at the
farm, where he resumed his habit of getting drunk
every day and bemoaning America's imminent humiliation.

Paul drank with him. In a daze that was almost as
bad as drunkenness, Hannah tried to make the old
farmhouse habitable. A series of overseers and their
families had lived in the house for the previous three

decades, leaving it a near wreck. Its age—it had been built around 1680—compounded her difficulties. Meanwhile, the fortunes of war underwent a startling reversal. George Washington won his miraculous victories at Trenton and Princeton, and the British retreated from most of New Jersey. But the war did not go with them. Bergen County became a frontier across which both sides waged a savage partisan struggle. Fear remained part of Hannah's days and nights.

Those were the days when Malcolm Stapleton began telling her his war stories. He stopped drinking and tried to organize the county's militia to give the civilians some protection. But age and brandy had sapped the physique that had once been indifferent to Canadian winters. In February the old man died of pleurisy, his last words a lament: "My poor country." His daughter-in-law and son were left to confront a war that now seemed endless. When Paul started drinking again after his father's burial, Hannah begged him to stop. "If not for your own sake, then for my sake," she had said.

To her surprise—she had had no hope of success—Paul stopped. He got out his easel and brushes, and announced he would make amends by painting the subject of her choice. "Why not that snow lark?" she said, pointing out the window at the familiar bird, sitting on a bare branch. Three days later Paul presented her with a superb watercolor of a male snow lark. He had caught with remarkable exactness the pinkish-brown back and darker tail, the pale yellow throat.

"I see you love birds as much as I do," she said. "In the spring you must paint my favorite, the

208

yellow titmouse." One June day, Paul gave her the painting framed and ready to hang beside the snow lark. Once more his perception of color was amazing. He managed to blend a subtle green into the golden-yellow coat, precisely as it was on the living bird.

"I can almost hear him singing," Hannah said.

That summer, with the British army back in New York, Paul went before a Bergen County magistrate and declared his neutrality. He took an oath not to speak or act against the interests of the United States and requested permission for a pass that would permit him to travel between New York and New Jersey at will. His friends in the British army had already assured him of a welcome in New York. Hannah could barely conceal her disapproval of this decision. Paul was clearly not a soldier. New York was the only place he could hope to earn money as a painter. But she found it hard to tolerate his abandonment of his country's cause.

Hannah concealed her opinion from Paul; they both tried to avoid politics. She told herself that his neutrality was a small price to pay for seeing him return to the practice of his art. She was fascinated by the mystery of his talent—how he could transfer life, in all its subtle colors and varied shapes, to a blank piece of paper or canvas. "It's a little like watching God at work," she told him. He said it was the highest compliment anyone had ever paid him.

Paul called the portraits he painted in New York money painting. The other pictures he called personal painting. They included more watercolors of birds and landscapes, portraits of his two nephews, and dramatic visions of his mother and father. His mother appeared as a sibyl in a classic fable, gold coins in one outstretched hand; the other hand dripping blood. His father was on a parapet, leading an assault. But Paul's favorite subject rapidly became Hannah Stapleton.

He painted a series of portraits of her. For the first, he asked her to put on the Quaker clothes of her girlhood. She found it strangely exciting to lift the old brown dresses and white collars from her trunk. The portrait restored her youth. It was uncannily close to how she remembered herself. Innocence shone from the unlined face. Hannah almost wept when she saw it.

Next Paul dressed her in her most expensive New York gown, a green paduasoy embroidered with cloth of gold. He recreated the elaborate hairstyle, the rouged cheeks, the pearls Hugh had given her on their first wedding anniversary. Again, the effect was mysterious. She felt catapulted back in time, yet facing a stranger.

For her third sitting, Paul insisted she put on one of the faded housedresses she wore for kitchen work. He sat her on a straight chair and painted her in winter light. It was chilling, dismaying. Did she look that gaunt, that tired? "Couldn't you leave out a few lines in my poor face?" she asked.

"I'm painting history here," Paul said. "Nothing should be left out of history."

While Paul painted they talked. Gradually Hannah lost her repugnance for this different brother. She began to admire his ruthless honesty. He was amazingly frank about the course his life had taken. He blamed it on his mother. She was a cold woman. She gave him everything but affection and meanwhile destroyed all his feelings for his father. Paul admitted what Hugh had told her—his sexual attraction for handsome young men. He now regarded it as an affliction. For one thing it was dangerous; the law made it a crime punishable by death. One never knew when a former lover, a secret enemy, would betray him. Since the war had driven him back to New Jersey, he had lived a celibate life. It had been difficult at first. That was why he drank. "For a time I considered killing myself."

She cried out at the thought. "Paul! You'd abandon your soul to—to—"

"Nothing. I don't believe in your hell—or heaven."

In a calm, empty voice Paul told her that he believed things happened in the natural world according to laws of cause and effect that men were gradually discovering. He described the universe as seen by Isaac Newton and other scientists—a vast, impersonal machine. "Newton called God the prime mover, the force that put the machine in motion. I'm inclined to think it's always been in motion. I think we're all part of it, including our minds. We're bound by cause and effect even when we think we're free."

Hannah refused to accept this vision of the world. "You weren't bound to risk your life to rescue me that night in Hackensack," she said. "You could have stayed here at the farm. You could have run when that monster Bogert threatened to kill you."

"What if I was really looking for death?"

"You could find that here at the farm, anytime."

"Why won't you concede the possibility of my explanation?"

"Because I see what you're doing. You won't let me—or anyone else—love you."

A few weeks later, Paul asked Hannah if she still prayed in spite of the war and his lectures on atheism. "I try to pray," she said. "I don't always succeed."

"How do you do it? Do you recite formulas?"

"No. I talk to God. Sometimes I argue with Him. I ask Him for faith."

The next day, Hannah sat for Paul again. Early spring sunshine streamed into the kitchen. He told her to look out the window and think about prayer. To pray, if she preferred. He wanted to capture the expression on her face.

"Are you praying?" he asked after a few minutes of silence.

"Yes," she said.

"Talk out loud," he said. "Or is it too private?"

She smiled. "I'm talking about you."

"I'm flattered. Let me listen."

She stared at the empty north pasture. "I haven't done it in so long. I don't have any light."

"Light?"

"That's what Quakers call bearing witness in church. When someone stands up and talks."

"Try."

She closed her eyes for a moment and tried to find her way back to the sunlit meeting house in Burlington. She imagined the surrounding green fields and orchards. The nearby shining river. She tried to remember the silence in the meeting house, the sense of the ingathered love she felt there.

"Heavenly Father," she said, "I'm thinking about my brother Paul. A man of great gifts. A man with a proud spirit. A man who has never known your love.

He's too proud to ask your help, Father. But you are too loving to refuse it. I believe that, Lord, even though I may never see a proof of it."

"Maybe God is an artist," Paul said. "He paints with light."

"You're laughing at me."

"By no means."

A sound from downstairs demolished these year-old memories. Achilles, Great Rock Farm's mastiff watchdog, began growling. Was it John Nelson and his monstrous friend, Bogert? Trembling violently, Hannah sprang out of bed and lit a candle. Achilles growled again. "Paul," she cried. "Paul."

She heard his feet strike the floor in his bedroom and come pounding down the hall. He burst into her room in his nightshirt, a pistol in his hand. "What's wrong?"

"Dear God," she said, relapsing into the Quaker idiom of her youth. "What art thou doing with that thing?"

"I sleep with it on my night table whenever they're on the farm."

The dog continued to growl. "Put it away," Hannah said. "I won't have thee die on my account."

"What I do for you is my affair."

"I—I love thee for it, nonetheless," she said.

Achilles stopped growling. The house was silent except for an occasional creak and groan in the northeast wind. Snowflakes whirled against the windows. Hannah shivered in the fireless cold. She got back under the covers. But she continued to tremble. Her heart pounded and rivulets of fear swelled in her throat.

"It's all right," Paul said.

The words only recalled the moment in the Hackensack town house, when those malignant faces ascended the stairs toward her.

"I told Walter Beckford to forbid them to come near the house. I'm sure he's done it."

Hannah could only shake her head while the fear flooded her body. "It's not just them. It's—everything. The war. Hugh. I've lost him, Paul. He blames me for bringing him back from the islands. I think he blames me for everything that's wrong. He—he loathes the sight of me."

"He's a spoiled bastard."

"I've begun to wonder if he ever loved me."

"He loved you. I considered it miraculous. Hugh Stapleton in love with something besides himself—or a chance to improve some moneys."

For a moment she almost told Paul the secret reason why she had lost Hugh. What he had said to her, on their first night together, after he returned from the West Indies. She had been in bed, waiting for him to join her, ready to give herself to him with all the ardor of their early years. He had come into the room and paused before the mirror. He had picked up a brush from the bureau and passed it through his hair. Facing himself in the mirror, he had said, "It's been three years. I'm sure you don't imagine I've been indifferent to other women for such a length of time. But I'll try to be as faithful from now on as I was before."

Why had he said such a thing? Hannah asked herself again. In spite of his worldly ways, did his conscience bother him? That was small consolation for the devastating impact on her feelings. Didn't he see that those words reduced their love from a sacred gift to a convenience? For a dizzying moment she hated him. A demon seemed to possess her. She wanted to denounce him, revile him.

Instead she had fumbled out words of mild regret, of humble hope that their love would soon be restored. But it proved impossible. She could barely kiss him that first night. Her lips had been dry and hard, as if they were caked with dirt. In the morning there had been none of the tender, bawdy talk with which he used to tease her. He had not sought her again for the better part of a week, and the result had been the same, perhaps worse. Behind her submission she found herself asking mad, raging questions about the other women he had known.

By day she had watched helplessly while the spiritual poison spread through their lives. They could agree on nothing. Hugh had glanced at the portraits Paul had painted of her and said she looked like a witch. He recommended burning them. She had been speechless with resentment. Paul, used to the cutting remarks that Stapletons aimed at each other, was unruffled. Hugh continued on his destructive way. He found fault with the education of their eight-year-old son, Charles. She had been teaching him herself since his local school had shut down because of the war. Hugh decreed that the boy should go to live with his Kemble cousins in Morris County, where the schools were flourishing beyond the reach of loyalist raiders. Then, within a month of Hugh's return, he had announced his decision to go to Congress.

When she had urged him to come home from the islands, she had not given a thought to Congress. She had wanted Hugh to replace his father as the man who could rally the county militia and protect her and her neighbors against nightly terror. But Hugh had no interest in such heroics. Philadelphia offered him an opportunity for the one thing that did interest him—a chance to do business on a grand scale. To be able to combine this opportunity with an escape from his long-faced, passionless wife and cloak it in the name of the patriotism she had inflicted on him was too delicious to resist.

Hannah saw through her husband's patriotic charade, which was now wearing thin. She recognized the dimension of his desertion, which was spiritual as well as physical. Suddenly she wanted to tell Paul everything.

Instead Paul told her the truth she had not been able to face. "I think the real trouble is not Hugh's failing to love you. I think you could bear that. I think you've stopped loving him."

Confessional tears streamed down Hannah's cheeks. "What shall I do, Paul? There are times when I only want to die."

"You'll do no such thing. You'll love me instead. I herewith give you permission." Almost casually, he slipped under the covers and held her in his arms. Her trembling gradually ceased. "You'll practice on me. A sinner who refuses to confess his sin, a cynic who sneers at patriotism. If you succeed with me, you'll soon be able to love Hugh again in spite of his hard heart."

"I love thee already. Not as a wife. I know that's not possible. But as a brother, a friend. I—would love thee perfectly if only—"

"I wasn't a neutral?"

"Yes. But I don't reproach thee. I understand."

"I'm not neutral. I haven't been neutral since that night in Hackensack."

He began telling her about his secret life as a spy.

fourteen

Mounted on Horace, the old plowhorse that had brought him from Lebanon to Morristown, Caleb Chandler rode slowly across snowbound New Jersey toward Bergen. The journey through the white landscape was dreamlike. Caleb kept lapsing into visions of Major Benjamin Stallworth's snarling face; he kept hearing his furious voice, compounding, magnifying the inner voice that whispered, *fool*. Stallworth was telling him that he had been, that he was, a fool on a continental scale. His idiocy had spiraled out of his stupid mouth and naive brain to become a whirlwind, threatening to engulf the army, the cause, the country.

But Caleb did not spend all his time writhing in humiliation. There was a middle region of rage and hatred into which he occasionally escaped. Stallworth was an abomination! What made him especially sickening was the uncanny way he parodied, with his denunciations, his apostrophes to military necessity, so many ministers Caleb had heard at Yale. Stallworth was a product of New England's theology even though he had ceased to believe it. He still spoke on behalf of that awesome God, in whose name human nature was damned with unrelenting severity. In pursuit of the same craven obedience Stallworth demanded, God's ordained servants howled down self-respect, affection. Stallworth made Caleb realize how much he loathed the faith he was ordained to preach. He detested it as totally as he despised Stallworth's military necessity. Yet that necessity, and the God of New England, still controlled his life. Here he rode, shivering in the blasts of the Great Cold, a pseudo-minister and a secret agent, a prisoner of both tyrannies.

For fragmentary moments Caleb escaped from both rage and humiliation, and glimpsed a zenith of icy doubt. What if Stallworth were lying? What if he was the British master spy and everyone—Caleb, Flora Kuyper, poor Joel Lockwood, even General Washington—was his dupe. Caesar had been killed only a hundred yards from Washington's door. Perhaps he had been on his way to headquarters to tell someone the truth and Stallworth or one of his confederates had killed him? Perhaps that was why Caleb was being shunted off to Flora Kuyper and from her to the British spymaster, Beckford.

Impossible? Was it any more impossible than Stallworth's sneer about Flora Kuyper: *She fucks for the King.* Could so much beauty, gentleness, kindness, survive that kind of corruption? In his student days Caleb had gone down to New Haven's waterfront and visited the taverns where the whores of the town picked up sailors. He wanted to test his feelings face to face with such women. He had felt nothing but revulsion. They were the sorriest, saddest jades he had ever seen; hair streeling, beer slopping down their chins; their desperate gaiety was as pathetic as it was false. He could not believe Flora Kuyper had anything in common with these women. He could not believe his feelings about another human being, even granted his pitifully small experience with the female sex, could be so misleading.

Down the road, across the salt marshes of Newark Bay, Horace plodded. A few gulls wheeled overhead in the gray sky, calling, *Ha-ha, ha-ha-ha,* in their brainless way. For a moment Caleb wondered what would happen if he simply kept going, if he rode past the gate to Flora Kuyper's farm and fled to his father's house. There, surrounded by friends, he could seek the aid of Congressman William Williams and dare Benjamin Stallworth to pursue him.

No. He could not bear the thought of his older brothers' condescension, the distress of his mother and father, his own humiliation as he tried to explain why, in four short months, he had turned from a patriot chaplain to a fugitive. Before it was over he would be a little boy again, pleading for his father's protection. He could hear his brothers saying: *Knew we should never have let Parson Lockwood send him to Yale. Now what we got to show for all that tuition money, Pap? A disgrace, that's what.*

He would see Flora Kuyper. He would perform the absurb part Stallworth had written for him. He hoped she would throw him out of the house and he could return to Morristown and ask: *What now?*

There was the Kuyper farmhouse on its little rise, the huge old oak beneath which Caesar Muzzey lay in the frozen earth. Suddenly Caleb was remembering the evening he had spent with Flora Kuyper. He was standing behind her at the harpsichord, his hands only inches away from those exposed shoulders, the graceful neck. He heard Stallworth snarling: *She fucks for the King.* No.

Caleb banged the brass knocker. The wind hissed across the porch like the stroke of a Continental Army whip. Cato in his blue-and-red livery opened the door.

"Ah, Cato. Is your mistress home?"

"No, sir," said Cato, blocking the Kuyper doorway. "Gone visiting."

"I'm on my way back from Connecticut," Caleb lied. "I had to escort a sick soldier home to Stamford. I thought it would not be amiss to say hello."

Cato said nothing. He continued to block the door.

"I brought along a copy of William Billings's songbook. For you."

Cato seemed to make up his mind about something. "That's very kind of you, sir," he said. "Won't you come in? Mistress may be away for some hours."

"That's all right. I would wait—several hours for the pleasure of seeing her," Chandler said.

Couldn't Cato hear the fumbling lie in those words? Caleb wondered. Apparently not. The black man ushered him into the warm parlor and soon returned with a flagon of mulled wine. "I'm glad to see you, sir," Cato said. "For a special reason. My wife and I have been praying and fearing for our mistress this past week. She's so melancholy, sir."

"Why?"

"That's not for me to say, sir. Maybe it's the bad times, the war. We think—it's also a trouble in her soul, sir. That's why we hoped someone like you—a man with spiritual training—might speak to her about it."

"These times are more than enough to trouble anyone's soul."

"Sir," Cato said after a moment of inner debate, "I can't give you more than hints. Caesar—he was bad, sir. A bad man. He let Satan rule him. Mistress feels guilty for some things he did. If you could talk to her, sir, you might free her soul from Caesar's sin."

Caleb was touched by Cato's concern for Flora. This black man was a caring Christian. He decided it was best to play the naive young cleric for the time being. "I'll do my best to help your mistress, Cato. But she must ultimately confess her guilt to God."

"I know that, sir. But she needs someone to lead her soul to it. Sometimes you've got to get down on your knees and work with sinners. You've got to feel their guilt and make them feel the Lord's forgiveness."

"You do that?"

"Yes, sir. Many a time I've done it."

223

For a moment Caleb saw the Reverend Joel Lockwood striding down the main street of Lebanon, Connecticut. Men hastily doffed their hats to him, ladies curtsied. Joel Lockwood bowed his head, acknowledging their obeisance. His word, his station, his presence, had been supreme in Lebanon. People may have gotten down on their knees before him, but never with him.

Cato left Caleb sipping his mulled wine, his mind in even worse turmoil. He did not want to think of Flora Kuyper as a troubled woman. He was not here as a minister of the gospel; he was a member of the army of the United States of America under orders. He was a servant of necessity. He stopped, appalled by what this meant, by what was happening in his soul.

About an hour later, Caleb stood at the window, watching snowflakes begin to fall from the gloomy sky, as they did almost every night at twilight. Flora Kuyper, driving a small one-horse sleigh, turned into the drive and approached the house. She was wrapped in the same purple cloak she had worn to Caesar's funeral. Caleb stayed in the parlor and let Cato tell her of his presence. A few minutes later, she entered the room. Her cheeks were flushed from the cold. She wore a formal smile on her lips. "Mr. Chandler," she said, "what a pleasant surprise."

"As I told Cato—"

"Yes. He told me. I hope, in spite of all my warnings, you haven't taken this dangerous route just to see me."

She frowned as she said this, and he noticed circles of sleeplessness beneath her eyes.

"I must confess—the answer is in part yes. But it

was also pastoral, madam. I promised to deliver a copy of William Billings's songbook to Cato. I think it will increase the devotion of his people."

"That is most kind. Religion is their consolation. Anything that adds pleasure to it is certain to be welcome."

He raised his wineglass. "To your health, madam. Have you been well?"

"As well as I deserve to be."

"Deserve to be? Madam, I can't believe you have any cause to be sent an illness."

"I'm flattered by your good opinion."

Cato came in with a cup of broth on a tray. Flora Kuyper thanked him and sipped it for a moment. Caleb Chandler found himself sinking beneath the spell of her beauty again. Her sadness stirred an irresistible tenderness in his soul.

He finished his wine and put the glass on a tea table. Solemnly, agonizingly aware of their crudity, he began reciting the lines Stallworth had written out for him and forced him to memorize like an actor in a play.

"I haven't been well, madam, since I saw you."

"Why not?"

"My mind has been disturbed, upheaved, more than I thought possible. At first I blamed it on your beauty alone. But the more I dwelled on it, night after sleepless night, the more I realized it was something else. Something far more terrible. I could bear loving you, madam, from a hopeless distance. But I can't bear the thought that I merited your contempt."

"Why do you feel such a thing?"

"For my pusillanimous attempt to defend my country, madam, from the charges, the just and terrible charges, you placed against it. In the matter of slavery and, linked to it in a mysterious way, the matter of Caesar Muzzey's death."

"Mr. Chandler," she said, "I hope you haven't been telling people that I'm an enemy of the United States. I've gone to such lengths to prove my patriotism—sending Caesar to the army, donating provisions from the farm."

"I'm not so obtuse, madam," Caleb said. "I know too well the jealous rage of fanaticism that such talk might loose on you. I've kept our conversation locked in my breast. But it has festered there, like an infection, destroying my smug assumptions."

"I'm sorry I spoke so frankly."

"On the contrary, such exchanges of truth, of true sentiment, are the heart of life, worth a million words of polite but empty conversation."

"I see you're like me. You value the motions of the heart above the cautions of the head."

Caleb was staggered. She was accepting his fake sincerity at its face value. He realized that she was also discounting the clumsiness, the labored style of his declaration. It was only to be expected from a country bumpkin.

He could not stop now. He could not quit the play. Stallworth and a horrified fascination kept him in his part. "The—the motions of the heart," he said. "Yes. I—I admire sincerity above all things. That's why I've decided to resign from the army and play no further role in the contest that's destroying us. In part it's a requirement of honor, in part a wish—a hope—to win your good opinion."

"Mr. Chandler," she said, "you overwhelm me.

I'm not worthy of—or capable of rewarding—such a sacrifice."

"Madam," he said, "you must have no mirrors in this house. Or else your modesty is so great you never bother to look in them."

Flora smiled, turning him speechless again. "Mr. Chandler," she said, in a voice measurably softer than the one she had been using, "your compliments are much too extravagant. But"—frowning again—"I'm serious. I felt—a certain affection for you when we met last week. In a better world we might have become friends. But too much separates us."

"Too much? A few dozen miles between New Jersey and Connecticut? Let me emphasize, madam, it's not only your person but the truth of your observations about my country that have demolished me. I will even confess to thinking—the unthinkable: going over to the King's side."

"No," Flora cried with intensity that sent hope thundering through Caleb's divided mind. She was not a spy.

"I thought that would be your reaction. That's why I resolved to withdraw from the contest. Yet we're all social beings. When one side or the other wins, we must live with them. Where can a neutral man go in a world ridden by fanatics?"

"Ah, Mr. Chandler, if you knew how many hours of sleep I've lost trying to answer that question. For a while I told myself that two—two lovers can make a world for themselves. But I've lost faith in that idea."

"Why, madam?"

"The world is too cruel. I think it hates—genuine

love, Mr. Chandler. Love that is ready to sacrifice everything, that is its own happiness. It fills many people with a kind of rage. Do you think I'm wrong?"

"Not at all," Chandler said. He had stood listening to her like one of those beings whom the ancient goddesses turned into trees or pools, thinking as her elegiac words and her emotion mingled, *She can, she will destroy me.*

"Perhaps death is the only place where lovers can find peace."

In two strides Caleb crossed the parlor and seized Flora's hand. He was improvising now. Nothing in Stallworth's narrow vision of this woman could have anticipated this response.

"My dear Mrs. Kuyper. Flora. I won't let you talk that way. This terrible winter has affected your mind. Life, love, will bloom again for you. No doubt with someone far more worthy of your beauty, your accomplishments than I. You heard me say I was ready, I was resigned to loving you from a distance."

She shook her head. "It's the other way around," she said. "It's I who am unworthy of your—your goodness, your admiration."

"Something—a memory, a fear—must be prompting those bizarre words," he said. "What is it?"

"Nothing—and everything," she said. "Come. Let us have some supper."

They dined on chicken, potted and baked in a pie with the lightest crust Caleb had ever tasted. There were side dishes of sweet potatoes and pickled beets. For dessert there were pancakes folded over a boysenberry filling and sprinkled with powdered sugar. The wine was a soft Moselle. Caleb's mind grew more composed as he ate. He began to wonder at the luxury Flora Kuyper seemed to take for granted. How could she afford it without some secret source of money? The war had made farming a profitable business. But for most Americans the perpetual inflation of the price of everything quickly devoured the surplus.

Meanwhile, she drew him out on his plans. Would he not be suspected if he quit the army? Would it make it difficult for him to obtain a living in Connecticut? Did he think that the army was as cruel as Caesar had made it sound? Caleb told her that he would feign an illness to protect himself from resentment at home. As for the army's cruelty, he was in complete agreement with Caesar. He described the constant whippings of the common soldiers, their starvation rations and wretched clothing. "Yet the country as a whole has never been so prosperous. There's talk of millions made by merchants in Boston and Philadelphia. The farmers' barns are overflowing from two years of magnificent harvests. But they hide their grain from the army commissaries in hope of seeing prices rise still higher. The universal lack of patriotism disgusts me."

Caleb stopped, bewildered, appalled by the realization that he was telling the truth. He *was* disgusted by the selfish devil-take-the-hindmost attitude that prevailed everywhere, even in Connecticut. He had heard his own father swear that he would not sell another barrel of flour to the American army until the Connecticut legislature doubled the fixed price.

Flora Kuyper nodded. "I was prepared to believe in the Americans at first," she said. "In spite of slavery. But the more I've seen of them, the more I'm convinced that they don't deserve this freedom they worship so loudly."

She stirred her coffee. Caleb decided it was best to say nothing.

"I have reason to loathe the British," Flora said. "And yet—I find myself—drawn to them, as you are."

Again, she hesitated, and he remained silent, tension knotting his chest.

"You're not a stupid man, Mr. Chandler. You must know I couldn't live here, so close to their lines, without some sort of arrangement."

"You mean you've taken a protection?" Caleb said. "I'm told that there are hundreds in this part of Jersey who have done the same thing."

"You might call it that," Flora said, studying him over her gold-rimmed coffee cup. "I have—rendered the British certain services, without compromising myself with the rebels. I own nothing in the world but this farm I inherited from Mr. Kuyper. Even a small risk fills me with terror. If I were condemned, the farm would be seized; Cato, the rest of the slaves, would be sold at auction."

"Yes," Caleb said numbly. He had a sudden sensation of sliding down an icy hill toward a precipice.

"If you've told me the truth, Mr. Chandler—and I believe you have—I don't think you'll betray me. Am I right?"

"Madam, you have my promise—to—to protect you at all hazards."

He could say that and mean it. He would protect her against Stallworth, against all the preachers and politicians in New Jersey and Connecticut, arrayed in righteous panoply. He told himself that her services to the British were probably trivial and eminently defensible.

"I think I could arrange—if we truly understand each other—I could arrange for you to render the British certain services, too. Without revealing your disaffection from the rebels. So that whoever wins, you'll be on the right side. That's the only way that I can see to survive in this chaos. For people like us."

"Yes," he said. "You're undoubtedly right."

"It would involve carrying messages between here and Morristown. There is very little risk. You would never see the men who send them or the men who receive them. You would pick up the messages in a certain place in Morristown—and leave them in another place, here on the farm. You could combine it with pastoral visits to Cato and his people. And with me."

Caleb put down his coffee cup to conceal his shaking hand. He was back in his part again, reciting words Stallworth had written for him. "Madam, are you mocking me?"

"Nothing of the sort."

"You know my visits to you won't be pastoral. Please don't joke at my—priestly profession. I took it seriously once. I still do, in some unhappy way."

Was *that* true? Caleb wondered dazedly as he saw contrition and concern on her lovely face. Or had Stallworth made him such a consummate liar even he could not tell the difference? All he knew was the sliding sensation, over the precipice now, falling through the darkness, with her green eyes impaling him. If she was sincere, what could he wish himself but death and ruin?

"Forgive me," she said. "I was only trying to make it seem—less terrible. There was such a stricken look on your face."

"Let us ban stricken looks, in the name of clever treachery," Caleb said, retreating to Stallworth's bombast again. "Madam, you've convinced me. I'm at your service. Together we'll outwit both sides and rescue affection from a worthless world."

"That calls for a toast," she exclaimed with a radiant smile. "Cato!

"Our best brandy," she said when Cato appeared. He returned with a green bottle that looked a hundred years old and filled two cordial glasses. Flora raised hers. "To treachery. And affection."

Caleb drank the expensive liquor, brewed by French monks of the previous century. Flora refilled his glass and her own, and told him to take the bottle with them to the parlor. There she sat down at the harpsichord. They sang only French songs. "It's what I sing when I'm happy," Flora told him. After a half-hour of cheerful rondos and caprices, she paused and let her fingers find a more delicate chord. "This is one I haven't been able to sing for a long time," she said. "It's called *Plaire à celui que j'aime.*"

As with earlier songs, Caleb translated the French poetry into English prose. But there was nothing prosaic about these words. There was an unmistakable invitation in them.

> *Pleasing the one I love*
> *Is my sole victory*
> *And my talents for him*
> *Are new tributes.*

I have cultivated them
Without thought of glory.
I have sought for love
A new, a better language.

Was she sincere? he wondered. Or had Stallworth been right when he predicted that Flora Kuyper would take him to bed with her to guarantee his loyalty to the King.

"Sing it with me," Flora said.

Caleb sang *Plaire à celui* in his barbarous French, telling himself that if Flora Kuyper was sincere, she would put her hands over her ears and burst out laughing at the thought of loving this provincial parson. Instead, when the song ended, Flora stared at her hands holding the last chord on the ivory keys and asked, "Do you think you could learn a new, a better language for love, Mr. Chandler?"

"I wish—I wish I had more confidence in my skill," he said.

"Much depends on the teacher," she said.

It was happening, as Stallworth told him it would happen. But there was so much that challenged Stallworth's cynical explanation. So much that made Caleb want to believe in Flora Kuyper's sincerity, even if she insisted on seducing him. What if it was not seduction, what if she was offering him genuine affection, what if everything she said about the Americans and the British was not only sincere but true? Then he would become her betrayer lover, her loving betrayer.

Caleb's next words owed nothing to Stallworth. "Madam—Flora," he said, "I never felt such a wish." He sat down on the harpsichord bench beside her.

"It's more than love. It's a desire to make you happy, to preserve your happiness—against all the powers of this world."

"Let's not speak of the world," Flora said. "There'll be time enough for that. Too much time."

"I—I can't ask you for the gift that would—be precious to me. Not yet. Not until I ask it with a clear—conscience."

"I thought you'd stopped believing in your New England God."

He stood up, hoping a few feet of space, several moments of silence, would somehow brake the momentum, would give her time to control her feelings (if she was sincere) and take advantage of his stated reluctance. But her eyes still challenged him. She forced him to give her the only answer his masquerade permitted.

"It's not that childish conscience," he said. "It's my inability to match my words. To make you genuinely happy. I—I have no living but my minister's profession, which I find more and more intolerable. I have neither money nor powerful friends. It's folly to talk of protecting you."

"Is that how you see it? As a kind of transaction, a bartering of my body for your protection? Is that all the feeling you have for me?"

"My God, no," Caleb cried.

Flora was standing beside the harpsichord now, anger and sadness mingling on her face, in her voice. "I have loved only two men in my life, besides my father," she said. "For both of them I was ready to do, to risk anything. I regret some of the things I did for those loves. But I don't regret why I did them.

For love, without any thought of my reward, my profit—or my future losses."

Caleb saw that they were going over the precipice. Whether she was taking him or he was taking her, he was no longer sure. Was Stallworth right—was he being seduced into the service of the King?—or was he winning a profound profession of love? Between the brandy and his conscience and Flora Kuyper's inviting breasts, Caleb was not sure of anything. He only knew that Flora was coming across the room and he was moving to meet her vowing that if she was sincere he would somehow purify this act, he would somehow live up to his promise to protect her. Simultaneously seeing her willingness as proof that Stallworth was right, unable to believe that this woman could really love Tom Brainless.

The kiss lasted so long Caleb began to drift in and out of time. He was home in Lebanon, seeing Deborah Hawley, knee deep in buttercups in her father's pasture, wanting her then, with a sharp, specific hunger that had shocked him. He was in New Haven, gazing at the trollops in the Long Wharf Tavern; he was in Morristown, looking down at a soldier who asked, *Do you think I'm damned?* He was staring up at Benjamin Stallworth's hatchet-edge of a face, hearing, *She fucks for the King.*

Upstairs, as he fumblingly undressed her, she interrupted him with a half-dozen kisses. In bed Caleb's clumsiness, his lack of knowledge of female anatomy, caused some awkward moments. Flora bridged them with more kisses, with patient whispers of affection. Her obvious experience only intensified his suspicion. As he entered her Caleb saw a vision of damnation, of flames leaping in a hell beneath the bed. But the terror vanished as a wild commingling of pleasure and desire, affection and passion, consumed him. He was in her, possessing her, but she also seemed to be within him, not only her tongue deep in his mouth, but her breasts, her thighs, her hands seemed to become part of his body. They were still over the precipice, still falling through the night like damned angels. But they were enjoying delights those bodiless creatures never knew.

Flora began to teach him the subtleties, the thousand smaller pleasures of love. The touches, the kisses, the bites, the teasing refusal and the sudden, laughing acquiescence. She made him aware of his body as he had never known it. Her fingers, her lips explored flowing muscle and soft flesh, and invited him to do likewise. He found the other meaning of the verb to know..

Caleb was infinite miles, ages of years from Morristown, where dirty, bitter men bared their backs at whipping posts in the blowing snow, where every path and road was guarded by bayonets, and an army's stench pervaded the icy air. Benjamin Stallworth's lash of a pulpit voice, his iron mouth demanding treachery in the name of victory, preaching love as a form of betrayal—all became ghosts, demons out of some nightmare. This alone was real, this woman giving herself to him, opening her sinuous arms, her languorous mouth to him, taking him into her body, with sighs of welcome, murmurs of praise.

At last there was that yielding and giving moment, that blending of wish and fulfillment. "Caleb, Caleb," Flora said after a few minutes, "now I must tell you everything. There can be no secrets between us.

They're the murderers of love. I know that from experience. But now I have another fear."

He cradled her in his arms, suspicion stirring again. Now, if Stallworth was right, she would tell him the whole truth. His answer was bombast. "That word—fear—is banned from this room, from this house."

"We'll see," she said. "We will see what love can risk—"

"I want to know why you're often so melancholy," he said. "I want to banish that word, that humor. Whatever its cause."

"What do you think is its cause? Have you guessed?"

They were speaking with their arms around each other, their lips only inches apart.

"It has something to do with Caesar Muzzey," Caleb said. "At the funeral I saw you weeping for him. Do you feel responsible for his death?"

"Yes. But it's more than that. Caesar was my lover."

Involuntarily, before his mind could do more than record the astonishing fact, Caleb felt his body stiffen in revulsion. She felt it, too.

"I knew it," she said, shoving herself away from him. "I knew it would disgust you."

"It doesn't," he lied.

"Don't deny it, in your stupid Protestant way," she said. "It's better to confess and repent, to admit your evil feeling. I felt the disgust run through your body. It disgusts you to think that Caesar's lips, his hands, his black thing, have been where you've just been. In spite of all your fine words about Negroes, you don't really like them. They disgust you. Isn't that true? Their blackness disgusts you?"

"Yes," Caleb said.

"Then let me tell you something even more disgusting. I'm one. White as I am, I have a grandmother, probably still alive in New Orleans, who's as black as Caesar. If we have a child by what we did together, your child could be black. Black as soot, black as mud. What do you say now?"

She was sitting up in the bed, the covers clutched around her against the cold. The firelight played on her face, which seemed to cast a light of its own, a blaze of pride and despair. Caleb lay on the pillow, gazing up at her, feeling more and more uneasy. He groped for something genuine. "Perhaps you're teaching me what love means," he said.

She began to weep, not tears of grief, Caleb saw, but of joy, hope. She fell back into his arms. "I wasn't sure of you," she said. "I wanted to turn you away now, when I could still deny everything."

Caleb's conscience leaped to savage life; a hell localized in his mind. How sound, how sure her loving instincts were. How many times would he have to stifle them with lies?

"There's no escaping it. You must tell me everything now."

"Promise me, no matter what you hear, you won't despise me."

Here it comes, Caleb thought. Stallworth's vindication. The true story of why Flora Kuyper wants Caleb Chandler to spy for King George. Did he want to hear it? "Stop talking nonsense," he said. "I'm ready to hear your life's confession and give you eternal absolution. For penance I'll command you to love me forever."

"Don't," she said, putting her hand over his mouth.

"Don't mock my Catholic faith. Caesar did that too often."

"Tell me," he said.

She began.

Flora's Story

"How dare you appear in public with that woman and child?"

"I'll appear where and when I please and with whom I please," my father replied.

Those words are my earliest memory. I heard them standing between my mother and father in the Place d'Armes, the dusty central square in New Orleans. I was about five and was wearing a blue silk dress with a red sash. My mother was wearing a much plainer white dress. My mother was not beautiful, but her height and bearing gave her great dignity. She glared at the black-mustached man who had just insulted us. He was Vincent Pierre Gaspard de Rochemore, *commissaire ordonnateur*, the second most powerful man in New Orleans.

Around us loomed the official buildings, the Church

of St. Louis, the mansion of the governor, the barracks of the garrison that de Rochemore commanded. On our right flowed the brown Mississippi from the heartland of my native continent, North America. Already I thought of myself as an American, even though I spoke mostly French.

"We shall see about your doing what you please, you and your fellow Hebrews," de Rochemore snarled at my father.

"Sire," my father said with a brief bow, "I am at your service any time you wish to discuss this matter with his excellency the governor."

De Rochemore muttered an oath and strode away. I looked up at my father's face. It reminded me of an old house, battered and worn, but wide and charming. "Papa," I asked, "what's a Hebrew?"

"A Jew," he said, "what I am. Some people don't like us. They blame us for killing the Lord Jesus, long, long ago. But that's not true. Don't worry your head about such things, my darling. Come on, now, let us go see the alligator Captain Dias Arias has brought from Pensacola. They say it's the biggest one ever caught."

We continued across the Place d'Armes to the wharf, where Captain Daniel Dias Arias had docked his ship, *Texel*. On deck was a huge alligator, over thirty feet long, its legs and tail tied to keep it from attacking anyone. Black seamen poured water on its head and the beast opened its small, glaring eyes, then gaped its great jaws with their rows of gleaming teeth. I was terrified and began to cry.

"Ah," my father said, "he can't hurt you. Watch this." He seized a stick and thrust it into the monster's mouth, propping its jaws open. The alligator thrashed its head back and forth until it dislodged the stick. "I wouldn't do that again, Moses, if I were you," Captain Dias Arias said.

Alas, my father did not listen. He liked to do daring things.

Captain Dias Arias, a small, sad-eyed man, died of fever in our house on Rampart Street a month later. Only when I was older did I grasp the whole story. Dias Arias was also Jewish. A war was raging between France and England. Under a flag of truce Dias Arias had sailed from British-owned Jamaica with French naval prisoners to be exchanged for captured British sailors. The captain also carried a cargo of merchandise he and my father hoped to sell in New Orleans. Monsieur De Rochemore claimed the cargo violated the flag of truce and seized the entire ship as an enemy vessel. When my father protested, the *commissaire* made an ugly attack on all the Jews in New Orleans, demanding their expulsion under Article I of the Black Code, which regulated slavery and religion in the colonies of France.

Most of the other Jews in the city—there were about a dozen—had been terrified and ready to abandon Dias Arias. But my father had dealt with petty bureaucrats in a dozen countries and colonies. He went to the governor, Chevalier Louis Billouart de Kerlerec, promised him a share of *Texel's* profits, and poof went Monsieur de Rochemore's seizure. As for Article I of the Black Code—it was an anachronism ignored in all the French colonies. The French were not inclined to fanatacism in religion. They regarded Jews as useful, valuable citizens. They stimulated trade—the chief reason for founding a colony in the first place.

But the second most powerful man in New Orleans became my father's enemy. For the next five years de Rochemore and his friends never missed a chance to insult "the proud Jew" Lopez. One of their chief weapons was the relationship he dared to call a marriage, his open alliance with a free woman of color and his public acknowledgment of his quadroon child. Even more infuriating to these bigots was the way my father had gone to the Ursuline sisters and persuaded them to admit me and other quadroon and mulatto children to their convent school. The gossips fumed but the sisters accepted my father's argument that we had souls that were eager for religion and minds ripe for learning. He paid for all of us at first, when he could afford it. This generosity and tolerance only aroused more antagonism. Not even the dinner for fifty or sixty people he gave to celebrate my first communion changed his enemies' minds. They called him a hypocrite, a *poseur.*

Over the next few years these slanders slowly diminished my father's business. He was a commission merchant, who sold goods shipped to New Orleans by Americans, Englishmen, Frenchmen. Gradually the word went out that Moses Monsanto Lopez was unpopular in New Orleans, that the best people in the city would not trade with him. More and more of his clients sent their wares to other merchants. He was forced to take cheap cloth, spoiled beef, shoddy goods that desperate ship captains dumped in New Orleans when they couldn't sell them elsewhere. Gradually my father's store, which had once been the favorite of the city's wealthy ladies, became known as the place the poor and middling sort went in search of bargains.

At home on Rampart Street, I never heard a word about these troubles. Each day at sunset I would race the whole length of the block to fling myself into his arms. Father would sweep me above his head and tease me about my name. "What flower are you today?" he would ask. "Rose, violet?" I would choose the flower and he would call me by that name for the rest of the evening. He loved music and could not hear enough of my playing and singing. "Encore," he would say, and join me for a reprise in his husky baritone.

Toward bedtime I would sit on his lap and he would tell me tales of the cities he had visited in his travels: London, Paris, Antwerp, and his birthplace, Lisbon. He had grown up speaking Portuguese, which was why he spoke French so badly. His family had lived in Lisbon as Marranos, converts to Christianity who ate pork and went to mass on Sunday but thought of themselves as Jews. They were forbidden to practice the Jewish religion under pain of expulsion.

While my father was on a trading voyage to London one of his brothers had been caught visiting a secret synagogue. From a fellow merchant, who warned him not to return, my father learned that everyone in his family had been arrested by the Inquisition and tortured until they confessed to being Jews. Some, including a favorite sister, were killed, the rest expelled from Portugal. Father settled in England, a country he soon admired. The government's power was limited; citizens had the right to vote and speak freely. Jews could practice their religion.

"Why did you leave England?" I asked him.

"I fell in love with a beautiful English woman who refused to marry me. It may have been because I was

245

Jewish. Or only because I was ugly and not very rich. I didn't think I would ever love another woman until I met your mother here in New Orleans. I came with a ship. I was only going to stay for a month, until I sold my cargo. Now I shall die here. The fever will get me one day, or your mother will poison my gumbo when she sees a chance for a younger, wealthier man."

The mere thought of his dying terrified me. I began to weep. My mother scolded him for frightening me. "She's only a child," she said. "You talk to her as if she's a grown woman."

He smiled at me and caressed my cheek. "I think of her that way," he said. "I have a feeling that I'll never see her as a grown woman."

Father gave me a squeeze and laughed at his own fears. "I'm in a gloomy mood," he said. "Just remember this, *chérie*, the important thing is to die in a place where you have been loved, where you leave some love behind you. I'm afraid that's all I'll be able to leave you."

One evening a year later, when I was about eleven, I came home from my music lesson and heard my mother and father talking in the sitting room. I stood in the shadows of the hall, unable to resist listening.

"What will become of Flora?" my father said. "That worries me more than the pain in my belly."

"She'll be very beautiful. She'll have no trouble," my mother said.

"I don't want her to be the plaything of some fat *commissaire* or wheezing judge."

"You must leave that to me. She won't have to

choose low. I'll make sure she has every protection the law affords."

My father sighed. "If I could get her to England, she could marry wealth. Even a nobleman might not ask questions. The English aristocracy often marry outside their class."

"But you can't get her to England," my mother said. "Your creditors will never let you leave New Orleans. We must bear what we can't change."

"Sometimes it's like a stone on my chest," my father said. "I can hardly breathe thinking about it. She's white, Madeleine. She could pass for white anywhere, especially in England."

"But not here. It's written on her birth certificate: F.D.C. You know that."

The next day, when I came home from school, I asked my mother what F.D.C. meant. "*Femme de couleur,*" she said calmly. "It is what you are, what I am."

My mother's skin was the color of coffee with milk in it. I looked at my hands and arms and said, "But we're not the same."

"Come with me."

She seized my hand and walked swiftly from Rampart Street to Chartres Street, in the heart of the city. There, in the hot sunshine, not far from the Ursuline convent, sat a fat old Negro woman as black as the mud of the Mississippi bank. In front of her were piles of fresh fruit. I passed her stand every day on the way to and from school. Often she called to me and gave me a pear or peach. I thought of her as a friend.

"*Bonjour, Mama,*" my mother said. "How are you?"

"I'm fine, daughter," the woman replied. "How is your good husband?"

"He's not well. He spits blood," my mother said. "Pray for him, will you?"

"Of course. But the prayers of this angel will do far more than my sinful croaks."

As she said this the old woman reached out to me. Her leathery black hand caressed my cheek. I recoiled. I could not believe this blackness was part of me. My mother soon convinced me that it was.

"My mother was a slave," she explained as we walked home. "She was very beautiful when she was young. Her master made her his second wife. When he died, he freed her and her children in his will. My brothers live in the country on a farm and are as black as she is. Because I was not black, she sent me to live with her cousin on Rampart Street. By law, women of color can only live there if they choose to stay in New Orleans. It's written in the Black Code that they can't marry white men. That's why your father angers people by calling me his wife. He hates the Black Code and often talks against it."

Our route back to Rampart Street took us through the quarter where the free Negroes lived. I stared at the glistening black skin of a tailor, sitting in front of his shop sewing a coat. "Who shall I marry?" I asked. "A black man?"

"No," my mother said, looking around her contemptuously. "Never. You are better than these people. You'll marry no one. You'll find love with a white man, one of the rich. I'll choose him for you. You'll have a house of your own and a servant and more jewelry and dresses than you can count. If you're clever, you may even get a plantation on one of the bayous, where you can live like a queen with dozens of black slaves at your call."

My mother didn't know that I had overheard my father's loathing for this future. Hour after hour in the following weeks I would lie awake, trying to imagine what this rich white man would be like. Would he be a fat *commissaire* or a wheezing judge? Would my mother condemn me to such a fate?

It was the end of girlhood for me, the harsh arrival of womanhood. It coincided with the coming of age of many of my friends on Rampart Street. There were numerous *femmes de couleur* in the quarter and many of them had children. Like my mother, they waited until we were close to maturity to explain the special future that awaited all of us. Most of my friends seemed to accept the part they were to play with unquestioning, often greedy expectations. A sickening competition sprang up between us, where before there had been nothing but girlish good nature. We began comparing each other's hair and eyes, and especially our skin color. I was envied because I was by far the whitest. Aware now of the nature of their mothers' friendships with their fathers, they talked incessantly of the presents some of them had recently received, silver plate and gold candlesticks and jewelry, expensive dresses. My father's worsening poverty left me with little to say in this competition. I grew to hate it and to doubt more and more the faith my friends seemed to have in the love of rich white men for their *femmes de couleur.*

Then news arrived from Europe that made all our futures a blank. New Orleans was no longer French. France had given it to Spain, had given all of Louisiana to the Spaniards. My father told us about it one night in the spring of 1766, his voice hoarse with apprehension and anger. The Seven Years' War had ended with numerous Spanish colonies seized by English fleets and armies. "In the peace conference," my father told us, "to compensate Spain for her losses, King Louis gave Louisiana to Charles the Third of Spain, his cousin. That was two years ago. Louis was so ashamed—or it meant so little to him—that no one in Paris even notified us." "What will happen now?" I asked.

"I don't know, *chérie*," my father said. "I only know this. Spain hates Jews even more than Portugal. To live in a Spanish colony you must have a certificate testifying to the purity of your blood. It's a detestable system. But they may hesitate to enforce it here in New Orleans. All we can do is wait and see."

Later in 1766 Don Antonio de Ulloa, Spain's first governor, arrived in New Orleans. He was an aloof, icy aristocrat, totally indifferent to the needs and interests of his new subjects. Without consulting anyone, he began issuing a stream of restrictive commercial regulations that were certain to extinguish most of the port's free trade. Excited crowds gathered on street corners to discuss the situation. There were mass meetings, at which my father was a frequent speaker. My mother took me to one of these gatherings in the Place d'Armes. It was thrilling to hear my father shout his detestation of Spain in his bad, guttural French.

"We're not a parcel of slaves to be sold to a new master at will," he roared. "Above all to Spain, the most detestable, most tyrannical power in the world. If France doesn't want us, we don't want France.

We've worked to build a city here. Why can't we govern it ourselves with rational laws, laws that are not based on old, blind prejudices and hatreds but on our brotherhood as *voyageurs* here on this great river, on this new continent? Let us create a republic of free men, free to trade with any country. We'll not only be happy, we'll be rich."

"*Vive la liberté*—long live liberty," roared the crowd.

To everyone's amazement, Governor de Ulloa did not even put up a fight. Panicking, he boarded a ship and fled the city. For a few months everything seemed possible. My father spent excited hours conferring with other leaders of the rebellion. He wanted them to write a liberal constitution for the Republic of Louisiana calling for freedom of religion and an end to restrictions against women of color and free blacks. He even urged a plan for the gradual abolition of slavery. Alas, these ideas only frightened and divided people. Some of the more daring spirits sided with my father. Others reacted to his proposals with suspicion and outrage.

One blazing August day, a fleet of twenty-four ships appeared on the river. They included transports and men of war, with menacing tiers of guns, all flying the flag of Imperial Spain. A boat came ashore and an arrogant young naval officer demanded the immediate surrender of the city in the name of the new governor, Lieutenant General Don Alejandro O'Reilly. If there was resistance, General O'Reilly was prepared to reduce New Orleans to ashes. But if the people agreed to accept the rule of His Majesty Charles III, King of Spain, General O'Reilly promised to forgive those "misguided troublemakers" who had forced Governor de Ulloa to flee.

Only my father and his small circle of friends wanted to fight. O'Reilly was an Irish mercenary in the pay of Spain. My father was convinced that he had orders to crush resistance to Spanish rule and would obey them literally. But the majority of the citizens of our stillborn republic, already divided by their quarrels and with few cannon to oppose the men of war, had no stomach for defiance. They accepted General O'Reilly's promise of forebearance and surrendered the city. We watched Spanish troops and artillery, well over two thousand men and fifty cannon, stream from the ships and parade to the Place d'Armes. As their red-and-white flag rose above the city, the hundreds of cannon on the ships in the river thundered a salute that was answered by the cannon and muskets of the men in the square. It was an awesome display. It left no doubt Spain possessed New Orleans.

That night, while we sat at supper behind the batten blinds of our house on Rampart Street, a fist pounded on our door. My mother opened it and a half-dozen squat Spanish soldiers carrying muskets with fixed bayonets crowded into the room. "Moses Monsanto Lopez?" asked the swarthy young man commanding them.

"I am he," my father said.

"You are under arrest by the order of Governor O'Reilly for treason against His Majesty."

"Put down your guns, gentlemen," my father said. "I'm not armed and have no intention of resisting you. Let me have a minute with my wife and daughter."

"Your wife?" mocked the young officer, eyeing my mother's tan skin.

"My wife."

The officer muttered something in Spanish. The soldiers laughed obscenely. But they filed out of the house. My father turned to me and took my hands. "I'll probably never see you again, my darling. Now all I can leave you is this kiss." He embraced me and in a choked voice said, "Remember how much you were loved by this old man. Never forget that you are worthy of love. Look for that before anything else."

"Are you sure it's so serious?" my mother asked.

My father nodded. "A Portuguese, a Jew, and a rebel all in one? That's too much for a Spanish judge to resist. Take the goods in the store to Isaac Solomon. He's a compassionate man and an honest one. He'll get the best price and take no commission. Good-bye my dearest."

"I won't say good-bye yet," my mother cried. Tears streamed down her cheeks, as they did down mine. "We'll pray day and night for you."

"I hope God is listening," my father said.

We prayed, and the Ursuline sisters in the convent prayed; not only for my father but for the dozens of other rebels that Governor O'Reilly had arrested during the night. But our prayers were wasted. My father and five other men were condemned to death. The rest received long jail sentences. All had their property confiscated. My mother stopped saying Catholic prayers. She called in Madame Levesque, the juju woman, who cast a spell. Then she read the cards. Each time she laid them out, spades were dominant. There was no hope. My mother paid Madame Levesque to put a curse on General O'Reilly. As we sat there in the darkness listening to her African chant, our neighbors told us that my father and his five friends had been executed in the court-yard of the army barracks.

The next few weeks were terrible for me. Night after night in the smothering heat of August I lay awake in my bed seeing my father before the firing squad. The guns blazed; my father's face spewed blood. I had nightmares in which I saw those grinning Spaniards thrusting their bayonets into him.

"We must accept God's will. What is to be will be," my mother told me. I found her fatalism outrageous.

No, I thought, no. I will never believe in the God who did not listen to my prayers, who let a good man, a loving man like my father, die while that florid-faced, gloomy-eyed monster, General O'Reilly—Bloody O'Reilly, we called him—walked our streets, unharmed, unchallenged, even fawned upon by the inevitable majority who were quick to bend their knees before a man in power. I detested my mother's gratitude to the governor because he had not persecuted us, and let us keep our house, which was, in the tradition of Rampart Street, in my mother's name. For me New Orleans became a huge Spanish prison, a place I loathed.

Nor could I accept the future to which my mother now saw no alternative. Next year, when I became seventeen, I would go to my first dance in the big ballroom on Condé Street. There, some wealthy young Frenchman—or perhaps a Spaniard—would fall in love with me. My mother would make the proper arrangements with him or his family. I would move to my own house on Rampart Street. Again and again my mother assured me that my beauty would win treasures for us both—servants, slaves, a huge plantation. But I only thought, No, no. I won't allow myself to be sold that way.

Early in September of that year, I was in our house, playing the harpsichord my father had bought me in his years of affluence. My friend Louise La Branche, who lived next door, called in the window, "Flora, there's a man out here who speaks only English. Come help him find his way."

Standing in front of the house was an extraordinarily handsome man of about thirty wearing elegant clothes—a powder-blue silk coat over a yellow waistcoat, with high-heeled red shoes. Lace ruffles rose from his shirt. He flourished an ivory-headed cane and dabbed at his sweating forehead with a lace handkerchief. "I am totally lost and about to expire from the sun," he said. "Can you direct me to the store of Mr. John Fitzpatrick, on Royal Street?"

"Of course," I said, pleased to be able to use some of the English my father had taught me. It was the first time I had spoken it since his death. Everyone in New Orleans knew Fitzpatrick's store. It was where people went to buy the finest cloth for suits and dresses as well as cutlery and china, delicious teas and spices from India—all the exotic and remarkable products of English commerce.

"Would you please be sure I go by a safe way?" the man said. "I have a great deal of money with me."

"If you will permit me," I said, "I will be happy to guide you."

"It will be my pleasure, I assure you," he said with a polite bow.

The man knew nothing of New Orleans and was obviously puzzled by the people he had seen on Rampart Street. "Why do you live there on the outskirts of the city?" he asked. "You're obviously a young woman of rank and breeding."

"I fear not, sir," I said, my eyes on the black mud of Royal Street.

"Come, come, my dear girl," he said. "Where did you learn to speak English? Whence came that lovely music I interrupted? The fine gown you're wearing?"

I said nothing.

"Is it—can it be—because I have not introduced myself?"

"By no means," I said. "Fitzpatrick's store is at the end of this block. It's been a pleasure to serve you, sir."

I turned and tried to leave him. He stepped playfully around me and blocked my path. "My dear young woman," he said, "my name is William Coleman. I would like the honor of your acquaintance. May I know your name?"

"Flora Lopez," I said. "But you don't want the honor of my acquaintance."

"No doubt your parents would prefer you to speak only to gentlemen whom they know," he said. "You have taken pity on a stranger in distress and fear a reproof from them. May I call on you and explain the entire incident to them?"

He spoke with such easy grace, his smile was so persuasive, I felt my body swell with shame and regret. Here was the sort of aristocratic Englishman that my father had yearned to find for me. But he was as unreachable, as untouchable, as if he had stayed in London. To be so close to him, to see how attracted he was to me, was almost unbearable. I could not explain my agitation to him.

"Thank you, Mr. Coleman," I said. "But no visit

will be necessary. Ask Mr. Fitzpatrick to tell you who we are, on Rampart Street. Then you'll understand my—my embarrassment. Good-bye."

At home I found my mother striding up and down the hall of our house. "Where have you been?" she cried. I was amazed. Her unshakable calm had been one of the bulwarks of my life. "Who was this Englishman? Where did you go?" she demanded.

At first I was bewildered, then angry. "You have no right to question me like a criminal, *Maman*. I'm not a child. I can go walking with whom I please," I said.

"Don't you see, you little fool, how that will ruin everything?" she shouted. "You have nothing to offer but your virginity. Lose that and you'll soon be walking the riverside selling yourself to sailors."

I asked my mother how she could say such a thing to me. "Because I must," she replied. She told me that other mothers on Rampart Street were eager to ruin my reputation so their daughters could win the men of wealth who were certain to bid for me. For the first time I told my mother how much I hated this idea. A tremendous quarrel exploded. She told me to accept the world into which I was born. She said I would eventually thank her for it. When I shouted that I would never thank her, that I would hate her for selling me like a slave, she ordered me to my room.

As twilight fell the rich smell of my mother's gumbo filled the house. It was my favorite dish. My mother was trying to placate me in the only way she knew. There was a knock on the front door. I heard a man's voice speaking to my mother. I recognized it instantly as William Coleman's. Then my mother's dark, deep voice answering him. I opened my bedroom door a crack, enabling me to hear William Coleman say, "Madame, I assure you my intentions are entirely honorable. Your daughter is the most beautiful woman I've ever seen. I ask only for a chance to see her again. She can send me away—"

"I've forbidden her to see you under any circumstances," my mother said. "You can sail for England any time you wish and leave her ruined. The man who chooses her must be a gentleman from one of the city's established families."

"Madame, I'm prepared to stay in New Orleans long enough to prove to you—"

My mother called him a liar. She had made inquiries and learned that he had arrived on a cargo ship that was helping Mr. Fitzpatrick transport the goods in his store to Pensacola, a move that had become necessary because the new governor had ordered all non-Catholic merchants out of New Orleans. William Coleman insisted he had only been a passenger on the cargo ship. He was an official of the British government and had a diplomatic passport. He could stay in New Orleans as long as he pleased.

"Madame, I understand your situation. Mr. Fitzpatrick has explained Rampart Street to me."

"Then you know the law," my mother said. "You can't marry my daughter here. And I'll never let you take her away from here unmarried. Go now. If I see you near this house again, I'll ask the authorities for assistance. We people of color are not without influence in this city."

That evening at supper I forced myself to be cruel. I ate the succulent crabs and shrimp and drank the soup of the gumbo, which never tasted more delicious, without a complimentary word to my mother.

I scarcely spoke to her for the rest of the night. The next morning was Sunday. We went to mass at the Church of St. Louis on the Place d'Armes. Louise La Branche and her mother went with us. As we knelt for the consecration and the priest raised the white host and gold chalice containing Christ's body and blood above our heads, I slipped a sealed note into Louise's stubby brown hand. Somehow in my mind it was the right moment to do it, the right way. To defy both my mother and the God who made me a woman of color.

On the way out of the church, while my mother was greeting several friends, I whispered to Louise, "Go to the English store. Give the letter to Mr. Fitzpatrick. If you open it, I'll put a curse on you. Your hair will fall out, then your teeth." Louise nodded, terrified. Everyone on Rampart Street believed in witchcraft.

The letter was addressed to William Coleman. Its message was brief:

> I heard you at the door last night. I will meet you tomorrow at 2 P.M. in Fitzpatrick's store.
>
> FLORA LOPEZ

The following afternoon, I went to my music lesson near the convent on Chartres Street and pretended to feel ill. My teacher permitted me to leave a half-hour early and I met William Coleman at Fitzpatrick's store. The place was full of men packing merchandise into crates. Mr. Coleman was wearing a suit of pure white Madras silk and a mauve waistcoat embroidered with roses. Once more he seemed to me the embodiment of aristocracy—and honorable affection.

"How kind of you to let me see you again," he said. "It will make my visit to New Orleans a happy memory. I don't envy your future in this city. Too bad your revolution didn't succeed. I hear it was led by a Jew who sounded like an English radical."

"He was my father," I said, almost weeping.

William Coleman was enormously distressed. He took an emerald on a gold chain from a tray of jewelry that was being packed and gave it to me. "I seem to cause you nothing but pain," he said. "Accept this as a token of—my regret. In another country we might have become more than friends."

I refused the gift. I knew my mother would never let me keep it. Mr. Coleman asked me about my father. I told him of his affection for England. "Since I was a child I've lived with descriptions of London in my head," I said.

William Coleman told me how much he wished he could show me London. He said that men and women could find more happiness there than in any other place on earth. They could also find unhappiness—if they lacked protection and guidance. He took my hand and said I had stirred something in him that he had never felt before—a wish to protect as well as to love a woman without any other motive but the reward of her affection. The women he knew in London presumed that he sought them for their wealth and influence because he himself was not a rich man. They had so disillusioned him he had retired to a government post in the West Indies to escape their mercenary ways. He had been on his way back to London when his ship was rerouted to

New Orleans to help Mr. Fitzpatrick. He had resigned himself to marrying one of these London women. Until he saw me.

Everything in my past combined to make his appeal irresistible. "When are you sailing?" I asked.

"Tomorrow at dawn," he said.

"I'll be there."

It was still dark when I crept from our white house on Rampart Street, leaving a note on my pillow to explain my resolution and to implore my mother's forgiveness. William was waiting for me on the dock. He had bribed the customs officers, who were conveniently absent. He rushed me aboard and hid me in his tiny cabin. By sunrise, the ship *Delilah* was in mid-river. Soon after we reached the Gulf of Mexico, the captain married us.

On the long voyage to London, William became the lover, the friend, I had dreamed of finding. We read novels and poetry. I taught him French. He perfected my English. We talked of London. It seemed, at times, that I was already there, so vividly did William describe it. He also told me about himself. He had been born poor. His father had been a printer and a drunkard, who started a half-dozen newspapers in the provinces and lost them all. His mother had died when he was three but she had powerful relations in London, men of wealth though not of noble blood. One of these, a merchant and member of Parliament, had paid for William's education at a school in the city and obtained a post for him in the British Treasury Office. But his life in London had been complicated by lack of money. Most of his friends were sons of noblemen and rich merchants. William's only hope of wealth was marriage. But he was determined not to sacrifice his happiness for security. Persisting in this determination, he had quarreled with a wealthy older woman who had wanted to marry him. In revenge she had slandered him and almost succeeded in driving him from society. His wealthy uncle had arranged for him to retreat to Jamaica, where he had served as comptroller of customs. Now, his purse replenished and his composure regained, he was challenging London to injure his happiness, with me at his side!

William asked only one indulgence of me. He hoped I would agree to keep our marriage a secret for a while. He would need time to explain it to his uncle, who might consider it highly imprudent. I agreed without the least hesitation. By this time I was rapturously, obliviously in love with him. I could not even imagine him telling me a lie.

We spent our first few days in London at an inn. Before long William regained his old rooms on the second floor of a broad-beamed house on Stonecutters Court in the Pall Mall section of the city. A stream of dressmakers and hatters appeared at his summons and set about making me the best-dressed woman in London. Morning gowns and evening dresses in painted satins, soft, lustrous velvets and brocades, all in that year's favorite colors—apple green, lemon yellow, and pink. There seemed to be no limit to the money William was spending. When I asked him about it, he told me that collector of customs in Jamaica was a very lucrative post; he had received a percentage of the duties paid by every ship that arrived or left the island. Money was no problem; William wanted me to create a sensation when he introduced me to society.

Create a sensation we did, the day we made our first visit to Ranelagh, the most popular pleasure garden in London. The immense rotunda—over five hundred feet in circumference—was illuminated by dozens of chandeliers. Brilliant colors glowed everywhere, from the green ceiling to the gilded boxes. In the center were four enormous black pillars. Around them strolled the social leaders of London, in their laced and ruffled best.

Many of the woman, usually the most extravagantly dressed, were masked. These were nobility, William said, and in spite of their masks he had no difficulty identifying them. "That's the Duchess of Kingston, Lord Grafton's mistress," he said. "There's Lord Hervey with his latest friend. Believe it or not, underneath those skirts you'll find a man. There's Lady Buckinghamshire, one of our great gamblers. They call her Faro's Daughter."

I was amazed by the amount of flesh these ladies displayed. I had protested when William insisted on getting my gowns cut quite low. Now I saw gowns that were transparent from waist to shoulder or cut so low that the least intake of breath would seem to have exposed everything. William recited a verse from a satire on Ranelagh in which the ladies were described as "Fair maids who at home in their haste/ had left all clothing else but a train."

At least a dozen times, in our progress around the rotunda, William stopped, made an elaborate bow, and doffed his small, sharp-edged tricorn hat to an acquaintance. Several did not acknowledge his bow, but William seemed unbothered by the rebuffs. He spoke to only one promenader, an army officer in the uniform of the Queen's Guards, Walter Beckford. He was with another soldier, a mere boy, extremely handsome.

"Good evening, Lieutenant. The prodigal has returned. How is our friend Lord Lyttleton and the other members of the club?"

"Well. And who is this gorgeous creature?"

"Her name is Flora Lopez. She's from New Orleans. The daughter of the richest planter in Louisiana. Her father sent her to visit relatives in Paris, but she has decided to see London first."

"You could not have found a better guide, Mademoiselle," Lieutenant Beckford said to me.

The boyish soldier with him laughed in a rather snide way. William ignored him and we resumed our promenade. He told me the boy was Beckford's latest love. They were both Williamites. Even when he explained the term to me, I found it almost incomprehensible.

The next night we went to Ranelagh's chief competitor in London's world of pleasure, Vauxhall Gardens, in Lambeth, across the Thames from the main part of the city. Here was a different kind of visual charm, a blending of nature and art. Lights shimmered through the trees, and there were delightful walks bounded by hedges and paved with gravel, ending in pavilions, groves, grottoes, decorated by pillars, statues, and paintings. At the main pavilion an orchestra played and a restaurant served delicious food. But the company at Vauxhall was much different from Ranelagh's. There were few great lords or ladies. London's lower classes felt at home here, and they came wearing their best clothes, usually garish imitations of the nobility's dress.

William sat us at a table near the orchestra and

made wry comments on the crowd's bad taste. "You could sit here all night and not see a single person above the level of a cheesemonger," he said.

"For that slur, Coleman you bastard, I demand satisfaction in Hyde Park at dawn," said a man's voice behind us.

William leaped to his feet, laughing. "My old friend Lord Madman," he said. "Why aren't you at Ranelagh?"

Lord Madman looked the part. He had a flaccid mouth, full of uneven teeth, and veined, dissipated eyes that glittered beneath wild tufts of eyebrows.

"Too damned boring, Billy," drawled Lord Madman. "Besides, you know how I love the people. How do you like this one?"

On his arm was a grinning blond girl in a red taffeta gown. She was obviously drunk.

"'Ere, now," the girl said in a strange accent, "is 'e really a lord?"

"I'm afraid he is," William said. "His father is known as the good Lord Lyttleton. He is the bad Lord Lyttleton. His friends call him Lord Madman."

"And who is this, Billy?" asked Lord Lyttleton, eyeing me.

William repeated the lie he had told Lieutenant Beckford about my wealthy father in Louisiana. "Flora," he said, "Lord Lyttleton. If he likes you, he'll let you call him Tom."

"How do you do," I said, trying to make it clear from the tone of my voice that I did not like Lord Lyttleton.

"I do very well," Lyttleton said. "But this doxy does not trust me. Can you imagine that? Not trust a man whose father was Chancellor of the Exchequer.

Ask Coleman here. He was a clerk of the Treasury in the great man's reign. Tell her how he could not count out twenty shillings to make a pound. Which is why he was the good Lord Lyttleton. He hadn't the brains to be anything else!"

"All true," William said.

"I don't care who 'is father was," the girl said. "'E wants to take me off somewhere but 'e made me promise not to cut 'is purse. 'E's so drunk I'm afraid if I go 'e'll accuse me of liftin' the money 'e lost at Boodles and I'll end up at Newgate on this great lord's testimony."

"How much did you lose, Tom?"

"I don't know. Say ten thousand. Fox lost fifteen. It was a night, let me tell you."

"That's more than Lord Madman usually carries in his purse," William said to the girl. "You have nothing to fear."

"I still shan't go," the girl said. "Any man who wagers ten thousand pounds is truly a madman."

William eventually persuaded the girl to risk a night with Lord Lyttleton. Back in Stonecutters Court, I expressed my distaste for this gentleman, who seemed the antithesis of the qualities my father had admired in the English aristocracy. William soothingly assured me that he found Lyttleton equally distasteful.

The next afternoon we went to St. James's Park, a lovely rectangle of green beside the palace of that name. Like Hyde Park, it was open on weekdays only to the gentry. Outside the iron railings, footmen sat on cream-and-gilt coaches while their mistresses promenaded in the mall. Here, too, the ladies wore masks and splendid dresses.

A fat, gorgeously dressed older woman, unmasked,

approached us. She was escorted by Lieutenant Beckford. "Good day, Mr. Coleman, I'm delighted to see you," she said. "Lieutenant Beckford tells us you've returned with promises of repentance."

"Indeed I have, madam," William said. "Flora, this is Mrs. Cornelys, an old friend."

"Everyone is talking about her," Mrs. Cornelys said. "You must come to my Society Night on Tuesday next. I'll send you tickets."

"We'll be delighted to come," William said.

In the hackney coach going home, William explained that Mrs. Cornelys was the owner of Carlisle House, in Soho Square, to which all the best people flocked for masquerade balls and musical entertainments. On the afternoon of Society Night, William insisted on my spending four hours at the hairdresser. He fussed over every detail of my gown, and his own clothes. Nothing but perfection would satisfy our hostess. We arrived in Soho Square to find it jammed with carriages. Carlisle House swarmed with brilliantly dressed ladies and gentlemen. All the ladies had dance cards, and I was startled by how swiftly mine was filled. A remarkable number of gentlemen, young and old, rushed to solicit my company. William was all smiles, bowing hello to Lady Grosvenor and Lord Stormont and Lady Archer and Lady Carpenter and Lord Lyttleton. We were all masked, but it was obvious that the disguises were nothing but an excuse to dispense with the usual formalities of society and permit everyone to speak and act as he pleased.

The orchestra struck up a country air, and the dances began. They were all violent gavottes and quadrilles, not at all what I expected aristocrats to prefer. But I was young enough to enjoy them. The activity and the crowd in the ballroom overheated me greatly and I asked William to get me some punch. I soon grew extremely giddy. The last thing I remembered was someone asking me a peculiar question: "Has William learned any new parts?"

William, solicitude itself, carried me upstairs and left me in a bedroom with a woman servant. I lay there, between sleep and waking, while the festivities continued downstairs. I heard applause, much laughter. As if the ballroom had become a playhouse. Later, William carried me downstairs to a hackney coach.

The next day, I was miserable, thinking I had failed William. But he assured me that my debut in society had been a success. Nevertheless, he seemed overwhelmed by melancholy all day. He sat staring out the window, occasionally sighing to himself and scribbling furiously in a copy book. That night he made love to me with uncommon tenderness.

We kept to ourselves for the next two weeks, seldom going far from Stonecutters Court. Only when I noticed in the paper that the great David Garrick was playing Hamlet did William consent to go out. At the Drury Lane I was surprised by the number of young men of fashion who swarmed around us, smiling and joking with William. Lord Lyttleton was among them. "You must take care to drink less the next time we meet," he scolded me. "Otherwise you shall never make your fortune."

"I told you—I've changed my mind," William said.

This struck everyone as amusing. Lord Lyttleton rattled some coins in his purse. "We have more confidence in that sound than we have in your mind, Billy."

William led me away from his friends to our seats in the stalls. "I shall have nothing more to do with them," he muttered. "We shall live quietly—I swear it."

He seemed to mean it. When another invitation arrived from Mrs. Cornelys, he tore it to shreds and took me to Vauxhall for a pleasant dinner. This time he did not sneer at the styles of the lower classes. We went to other gardens, Marylebone, Kensington, on other nights. But William was seldom free of his melancholy mood. When I asked him why he was so gloomy, he said that his uncle was having trouble obtaining a new post for him. He had come home with the assurance that he would have an undersecretary's rank in the Colonial Office. But the noble lord who controlled the posts in that department had quarreled with William's uncle about Britain's policy toward America. Even then—this was 1771—America was creating divisions in England.

One night Lord Lyttleton appeared, drunk and bawling William's name in the street. "I won ten thousand at Boodles last night," he roared. "Tonight it shall be a hundred thousand. Half yours if you will reopen the Church."

I had no idea what he was talking about but William found his offer irresistible. He dressed in his most expensive suit and left with Lyttleton. He returned at dawn, drunk and disheveled, and poured an astonishing pile of guineas on our bed. "Look at them," he said. "Aren't they beautiful? Have you ever seen anything more beautiful?"

"Where did they come from?" I asked. There must have been a thousand of them.

"From Boodles," he said. "Lyttleton lost twenty

thousand but I made all this. I give you the credit. You've brought back my luck. Watch what I'll do with this. We're going to be rich, Flora."

Eventually I looked back on that night as a fatal turning point in both our lives. William had tried to resist, for my sake, a world that had almost destroyed him once. But he could not do it. London itself, with its wealth gleaming in every shop window, was a vast seductress. His friends, rakes and dissolutes to a man, could not tolerate the thought of his defection from their desperate ways. Above all he could not resist the passion for gambling, which they all shared.

At first I really seemed to have brought William luck. He was amazingly successful. Each night I met him at a convenient tavern around 4 A.M. to count his winnings and celebrate past dawn. For a few months he seemed to be as rich as Lord Lyttleton. He hired a coach and spent hundreds of pounds on clothes and jewelry for both of us. He convinced me that he was a genius at computing odds, that he had found a way to outwit fate. I believed in him, in spite of stories I kept hearing of men who had lost their ancestral estates or their father's hard-earned fortunes at Boodles, Almack's, or one of the other gambling clubs. More than a few of these losers completed their ruin by committing suicide.

One night, in the fall of 1771, William appeared at our favorite tavern in Covent Garden without his usual smile of triumph. He took me to our coach immediately. As we jounced through the deserted streets he told me he had lost five thousand pounds at Boodles. "Lyttleton says he'll cover a thousand for me on one condition. That you spend the night with him."

"You can't be serious," I said.

"My dear, he's so drunk he'll do nothing but undress you," William said. "Even when he's sober, there's little that he can do, for all his talk." He seized my hands and swore he would love me forever if I agreed to do it. No matter what happened, he would love me no less. Wildly, he told me that his only wish had been to make a fortune so he could support me in the style that my beauty deserved. He had shared his good luck with me. Now I must share his bad. If I refused him, there was no hope. The bailiffs would be at our door to seize everything we owned and take him to debtor's prison. He had been there once before. He preferred death to another visit.

I agreed to the bargain. At Lord Lyttleton's mansion we were escorted to his lordship's bedroom. He seemed anything but drunk and he announced an adjunct to his bargain. William must stay and perform with me to arouse him. "I told you I wouldn't do that," William said as I stared at him with dazed disbelief.

"I'll double the money," Lyttleton said. He looked at me, his ugly mouth working. "He's famous for his performances, you know. He was high priest of the Church of the Cunt and we were all his acolytes until someone ratted on him and we came near to ending in the pillory for blasphemy. I trust he'll repeat some of the flourishes he displayed at Mrs. Cornelys's masquerade ball. The one where you got so drunk. I for one have been offended by his refusal to share you since then. Would you like some laudanum before we begin?"

"A good idea," William said. He put one or two drops of the drug in a glass of wine and ordered me to drink it. In a few minutes I seemed to drift out of my body. I watched them undress me and perform acts that I cannot describe to you. I found myself welcoming the most obscene commands. Lord Lyttleton's revelation about William made me want to become completely loathsome, beyond redemption. It was what I thought I deserved for defying God and my mother, for believing I had the power to escape my fate. I saw myself as both a sinner and a fool.

Back in our rooms, I discovered that I was neither damned nor completely loathsome, but simply miserable. I demanded the truth about his past from William. He confessed the real reason for his sojourn in Jamaica. He had won a reputation among the aristocracy as a performer in plays that were little more than sexual exhibitions. Such shows were among Mrs. Cornelys's many illegal sidelines at Carlisle House. When William lured away some of her noble clients to his blasphemous "church," she had informed on him, forcing him to retire to Jamaica until the scandal subsided.

I accused William of bringing me to London to sell me to the highest bidder. He vehemently denied the charge. "What I told you in New Orleans was the truth," he vowed. "You stirred the first genuine feeling I've ever known for a woman—for anyone. But Mrs. Cornelys, Carlisle House, still haunted me. I wanted to go back there with you and defy them, mock Lyttleton and Lady Grosvenor and the rest of them to their faces. Unfortunately, when I got there, they insisted on my performing one more time. They offered me five hundred pounds. I couldn't resist the money. But I put laudanum in your punch to keep you from seeing me."

William begged me to regard the episode with Lyttleton as a nightmare, a thing to be forgotten as quickly as possible. He swore that I would never have to do such a thing again, although it had made him love me all the more. This declaration caused enormous confusion in my mind and spirit—to be told my debasement was treasured, revered, by my husband. I tried to believe him. But the events of the next few months made it impossible.

William's vow to change his life was as empty as his promise to me that I would never be sold again. He was still horrendously in debt, and he continued to gamble, hoping a run of luck would rescue him. But luck deserted him to an unparalleled degree. Not all his skill at computing odds could recapture it. Meanwhile, Lord Lyttleton was bragging to all his friends about the delights of Billy Coleman's quadroon.

More and more of Lyttleton's fellow aristocrats wanted to share his pleasure. Their pleas coalesced with William's ever-mounting debts. One more time, a second, a third, I was entreated into spending the night with some baronet or marquess and returned home to pour a shower of golden guineas onto our bed in Stonecutters Court. William took the money and lost it at Boodles or Almack's the next night, clinging to his gambler's faith that his luck had to turn.

To calm me, he began giving me laudanum regularly. I took even more of it after I became pregnant and William sent me to a midwife, who prescribed some herbs, which caused me to abort the child so violently that I lost a great deal of blood. A doctor who had to perform delicate surgery to save my life prescribed laudanum for the pain. The drug soon became so necessary to me I could not live without it.

My illness made William vow to stop selling me. I begged him to give up trying to live like an aristocrat, to move to another part of London. He had been given a place in the Colonial Office—not the undersecretary's post that he had wanted but respectable enough to enable us to live decently. William shook his head. Moving would not save him from his debts. It was too late for preachments. But he agreed to quit offering me to his friends. "There are other ways to raise money," he said.

For another three months we continued to live in the same extravagant style. William continued to gamble. But there were no more assignations required of me. Then came the day I might have foreseen, had I known more of London life. A half-dozen bailiffs arrived at our door with William in manacles. They informed me that he had been arrested for forging Bank of England stock certificates with the help of "persons unknown" at the Treasury. I was taken into custody as his accomplice. My claim—that I was William's wife and as innocent as any wife might be of a husband's crime—was overruled by the judge because no record of our marriage existed. Apparently the captain of the *Delilah* had never bothered to register it when he arrived in London.

In a few hours we were in Newgate Prison. Its three gray-stone floors were filled with the most vicious criminals in England. When we could not pay the "garnish," as they called it, a sort of entrance fee demanded by the inmates, we were stripped of our fine clothes, William to his shirt, I to my shift. I was shoved into a room full of prostitutes, many of them convicted of murder and theft, and awaiting sentence.

Our trial in Bow Street was a formality. The judge was unmoved by our attorney's plea that my youth and beauty called for mercy. We were both sentenced to hang. I felt nothing, thought nothing. I had returned to the blank fatalism of my first night with Lord Lyttleton. I accepted, even welcomed, my doom.

A death sentence makes a person a grisly sort of celebrity in London. William's friends showered money and presents on us. I had all the laudanum I needed to make dying a matter of indifference, just another darker dream. We were moved to the master's side of the prison, and given a private room with beds and other furniture to replace the filthy straw on which we had been sleeping. Lord Lyttleton, Lady Grosvenor, Mrs. Cornelys, and others visited us, more from a ghoulish interest in our appearance, I think, than from any genuine sympathy for our situation.

On our execution day William begged me to forgive him. He said he could bear death if I believed he had acted out of love for me. We embraced each other one last time, and were led to the prison chapel, where the criminals condemned for that day sat in a special pew with a coffin draped in black in front of them. The chaplain preached a sermon urging us to repent while our fellow prisoners shouted blasphemous encouragement to us from the galleries. With our black death caps on our heads and our unread prayer books in our hands, we were mounting the cart for the procession to Tyburn when a horseman galloped up to the deputy sheriff in charge of our execution. He shouted an order and William and I were dragged from the cart by the keeper and hurried back into the prison. The crowd sent up a roar of protest. They had been looking forward to seeing the "amorous quadroon," as the newspapers called me, hanged.

We soon discovered that William's relations had used their influence to have our sentence commuted to transportation to the colonies for life. We were transferred to a ship in the Thames and early in the spring of 1772 we sailed for America. I returned to the continent of my birth in irons, as enslaved as the most miserable black from Africa. In New York we were released from our chains and fed fresh food for a few days, then sold to the highest bidder. William was bought by a Connecticut man, I by Henry Kuyper. I told him enough of my story to arouse his sympathy, and he soon fell in love with me. He consulted a lawyer, who told him my unregistered shipboard union to William Coleman had no legal merit. We were married on New Year's Day, 1773.

Though I never learned to love Mr. Kuyper, I did not hate him. I tried to be a good wife to him. His mother considered me a fallen woman, and despised me. This only made Henry love me more ardently. Our marriage was his way of declaring his independence from his mother, a domineering old *vrouw* if I ever saw one.

Before the year 1773 was over, the rebellion broke out in New England, with the dumping of tea in Boston Harbor. The upheaval swirled around us like a rising sea. Henry Kuyper and his mother were loyal to the king, like many of the Dutch in Bergen

County. They were astonished and dismayed by the rebel victories at Lexington and Bunker Hill in 1775.

When Henry Kuyper refused to support the rebels in New Jersey, he was dragged before a revolutionary committee and cowed into recanting his loyalty to the King. The old lady received so many insults from her rebel neighbors and was so ashamed of her son's cowardice, I think she died of mortification, although the doctor called it pleurisy. This placed the direction of the farm in the hands of Caesar Muzzey.

To some extent Caesar had been running the farm already. But Mrs. Kuyper was a sharp supervisor, almost to the day of her death. She would ride out to the farthest fields on her little pony and criticize the planting, the drainage, and the fertilizer with an experienced eye that even Caesar respected. But respect vanished into the grave with her.

Henry Kuyper had no interest in farming. If any evidence is ever needed of the bad effects of slavery, Henry would be a prime example. With blacks to labor for him, he grew accustomed to spending most of each day at the Three Pigeons Inn or some other local tavern, drinking and smoking and talking politics with cronies who had equally large amounts of leisure time.

His only work was his weekly trip to New York to sell his meat and produce. The rebellion diminished but by no means eliminated his social life. The secret loyalists among the Bergen Dutch formed their own society.

Caesar and I had had little to say to each other while Mrs. Kuyper was alive. After her death Henry made only a pretense of supervising him. He was fond of Caesar, who had been his body servant as a boy; they had been raised almost as brothers. Henry often boasted of his good fortune, having a manager who took all the worries of farming off his shoulders. Nevertheless Caesar made a point of consulting Henry on when to plant, when to harvest, when to prune the fruit trees. I thought he was being tactful. I gradually realized he was looking for reasons to come to the house to see me.

When he found me alone, Caesar quickly turned the conversation to other matters, such as my opinion of slavery, the progress of the war, my personal history. He was fascinated to learn that in New Orleans free blacks and mulattoes had their own quarter, that many of them practiced trades as skillfully and profitably as whites and some owned substantial farms in the countryside. The few free Negroes Caesar knew in New Jersey led miserable lives. He told me that I had given him a paradise to dream about.

It soon became evident to both of us that the sympathy I had expressed for Caesar's enslaved state was turning into something more profound. Now I realize I desired him not only as a man but as Africa, as a turning within me to my black blood, after so much abuse and humiliation as a white woman. I told myself the happiness my father had urged me to seek in love was there, where I least expected it. When I confessed to Caesar the truth about my ancestry, we both knew what must follow.

But I never told Caesar the whole truth about England or William Coleman. I was afraid he would despise me. Caesar was enormously proud. He would have had no use for a degraded woman. I invented a story about a trip to London to seek out my father's relatives, being rejected by them, and forced to become a redemptioner. But I was able to tell Caesar, with complete sincerity, that I was ready to flee with him to New Orleans, where we could live together as man and wife.

Then the war rumbled closer and at the end of the summer of 1776 it swept over us. The Americans were routed from New York and New Jersey, and Henry, unwisely thinking the British had won, recanted his oath of loyalty to the rebellion and again pledged his allegiance to the King. Before the year was over, British fortunes underwent an astonishing reversal and most of New Jersey was in American hands once more. The rebels threatened to confiscate Henry's farm. I persuaded him to feign enough contrition to convince them that he was only a weakling. There were hundreds of others who did the same thing. But Henry became a suspected person, whom the rebels were determined to punish in some way.

In the spring of 1777 the rebels ordered every tenth militiaman drafted to fill the ranks of Washington's army. Henry's name was among the first on the list. This seemed strange policy, to try to make a soldier out of a man who had no love for their cause. Now that I know more of the army, I understand that a soldier's opinion of the war has little to do with his usefulness. On a battlefield there is no time to debate ideas. Every man fights for his life. But Henry had no intention of going near a battlefield. Under the law he could send a substitute, and he announced that he was sending Caesar.

When I told Caesar, he uttered a terrible oath. "That decides it," he said. "I've been thinking for a long time that there's only one way we'll ever get to New Orleans. You must become a widow."

That night, I left the back door unlocked. When Henry went to bed, I stayed downstairs, pretending enthusiasm for a novel. I heard Caesar's bare feet go up the back stairs and down the hall to Henry's bedroom. There was a muffled cry, then silence. Caesar smothered him with a pillow. He was careful to leave no marks on the body. It was easy to convince the doctor that Henry had died of apoplexy.

Caesar forced me to come upstairs and look at Henry's dead face. "I wish I could cut him open and make you drink his blood with me," he said. "Swear on his eyes that you love me."

He forced me to put my hand on Henry's eyes and swear. The hatred slavery creates is monstrous. That night it poisoned my love for Caesar. I was never able to regain the feelings that drew me to him.

Shortly after Caesar left for the American army, William's London friend, Walter Beckford, walked into this house. He was still in the British army, a major now, serving with the garrison in New York; Beckford informed me that he was making the house a way station for escaped prisoners. He told me that William had joined the American army and was working for him as a spy. He asked me if I knew anyone in the army who might make a good courier. I volunteered Caesar. I saw it as a way of securing Beckford's protection and earning money to reach New Orleans. By now our plan included taking Cato and Nancy and the field slaves with us and freeing them in Louisiana.

I don't think, even as I taught Caesar French and talked of the happiness we might find in New Orleans, that I really believed we would succeed. I always saw

Henry Kuyper's smothered face, with its gaping mouth and bulging eyes. I remembered things Lord Lyttleton—and others—made me do in London. Now do you see why I need forgiveness?

sixteen

The candle beside the bed was a guttering stump. Caleb Chandler had no idea what time it was. Time—and space—had been annihilated. Flora Kuyper's whispered words had changed the shape and dimension of his world. It no longer rested on traditional ideas of good and evil, salvation and redemption. Flora's life could only have been created by a God of darkness and mystery, a being whose purposes and powers were infinitely beyond the comprehension of the human mind.

As Flora talked Caleb had had a sense of God receding from this world. It was a new experience for him. Before, he had been certain of God's presence; his argument had been with those who saw Him as a harsh, relentless tyrant. God's absence was a new idea. It aroused in Caleb an awed pity for human loneliness.

For a few minutes this loneliness made his promise to protect Flora loom larger than victory or defeat in this stalemated war. What she had just told him was both a confession and a pledge, a kind of covenant. But how could he honor it? How could he respond to her trust and simultaneously plan to betray it?

Necessity, roared Benjamin Stallworth's iron mouth. But his cynical assumptions about this woman had proven to be as narrow and as sterile as his soul.

"My dearest love," Caleb said, "if ever I've seen or heard of a woman who's been more sinned against than sinning, it's you."

Kissing her, he realized her face was wet with tears. "I have one more sin to confess," Flora said. "The congressman, Hugh Stapleton, whom you sent here with Caesar's body. Walter Beckford ordered me to seduce him. Now he's in love with me. He wants to take me to Amsterdam with him."

Caleb heard Stallworth's triumphant sneer: *She fucks for the King*. But the fact was not the truth. The truth was as remote from Stallworth's sneer as it was from most pulpits, where sin and sinners were equally condemned.

Fact or truth, Flora's final confession made Caleb writhe with redoubled desperation. She had to be extricated from this maze of deception and corruption as soon as possible. But even if he abandoned Stallworth's necessity, turned his back on the dubious revolution, how could he tell her that the man who had just made love to her was a patriotic liar?

No. He turned to the hope that he could somehow

284

persuade her to accept the cause, the revolution, and then confess what he had done in its name. It was still, in spite of its Stallworths and Stapletons, a struggle for liberty, the rights of man—the same sort of struggle for which her father had died in New Orleans.

"I understand—about Stapleton," Caleb said. "Too bad the rebels have congressmen like him. What we—they need are more men like your father. A man who really believed in liberty."

"I don't think my father would be any more popular in Philadelphia than he was in New Orleans. He'd still be opposed to owning slaves. He'd never use liberty as a catch phrase to justify persecuting and robbing those who disagreed with him."

"He didn't fight a war. Perhaps a war forces people to do things they—dislike."

"You sound like you're changing your mind. Are you thinking of going back to the Americans and betraying me?"

"Don't say such a thing. I—I'm only trying to honor your father's memory."

"It needs no honoring, as far as I'm concerned. What happened to him is a better lesson. Anyone who trusts the people is a fool. There's no virtue—or courage—in them."

Caleb retreated to agonized silence. The cage of circumstances in which he found himself seemed to have no exit. Stallworth had made him a liar and seducer. Without the lies and seduction, he would never have learned the truth about Flora. Now the lies and seduction made it impossible to tell her the truth about himself.

At dawn Flora rose and ordered Cato to get out

her sleigh and horses. She was anxious to leave for New York to see Major Beckford. "How will you get past the rebel militia guards on the road to Powles Hook?" Caleb asked.

"They've been bribed long since," she said. "They think I'm just replenishing my wardrobe with a little London trading."

Flora returned in the late afternoon, trembling from the savage cold. "Beckford was skeptical at first," she said. "But he's desperately in need of a courier. I convinced him of your sincerity. He'll send for you tonight."

"Good," Caleb said.

Flora accepted some hot broth from Cato but did not drink it. She put the cup down on a side table and waited until Cato left the room to begin a new topic.

"All day, on the road, in New York, I've been thinking—about our future together. Now that you know the truth, you can see why I wanted to retreat to New Orleans with Caesar. If the British win this war—which begins to look more and more probable— William will attempt to reclaim me again, with Beckford's help. It seems to me we have no alternative but to follow the same plan. I see no refuge but New Orleans."

Caleb nodded. He was finding it harder and harder to lie to this woman.

"They won't let you marry me. I'm still a woman of color," Flora said. "But we won't need priests or ministers to seal our marriage. We'll buy a plantation on one of the bayous and live quietly. Perhaps I'll have babies. If not, we'll adopt some children of color."

"Yes," Caleb said.

Flora heard the falling note in his voice. Her eyes filled with tears. "You don't think we'll ever do it," she said. "You think the whole thing is mad."

"No," he said, "I think it's—desperate. I fear it will be much more difficult than you think. What if the British win the war before we can leave? Won't Major Beckford—or William Coleman—detain you?"

"Do you think it's possible—that they could win so quickly?" she said.

"All too possible," he said.

"I—I don't want to see William again. Beckford I can deal with. But William is different."

"What do you mean?"

"It's hard to explain. There are certain memories—"

"You still love him?"

"No!" Flora looked past Caleb at the parlor's dark, ice-coated front windows. For a moment Caleb had an eerie feeling that William Coleman was out there, his face pressed to the glass. "I don't love him. But I don't hate him, either," she said.

"Let me hate him for you," Caleb said. "He deserves someone's hatred. If anything makes me dubious about our future, it's the thought that this man could somehow reclaim you."

For a moment Flora seemed to waver toward a declaration of her detestation of William Coleman. But before she could answer him, there were footsteps in the hall. Two men in white greatcoats clumped into the parlor. One was short and middle-aged, and had corruption written on his face in a hundred brutal lines and creases. His companion was huge, with the staring eyes and expressionless face of an angel in a bad religious painting.

"These are Beckford's guides. John Nelson," Flora said, gesturing to the older man with evident distaste, "and Wiert Bogert."

"Let me get a good look at you, Parson," Nelson said, advancing into the parlor until snow from his boots formed rivulets on the Oriental rug. "You're a seven days' wonder, you know that? A week ago we had orders to cut your throat. Now we're told to bring you to New York like a bloody escaped colonel or general."

Caleb did not know what they were talking about. "Orders to cut my throat? Who gave them?"

"Major Beckford, who else? At the request of his friend in Morristown, the one they call Twenty-six. Mistress Kuyper was supposed to keep you busy till we got here to do the job. But for some reason she sent you away ahead of schedule."

"I don't know what you're talking about," Flora said. "I had no control over Mr. Chandler. The funeral service he came to perform was over and I could think of no way to detain him."

"You could think of no way to detain him," Nelson said, sneering. "There's one way you could have tried, if you'd been so inclined."

"Shut your mouth. Major Beckford has ordered you to treat me with respect."

"I've obeyed the order like a good soldier," Nelson said. "But respect works both ways and so does obedience. If you'd obeyed orders, we'd be fifty guineas richer."

While they argued Caleb was reconstructing the events of his first visit: Flora's decision to have the funeral the morning after his arrival, her impatience to see him on the road to Morristown. He realized she had saved his life.

"I saw that Mr. Chandler was a servant of the King. Or ripe to become one," Flora was telling John Nelson. "I saw what a mistake it would have been to kill him."

Lying again? Chandler wondered. This time he was not sure. He looked at her and heard Stallworth's sneer.

Nelson grunted skeptically and pulled a white greatcoat and boots from his knapsack. "Here," he said, flinging them at Caleb's feet. "Get these on. We've orders to run you back to New York without delay. Can you use snowshoes?"

"I used them in the woods as a boy," Caleb said.

"We've got some outside for you."

As Caleb walked to the door Bogert stepped in front of him, glowering. "Tell me truth. You kill Caesar?"

"No."

"John think you did."

"John's wrong. I'm on the side of the King. So was Caesar. There was no reason for me to kill him."

"I find out you kill him, I kill you no matter what Beckford say."

"Forget it, lad. I was just talkin' to hear meself," Nelson said. He grinned mockingly at Flora. "Old Caesar and Bogert was friends. They did some carousin' in New York that it took half the watch to stop. He was a wild one, old Caesar. The whores all loved him. Black and white."

Flora looked like she might start weeping. "Let's go," Caleb said.

Outside, the cold was the worst Caleb had felt

since the winter began. It assaulted every inch of exposed skin. He bound a scarf around his nose and lips, stepped into his snowshoes, and followed Nelson and Bogert into the dark fields north of the Kuyper farm. They kept to the fields and woods, avoiding the roads, stopping only to consult a small luminous compass. They were traveling east to avoid the heavily patrolled roads around the British fort at Powles Hook. East was also the direction of Connecticut but Caleb felt the journey was away from, not toward, the state of his birth. He kept thinking of home as a place from which he was receding, perhaps forever. He remembered other winter journeys, when his father joined twenty or thirty fellow farmers for a trip to the New London market. He could see the slim figure of his father on the back step of the two-horse sleigh that Caleb and his brothers had spent hours loading with frozen hogs, poultry, firkins of butter, casks of cheeses, skins of mink and fox, baskets of nuts, hand-cut shoe pegs, and yarn their sisters had spun. How he had envied his father those journeys. Even then Caleb was dreaming of a way to escape Lebanon. But his father returned from the city untouched by its sophistication or its vices, the same simple, earnest man who trembled at the thought that he or those whom he loved might not be among the saved. Caleb was certain he would not return from this journey the same man.

The three travelers came out of the woods onto a road. Bogert caught Caleb's arm and dragged him back into the trees. They waited for a moment and Caleb heard the irregular thud of horses' hooves on the snow. Five minutes later a sleigh, loaded not unlike the one Caleb's father used to drive to New London, rounded the bend and passed them. "Contraband trade," Nelson muttered. "If we didn't have special orders to bring you straight in, we'd wait here for the bastard to come back. There's sixty guineas in fresh beef on that sleigh. I'd be happy to extract the cash from his pocket on his way home."

"Wouldn't that discourage other loyal traders?" Caleb said, trying to sound like a thorough King's man.

"Nothing'll discourage them as long as the money's at the end of the road," Nelson said. "That's what we're all in this for, right, Parson? The King's shilling?"

"I'm here because I believe the King can rescue America from ruin."

"Listen to'm," Nelson hissed. "I was that way in 1775, Chaplain. But when I seen the way this war was being fought, I decided, Nelson, it's every man for himself. Why shouldn't you try to get as rich as a bloody commissary or a secret service director? That's all they're doin' here. Gettin' rich. They ain't fightin' a proper war like we did against the Frenchies. If they was, they'd have hanged, drawn, and quartered old Washington in London four years ago."

Eventually they turned south and reached the rugged bluffs above the Hudson. They descended a winding slippery path and crossed the river on the thick, silent ice. On the other side, they exchanged the sign and countersign with a British sentry and soon reached the door of a safe house kept by Major Beckford on Bowerie Lane, on the outskirts of New York.

There, Caleb's escorts left him and a surly soldier with an Irish brogue showed him into a sitting room. A fire burned briskly in the fireplace. Caleb stood before it, grateful for the warmth. The door opened and a fat, ruddy-faced man wearing an officer's red coat entered the room. Caleb disliked the arrogance on his face. "The Reverend Chandler?" he said.

Caleb nodded.

"I'm Major Walter Beckford. You're under arrest as a spy."

Caleb remembered Stallworth's warning: *They'll run you through a gauntlet worse than the one I'm giving you.* The memory offered neither comfort nor reassurance. Worse, there was no way to tell if this was only a test.

"You can't be serious, sir," Caleb said. "The mere suggestion is a travesty. I'm here to offer my services to you—and His Majesty."

"Do you think you're dealing with children, Mr. Chandler?" Beckford said. "We're aware of almost everything Mr. Washington and Mr. Stallworth attempt. You were sent to Flora Kuyper's with orders to persuade her—knowing the utter lack of morality that characterizes this rebellion, perhaps even to seduce her—and thus insinuate your way into our service as a double agent. Did you enjoy our little Flora? She's quite a piece."

"My feelings for Mrs. Kuyper," Caleb said, struggling to control his panic, "are of the purest sympathy and admiration. If I ever merit her—her favor, it will be within the bonds of holy matrimony. She has done nothing but help me confront in myself what I already half knew—what thousands of my countrymen half know—that our revolution has become a travesty

292

of the glorious hopes of 1775, and there is no recourse for America but the King's forgiveness and protection."

"They teach you pretty speeches in Morristown," Beckford said. "I'll give you a chance to recite some of them tomorrow, when we hang you. Guard, take him away."

Two ugly soldiers with fixed bayonets strode into the room. "I demand a trial," Caleb said. "The right to call witnesses, including Mrs. Kuyper, who will attest—"

"She'll attest to whatever we tell her to. You'll have a trial. A military court will judge you guilty in five minutes. We have the proof, Chandler, from our agents in Morristown."

"My proof is here, in my heart," Caleb cried, pounding his chest.

"You should have been an actor," Beckford said.

The two soldiers marched Caleb through the dark, snowbound city to the three-story stone Provost, the most infamous of the several British prisons in New York. He was shoved into a bare cell, with straw for a pallet, and left to spend the night trying to choke down his terror. His anguish was not assuaged by the conduct of the provost marshal, William Cunningham, who came in drunk from dinner and proceeded to beat and kick several other prisoners. The place echoed with the screams of the victims. Later, Cunningham stopped outside Caleb's cell and asked his identity. "A Yankee spy?" the provost marshal said. "I'll look forward to putting a hemp collar on him tomorrow or the next day."

Caleb lay on his bed of dirty straw, thinking of Flora's description of her execution day in London.

He had been sympathetic, of course, but how pale sympathy becomes when the listener is far removed from the experience.

At dawn the cell door opened and a small, shabby man in black introduced himself. "I am the Reverend Jonathan Odell," he said. "Major Beckford, out of sympathy for your clerical status, has asked me to minister to you. Although we're of different churches—I am an Anglican priest—we share a common faith in Jesus Christ. The major thought you might find your mind eased by telling me the truth."

Caleb gasped out another explosion of lies and half-truths. "My mind will not be eased because the truth is that I am about to die for my loyalty to the King. For my discovery of that loyalty in my heart through the love of a brave woman. Major Beckford is so far gone in cynicism—or hatred of Americans—that he can't believe such a thing could happen. You can't help me, sir, unless you can change his mind about murdering me. Failing that, I ask you to tell my story to the world and see that Beckford receives the punishment he deserves."

"The major is only doing his duty, as I'm doing mine," Odell said. "We have proof that you're a rebel spy. Your one hope of life is to tell us everything you know of your army's secret service. Even if you know very little, a sign of repentance may go far with the court-martial officers. They don't want to hang a clergyman."

Caleb struggled for breath. For a moment he lost touch with the world he had discovered in Flora Kuyper's arms. He reverted to the terrified fourteen-year-old, begging the Reverend Joel Lockwood to help him win God's forgiveness for his sinful, lustful nature. He deserved damnation for the sin he had committed with Flora Kuyper. This doleful man of God was trying to rescue him from that fate and its grisly counterpart in this world—the gallows. Why was he trusting Flora Kuyper, a woman who admitted infidelity, adultery, with not one but a half-dozen men? *She fucks for the King*. Stallworth's words whined like a passing bullet.

Then Caleb remembered John Nelson's truculent argument with Flora last night. Her anxious, evasive replies. She had saved his life. Before treachery, before lying began, she had refused to let him be murdered. The existence of this act of primary generosity steadied him. He continued the masquerade.

"I can only say that I'm innocent and have nothing to confess but love for a lady who convinced me to risk my life for the King."

Odell sighed. "It's sad to see what rebellion can do to a man's soul."

The clergyman departed. The iron door clanged behind him. A half-hour later, Major Walter Beckford appeared. "Well, Chandler," he said, "you have one last chance. Will you confess?"

Caleb only shook his head. Beckford looked annoyed. He consulted his pocket watch and paced the cell for several moments. "I suppose you're encouraged by Mr. Odell's inept performance. I was outside, listening to him. You think because he admitted we dislike hanging a clergyman you can continue to bluff me. You're wrong, Mr. Chandler. Unless we get a complete confession from you—names, tokens, places of rendezvous, including, if it happens to be the case, Mrs. Kuyper's guilt—you're a dead man."

"Mrs. Kuyper is responsible for my decision to

come here. I responded to her—courage, her example. To her arguments on behalf of the King. If you call that guilt, Major, I wonder about your loyalty."

"Mr. Chandler, you're almost amusing," Beckford said. "We'll let you think things over aboard the *Jersey* for a month or two. Then we'll talk again—if you're still alive."

It was a sentence of death, without entangling legalities. By now stories of the *Jersey*'s horror had crept through every town in Connecticut. It was a prison ship, primarily for American sailors captured while privateering. The few who emerged from it alive, exchanged for British sailors, were walking skeletons, who often died before they reached their homes.

About 10 A.M. two soldiers escorted Caleb to the Brooklyn ferry landing, where a sled was waiting for them. Riding behind two horses on the ice covering the East River accentuated the feeling that he was caught in a waking nightmare. In a half-hour the sleigh reached the hulk of the *Jersey*, tilted ten or fifteen degrees in the ice of Wallabout Bay, near the Brooklyn shore.

Caleb mounted the ladder to the deck, where he was handed over to his jailers. A grimy Scotsman in the captain's cabin recorded his name in a large ledger, writing beside it, "suspected spy." He was then hustled down the ladder to the main hatchway, where two more Scotsmen searched him and ordered him below. He descended the almost vertical ladder and found himself in the nether world of the *Jersey*.

Around him, their heads to the hull, lay gaunt men in rags. Some shivered and shook with fever, clutching tattered blankets to their throats. Most were listless as corpses. They stared indifferently at Caleb like phantoms in the Hades of the ancient Greeks, no longer interested in the world of the living. Around them rose a stench worse than anything Caleb had ever encountered at Morristown, a compound of urine and excrement and human sweat and rotting garbage. Pervading it, somehow worsening it, was a dull, terrible cold. There was no fire anywhere on the ship. The temperature was not much above the zero mark at which it hovered outside. Only the cutting wind was absent.

"News, mate?" called one man, shoving himself to a sitting position. "Any news of a peace treaty?"

Caleb shook his head. A man wandered past him, jabbering to someone. "Father," he said, "I'll do the milking this morning. It be too cold out there for you." In the gray light spilling down the hatchway, Caleb saw the reason for the man's delirium. His face was covered with the oozing sores of smallpox.

Caleb retreated into the darker section of the hold, where he found an open space along the hull. He settled against the timbers and felt their cold penetrate his cloak. A voice beside him asked what ship he was from. "No ship. I'm a civilian," he said. "Captured in New Jersey."

"There's more like you down on the next deck."

The man on the other side of Caleb was racked by a fit of coughing. He groaned, struggling for breath. "I doubt my shipmate will last the night," said the first prisoner. As his eyes adjusted to the semidarkness Caleb was able to see him. He was about seventeen years old. Most of his hair had fallen out; his neck was withered like an old man's. The skin on his face, his hands, seemed almost transparent, the bones beneath it were so visible.

"How long have you been here?"

"Six months, I think. What day is it?"

"February 18, 1780."

"Ten months. When my shipmate goes, I'll be the last of our crew. There was twenty-six of us from the privateer *Independence*. Most died in the summer."

Toward the end of the afternoon, the prisoners received their rations. Meat, bread, and some faintly flavored water supposed to be coffee. "Fire, we must have fire to cook," several men shouted to the guards as they passed the hatchway, where the food was handed out.

"You'll have to dine on raw meat like the animals you are," the guard said. "There's no fuel to be had. Many a loyal man in New York is doing the same thing."

The meat had a nauseating smell. As Caleb lifted it to his mouth something moved beneath his finger. He saw a maggot shoving its head from beneath the slimy mass. He flung the meat aside, gnawed morosely on the bread, and drank the cold, watery coffee. A few hours later, the day faded and darkness engulfed them. The man next to Caleb kept struggling for breath and at last descended into his death rattle. Cries of delirium, groans of the dying, drifted from other parts of the ship. Again and again, Caleb found himself fighting back surges of terror.

In the morning the hatches were flung back and the guards awakened the prisoners with the shout: "Rebels, turn out your dead."

The boy next to him joined a six-man working party of fellow skeletons. They made the rounds of the ship, taking away a dozen bodies, including the man next to Caleb. It took the strength of all seven to lift a single corpse. When one of the working party collapsed, Caleb took his place. They had to struggle to drag the bodies up the ladder to the top deck. As they deposited the last one Caleb glanced down at his coat. It was crawling with lice. He looked at his hands. They were swollen with bites. "I'll pick you clean if you do me," said the boy. "That's how we pass most of each day. If you don't get them, they suck the blood out of you."

For the next three days Caleb endured this ordeal. Hunger settled into his bones and he began to eat the maggoty meat. It produced violent cramps and fever. On the morning of the fourth day, as they carried the night's usual harvest of dead to the top deck, he was summoned to the captain's cabin. There stood well-fed Major Walter Beckford, a mocking smile on his face. "Well, Chandler, are you still a loyal servant of His Majesty?"

Caleb had to resist an impulse to spring at his throat. "Yes," he said. "And your enemy, who'll haunt you when I die."

"Mr. Chandler, I am, appearances to the contrary, a humane man. I don't wish to kill you, and you have done no spying worthy of the name. Tell me what you know and I assure you that I'll arrange for you to be released on your promise to remain neutral for the rest of the war."

For a moment Caleb almost succumbed. Why not accept defeat, go home to Connecticut, and try to forget this nightmare? Then he heard Stallworth's voice: *The same gauntlet*. How could he trust Beckford?

Once he confessed, he was his creature, to hang or abandon in this hell ship.

Caleb shook his head. "I've risked too much to serve His Majesty. I won't yield to your perverse hatred of Americans, Major."

Beckford smiled and held out his hand. "Mr. Chandler," he said, "welcome to the gratitude and protection of King George the Third."

seventeen

"Say, Stapleton," drawled Congressman Samuel Chase of Maryland, "did you hear what that slimy bastard Tom Paine called me t'other day? A voluptuary! How's that, eh? A voluptuary! Just because a female can't look into his ugly phiz without losing her dinner, he calls me a voluptuary. How are things in New Jersey, Stapleton? Were you overwhelmed by the rising spirit of patriotism? Did your constituents pledge to you their lives, their fortunes, and their sacred honor? Hah?"

"They did better than that," Hugh Stapleton said. "They told me if I didn't find a way to raise our paper dollars to par with specie in three weeks, they'd reenact the Crucifixion."

Chase chuckled. "Where have you been hiding, Stapleton? We've missed you."

"Some business I couldn't afford to pass up came my way."

Chase chuckled even more knowingly. He had replaced Benjamin Harrison of Virginia as the Falstaff of Congress. Chase's shape was virtually spherical, and his complexion was not much different from the color of the brimming glass of French claret he had in his hand. The two congressmen were sitting in the Long Room of the City Tavern, the best hostelry in Philadelphia. A huge fire leaped in the massive fireplace. Delicious odors drifted from the kitchen. The Continental Congress had just adjourned for the day and the room was rapidly filling with delegates.

Hugh Stapleton preferred the company of cynics like Samuel Chase because he could speak frankly to them. When he had returned to Philadelphia two weeks ago, Robert Morris, the city's leading merchant, had invited Stapleton to join him in buying out an importer who had just gone bankrupt and was desperate for cash to pay his creditors. Morris, busy with a dozen other ventures, had let Stapleton conduct the negotiations and take title to the man's warehouse. It was a tribute to Stapleton's increasing reputation as a businessman.

Limping across the room toward them now was Philip Schuyler, who had been Congressman Stapleton's fellow guest at General Washington's dinner table in Morristown. "Mr. Stapleton," said Schuyler, "I've been looking for you in Congress. Have you just arrived in town?"

"More or less."

"I've been laid up with an attack of the gout myself. I'm anxious to have a talk about the army. I received a letter from General Washington today. Things are no better in Morristown."

"I'm at your service," Hugh Stapleton said, although he had no desire to discuss the army or anything else connected with the government of the United States.

Schuyler gave Chase a rather chilly nod and sat down with several Carolinians at another table. "What's this—are you turning soldier, Stapleton?" Chase said. "Schuyler enlisting you? Livingston, come help me save Stapleton from Schuyler's clutches."

Robert R. Livingston of New York, one of the great landholders in the Hudson River Valley, joined them. The elegantly dressed aristocrat was trailed by a half-dozen other congressmen from the middle states. It reminded Hugh Stapleton of the way the English lords promenaded in St. James's Park or at Ranelagh, followed by their crowds of retainers. In his most condescending tone, Robert Livingston told Stapleton that Philip Schuyler had been "hectoring" his fellow congressmen as if they were privates and he was still a general. "He's simply not a politician," Livingston said.

After eighteen months in Philadelphia, Hugh Stapleton was inclined to think such a remark was a compliment. But he did not contradict Robert R. Livingston. Few people did. "What has been happening in Congress?" Stapleton asked.

"Nothing but declamations from the fanatics of Yankeeland," Chase informed him. "They say every man who has earned a dollar from the revolution is a traitor. Death to aggrandizers and monopolists! I tell you they're enough to make me think Maryland's greatest mistake was joining this confederacy."

"The radicals here in Pennsylvania echo the Yankees' cry," Livingston said. "They've threatened Robert Morris and other merchants on the street."

"There's no question those fanatics are a disgrace to the province," agreed lanky James Wilson in his Scots burr. Dismissed from Congress by Pennsylvania's radicals, Wilson was getting rich as a lawyer. His chief client was America's ally, France, for whom he often acted as unofficial spokesman. He proceeded to do some impromptu pleading on the spot. "There's surely no crime in making an honest profit from a well-conducted business," Wilson said. "But there are some among us who would endanger our alliance with France—the one thing that keeps us politically alive—to make a few rotten dollars."

"Why, damn you, Wilson," Chase roared. "Are you referring to the gentlemen of Maryland?"

"If the shoe fits so that you recognize it at the first pinch—"

They began a violent argument about several thousand pounds of flour that had been bought before prices began to rise at a gallop and stored in Maryland by the French ambassador to supply the French navy when it operated on the American coast. Chase and some fellow Marylanders had seized the flour a few months ago and resold it to the American army at a huge profit. "How can we hope to persuade a French fleet or a French army to come to our assistance," Wilson raged, "when we can't honor a simple contract?"

"Oh, pshaw, Wilson," Chase said. "'Twas just good business. Your client can buy again at the new prices. His Most Catholic Majesty can afford it."

For a moment Hugh Stapleton thought of the

starving army in Morristown and the tall, diffident Virginian who was trying to hold it together. He looked at the complacent faces around the table and wondered why they could not see where the United States of America was going. Down, down, down into ruin and defeat. Something stirred in Stapleton—a confused but nonetheless real regret for what was happening. He almost became angry at these politicians, so busy looking out for themselves. The impulse was stifled by the realization that he was no different. During the past year he had spent far more hours fretting over his privateers and his profits than he had spent thinking about Congress.

But for Hugh Stapleton the time for conscience-stricken reproaches was almost over. For the past two weeks, as he toiled over inventories and accounts receivable, his imagination was in New Jersey, recalling sounds, sights, touches from his most recent visit to Flora Kuyper. He had stayed with her for two nights and found her as amorous, as eager to please him, as adept at agreeable conversation as she had been on his first visit. He had used the press of business as an excuse to return to Philadelphia and see if time and distance altered his feelings for her. The delay only confirmed the intensity, the insistence of his desire. Within a month, when spring sunshine melted the ice on the Delaware, he would say good-bye to this floundering rebellion—and his sullen New Jersey wife—forever.

At the dinner table the talk had turned to the British invasion of the Southern states. Several congressmen condemned the Southerners, particularly the South Carolinians. They had failed to support Georgia the previous year, when the British overran it. Now Charleston was under siege and the response of most of the Carolinians seemed equally apathetic. "Not one in twenty of their militiamen have turned out," Robert Livingston said. "I heard confidentially from the President of Congress that Governor Rutledge wrote demanding to know what aid South Carolina can expect from her sister states. Unless he got an immediate answer, he said, he was prepared to negotiate a separate peace."

"Can you blame him?" bellowed Chase. "Has South Carolina seen any evidence that the rest of the country gives a damn for her? I sympathize with Rutledge. In fact, if a member of the British ministry entered this room at this moment, I wouldn't hesitate to treat with him on Maryland's behalf, let Congress fulminate how they please over it."

Some congressmen at the table were shocked by Chase's boast. Since 1776, when the British almost forced New Jersey to drop out of the war, the idea of any of the supposedly United States signing a separate peace had been anathema. But Livingston, whose family had been one of the rulers of New York before the revolution, was unruffled. "I'd negotiate for New York, Chase, and outbribe you ten to one."

The waiter came and went with fresh bottles of claret and Madeira. The congressmen were all a bit drunk by the time dinner was served. A goose, a turkey, a ham, and several succulent meat pies were among the main dishes. French Burgundy went down in literally staggering quantities. "Tell us what you found at Morristown, Mr. Stapleton," Robert Livingston said.

"The total opposite of this plenty," Stapleton said, gesturing to their feast. "General Greene told me the commissary had only enough flour to bake a single day's supply of bread. There wasn't a piece of fresh meat in the entire camp—"

"Good God, you sound like Schuyler," Samuel Chase said. "A little hardship has never done soldiers any harm. It toughens 'em for battle." He began needling Robert Livingston for his frequent meetings with Peggy Shippen Arnold, wife of Major General Benedict Arnold.

"Aren't you worried about the danger of retaliation?" Chase asked. "I hear Arnold is a dead shot. But I suppose she's worth the risk."

"You're an incorrigible rumormonger, Chase," Livingston replied. "The lady has consulted me on matters purely political."

"Ho," roared the Marylander. "And what are you consulting her on? I'll wager it's a mattress."

Before her recent marriage to General Arnold, the blond, moody Miss Shippen had flirted with Congressman Stapleton at several dinner parties. Now, comparing her in his mind to Flora Kuyper, he infinitely preferred Flora's dark beauty to Peggy's pale good looks. Peggy was too familiar, too American. In the play of somber light between Flora's black hair and her green eyes, in her European sophistication, there was the promise of more than pleasure. She was a woman who could enrich a man's soul. She was a world that a man could explore and enjoy for a lifetime.

After dinner Hugh Stapleton excused himself from the inevitable round of toasts and hired a small sleigh and driver from the City Tavern's stable. He directed the driver to a house in narrow Strawberry Alley and advised him to seek shelter in a nearby tavern until he called him. A knock on the door produced a wary request for his identity. As soon as he said, "Hugh Stapleton," the door was opened by a husky, middle-aged man with a bad limp. "How be you, Congressman?" said Captain William McPherson with a broad smile.

"I'm fine, Mac. How's the leg?"

"Not so good as new. But it'll hold me on a quarterdeck," McPherson said.

On his last voyage aboard Hugh Stapleton's privateer *Common Sense*, McPherson's right leg had been shattered in a running fight with a British cruiser. Ignoring his wound, he had beaten off the enemy and outsailed him to safety. There were few tougher, shrewder ship captains in America than this Belfast-born Scotsman. The congressman had paid his doctor's bills and living expenses during his convalescence. Although he had made a hundred thousand dollars on privateering during the past year, McPherson was broke. As fast as he made money, he threw it away on faro and girls.

"Hey, Sal," the captain shouted, "fetch me the port and two glasses." He winked at the congressman. "Wait'll you see this one."

A high-bosomed redhead swept into the room with the port and glasses. She wore a fashionable French gown without stays or petticoats, and it revealed her figure to a startling degree. She patted her hair and smiled as McPherson introduced the congressman. "She can't cook worth a damn," McPherson said. "We eat all our meals at the Pewter Platter. But she does everything else well enough, right, Sal?"

"Sure I don't know what you mean, Captain."

She flounced out of the room. "Scotch-Irish from

Reading, out in the back country. Father kicked her out of the house and she turned up in Philadelphia, naturally. Reminds me of Polly, the redhead I had in New York in '74. You remember that one?"

"Yes, of course," Hugh Stapleton said. For a few seconds he was uneasy. Was he about to wander the world like McPherson, picking up his women wherever wind or weather beached him? No. Flora Kuyper was not a casual flirtation.

"What's on your mind, Congressman?" McPherson asked, pouring the port.

"I want you to hire a crew for *Common Sense*. Not too many Americans. French, preferably. Hire them now, and have the ship ready to sail the moment the ice breaks."

"Why the hurry, Congressman?"

"I'm planning to resign my seat and go to Amsterdam on private business. You know what some people in this town are liable to say about that. They wouldn't be above giving the British word of our sailing, and we'd find a squadron waiting for us at the capes of the Delaware."

"What do we do when we sound Amsterdam?"

"I'll get you a commission from the French government or from Benjamin Franklin, our ambassador in Paris. You can make a million on British shipping in the North Sea."

"Sounds good to me, Congressman. Will Mrs. Stapleton and the boys be sailing with you?"

"No!"

The mention of his sons flustered Hugh Stapleton. He had tried to convince himself that he was not abandoning them, that he would bring them to Holland as soon as the war ended. But his plans for them were vague at best.

"There may be other passengers. What do you care?" he growled.

"I don't," McPherson said. "It's your ship—and your money, Congressman."

"If all goes well, you'll be able to buy her from me, Mac."

"Is that a promise, Congressman? You'll give me first crack and a good price? Sometimes I think it's what I've always needed—a ship of my own. It might make me think twice about throwing cash on a faro table. No true sailor would bet a ship like *Common Sense*. For the chance to own her, I'd run the British channel fleet in line of battle formation."

"I'm depending on you to do that if necessary, Mac."

"Planning to stay in Amsterdam awhile?"

"It's hard to say. A lot depends on the war."

"Amsterdam will be a healthy place for a Continental Congressman to be when the rebels go smash." The captain gave him a knowing grin. "Don't worry, the secret's safe with me. I've never lost money on a voyage with you yet. And money's the name of the game, ain't it?"

"Money is—important," Hugh Stapleton conceded.

McPherson held out his hand. "I'll let you know how the recruitin' goes."

Hugh Stapleton found his driver and rode back to the City Tavern through the frigid, deserted streets of Philadelphia. It was ridiculous, but those last casual words of Captain McPherson rankled him. *Money's the name of the game.*

Everyone, particularly his wife and his brother,

Paul, assumed that Hugh Stapleton cared about nothing but "improving some moneys." He was about to prove that he, too, had visions, that he was ready to take risks in his private pursuit of happiness and beauty. Mercenary Hugh Stapleton would show them all what he could do with his money. He would even show his mother, with her endless preachments on prudence, and his father, who had seldom concealed his opinion that most businessmen lacked courage. Amazing how many wars a man fights in his own mind with ghosts of the dead, phantoms of the living.

Back in his room at the City Tavern, the congressman wrote Flora a letter.

My dearest:

I was not in this city three hours when I set about the business of preparing my privateer *Common Sense* for our voyage. The winter weather makes our plan only a future promise. But it is as sealed by your kisses as the most solemn oath. My only worry is whether I shall be able to make you as happy as I know you will make me. I almost tremble at your discovering the full power of your enchantment and wonder whether I am quitting a war with one tyrant to put myself under the power of another one. But your tyranny will be tempered by a natural goodness of heart. Send me by return post an explicit agreement to my plan. Without it I will find the petty politics of this place unendurable.

Your devoted
HUGH S.

A knock on the door. One of the City Tavern's porters with a note. General Schuyler was hoping he could see Mr. Stapleton for a few minutes. The congressman ordered a bottle of Madeira and said he would be happy to see the general. The wine and Schuyler's bulky figure arrived simultaneously. The general was wearing a blue coat and buff breeches, a distinct echo of a Continental Army uniform. It was an impolitic costume to wear in a Congress that was extremely touchy about its independence of the military.

"I need your help," Schuyler said as Stapleton poured the Madeira. "I can make no impression on Congress. They dismiss me as a special pleader, a soldier. The Yankees ridicule and revile me behind my back."

"I don't see what I can do when someone of your reputation can't gain a hearing," Hugh Stapleton said.

"You've been to Morristown—and, unlike me, you have no connection with the army," Schuyler said. "I gather that you've said little in Congress."

"I'm not an orator—or a politician, for that matter," Hugh Stapleton said.

"All the more reason why they may listen to you. If I bring up the question, will you speak tomorrow on the state of the army?"

"I—I've made no notes. One visit to Morristown hardly makes me an expert—"

"I'll give you all the information you need. Colonel Hamilton—who I begin to think may soon be my son-in-law—tells me you have a reputation as a man of business. Put it to them as a business proposition. Tell them that the army is going bankrupt, literally and spiritually."

Somewhat to his own amazement, Hugh Stapleton heard himself saying, "If you think Congress can endure my ineptitude as a speaker, I'm at your service, General."

Why not? he thought as Schuyler thanked him. George Washington deserved respect, even pity, for the stoic steadiness with which he was confronting almost certain defeat. A soldier's son—Hugh Stapleton could not deny that part of his heritage—owed the weary Virginian at least a farewell gesture of support, of personal appreciation, no matter how futile it was certain to be.

The next morning, Congressman Stapleton breakfasted on buckwheat cakes and coffee in the Long Room of the City Tavern and trudged through the snow to the Pennsylvania State House, three blocks away. He had spent much of the night going over facts and figures on the army that Schuyler had given him. In the ground-floor chamber of the familiar red-brick building, the delegates were gathering for the day's session. The twin fireplaces along the east wall combated the relentless cold. Stapleton sat down beside the other two members of his state's delegation, tall, long-nosed John Witherspoon, the president of the College of New Jersey, and stumpy Abraham Clark, the self-styled "people's lawyer." Stapleton had never seen a smile on either face.

"Ah, Stapleton," Clark said, "I trust you communicated to the Great Man our disapproval of his looting and brawling soldiery."

Washington's enemies frequently referred to him as the Great Man. The epithet made it difficult for Hugh Stapleton to conceal his dislike of Clark. "I had dinner with the general. We discussed the matter at length. I made him aware of our concern."

"Concerrn," Witherspoon said in his thick Scots

burr. "Oootrage would have been a better worrrd. I still think we should have put our sentiments in a formal resolution of condemnation rather than send a mere emissarry."

Clark and Witherspoon regularly joined the New Englanders in their attempts to embarrass and humiliate Washington. The Southern congressmen, with the aid of New York and Pennsylvania, managed to block most of these petty moves. Hugh Stapleton always voted with the Southerners but Witherspoon and Clark invariably put New Jersey in the Yankee column. How delightful it will be, Hugh Stapleton thought, to wake up in Amsterdam with Flora Kuyper beside me and mentally thumb my nose at these two sour Presbyterians.

The president of Congress, lean, tight-lipped Samuel Huntington, a Connecticut Yankee best known for his parsimony, sat down behind the small table that served as his desk, his back to the twin fireplaces. With a rap of his gavel, Huntington called the Congress to order. Members who had been hobnobbing with friends hurried to their seats. Philip Schuyler asked for the floor and was recognized by the president. Schuyler said he had received another letter from his "good friend," General Washington, about the state of the army. It had alarmed him a great deal and he had planned to give a speech to the honorable members about it. But another honorable member had recently visited the army's winter camp at the request of Congress and had now returned. He therefore yielded the floor to Congressman Stapleton of New Jersey.

Hugh Stapleton rose and looked around the room. Gray winter light from the long windows on two sides of the room gave almost every face a melancholy cast. Most of his fellow congressmen were obviously as tired of this endless war as he was. There were numerous yawns, even though it was only 10 A.M. Many of the members had been at work since 7 A.M. on committees that met before Congress went into session. At least a dozen delegates sniffled and coughed, fighting colds. One man had a gouty foot wrapped in wool.

Stapleton began by reminding them that he had been sent to Morristown to investigate the charge that the army was abusing and robbing civilians near the camp. He acquitted Washington's men of deliberate wholesale looting. Describing the army's desperation after the four day blizzard, he somberly declared that the situation was only a little less desperate now. Carefully, methodically, he translated the pay of each rank in the army from its paper value to its real value. By his calculation, a captain was getting paid seven and a half real dollars a month; an enlisted man received less than a dollar. Stapleton described the bankrupt commissary department, without a cent to buy food from nearby New Jersey farms. Next he described the army's "spiritual bankruptcy." He enumerated the desertion rate, the brawls between soldiers from different states.

"A private was stabbed to death with a bayonet, not a hundred yards from General Washington's headquarters, the night I visited him," he said. "Can you blame the men? Unable to vent their rage on the enemy, they're wounding and murdering each other. Can anyone doubt that the contagion of discontent will soon unleash a like violence on the officers—yes, even on General Washington himself? And the next

315

target, gentlemen, will be the members of this body, whom the army sees as the authors of so many of its woes. Nothing poisons a man's mind more than resentment; nothing will demolish the principles on which we have tried to build a government more quickly, more totally, than neglect of the men who are commissioned by the civil officers to defend it. You have a commander in chief who has demonstrated the patience of Job. But the rest of the army are not such extraordinary mortals. Something must be done, and done immediately, to show the army we are still with them in this cause, heart and soul."

It was, members told Stapleton later, the best speech made in Congress in a year. A delighted Philip Schuyler sprang to his feet and said that the chief reason for the breach between the army and Congress was lack of knowledge. There was only one way to remedy it. A committee should immediately be formed to work with General Washington in Morristown on a permanent basis. One of its members should always be in residence, and the others would report back to Congress at regular intervals.

The motion was ferociously opposed by Abraham Clark of New Jersey. It would give the army dangerous delusions of its power and influence if Congress waited upon them like humble servants. If the army wanted anything, let them come to Congress, not vice versa, he shouted. Roger Sherman of Connecticut agreed in his creaky, anxious voice. Other New Englanders sounded the same note of alarm at the danger of encouraging the military. Southerners, notably young James Madison of Virginia and Thomas Burke of South Carolina, supported Schuyler's motion. Were the honorable gentlemen from New England afraid they might be put upon the committee? Burke inquired in his rough Irish way. Were they more worried about forsaking the comforts of Philadelphia than about the dangers of military dictatorship? Samuel Chase of Maryland arose to declare he was ready to go to Morristown and live in a tent if necessary, a lie so outrageous that most New Englanders were temporarily speechless. Samuel Adams of Massachusetts, the leader of the Yankee phalanx (known as Judas Iscariot by those from rival sections), rose to put the Bay State behind the idea. The motion to send a committee was put to a vote and carried, seven states to five, with Rhode Island abstaining.

Who would serve on the committee? Philip Schuyler volunteered his services. The New Englanders pushed forward one of their most dependable yes-men, Nathaniel Peabody of New Hampshire. A third member inevitably came from the South—pugnacious John Mathews of South Carolina. Schuyler rose again to note that the duty in Morristown would be severe and the committee should have at least one more member, lest illness hamper its effectiveness. There was in his opinion only one possible choice for the additional member: Mr. Stapleton of New Jersey.

The motion passed unanimously. Hugh Stapleton sat stunned in his seat. He had too many other things on his mind to get involved with George Washington's problems. He had intended no more than this single gesture to appease his conscience. On the other hand, there was one consolation. Morristown was much closer to Flora Kuyper than Philadelphia. Perhaps his goddess of spring would make a winter of politics endurable. Perhaps when he sailed away he could leave behind him an American army that would survive another year or two of war and force the British to quit in disgust. Perhaps he could be both a patriot and a scoundrel.

eighteen

Outside the red-brick British headquarters at One Broadway, New York traffic was in its usual tangle. Drivers of sleighs and army wagons cursed one another and any pedestrian foolish enough to risk crossing the street. Inside British headquarters, there was almost as much turmoil. Lieutenant Colonel John Graves Simcoe's face was scarlet. His fist descended on Major Walter Beckford's desk like the gavel of a hanging judge. "Outrageous," Simcoe roared. "The plan's been on your desk for two weeks. And you say General Knyphausen hasn't seen it?"

Simcoe was talking about his plan to attack the American outpost at White Plains—the dress rehearsal for the strike at Morristown that General Knyphausen had demanded. The search for another courier to restore communications with Twenty-six had forced

Beckford to delay submitting the plan to the commander in chief. He knew that he had to have his own operation in a state of total readiness if he were going to participate as an equal in the foray to Morristown. Simcoe and his Queen's Rangers were more than capable of executing a brilliant sortie against White Plains that would win Knyphausen's soldierly admiration. He might decide to let Simcoe proceed to Morristown without the dubious assistance of agent Twenty-six and his men. The German's opinion of intelligence work was not much higher than Simcoe's.

"You seem to have lost sight of the reason you were assigned to General Knyphausen—to provide liaison with the British army. You act as if you're getting paid by the Landgrave of Hesse," Simcoe bellowed.

Beckford displayed just enough indignation to repel this accusation. "I assure you, Colonel, all my efforts since I accepted this thankless post have been directed toward serving both armies effectively."

"I'd like to see some proof that your efforts are *succeeding*, Major," Simcoe said.

The lieutenant colonel stamped out of the office. Several agents had reported that Simcoe was abusing Beckford in taverns and at dinner parties all over the city. It was becoming very clear that the commander of the Queen's Rangers would never share the credit for inviting James to New York. The coup of capturing George Washington would belong to him and his loyalist warriors exclusively. If Walter Beckford were assigned even a minor part in the drama, it would be the role of obstructive paper

shuffler, the stupid spokesman of the German dunderhead Knyphausen.

That afternoon, after dinner, Beckford climbed
into his sleigh and maneuvered through Broadway's
traffic to the outskirts of the city. There, in a battered-
looking farmhouse on the Bloomingdale Road, lived
Brigadier Samuel Birch, commander of the British
cavalry. Birch's batman directed Beckford to the barn,
where the brigadier and an aide were dueling on
wooden horses. Beckford stood in the doorway,
watching the fearsome sabers whoosh and clang for
several minutes, letting Birch ignore him. Brigadier
Birch did not welcome visitors from headquarters.
They usually meant trouble.

Like too many other members of the British high
command, the stocky, short-tempered cavalryman had
come to America to get rich, and was working hard at
it. In his files Beckford had a dozen complaints from
outraged loyalist farmers on Long Island who claimed
Birch had confiscated tons of hay and grain for his
horses, then forged receipts and pocketed the cash
he should have paid for them.

Another Birch maneuver was the great sheep roundup of 1779. The brigadier had had his dragoons herd
over two thousand sheep to Hempstead Plain, where
the troopers cut off their ears. Birch then summoned
local farmers to claim their animals. Not a man could
do so because the sheep, which were allowed to
forage on common land, had had the owners' brands
on their ears. Birch declared all the fleecy vagrants
His Majesty's property and sold them for five thousand pounds.

The brigadier finally quit his saber-clanging and
dismounted, eyeing Beckford in a most unfriendly

way. "Well, Major," he growled, "what's the bloody problem this time?"

"Nothing whatsoever, Brigadier," Beckford said. "On the contrary, I thought you'd be pleased to hear that those troublesome sheep owners in Hempstead have been told to bite their thumbs. My investigation supports your charge that they're all secret rebel sympathizers."

"Damn me if they aren't," Birch said, barely concealing his amazement at his luck in accidentally selecting genuine rebels to be gulled. "I can smell treason in these Americans by just looking'm in the eye."

"We could use your expertise in intelligence, General," Beckford said. "But I'm here to seek your advice on a cavalry matter. A question that requires professional judgment. It's also highly confidential."

"Quimby, go find that punk you were fucking last night," Birch said to his aide, who was still on his wooden horse. "On your way, tell my batman we want two tankards of flip. Do you like that bloody American drink, Beckford? It'll blow your head off if you're not careful."

The barn was unheated, and Beckford was beginning to shiver from the cold. Birch jammed a scarecrow's stuffed head on a pole, positioned it in front of his wooden horse, and remounted. He swung his saber and took off the right side of the scarecrow's face. "Now, what was this professional, confidential matter, Major?"

"A certain American commander has situated himself dangerously far from his army. Would the cavalry be willing to risk a winter raid to seize his person?"

"If the cavalry is given a direct order, it will obey it."

Whirsk went the other side of the scarecrow's face.

"More to the point, could it be done? Can your horses cover eighty miles of snow-covered roads in one night? Or would it be necessary to have a change of horses, at least for some of the party, those immediately guarding the prisoner?"

Chunk—what was left of the scarecrow's head was split down the middle by Birch's saber.

"A change of horses would be most advisable. Our mounts have been on short rations and this barbarous cold has done nothing for their health. But what makes you think this idea can succeed? That certain general may be dangerously far from his army. But he surely has his personal guard about him. Three or four hundred picked troops?"

"More like two hundred. What if there were a way to guarantee complete surprise? Not a shot fired until you were within a hundred yards of his headquarters."

"That would be another matter entirely. We could cut the guard to pieces as they came out of their huts. It would be all over with a single charge. But can it be done?"

"We have men in Morristown who can arrange it. You must realize, Brigadier, that the stroke, if successful, would virtually end the war. The man who executed it would merit His Majesty's gratitude as would no other soldier in the army."

"Damn me if I don't," Birch said, climbing down from his wooden horse. "I'm not stupid, Major. You want someone in on this who can keep his jaw shut tight and stand ready to pull off the trick when General Knyphausen gives the signal."

"Precisely."

The batman arrived with two tankards of flip. Beckford's stomach almost rebelled. On several trips through New England to set up intelligence networks he had had to drink gallons of the stuff, made of raw rum and egg yolks stirred with rusty pokers. But at least it was hot. He raised his tankard. "To the cavalry," he said.

"The only branch of His Majesty's forces in America that has a record of unblemished victory," Birch said. "That's why you're here, isn't it, Major? You want someone you can depend on. Well, you've got him. You've got him here with Birch and the Sixteenth Dragoons. What about guides? In this bloody weather one road looks like another. You've got to give me good guides."

"They'll be the best. Men who know New Jersey as well as you and your troopers know the Holy Ground."

"By God, the buggers must be bloody mapmaking geniuses in that case," roared the brigadier.

Back at his office at One Broadway, Walter Beckford found Paul Stapleton waiting for him, his palette and case of brushes and oils at his feet. Paul was dressed in his usual high style, his blond hair craped and rolled. For a moment Beckford felt a demoralizing flush of desire. He paused long enough for it to subside. Dealing coolly, even coldly, with Paul Stapleton was necessary to prove to himself—and to others— that Walter Beckford was a new, serious man.

Paul was the reason Walter Beckford had come to America. They had become lovers in London, brought together by mutual detestation of martial fathers, mutual flight from oppressive mothers, mutual passion for art. Through his mother's relations, Beckford had arranged for Paul to meet Gainsborough, Reynolds, and other English painters. Armed with letters of introduction from Beckford's father, the lovers had toured the Continent together, visiting aristocrats with notable art collections. When Paul returned to America, Beckford had outraged his father by resigning his commission in the Queen's Guards and buying a lieutenancy in the nondescript 10th Regiment, which was stationed in New York.

The war—and Edward Gibbon's history of Rome— had changed everything. Ambition—his vision of ruling humbled Americans, of possessing a proconsul's power over this immense continent—had forced Beckford to see that his infatuation would be fatal to his career. Sodomy was not popular in the officer corps of the British army. A general's son might be immune from prosecution, but the habit exposed him to insults and character assassination. So Beckford, not without a wrench, had ended his affair with Paul Stapleton.

For a while he had frequented the houses in the Holy Ground to publicize his change of allegiance. Now he was in the process of acquiring an American fiancée—a logical step for a would-be proconsul.

"You're late, Becky dear," Paul said.

"I've told you not to call me that, even in private," Beckford snapped.

"Sorry," Paul said. "It's hard to break old habits."

"Not if one has the will, the determination. Let's go. The general can be impatient."

They rode up Broadway past acres of charred and

325

crumbling ruins. The Americans had burned the west side of New York City in 1776. Trinity Church was a gutted hulk. On the corner of Barclay Street, a crowd had gathered. A woman and a tattered boy with rags for shoes were wailing over the body of a man in the snow. "Another refugee frozen to death?" Paul asked.

"No doubt. Ten or twelve have been dying every night lately."

"Why don't you stop them from living in the cellars of those burned-out buildings or give them some fuel?"

"The British army isn't a poor-relief society. We didn't ask them to flee to our protection. Do you think you'll finish Knyphausen's portrait today?"

"Probably. Why? Do you have another commission?"

"Yes."

"Someone with ready money, I hope. I'm tired of taking promissory notes."

"The general will pay promptly. I'll see to it," Beckford said. "So will your next subject."

"Who is he?"

"You're sitting beside him."

"A miniature for your lady love, Miss Fowler?"

"By no means. A formal portrait."

"What's the occasion? Most of my subjects want to commemorate a martial feat. I don't think you have one to your credit."

"I'll have one by the time you finish the portrait. It will be substantial enough to win a display at the Royal Society if you take the job seriously enough to do your best work."

"You're inspiring me."

They were crossing Harlem Heights. To the west,

beneath its foot-thick gray armor of ice, the Hudson sluiced from the heart of the continent. The reddish-gray Palisades, splotched with patches of snow, loomed above the silent river.

"Look at that view," Beckford said. "There's nothing in England to compare to it."

"I prefer a summer landscape, myself," Paul said.

"You Americans lack a sense of grandeur," Beckford said. "Vision."

In a few minutes they reached the white-columned Morris mansion. The black-uniformed Hessian sentry ran down the steps to lead their horses to the barn. In the house, General von Knyphausen greeted them and declared himself pleased with his portrait, even in its semi-finished state. Beckford quickly translated this good news for Paul. It was encouraging to see the general in such a jovial humor. Knyphausen sat his aide behind his desk and assumed the sitter's pose in front of the parlor window. While Paul painted, Beckford plowed briskly through the usual business—courts-martial and European correspondence, commissary and police reports. New York was under martial law, which meant the commander in chief was responsible for its internal order as well as for its defense.

Beckford stuffed the routine papers into his portfolio and with a small flourish produced another document. "You've asked me several times about Colonel Simcoe's projected attack on White Plains," he said in German. "I've finally extracted a plan from him."

"Read it to me," Knyphausen said, staring uncomprehendingly at Simcoe's beautifully inscribed sentences. The colonel had had his plan copied by a professional clerk; it must have cost him several pounds.

"I don't think it's necessary, General. It's a rather impertinent document. After outlining his plan, for which he says he will need a regiment in support, Colonel Simcoe argues most aggressively that the attack is unnecessary. He says he's consulted one of the English generals—he declines to name him—and the officer agrees. He ends by implying that if you don't give him permission to strike at Morristown immediately, he'll rely on the English general's approval."

Knyphausen's pale eyebrows rose. "You mean launch an unauthorized attack?"

For a moment Beckford savored the German word for unauthorized: *unbefugt*. It had an explosion of outrage in it.

"Not only would it be insulting to you—it would demoralize and endanger the men I've placed in the American camp—with your encouragement and advice."

"Of course." Actually, Knyphausen had allowed Beckford to develop his intelligence network entirely on his own. But he was complacently willing to accept the credit for it.

"We're close to accomplishing a feat that could end the war, General. I don't want to see you deprived of your just share of the honors you so richly deserve," Beckford continued.

"I think you had better arrange to watch Simcoe and his friends a bit more closely," Knyphausen said. Then he nibbled at the bait Beckford was dangling in front of him. "Is there some way we could make the attempt without this fellow Simcoe?"

"We could use cavalry," Beckford said.

"Why don't you talk to Brigadier Birch about it?" Knyphausen said.

"An excellent idea, General."

Eine ausgezeichnete Idee, mein General. The German words echoed triumphantly around the high-ceilinged room.

Paul Stapleton looked up from his palette and paints. "I marvel at your skill with that dreadful language," he said. "What were you talking about just now?"

For a moment suspicion coiled in Walter Beckford's mind. He dismissed it. Where could Paul have learned German? "We were discussing your work. The general likes it so much he's commissioned you to do that portrait of me."

"Lovely," Paul said.

nineteen

Flickering lanterns threw shadowy light across the hospital's crowded floor. The sick men tossed on their straw mattresses; several called feebly for water. A fat orderly dozed on a chair tipped against the wall. Major Benjamin Stallworth kicked the chair out from under him. He crashed to the floor, arms and legs flailing like some species of stupid bug. "Get off your ass and give these men a drink," Stallworth said.

While the orderly scrambled to obey his order, Stallworth took one of the lanterns and stepped through a rear door into a room permeated by a cold dramatically different from the wind-whipped winter outside the hospital. This cold was silent, still. Around him were tiers of raw pine coffins. The hospital's dead waited here to be buried in a common grave as soon as the ground thawed.

Stallworth sat down on a coffin. He cocked his pistol, blew out the lantern, and waited in the frigid darkness. In spite of the cold his eyes began to droop. He pressed the icy gun barrel against his forehead. Using one of the letters Caesar Muzzey had passed, Stallworth had spent the last forty-eight hours trying to break Walter Beckford's code—without success. Two days ago he had received a message from the network assigned to watch Major Beckford's safe house on Bowrie Lane. The Reverend Caleb Chandler, looking somewhat the worse for wear after spending a week on the prison ship *Jersey*, had been seen entering the house with Beckford.

By now Chandler was back in Morristown, supposedly returned from a visit to his sick father in Lebanon, Connecticut. A message had already been left at his quarters that one of the soldiers in his brigade was ill. He would come to the hospital like a dutiful chaplain, pray beside the soldier, and then meet Stallworth here in the burial shed. If anyone from Twenty-six's network was watching him, they would conclude only that Chandler was making good use of his chaplain's cover.

Fifteen minutes later, the mortuary door opened, then swiftly closed. "I have a gun aimed at your middle," Stallworth said. "What's the password?"

"Mercury," Caleb Chandler said.

Three clicks of Stallworth's flint and the lantern glowed. He motioned and Caleb sat down on another coffin, clutching his cloak around him. He looked haggard, ill. His eyes were as blank as nailheads. For a moment Stallworth felt sorry for him. He suppressed the emotion. The would-be prophet was getting just what he deserved. "Did you stop to comfort a few of the sick?" Stallworth said.

"Yes. I obeyed your orders, Major, down to the most minute detail."

"They're designed to keep you alive, Chandler. Remember what happened to Caesar Muzzey."

"How well I remember."

"Are you carrying a message?"

"Yes."

He drew a sealed letter from a pocket of his cloak. "Beckford told me to leave this at a drop in the woods within twenty-four hours of my arrival here or I would be a dead man."

"You'll leave it, tomorrow morning," Stallworth said, taking the letter. "We'll copy it tonight and reseal it. Thanks to Muzzey, we've got a perfect duplicate of the seal they use."

"You'll follow me into the woods and arrest the man who collects it?"

"Don't be ridiculous. He's only a courier, like you. Arresting him would drive the big game to cover. We'll let him deliver it, on schedule."

"And use the information to arrest the whole network?"

"Hardly. We haven't been able to break their code."

Chandler sprang up, trembling. "Then what's the point of all this? I've gone through hell for nothing."

"It's not your job to think about the point of it all, Chandler. And you aren't out of hell yet. What about Mrs. Kuyper? Have you mounted her ramparts?"

"I—I refuse to talk of her that way. I respect—and pity her. She's politically innocent. In fact—innocent in almost every way. She—she has an excellent heart."

"An excellent cunt is more like it. Grow up, Chandler."

"I've grown up considerably. Enough to tell you I'll quit this business right now unless you agree to protect that woman. Beckford will destroy her unless—"

"Who else is she pleasuring that has you so upset—Congressman Stapleton?"

"Yes. He plans to quit the country and take her with him to Holland."

"Oh? Now, that kind of news would earn you a commendation if we could give one to a spy. Well done, Chandler."

"Well done?" Chandler said. "Well done? I tell you that a beautiful woman is being forced to give herself to a man she despises, that one of our congressmen has compromised himself with the enemy and is ready to desert our cause—"

"Think of it as a battle, Chandler," Stallworth said. "Every item we learn is like a well-aimed bullet that brings down one of their men. Already you're advancing in wisdom and age and grace with me, Chandler."

"Delightful news, Major. I wish I could say the same for you."

"Your opinion is a matter of utter indifference to me."

"Good. I won't hesitate to express it."

For a moment Stallworth wanted to smash his fist into Caleb Chandler's face, beat the last shreds of idealism out of this young fool. "Judge not, lest you be judged, Chandler," he said.

"Sometimes, Major, you're almost amusing."

"What else did Mrs. Kuyper tell you?"

"She told me the story of her life—which I'm sure

334

is of no interest to you. It's a sad story, Major. It stirs pity in the normal heart. You'd probably find it boring."

"Tell it to me."

"The whole thing? It could take half the night."

"I want to hear every word you can remember."

Chandler told the story in a voice that grew more and more leaden. Flora Kuyper's life was sad. It would stir a normal heart to pity. But Stallworth ordered himself to listen with his head, not his heart. As the chronicle of deception and degradation wound to its close Stallworth heard another voice in his mind. It belonged to George Washington. He was sitting in his office wearily musing: *Whoever killed Caesar Muzzey wanted us—or someone else—to know about it. Even to implicate us in the crime.* Stallworth heard himself saying, *I can't imagine who that someone else might be.*

That someone else, he saw now, had to be Flora Kuyper.

"Chandler," Stallworth said as the chaplain finished the story, "you're a good spy in spite of yourself. You've just explained Caesar Muzzey's murder. Twenty-six killed him, to prevent him from debouching to New Orleans with Mrs. Kuyper. He took the risk of killing Caesar more or less in front of our eyes to guarantee her hatred of Americans and her dependence on him and Beckford."

"How did Twenty-six find out about Caesar's plans? He wouldn't be stupid enough to tell him."

"Muzzey never got any closer to discovering Twenty-six's identity than we have. But standing at the bar at Red Peggy's or talking in his hut in Jockey Hollow,

335

he may have been face to face with him without realizing it."

"What can we do about all this?"

"You can do a great deal, Chandler. You can—in fact, you must—convince Mrs. Kuyper that Twenty-six is Caesar Muzzey's murderer and persuade her to come to Morristown to expose him."

"Do you believe women have souls, Stallworth?"

"I only believe in this war. When it's over I'll sort out what else I believe. I advise you to do the same."

"I love this woman. Do you understand what that means?"

"She's a whore, Chandler. You're telling me a man with a Yale education, a minister of the church, is in love with a whore?"

"I knew the idea would be beyond you. Loving anything or anyone is beyond you."

"You son of a bitch!" Stallworth grabbed Caleb Chandler by the throat and hoisted him off his feet. "I love this country! I love the men who died for it! I'm not going to let those deaths go to waste even if Congress and most of the supposedly virtuous American people have lost interest in winning this war. We're going to win it, Chandler. If that means the loss of Mrs. Kuyper's soul or your own precious soul, I don't care. Do you understand me, Chandler? I don't care."

Caleb Chandler was gasping and gurgling like a fish with a hook in his throat. Stallworth realized he was close to asphyxiating his most valuable spy. He flung him into the darkness beyond the lantern's light. "Get out of here," he said. "You desecrate this place."

"I'll—talk to Mrs. Kuyper," Chandler gasped. "I'll do what I can."

He was gone. Stallworth sat alone with the dead. Was that how he was going to spend the rest of his life? he wondered. He was appalled by what he had just done. He rode numbly back to headquarters, where he found George Washington at his desk, writing the usual midnight letters. "Your Excellency," he said, "I want to be relieved."

"For God's sake, Stallworth, why?"

"My nerves are gone, General. I can't handle the strain of this work."

"Stallworth, I'd sooner lose this," Washington said, holding up his right hand. "What's happened?"

Stallworth described his assault on Caleb Chandler. Washington shook his head. "Flint against flint. When two Yankees disagree, there's bound to be sparks."

"It's more than that, General. The boy exasperates me in some way that threatens my self-respect, my—my sanity. I can't explain it. What else can it be but my nerves?"

"Perhaps you don't like tampering with souls any more than I do, Major."

"That may be."

"But we have to see the business through now," Washington said. "When it's over, we'll try to repair the damage if it's in our power."

"And if we can't, I'll have to live with it, somehow."

"Both us will, my friend."

Tears welled in Stallworth's throat. He realized how much he had wanted to hear those words. "Your

Excellency," he said, "I've loved only two men in my life. One of them was Nathan Hale. I think you know the other one."

"Get some sleep, Stallworth," Washington said.

— twenty —

Cato's bulk filled the doorway of the Kuyper farm-house. For a moment he seemed to consider blocking Caleb Chandler's entrance. It was easy to imagine this black moralist's disgust with the Reverend Chandler's conduct. Too bad Cato could not imagine the Reverend Chandler's own disgust. Instead they communicated in formal terms.

"Good morning, Cato. I'm here to see your mistress."

"Yes, sir."

"Have you used the Billings songbook I left with you?"

Cato's face brightened slightly. "Yes. It's done wonderful things for the hearts of my people. That man must have written those songs under the inspiration of the Lord."

"Yes," Caleb murmured. "May I come in?"

"Of course, sir. Mrs. Kuyper is in the parlor."

The plangent tones of the harpsichord drifted into the hall, along with Flora's delicate contralto, a sound between a chime and a sigh. She was singing "*Plaire à celui que j'aime.*" Caleb felt a thickness in his throat. He had to struggle for breath. It was almost as if Stallworth were strangling him again. He forced himself to walk briskly into the parlor.

Smiling, Flora turned to greet him. "I was hoping it was you," she said. She was wearing a simple country dress, a soft red, without lace or pleats. Her hair was tied with a matching red ribbon. It made her look girlish. She acted the same way, throwing herself into Caleb's arms for a long, enthusiastic kiss.

"I haven't slept a whole night since you went to New York," she said. "Nelson told me Major Beckford arrested you and put you on one of the prison ships."

"A little test of my nerves and loyalty," Caleb said.

"I almost went to New York—to berate him," she said. "But I decided it might arouse his suspicion."

"Possibly. Anyhow, I survived the major's auto-dafé and his suspicion has turned to trust. He's paying me twenty guineas for a trip to Morristown and back."

"I feared for you at Morristown, too," she said. "You're new at this business of deception."

"I proved myself a talented liar there, too."

Flora caught the pain in his voice. "It troubles you, doesn't it?"

"Sometimes," he said.

"That's been my worst fear," she said, her arms still around him. "I saw your New England conscience getting the better of you, once we parted. I imagined you starting to think: Is she worth the risk of my soul, this Portuguese-Jewish baggage, this amorous quadroon, this mere woman? Has she tricked me into abandoning my country's cause?"

"I begin to think you are my soul," he said.

Was that true? Caleb wondered. It was what Flora wanted to hear. The extravagant words came so naturally to his lips he found it impossible to qualify them in his mind. This woman was so alive, so vulnerable, she blurred the boundary between truth and deception.

"Let's have a late supper," she said. "I'll tell Cato to light the fire in my bedroom."

"I—yes. That sounds lovely."

He dangled between opposing wishes, between desire and conscience. On the road he had vowed to avoid another visit to her bedroom, where the boundary between truth and deception was certain to vanish. He had hoped for a chance to resume the talk they had been having when Major Beckford's emissaries had interrupted them two weeks ago. Caleb was still convinced that he could use her father's death to change Flora's loyalty.

But Flora only wanted to talk about, think about, love. As they drank mulled Madeira, waiting for the bedroom to warm, she dismissed Caleb's halfhearted attempts to discuss the war. She wanted to know if he had thought about her as he shivered aboard the *Jersey*. Had he hated her? Did he think she had betrayed him? Even now, did he feel some resentment? She wanted to analyze their love, learn its precise shape and quality. In spite of his conscience, his opposing wish, Caleb began to experience the transported sensation again. Every smile, every change of mood in Flora's green eyes, took him further away from the winter world of Morristown, where he had so recently sat surrounded by corpses and discussed betrayal with Major Benjamin Stallworth.

Up the stairs they went, arms entwined, tongues exploring, his breath filled with her perfume. They undressed each other before the fire. *Eden*, Caleb thought. She recreates Eden with her freedom from shame, with the pleasure, the joy, she invests in this sacred act. He saw that Flora wanted to consume with her kisses, her breasts, her welcoming thighs, the memory of his ordeal on the *Jersey*. She wanted to restore the purity of the mutual gift, the passionate trust they had exchanged on their first night together.

When it was over, the transported experience was complete. Caleb lay in her arms, trying to think of some way to escape with this woman, to avoid returning to the real world of Stallworth and Beckford, to the guns and bayonets of New York and Morristown.

"We have so little time together," Flora whispered.

"So little? I'm thinking of the rest of our lives," Caleb said.

"John Nelson and Wiert Bogert were here today. They told me to leave the usual signal the moment you arrived. Major Beckford is very anxious to see you."

"What's the usual signal?"

"Two candles in this window."

"Let's ignore them all and think of some way—"

Stallworth's hands seized Caleb's throat. He heard him roaring, *I love this country. I love the men who died for it.*

"There is no way," Flora said. She got up, lit two

candles, and put them in the window that faced the British fort on Powles Hook. "Let's have supper."

Downstairs, distanced by the table, Caleb regained control of his emotions. She was right. There was no way—except the one Stallworth had already chosen for him. He had to persuade Flora to return to Morristown and expose Twenty-six. Caleb waited until Cato had finished serving the modest supper—beef and kidney pies—and they were having coffee. He began talking about the situation in Morristown. The army had run out of meat again. Several regiments had refused to obey their officers. The men had stayed in their huts, chanting, "No meat, no meat." A mutiny seemed more probable every day.

"That's always been part of Walter Beckford's plan," Flora said.

"Congress is sending a special committee to Morristown to see if they can solve some of the army's problems. Your friend Hugh Stapleton is on it."

"He's not my friend."

"I'm being ironic, my darling."

"Why mention him at all?"

"I'm just wondering what Beckford plans to do with him."

Flora was looking confused and hurt. "I have no idea. Perhaps all he wanted was the letter Mr. Stapleton wrote to me about going to Amsterdam. Beckford can use it to blackmail him."

"I hope that's all."

"If I must meet Congressman Stapleton again, I'll do my best to avoid inviting him upstairs. Even if that's necessary, can you believe he could change my feelings for you?"

Caleb writhed. He could hear Stallworth's rasp: *She's a whore*. He found some small consolation in an answer that was the literal truth. "I can't—I won't—tolerate that man—or any other man—in this house, much less in your bed. Sometimes I think you're still under William Coleman's influence."

"Caleb—what's wrong? After we just—"

"I know what we just did. It makes me all the more determined to speak—out of love for you. I wonder why you go on working for William Coleman, knowing that if he succeeds, he may try to claim you as his wife, knowing—you must know it—that he killed Caesar Muzzey."

"William didn't kill Caesar. The Americans did. Walter Beckford told me."

"Beckford wouldn't tell you the truth. Even if he knew it. But I don't think he knows. You must have known, though, or at least suspected in some part of your mind."

Flora grew agitated. She obviously did not want to think about William Coleman as a murderer. "You'll never convince me—unless you give me some proof."

"Did Caesar ever talk of buying a discharge from anyone?"

"Yes. From a woman they call Red Peggy. She keeps a grog shop."

"Do you know what buying a discharge involves?" Flora shook her head.

"Forgery. The certificates themselves are easy to counterfeit. Any printer can run them off. But there must be two signatures on each one—George Washington's and the colonel of the man's regiment."

"Forgery," Flora said.

"William Coleman was convicted of forgery, was he not?"

Flora nodded numbly.

"Caesar knew nothing of your marriage to Coleman."

She nodded again, passive, almost defenseless now. Caleb struggled to control his guilt, his regret for the pain he was inflicting on her.

"Caesar didn't know what Twenty-six looked like. He talked carelessly to him—or to someone in his network—about you. He was proud of having a woman like you. Even if he didn't mention your name, even if he simply said he needed his discharge to get to New Orleans with his beautiful woman—Twenty-six would have known who he was talking about."

Flora's anguish was almost unbearable to watch. But Caleb pressed on to the climax of his prosecution. "When I found Caesar, he whispered two words: 'Forty—Twenty-six.' The second number was unmistakable. Now that I know what it means, I think the first word wasn't 'forty'—it was 'Flora.' Caesar was trying to say, 'Tell Flora Twenty-six killed me.'"

"Stop—please!"

Flora fled from the dining room into the parlor. Caleb found her on the couch, her arms wrapped around her body, rocking back and forth, weeping. "Caesar, Caesar, I let you go, I let you go to your death," she sobbed. "Why didn't you stop me? Father, why didn't you warn me?"

Caleb sat down beside her and took her hands. "Flora," he said, "I think William Coleman deserves to die for what he did to you in London. Now he deserves hanging twice over."

"Hanging?" Flora said.

Caleb saw the word was a mistake. It revived

345

memories of Newgate. But he could not retreat from it now. "Hanging," he said. "Come to Morristown with me. We'll find him and expose him to the rebels. They'll hang him for us."

She shook her head, still half objecting to the word "hang." "I only know he's in Morristown. I have no idea where. No one knows except Major Beckford."

"Can you send him a message, asking him to come here?"

"He'd never come. If you're right about Caesar, he already suspects me."

"Has Coleman given you a way of getting a message to him if you ever need help?"

Flora stopped weeping. She struggled for another moment against some inner resistance. "Yes. He told me to go to Red Peggy's, on the Vealtown Road, with this token."

She went to a sideboard in the dining room and took out a playing card—the Queen of Hearts. Someone had scribbled a beard on the face. There were similar scribblings on other cards in the deck.

Caleb realized that this was Flora's final secret—the one she had withheld even from him. He took her hands again. "My dearest love, you must trust me. I'll be with you. This is your chance to free yourself from an incubus, an evil spirit—"

"No!" Flora cried, pulling herself free. She backed away from him, shaking her head. "I can't do it to him. I couldn't bear the thought that I was directly responsible for his death. Especially a spy's death—hanging. I remember how we waited in Newgate. He told me he loved me."

"What about Caesar's death? Do you think that

was pleasant? A bayonet in the chest. Left to die in the snow."

Caleb could not believe his own voice. It was a lash. It might have belonged to Stallworth.

"That was—war. The Americans offered Caesar a hundred guineas to betray William. I never thought Caesar could find him. I never gave him any help. I even begged him—not to try."

"Will you help me? Will you give me that token? I don't want to find William Coleman for money. I want to do it for your sake—and Caesar's sake."

He took the token from her paralyzed hand. Something in her look—an edge of puzzlement—tempted him to tell her the whole truth. But he had come too far. There was too much at stake. There were too many deaths that had to be justified. It was infinitely better to find Twenty-six, destroy the monster and his mutiny, and then reveal himself.

Someone kicked the front door. Caleb knew who it was even before Cato appeared in the parlor with John Nelson and his huge shadow, Wiert Bogert, behind him. They wore their hooded white greatcoats, making them look like evil spirits out of some ancient saga.

"Good evenin', Reverend," Nelson said. "Major Beckford sends his compliments. He's eager to have you preach him a little sermon on the odor of turncoat sanctity and the like at his church in the Bowrie Lane."

Caleb nodded. "I'm ready."

He put the token in his pocket, his eyes on Flora. Now was the moment when she could stop him. All she had to do was tell these two killers that Caleb Chandler had become the hunter of William Coleman, agent Twenty-six, and he would be dead. But Flora only rang for Cato and told him to fetch Mr. Chandler's greatcoat, boots, and snowshoes. "It was very nice to see you again, Mr. Chandler," she said. "I hope you have a safe, swift journey to New York."

twenty-one

In his darkened study on Jane Street, Walter Beckford finished decoding the message that the Reverend Caleb Chandler has brought him from Morristown.

We can do what you propose, though I don't see its necessity. We have the men in Washington's guard, as I told you in my last message. Beginning midnight, Sunday, and every seventh night thereafter, the watch will consist entirely of our men. I presume from the urgency of your last message that the attempt will be made immediately. We will expect you this Sunday unless we hear to the contrary. I am glad that this body-snatching expedition does not supersede our mutiny. But it worries me. If your scheme fails, it could stifle the mutiny by arousing solicitude for Washington. We have been laboring night and day to break down the men's devotion to him, and in many brigades have partly succeeded. I distrust the new courier Flora recruited. I no longer trust her as an agent, although she remains at the center of my plans for the future. Without her this miserable ordeal could never have been borne. I told you when it began that it was not worthy of a gentleman. Now, with success so near, don't deprive me of my just reward, or you will make me an enemy for life.

William Coleman was as arrogant as ever. In spite of the humiliations that had forced him to assume his present role, he still considered himself the equal of Walter Beckford and every other Englishman of wealth and station—including titled lords. Major Beckford was unbothered by his threat. More to the point was the information that Coleman's men were in place. The moment of decision had arrived.

Pulling on his fur-lined boots, Beckford went out the back door of his house to the barn. There, as he expected, he found Major Henry Whittlesey at work. Since his escape via the Liberty Turnpike six weeks ago, Whittlesey had been toiling in Walter Beckford's barn eighteen hours a day, dismantling and studying a curious machine. Basically it was a barrel of gunpowder. Inside it were a clock and a device that struck a spark when the clock had run a set number of seconds or minutes, detonating the whole thing with lethal effect. In 1777 the Americans had sent a number of these time bombs floating down the Delaware in an attempt to sink the British fleet. This one had failed to explode.

A spy had identified the wizardy thing as essentially the same weapon a Connecticut tinkerer, David Bushnell, had used in conjunction with something even more fiendish, a submarine, to attack the British fleet in New York in 1776. Bad luck had frustrated Bushnell's attack, but his mine had detonated when he released it during his retreat from New York harbor. A British agent in Connecticut had obtained a sketch of the mine from Bushnell's papers. Major Beckford had presented it to Major Whittlesey with instructions to produce a smaller version that could be carried on horseback and detonated where and when its owner chose.

"Are we ready, Major?"

"Virtually, virtually," Whittlesey said. "There are only a few minor defects, but they can be corrected in a day or two, by amputating some parts from a musket and having a blacksmith shape them per my directions."

"Good."

"What do you plan to do with this weapon, Major?"

"I can't tell you that, my dear sir," Beckford replied. "But rest assured, it will, as I promised you, help to end the war."

"Nothing else will recompense me for the rheumatism I've acquired from sleeping in those unheated barns along Liberty Turnpike."

"There will be other rewards, Major, when you return to London."

Back in the house, Beckford studied another decoded message, this one from an agent in Philadelphia.

There is a report abroad that Robert Morris has proposed founding a bank to finance the army's purchases. He is soliciting hard money from other leading merchants. Congress continues to quarrel along the usual lines. The Yankees are accused of preparing to abandon the Southern states and vice versa. Massachusetts has banned the export of food beyond its borders. A special committee has been appointed to go to Morristown and confer with Washington. Its members are Schuyler, Mathews, Peabody, and Stapleton.

That last sentence had made Beckford's pulse leap when he had read it earlier in the day. How convenient of Congress to put Hugh Stapleton within easy reach. Was there need for more proof that Fortuna, the goddess who guided the destiny of nations, was standing beside him, a reassuring hand on his shoulder?

For a moment Beckford remembered standing in the smoky tension of Boodles, watching gamblers like Lord Lyttleton and Charles James Fox risk ten thousand pounds on a single card. That was where he had met Paul Stapleton, the night he lost the last thousand pounds of his inheritance. It was where he had watched William Coleman challenge fate, to his ultimate ruin. Fools, all of them. They misunderstood the value of patience, the steady accumulation of power and money. Another of history's lessons.

Beckford strapped a pistol to his waist. No one went out in New York after dark without a weapon. He strode down Broadway past staggering soldiers and equally drunken civilians. On a side street, a man cried for help in German. The cry was quickly smothered by English curses. Another brawl between soldiers of the supposedly allied armies. Beckford paid no attention to such trivialities. Petty murders were the bailiwick of Major General James Pattison, the commandant of the city's police.

Across Pearl Street the major strode, ignoring numerous invitations from wandering prostitutes. Soon he was on the east side of the city, in a neighborhood of three- and four-story warehouses. He knocked on the side door of one of them. The door opened a wary crack, and a lantern glowed in his face. A relieved voice whispered, "Ah, Major Beckford. Come in."

Beckford stepped into a warm office; a fire crackled in the grate. In one corner a plump blond girl with a plain, pale face labored over a ledger. Another ledger lay open on the table; beside it stood lean, spindle-shanked Abraham Fowler, once the most prosperous merchant in Perth Amboy, New Jersey. He had fled to New York in 1776, a stowaway on one of his own ships. The rebels had driven his family into the British lines a month later. Fowler had run out of money in 1778. Reduced to living in a cellar, he had watched his wife die of exposure and discouragement. His two sons had enlisted in the British army. He was close to suicide when Beckford had made him his secret partner in the business of London trading.

In two years, using secret-service funds for capital, Fowler had sold thousands of dresses and pairs of stockings and gloves to rebel women in East Jersey and Connecticut and New York. He doubled his profits by selling the meat and vegetables their husbands traded to the British army at prices that Beckford, on excellent terms with the commissary general, made sure were doubled and sometimes redoubled. After all, the commissary general was making a hundred thousand pounds a year renting wagons on a per-diem basis to the army—wagons he had bought for a fraction of that price in 1776. If a secret-service director did not know the secrets of his own army, what good was he?

"How are you, my friend?" Beckford said. "And how is my dear girl?"

He bowed to the blond girl, who smiled shyly. Beckford had asked Abraham Fowler for permission to marry his daughter. Fowler had all but thrust her into the major's arms, so eager was he to solidify their partnership. Alice Fowler, wholly submissive to her father, had made no objection. But Beckford preferred to wait until the war was won; then he would decide whether it was advantageous (as he suspected it would be) for a proconsul to have an American wife. In the meantime, Alice was a convenient companion at the numerous dinners to which he was invited in the course of garrison life.

"I hope you're not keeping two sets of books," Beckford said, glancing at the ledger on the table.

"By no means," Fowler said, almost cringing at the suggestion. "Alice is balancing out the old year. This is the account for the current year."

"I trust things still stand in our favor."

"Handsomely. What is the balance for '79, Alice?"

"One hundred and twenty thousand," Alice said.

"Excellent."

In 1778 they had cleared eighty thousand. Allowing twenty-five percent to Fowler, this left Beckford with a hundred and fifty thousand pounds. A good beginning for an independent fortune. In the imperial scheme of things, money was as essential to keep power as power was necessary to get money.

"Has anything of interest arrived from London—something that one of my particular friends in the garrison might like to see first?"

"At your suggestion, Major, we've made a beginning in the jewelry line. Let me show you."

He seized the lantern and led Beckford through an inner door into the well of the warehouse. Boxes and chests were stacked in neat, numbered rows. Fowler was an extremely competent businessman. He led Beckford to the rear of the first row and opened a chest from a ring of keys at his waist. The lantern's glow revealed pearl necklaces, diamond and emerald brooches. Beckford lifted a particularly fine pearl necklace from the pile. "Governor Robertson would love this for one of his young ladies. Send it to him with my compliments."

"Certainly, Major."

Beckford took a pearl brooch, considerably less costly. "Give this to my dear Alice, and debit my account accordingly."

"If there is to be a debit, Major, it will be on my account," Fowler said.

"Out of the question, my dear sir."

"I insist."

"Very well," Beckford said.

Back in the office, Fowler displayed the brooch like a trophy. "Look at this, daughter. Major Beckford wants you to have it."

"Oh, thank you," Alice said. Beckford noticed that her eyes strayed to the pearl necklace; obviously she wondered who was getting that.

"And this," Beckford said, taking the necklace out of Fowler's hand. "I pretended I was going to give it to Governor Robertson because I knew your father would forbid it as too extravagant."

"What can I say?" Fowler murmured as Alice gasped with delight.

355

"Let us hope she can soon wear it at the happy event we all anticipate."

Alice blushed. With the necklace and brooch enhancing her complexion, she looked almost pretty. For once Beckford had no difficulty imagining her as a reasonably satisfying wife.

"We civilians hear a thousand rumors a day, Major. Is it possible that our prayers will soon be answered?"

"Quite possible, Mr. Fowler. Did you see the poem by the Reverend Odell in the *Royal Gazette* the other day?"

Striking an actor's pose, Beckford recited it:

Seen or unseen, on earth, above, below,
All things conspire to give the final blow.
Myriads of swords are ready for the field;
Myriads of lurking daggers are concealed;
In injured bosoms dark revenge is nursed.
Yet but a moment and the storm shall burst.

Well pleased with his performance, Major Beckford said good night to his wide-eyed audience and strolled into the wintry darkness. He strode north, feeling colossal, a giant looking down on the shrouded city, the frozen continent. The cold was incredible. The frigid air seemed almost ready to condense into black sheets of ice. It pressed relentlessly against Beckford's fur-lined greatcoat. He exulted in resisting it.

By the time he reached Brigadier Samuel Birch's quarters on the Bloomingdale Road, it was dawn. Beckford kicked the front door and roared, "To arms, to arms. Dragoons, turn out."

Much thrashing and clattering. The door was flung open by Birch in his nightshirt, saber in hand. He flung his weapon into a corner when he saw Beckford.

"What the devil do you think you're doing, Major?" he said.

"Testing you, Brigadier," Beckford said. "Testing your capacity to act on a moment's notice."

"You're drunk. Come in and have breakfast. It will clear your head."

"I'm not drunk," Beckford said. "I'm merely ebullient. We've received our orders from General Knyphausen. You've been entrusted with the greatest opportunity given a British officer in this war."

"When?"

"I can't tell you. It depends on news from Morristown," Beckford said. "But it will certainly be one night this week. You must have your men lie on their arms each night. Make them think it's part of a training exercise. This must be the deepest secret you've ever kept, Brigadier."

"Do you doubt my ability to keep my mouth shut?"

"With all due respect, Brigadier, yes. You've gotten drunk and talked about making Washington your prisoner, at least twice. I have agents about town who tell me these things. You must promise me that you won't take a drop of liquor between now and the night we act."

For a moment Birch's temper rose. It did not sit well with any officer, above all a general, to learn that his own intelligence service had been spying on him. As for being lectured on his drinking habits, this was something not even the lowliest private would tolerate. Getting drunk was an Englishman's proof of his liberty. It was practically guaranteed in the Magna Charta. But the present opportunity was so large, so historic, Birch swallowed his outrage. "You have my promise," he said. "What would you like for breakfast?"

"Some coffee will do for me," Beckford said.

"My taste precisely."

Birch bellowed for his batman. When the coffee was served he took a decanter of brandy from the sideboard and dosed it liberally, by way of defying Beckford's ban on alcohol. "Our last potation," he said, "until we raise our glasses to our prisoner, General Washington."

"Agreed," Beckford said. They drank the doubly scalding brew. "Now let's get down to business. How many horsemen can we muster?"

"Four hundred, give or take a dozen."

"Admirable. You must select forty of the most dependable troopers for an advance guard. They should be men hardy enough to give no quarter to anyone they meet on the road—man, woman, or child. We must use terror to guarantee the militia makes no attempt to block our return."

Birch nodded. "What about the reserve horses we talked about?"

Beckford took a detailed map of northern New Jersey from his cloak. It had been drawn for him by a lieutenant of the engineers, who had ridden the roads himself under the protection of Wiert Bogert and John Nelson. Beckford pointed to Great Rock Farm. "The horses will be waiting here, in a large barn guarded by my men."

"Why take such a roundabout route? There's the shortest and most direct way," Birch said, running his finger from Elizabethtown to Morristown.

"That route is guarded by a regiment of Continentals in Elizabethtown," Beckford said. "And it requires us to use a pass through the mountains, where a company of men can hold the road. This way"—he ran his finger from the fort at Powles Hook, up the shore of the Hudson, across the New Bridge to Hackensack, and across Bergen County to Boonton, then south on the Warwick Road to Morristown— "offers us a route guarded only by militia. We avoid the mountains and appear on the road that they worry least about."

"You're coming with us, Major?"

"Of course."

They clinked their brandy-laden coffee cups once more and Beckford strolled back to his house on Jane Street. Birch was a fool, but he was a necessary part of the machinery of war. A man had to be something of a fool to lead a cavalry charge.

In his study, Beckford summoned his batman, Kiphuth, to make a fire while he wrote a letter to Flora Kuyper.

> This order must be obeyed the moment you receive it. Send your most reliable servant to Morristown with an urgent request for Congressman Stapleton to visit you tomorrow, without fail. I will join you at the house about noon.
>
> BECKFORD

The major gave the letter to Kiphuth and ordered him to take it to John Nelson at the White Horse Tavern immediately.

The batman had just departed when the Reverend Caleb Chandler came down the stairs looking as haggard as he had when he arrived. Espionage obviously did not permit him to sleep soundly. "Good morning," he said. "Am I to return to Morristown today?"

"Tomorrow. You must wait for Bogert and Nelson to return and escort you across the Hudson."

"Is there another message for me to carry?"

"No. We no longer need to send messages, Mr. Chandler. But I want you back in Morristown in the hope that you can play some part in the mutiny that will take place there in a few days. You can add to the confusion by siding with the soldiery and urging them to further defiance of their officers."

"A mutiny? That's your plan?"

"Yes," Beckford said. "That's our plan. You seem inordinately interested, Chandler. It reawakens suspicion in my mind."

"I—I was only expressing my surprise. At the mutiny. Let me congratulate you. The army is ready to revolt. They'll join you in hanging a congressman from every tree in Morristown."

"If you're playing a double part, Chandler, now is the time to quit the rebels. A successful mutiny of your Connecticut brigade will be worth a thousand pounds. Do you hear me? A thousand pounds."

"I'm deeply grateful. But to prove my loyalty to you, to His Majesty, I'm prepared to play my part for nothing."

"I insist on being generous. You may go now."

Caleb Chandler retreated upstairs and Beckford lay down on his bed in the room next to his study. He dozed for a few hours and awoke at Kiphuth's knock. "Major," the batman said in his precise German, "the American painter, Mr. Stapleton, is in the parlor."

"Tell him I'll be down in a moment."

Beckford found Paul Stapleton setting the half-finished portrait on an easel. The major admired the skill with which Paul had subtracted flesh from his face and belly. He looked like the hearty young man who had loved Paul in London ten years ago. "It's magical, the way you recall the past," he said. "It's almost like seeing a ghost of myself."

"I paint to please, Major," Paul said.

"Remember, there must be some severity in the eyes," Beckford said. "A sense of command about the mouth."

"I'll do my best to disguise your true character, Major."

Beckford laughed. Paul's sarcasm no longer stung. He was armored against him now. Paul was part of his childish past. "In a day or two you'll see my true character."

"We haven't decided on an appropriate background for this masterpiece," Paul said. "How about the Battle of Long Island?"

"Piffle," Beckford said. "I was a nobody then. A very junior captain. I have something else in mind. A mansion in flames, a rabble of Americans fleeing from a half-dozen huts in its vicinity."

"Something like this?" Paul said, rapidly blocking out the scene on his sketch pad.

"Exactly. With British soldiers—cavalry—charging the peasants."

"Easy enough. But I don't know the incident. Is there an account of it I might read—for detail?"

Beckford laughed again. "Not likely. It hasn't taken place yet."

Paul Stapleton gazed at him for a moment. A slow

smile spread across his face. "I'll be damned," he said. "Maybe you're a great man after all, Becky."

"Let's get on with it," Beckford said.

He sat down at one of the parlor's west windows and fixed his eyes on the frozen Hudson and the shore of New Jersey, the beckoning edge of the continent. Suffusing his profile with determination, he concentrated on the future. He saw the painting in the gallery of the Royal Society in London, admired by awed visitors, including His Majesty, King George III. So that's how Beckford did it, they would murmur. But how could he fail? Look at that expression on his face. There was a man born to rule.

"You have a part to play in this final act, Paul dear," Beckford said. "At long last you'll see the point of your dreary interviews with Major Stallworth, feeding him all that useless information you supposedly picked up painting portraits. Tomorrow morning I'll have some papers for you to take to that safe house in Elizabethtown."

"Oh?"

"You can say you stole them off my desk. They'll detail an attack from Staten Island. There will actually be a diversion by the Queen's Rangers—designed to keep the Americans looking in the wrong direction."

"I'm at your service, Major," Paul said, continuing to paint.

"Precisely," Beckford said. "I hope you not only mean that, but understand it. You were once rather dear to me, Paul. But those days are gone, beyond recall. I've always been aware of the possibility that you were doubling me instead of Stallworth for the

362

past three years. If you double me now, I'll have you killed. One way or another, I'll have you killed. Do you hear me, Paul?"

"I hear you," Paul said.

twenty-two

"Congressmen? Congressmen?" bawled the ragged Connecticut soldier. "Hey, lads, some fucking congressmen have come to inspect us!"

Congressmen Schuyler, Peabody, Mathews, and Stapleton were spending their first day in Morristown making a tour of the Jockey Hollow encampment. They had been growing more and more solemn as they trudged from one brigade to another, seeing again and again gaunt men with empty bellies and improvised uniforms. Colonel Alexander Hamilton, General Washington's aide, was their guide. Without consulting a note he recited the number of men lacking shoes, coats, breeches, even guns, in each regiment.

Neither Colonel Hamilton nor anyone else was prepared for the reception they met on the parade ground of the 2nd Connecticut Brigade. Within sixty seconds they were surrounded by a mob of several hundred angry men.

"How do you know they're congressmen?" someone yelled.

"From the fat on them," roared someone else.

"Hey, be any one of you plump turkeys from Connecticut?" demanded another voice.

"What does it matter? They're all alike, swilling in Philadelphia while we starve," shouted a man with a face as dirty as a blacksmith's.

"Where are your officers?" Colonel Hamilton snapped. "Get back to your huts."

"Our officers are down at Red Peggy's getting drunk, like as not," bellowed the dirty-faced man.

"They are not," shouted a captain and two lieutenants, trying to fight their way through the mob. "Form on the parade ground. Disperse this mob and form."

"Blow it out your asshole," howled a voice on the far side of the crowd.

The officers began smashing to the right and left with the flats of their swords. A half-dozen more officers came running from their huts and joined the assault. The press around the congressmen was broken and the soldiers sullenly drifted away. The visitors hastily departed for the nearby camp of the 1st Connecticut Brigade, where they were introduced to the acting commander, Lieutenant Colonel Return Jonathan Meigs. He told them the same story they had heard everywhere. Given the opportunity, the whole army would go home tomorrow. The men were disgusted with no pay, poor provisions, and worse clothing. Meigs told the congressmen this in his laconic country manner. Standing beside him was another Connecticut lieutenant colonel, Ebenezer Huntington, who had a much different style. The son of a wealthy Norwich merchant, Huntington had a cosmopolitan swagger. "Gentlemen," he said, "I used to glory in the name American. Now I'm ashamed of it. The abuses that this army has suffered at the hands of this country beggar description. Tell that to your colleagues in Philadelphia!"

At the end of the tour the congressmen rode back to O'Hara's Tavern, on the Morristown green, in Hugh Stapleton's sleigh.

"Something must be done and done quickly," murmured usually optimistic John Mathews of South Carolina.

"By God, I wish I could persuade some great men from New England to come down here," growled Nathaniel Peabody of New Hampshire. "They'd stop talking through their sainted noses about General Washington."

"Can I believe my ears? We've converted Yankeedom?" Stapleton said.

He had already discovered Peabody did not fit his fixed image of the New Englander. He was a sophisticated, skeptical man with a wry sense of humor.

"There's an old saying: Seeing is believing," Peabody said.

The four men debarked from the sleigh and hurried into O'Hara's Tavern. The proprietor rushed up to Congressman Stapleton waving a note. "A black fellow left this for you not an hour ago, sir," he said. "He's waiting in the stable for your answer."

While his fellow congressmen warmed themselves before the huge fireplace in the tavern's taproom,

Hugh Stapleton read the letter and felt another kind of warmth stir his blood.

> My dearest:
> I beseech you to come see me soon. Tomorrow if you can. Something has occurred which may enable us to obtain the happiness we have discussed much sooner and with more ease than either of us has dreamed possible.
>
> FLORA

Hugh Stapleton excused himself and walked out to the stable. Cato stood beside Flora's horses feeding them oats from his hand. "Tell your mistress I'll be there at noon," the congressman said.

For the rest of the day and night Hugh Stapleton was a divided man, bodily present in Morristown at General Washington's dinner table, nodding sagely at the exhortations Congressman Schuyler was issuing on the army's behalf, listening with apparent attention as Washington described the kind of help he needed from Congress—a consistent supply of hard money, a new enlistment policy, a committee that could plan with the army the amount of men and money needed for the next campaign and do something about getting both in hand before summer. "This will take hard work, gentlemen, damn hard work," Washington said. "I hope you plan to stay for the rest of the winter."

"That's the least we can do," Hugh Stapleton said.

The words rang in his ears with a hollow clang. They were pure fraud. He was a total hypocrite. What would the other soldier in his life, the late Malcolm Stapleton, have said about a son who lied that way? Hugh Stapleton saw that the love note in his pocket and George Washington, somberly presiding at the head of the table, were two contradictory futures. The congressman had gone too far, he had made too many promises to himself, to others, to resist Flora Kuyper's invitation. The realistic side of his mind told him it would take months of wrangling with the army's enemies in Congress to translate Washington's words into action. A woman with no interest in politics would hardly accept politics as an excuse for delaying the happiness she had been so confidently promised. But from another part of the congressman's mind or body rose a wish for some way to voice his regret, to explain himself to the soldier at the head of the table.

No explanation was possible. Stapleton did not say a word for the rest of the night. He and his companions shrugged into their coats for the cold walk back to O'Hara's Tavern. Washington stood at the door and shook each man's hand as they departed. Hugh Stapleton was the last man out the door. Washington gripped his hand for an extra moment and said, "Mr. Schuyler told me about the speech you made on our behalf. You have my gratitude. Eventually I hope you'll have your country's gratitude."

"Thank you, General. I—I merely wished to be of some service. It was—is—the least I can do."

The least and the last, he thought.

Washington cleared his throat. He seemed suddenly uneasy. "There's another matter I've wanted to discuss with you. A thing of some delicacy. Perhaps we could meet tomorrow morning."

"I—I'm afraid that's impossible, General. I must make a flying visit home. My—my wife is ill."

"I'm sorry. The next day, perhaps. Ask Colonel Hamilton to arrange a time."

The next morning Hugh Stapleton was up at dawn, gobbling a hasty breakfast, impatiently asking innkeeper O'Hara why his horses and sleigh had not been ready at 6 A.M. in accordance with the orders he had left the night before. By 6:30 he was whipping his two black geldings down the road to Bergen so swiftly their bells fairly clattered out the opening bars of his old favorite, "The Good Fellow."

By noon he was past Newark, skimming down the packed snow of the new road across the marshes to the heights of Bergen. For the first time the gray clouds that had dominated the sky for so long had broken, and ragged sunlight gleamed on the white, silent world of winter. The congressman was egotistic enough to think it was an omen of his coming happiness.

The messenger of the day before, Cato, met the congressman at Flora Kuyper's door and bowed him into the familiar center hall. The air was rich with the scent of burning cedar. Flora appeared in the doorway of the parlor, wearing a dark blue gown with the skirt modishly bunched and flounced and looped. The loops exposed a scarlet flash of petticoat at the front, and beneath the petticoat hem peeped a delicate ankle, in white silk stockings with gold clocks. "My dear friend," Flora said, "I'm so glad you could come."

To the congressman's eyes her smile promised everything. He swept her into his arms. But she avoided his kiss and slipped from his grasp. "There's someone here—whom you must meet," she said. "To

370

whom I referred—when I mentioned achieving our happiness. He's an old friend of mine from London."

She took Hugh Stapleton's arm and led him into the parlor. A fat man wearing the red coat and white breeches of a British officer rose from a wing chair, a confident smile on his spherical face. "Mr. Stapleton, I'm Major Walter Beckford, aide-de-camp to General von Knyphausen. You don't know me, but I've often heard your name. Your brother, Paul, and I were good friends in London."

"And in New York for a while, I believe," Congressman Stapleton said.

"I, too, met Major Beckford in London," Flora said. "When the war began, we renewed our acquaintance. He offered me—his protection."

"There's no need to be discreet, my dear," Beckford said. "Congressman Stapleton is a man of the world. He knows what a dunce your husband was. Without me this farm would be a burned-out ruin. In return, Mrs. Kuyper has assisted us in small, harmless ways—such as arranging this meeting."

"I understand, of course," Stapleton said. But he realized that he understood very little. He could be certain of one thing. Major Beckford was not risking his safety within the American lines merely to exchange polite compliments.

"Would you like some wine?" Flora said, her manner still strained.

"Sherry, thank you," Stapleton said.

"The same," Beckford said.

Cato served it promptly. He had obviously been waiting in the kitchen for the signal. Beckford raised his glass. "To peace," he said. "And the happiness of both England and America."

"I can drink to that most heartily."

"Surely you can join us, Flora," Beckford said.

Flora stared at the glass in her hand as if it were some loathsome object. With a choked cry she flung it into the fire and ran from the room.

"What—is going on?" Congressman Stapleton asked.

Beckford sighed. "Women are such unpredictable creatures. You never know what idea will pop into their heads. Flora thinks that I—or one of my agents in Morristown—had something to do with the death of Caesar Muzzey, the slave you found in the snow near General Washington's headquarters. She seems to have been extraordinarily fond of the fellow for some reason. I hope, for your sake, it's not the one that comes obviously to mind. I've told her she's being ridiculous. Caesar was one of our couriers. It would make no sense for me or one of my men to kill him."

"I begin to see you're more than the general's aide-de-camp, sir," Hugh Stapleton said.

"Intelligence matters have been my province for the past three years. If you wish, I can give you a verbatim copy of the excellent speech you recently made in Congress, which resulted in the appointment of the special committee to confer with General Washington on army affairs."

"Remarkable," Stapleton said dryly.

"We also have the letter you wrote to Mrs. Kuyper, discussing your plans for sailing to Holland with the first spring breeze. But we're men of the world. There's no reason why there should be the least unpleasantness between us. I would do precisely the

372

same thing if I were in your position and with the possession of Flora's affections. In fact, I must confess a certain envy. She has never so favored me."

"The more I hear, the more I begin to wonder about Flora's affections," Stapleton said.

"Oh, they're genuine," Beckford said, pouring himself more sherry from the bottle Cato had left on the table beside his chair. "She's an extremely difficult, independent creature. She doesn't dispose of herself casually at my command, let me assure you."

"But she informs you the moment that she does."

"Even if she wished it, she couldn't have kept it a secret. We have men watching this house. It's rather important to several of our operations. But I'm not here to discuss Flora with you, Mr. Stapleton. You must know that. Charming though she is, she's only a minor matter between two men of the world. Two men of affairs. Large affairs."

"You may be right. It depends on what else you propose to discuss."

"You're disillusioned, disgusted with your rebellion, Mr. Stapleton, like a great many Americans. It has turned out to be more of a revolution"—Beckford made a flip-flop motion with his hands—"and less of a rebellion than you imagined. The wrong sort of people have *revolved* to power and influence. No?"

"In many ways you're right."

"If the war drags on, the only victor will be France. England and America will be bled white, of men and money. I can't believe you love the French, the nation your father fought in Canada. It's time, in short, for negotiation."

For a moment Hugh Stapleton was back in the City Tavern in Philadelphia, hearing Samuel Chase of Maryland drunkenly declare that he was ready to negotiate with any representative of His Majesty on Maryland's behalf and Robert R. Livingston saying the same thing for New York.

"You can be the means, Mr. Stapleton, of restoring peace and concord between England and this continent. Can you imagine what His Majesty would do to express his gratitude for such a feat? There's no office in his power that he would deny you—no title."

"It's a flattering part you write for me, Major," the congressman said. "But it seems too large for me to play. What can I do?"

"You can carry proposals from us to Congress. Proposals which will have the endorsement of General Washington."

"Washington? Are you in correspondence with him?"

The congressman was staggered but not disbelieving. Anything was possible after five years of a stalemated war. Washington was the wealthiest man in Virginia. He might be delicately exploring the terms on which he could keep his lands—and his head.

"We'll soon be in correspondence. Such close correspondence that there'll be no need for pen and ink. We'll talk as you and I are talking now."

"He'll come here?"

Beckford shook his head. "He'll come to New York. Tomorrow night—he'll be our prisoner. We have his guards bribed, a force ready to seize him. You'll be in New York to greet him, Mr. Stapleton. To urge him to agree to our terms. You'll then take these terms to Congress and urge their acceptance, with all the eloquence at your command. Meanwhile, the American army will be racked by an explosion of mutinies in every brigade. The Congress, if there are enough men of the world like you among them, will accept our terms and this rebellion will be over. Your name will be blazoned across England as the great peacemaker."

"A fantastic scene, Major," Stapleton said. "But what are the terms?"

"The immediate disbandment of Congress and the Continental Army. A return of the old royal governments in all the colonies except New England. The Yankees began this ruinous war by dumping private property into Boston Harbor and firing on His Majesty's troops at Lexington and Concord. They must be punished accordingly. Civil government will be dismantled, from Connecticut to Boston. New England will be under military rule for the next ten years at least."

"Their commerce, trade?"

"Banned, except for their fishing fleet, which will help feed them—and us."

"And the commerce of the other colonies?"

"Permitted, under strict regulation by Parliament."

"What of retaliation against persons?"

"Those guilty of heinous crimes will stand trial in their respective colonies. Those who merit the King's forgiveness, such as yourself, will receive it. Those who do not—such as Mr. Washington—must take their chances."

"I don't think much of those terms, Major, even assuming you can manage your coup against General Washington."

"That's precisely what I *am* assuming, Mr. Stapleton. And what you should assume as well. The terms are as generous as the situation allows. More than generous, in fact."

"I don't think so. Nor will General Washington even if he's your prisoner."

"Mr. Stapleton, what he or you actually think is irrelevant. You will go to Congress and tell them that Mr. Washington accepts the terms. You will have a letter from him attesting to this fact, with his signature forged by an expert. If you do not, your wife and the whole world will know of your plan to retreat to Holland with Mrs. Kuyper. We'll send another emissary to Congress, someone such as the rebel chief justice of Rhode Island, who's already in our employ, and the result will be the same—except for you. Your great opportunity will have gone glimmering. You'll die on the gallows, your property will be confiscated, your sons condemned to lives of disgrace. People will say, 'With a whoremaster for a father, what can you expect?' Your absurd little fit of loyalty to America will be unknown unto eternity."

Hugh Stapleton sat back in his chair. The impact of those words thrust him there. Not merely the words but Beckford's confidence. Dazedly, mechanically, trying to show at least a shred of insouciance, the congressman sipped some sherry. The gesture was meaningless, absurd, before Major Beckford's mocking smile.

"Are you telling me that I'm your prisoner now? You're unarmed, sir. What's to stop me from walking out of this house at this moment?"

"Two men—who will cut your throat if you try it. One is a citizen of Bergen County. He'll publish an account of how he waylaid you here, to protect the virtue of Mrs. Kuyper, whom he loved. We'll publish your letter, attesting to your pursuit of her. She'll confirm it and accuse you of ravishing her. It will add to the demoralization and disgust of your people with their so-called cause."

Think, Hugh Stapleton told himself. Think. His eagerness to overwhelm you, to make you his accomplice, means you are far less superfluous to him than he claims. But the congressman could not get beyond that obvious point. His world was crashing in ruins around him. Hugh Stapleton—congressman, merchant, man of the world—was about to become Hugh Stapleton—prisoner, traitor, fool.

"I regret the disagreeable turn our conversation has taken," Major Beckford continued. "I had hoped that we could go back to New York as friends, fellow peacemakers. To be blunt, you are in no position to negotiate, Mr. Stapleton. Your only choice is to help me negotiate. What possible objection can you have to our terms? You've damned New England to your comrades in Philadelphia a hundred times. You and others of your congressional friends have declared yourselves open to the idea of a reconciliation."

"This isn't reconciliation you're suggesting, it's surrender," Stapleton said.

"It's reconciliation on the parent's terms. You Americans have been wayward, froward children and must be treated accordingly. Perhaps it's your wild country, but there's a certain element of the barbarian in you, like the Irish and the Scots. You must be tamed, civilized."

"I see," Stapleton said. He was seeing a great many things. Some of them were things he had known before but had conveniently forgotten, such as the arrogance of imperial England. He had sat at dinner tables in London and heard British aristocrats sneer at every other nation in the world. But he had declined to realize their condescension included him, the American. On the contrary, he had been inclined to join them, to deny the difference between the two names, English and American. The congressman remembered the conversation with his brother, Paul, about his father's fear that the Americans were in danger of losing the respect they had wrung from the British in previous wars. What else explained the contempt with which Major Beckford was treating him, and the repression the British government obviously planned for all of America? *Wayward, froward children. A certain element of the barbarian in you.* There was a century of future contempt and abuse in those words.

This realization was not so painful as another, more personal one, another sight or insight, created by the congressman's new, agonized perspective. "Mrs. Kuyper—she is really in your pay?"

For a moment Beckford's lips twitched. He was about to permit his mocking smile to reappear. But he suppressed it. He did not want to humiliate Congressman Stapleton completely. "Of course," he said. "But let me promise you, my dear sir, as a gentleman, the matter will remain utterly secret if we're assured of your cooperation in this business. It's even possible, when everything is settled, that you might make an arrangement with the lady, to your mutual satisfaction. Like most women of her sort, she wants security, the protection of a wealthy man, above everything. This you most assuredly will be. In fact, when the King creates an American peerage, as I am certain he will do, I wouldn't be surprised to see you named the first baron."

There it was, the judgment of a man of the world

on Hugh Stapleton. Even if he ended his days as a baron, he would never be more than the kept fool of his conquerors. But his personal humiliation was nothing in comparision to the event that was about to transform the future of America. He was powerless to prevent it. All he could attempt to do was discourage it.

"Major Beckford," he said, "your solicitude for my feelings, my future welfare, is touching. But I'm inclined to think that a man who would trap another man in this fashion is no gentleman, and neither his sympathy nor his word is to be trusted for ten seconds. I despise your smirking condescension, sir, and I defy you to force me to cooperate in my country's betrayal. If you're so fortunate as to seize General Washington, I am sure you'll find him of the same temper."

"We expected no less of Mr. Washington," Major Beckford said. "I must confess I had better expectations of you. My genuine affection for your brother— no matter what your opinion of it—also led me to hope we might negotiate as friends. But now it seems as if you are giving me no choice."

Major Beckford drummed his fingers on the table beside him. "Perhaps a day or two in the Provost Prison will change your mind."

twenty-three

At 1 A.M. the following morning, Caleb Chandler began his journey back to Morristown. Wiert Bogert and John Nelson escorted him across the Hudson at the usual place, several miles north of New York City. Above them, for the first time in months, a few random stars glinted through broken clouds. The Great Cold was gradually retreating to the Canadian northland, from which it had come.

As they reached the middle of the river an unnerving groan filled the night. It was followed by cracking and crunching that Caleb found even more demoralizing. He was tempted to run, but his escorts accepted these unearthly sounds as routine. The ice was shifting.

"Soon dis be water," muttered Bogert.

"Aye," growled Nelson. "Then we'll have to worry about bloody boats again."

Nelson began condemning Beckford for refusing to reimburse him for a boat the rebels had discovered and sunk last summer. To Nelson the war was a business. Listening to him talk about the amounts of money various British officers, particularly the commissaries, were making from the stalemate, Caleb could not blame him for his attitude.

They struggled up the New Jersey bluffs on a path made doubly treacherous by the snow that had melted during the day, then frozen with a crust of ice over it. Nelson's humor improved once they reached the woods and put on their snowshoes. "Let's hope that this is the last bloody time I have to make that climb, Parson," he said. "This old soldier's nose tells him the end of the campaign's gettin' closer every minute. I'll be glad of it, let me tell you. These bones can't take much more of this cold. There's mornings when every joint feels like Bogert here's been poundin' me with both fists. I'm takin' the lad home with me, Parson. Goin' to show him London from Guild Hall to Vauxhall. Then we're goin' to take our sock and buy ourselves a farm in the West Country or maybe Ireland. We'll—"

A blast of musketry erupted a few feet away. Bullets ripped through the branches above their heads, showering them with splinters. Wiert Bogert flung Caleb facedown in the snow and dropped beside him. Nelson joined them. "God damn me and my big mouth," he muttered.

"Militia patrol," Bogert grunted. "Best go get dem first."

"You take the right flank, lad. I'll take the left,"

Nelson said. "You keep your nose close to the ground, Parson."

Bogert crawled off to the right. Nelson vanished to the left. In about sixty seconds they let out simultaneous yells and opened fire. They were answered by random musketry, then cries of pain and shouts of panic, then the pounding of numerous feet. A minute later Nelson clumped back to Caleb and hauled him erect.

"Not much fight in them, Parson. A good sign," he said.

Out on the road, three elongated objects lay in the snow. It took Caleb a moment to realize they were men. One of them was still alive. "Quarter," he whimpered. "Quarter."

"Here's your quarter, rebel," Nelson said, and smashed the man's head with the butt of his musket.

They reentered the woods and as dawn broke reached the Kuyper farm. "This is where we part company, Parson," Nelson said. "We've got business up Hackensack way. Get your nag out of the barn and head for Morristown without delay. Them's your orders, ain't they?"

"Yes," Caleb said. "Thank you for your protection. I hope we'll be toasting our success in New York in a few days' time. God save the King."

"God save your ass, Parson," Nelson said.

In the barn, his old plowhorse, Horace, welcomed Caleb with a friendly whinny. He fed the horse some oats and wondered if he could risk a visit to Flora. In their last conversation he had seemed so close to cutting the twisted shreds of sentiment that bound her to William Coleman. Caleb tiptoed to the side door of the barn, which was closer to the house. The windows were dark. For a moment he was in Flora's bedroom, holding her in his arms. What a strange, dangerous compound his love was: pity and desire and treachery—and atonement. Above all atonement.

"Parson," called Nelson from the front of the barn, "where the hell are you? What's taking you so long?"

"Just giving Horace some breakfast. Those damn rebels I board him with in Morristown have been starving the poor animal."

"Get on with it. Beckford's promised us fifty guineas if you get to camp in time to do some good. He told us to take particular care you didn't waste any time with Madam Kuyper."

A half-hour later, Caleb rocked in Horace's saddle as the old horse plodded down the winding road from the heights of Bergen to the salt marshes of Newark Bay. In his pocket was the bearded Queen of Hearts, the token that would have given Flora access to Twenty-six. Would it also give him access? This unanswerable question tormented Caleb as he rode toward Morristown. Should he report to Benjamin Stallworth at once and tell him of his discovery of Beckford's token? He remembered Stallworth's insistence that they were fighting a battle and each fact was a well-aimed bullet. Stallworth was his commanding officer. He was also the man who had declared himself indifferent to the fate of Flora Kuyper's soul.

For Caleb that declaration was decisive now. Stallworth's mind ran to the obvious. Caleb suspected that he would dismiss the token as useless without Flora. He would reiterate his order to get Flora to Morristown, one way or another, without any concern for her feelings. In his desperation Caleb concocted a plan that was closer to a leap into the dark. He would use the token to uncover Twenty-six on his own. By now, he reasoned, the spy must trust him. Beckford would never have sent him back to Morristown with orders to cooperate with the mutiny if the master mutineer, Twenty-six, suspected or opposed him. He would pretend to be carrying an urgent verbal message from Flora. Face to face with Twenty-six, he would put his pistol to the spy's head and march him to Stallworth. Then, the mutiny aborted, Washington and the army safe, he could return to Flora and tell her the truth about himself.

Horace soon complicated this plan. The old horse really had been half starved by the farmer who was boarding him. Beyond Newark, Horace's pace declined from a plod to a crawl to a stumble. Caleb tried to buy some oats from a Dutch farmer, who contemptuously turned him away when he admitted he had only Continental money. When he invoked George Washington's name, the man seized a pitchfork and showered him with Dutch curses. The glorious cause was clearly no longer popular in this part of New Jersey.

Winter twilight was falling fast as Horace crept into Morristown. Caleb left his feeble steed at the stables of O'Hara's Tavern and paused to load and prime the pistol he carried in his saddlebag. He tucked it in the waistband of his pants, under his waistcoat. The loose drape of his old frock coat concealed the bulge.

It took him another hour to walk the four miles to Red Peggy's groggery, on the Vealtown Road. It was Saturday night. The place was crowded with drinkers, both soldiers and civilians. Red Peggy presided at the bar, rouged and powdered as usual. If she was an accomplice of Twenty-six, she was almost certainly a halfhearted one. He had probably frightened her into cooperation.

Red Peggy greeted Caleb with a wary smile. "Why, Chaplain," she said, "what brings you this far?"

"Just looking for a little company," he replied. "By the way, I found this pack of playing cards outside in the snow. Does anyone here own them?"

Caleb held up the cards so everyone in the taproom could see them. Blank looks predominated. "Ah, well," Caleb said, "I suppose no one wants to claim them because they're so thoroughly marked, front and back."

He flipped the top card and turned up the bearded Queen of Hearts.

"For sure," Red Peggy said, "they look like the kind of cards that lead to killing." She took the deck away from Caleb and put it in the pocket of her apron. "I'll start my bedroom fire with them tonight and good riddance. What would you like to drink?"

Caleb ordered a tankard of flip. Having eaten nothing all day, he liked the way it filled his stomach. The eggs were well beaten and the rum was hot. He drank it rapidly and did not object when Peggy served him a second one.

In a corner of the taproom, the dwarfish waiter in the Continental Army uniform leaped up on a table and began singing a liberty song. Other drinkers joined him. Beneath the noise, Red Peggy murmured, "You must wait while we set the signal. It's a special one for that card."

"Tell him I have a message from Mrs. Kuyper, too important to be put in writing," Caleb said.

An hour passed, during which the waiter sang more songs praising General Washington and abusing the British. Red Peggy served Caleb another tankard of flip. She made numerous trips into the rear of the house through a door behind the bar. Finally she emerged and called to the waiter, "Ned, I'm low on rum. Get me a cask from the cellar. Who'll help him?"

There were several volunteers. But Peggy turned to Caleb and gave him a friendly shove. "Here, Chaplain, you're falling asleep there. You could do with a bit of exercise."

Caleb and Ned ducked under the bar and followed Peggy through two sparsely furnished rooms to the rear of the house, where stairs descended to the cellar. Caleb kept a hand on his pistol, certain that at any moment he would be face to face with Twenty-six. But there was no trace of the master spy in the crowded cellar. Casks of rum and other liquors were stacked against the walls. Red Peggy pointed to one and Ned rolled it into the center of the room. "You must follow Ned to your rendezvous in the woods," Peggy said. "First get the cask upstairs."

With Caleb doing most of the lifting, he and Ned wrestled the cask up the steep stairs and down the hall to the taproom. They rolled it into position behind the bar and Red Peggy expressed her satisfaction. "For that you can both drink your fill," she said, handing them brimming tankards of flip.

Ned downed his tankard in one startling swallow and disappeared behind the bar. Caleb drank at a more civilized pace to give Ned time to get in position outside the house. With a cheer he did not have to pretend after four strong drinks, he said good-night to Red Peggy and departed. Ned was waiting for him in the yard.

"God save the King," Caleb said.

"Amen," Ned replied.

Caleb clutched the butt of his pistol for reassurance. He had hoped to meet Twenty-six at Red Peggy's, where he could have called for help if he needed it. Ned scampered ahead of him, moving through the dark woods with the sureness of a fox. At last they came to a humplike hill, which they circled for a good quarter of a mile.

A growling voice challenged them. "Who goes there?"

"Liberty," Ned replied.

"Advance, Liberty," said the voice. Caleb thought it sounded familiar.

Before he could be certain he felt the tip of a bayonet against the small of his back. "Just walk straight ahead," the voice said. Caleb obeyed. "Now turn." He obeyed again.

Ned, just ahead of them, tugged at some shrubs growing out of the side of the hill. A door creaked open. Caleb found himself facing a small cave with a mass of glowing coals in a pit in the center of it.

Caleb cocked his pistol. As he whirled to capture agent Twenty-six the butt of a musket struck him in the side of his head. He reeled into the cave and the musket struck him again, this time in the shoulder. He hurtled against the side wall, the pistol flying out of his hand. Another blow on the head knocked him face down beside the pit of coals. Someone much larger and stronger than Ned jammed his knee in Caleb's back and tied his hands behind him.

"All right, Chaplain," said the voice. "What's your message from Mrs. Kuyper?"

Caleb's ears whined; the cave was a whirling blur. The heat from the coals was searing his face. "She's—she's being seduced by Major Beckford."

"Stuff. Beckford coudn't seduce the most willing whore in New York. Twenty-six has talked about the kind of lovers he favors."

A hand grabbed Caleb by the collar and rolled him over on his back. He blinked up at a skull-faced man wearing a Continental Army uniform with the buff trim of the New Jersey Brigade. It was Case, Caesar Muzzey's hutmate, the man who had dominated the other men in the hut when Caleb visited them. Could this be William Coleman, whom Flora had called the handsomest man she had ever seen?

Case jammed his musket into Caleb's chest. "Where'd you get them cards? Did you find them by accident?"

"Flora—Mrs. Kuyper—gave them to me. She needs help. I'm telling you the truth."

"I don't think you've been acquainted with the truth for a long time, Chaplain. You've been visiting Mrs. Kuyper's thingy the way Caesar Muzzey done. That don't sit well with Twenty-six. I expect you're going to end up like Caesar, Chaplain."

"It's Mrs. Kuyper. She must have deceived me. I'm a servant of the King, so help me God."

"Sure. That's why you had that pistol in your hand. I suggest you start talking to God. I'll give you ten seconds."

Caleb heard the click of the hammer as Case cocked the musket. Suddenly something or someone transfixed the skull-like face above the gun. The eyes bulged; the mouth gaped. Simultaneously a foot flashed into Caleb's field of vision, kicking away the barrel of the gun. The musket crashed and a blast of hot air and gunpowder sparks scorched Caleb's cheek. Case toppled out of sight. Caleb stared up through a swirl of gunsmoke at Major Benjamin Stallworth.

"God damn you, Chandler. What are you trying to do?" he said.

Case writhed on the ground beside the pit of coals. Stallworth had bayoneted him. The major cut Caleb loose, reiterating his demand for an explanation. Caleb told him about the bearded queen and his decision to hunt Twenty-six alone. Stallworth groaned in frustration.

"How many times do I have to tell you to stop worrying about Mrs. Kuyper's whorish soul? With that card we might have flushed the bird if you'd given me time to work out a plan. Now you've driven him into deeper cover."

"Too deep—for you, Major," gasped Case.

Stallworth glowered at him. "I assume this isn't Twenty-six."

Caleb shook his head. "One of Caesar Muzzey's hutmates. Probably the man who killed him."

Stallworth propped Case against the wall of the cave. "Who's Twenty-six?" Stallworth demanded. "Have you ever seen him?"

"He's a fine and generous gentleman. Which is more than I can say for any whoremaster of an officer in the American army."

Stallworth cuffed the man in the face.

"Who is Twenty-six? Where do you meet him? Tell me and I'll get you to a doctor."

"Too late for that, Major. I'd rather die loyal to the

man who paid me—enough to keep my wife and children alive these last two winters. No fucking American paymaster—or congressman—has done that."

"We'll see how loyal you are," Stallworth said. He thrust the tip of his bayonet into the coals. In a few seconds it was white. He held the glowing metal an inch from Case's eyes. "If you don't want to die cursing, tell me the truth."

"I'll meet you in hell, Major."

Caleb looked away as the bayonet moved forward. Case's scream was horrendous. It leaped around the walls of the cave like a berserk animal. Then it was gone. Caleb looked back. Case was dead, his head lolling to one side, blood drooling from his right eye.

"Couldn't you see he was already dying?" Caleb said.

"Shut up," Stallworth muttered. "Just shut your mouth and come with me."

In an hour they were in the Ford mansion. The upstairs windows were dark. One or two lights glowed on the first floor. A black servant led them past a room where an aide was hunched over a desk to the rough log office Washington had added to the west wing of the house. The general was at his desk writing letters. He looked up, a polite smile on his face until he saw Stallworth's scowl.

"What's wrong, Major?" he said.

"A great deal," Stallworth said. He told the commander in chief how one of his men had warned him that Caleb Chandler was making an unauthorized visit to Red Peggy's groggery. He had rushed there, trailed the Reverend Chandler through the woods, and rescued him from execution—a deed that unfortunately required killing the man who might have led them to Twenty-six.

Stallworth glowered at Caleb. "Your Excellency," he said, "I give up on this fellow. He ignores my orders. He scorns my advice, criticizes my methods, while he consistently proves himself to be the most infuriating fool I've ever seen. I've brought him here in the hope that he'll take a direct order from you."

"What's the order, Major?"

"I want him to write a letter to Mrs. Kuyper, telling her that she must come to Red Peggy's immediately. His life is at stake."

"What do you think of that, Mr. Chandler?"

Caleb found himself confused and surprised by Washington's mild, calm manner. From a distance the man had looked so severe. "I would hate to do it, Your Excellency. I'm afraid it would cause her considerable pain if she discovered I'm—an American agent."

"Isn't that too damned bad," Stallworth said. "If anyone deserves a shock to the nerves, it's that bitch. Tell him what she did today, Your Excellency. He won't believe me."

"Mrs. Kuyper seems to have persuaded Congressman Hugh Stapleton to pay her a visit," Washington said. "A British officer and several men were waiting for him. He's now their guest . . . or their prisoner—we're not sure which—in New York."

Exhausted—he had not slept for twenty-four hours—battered by musket butts and muzzle blasts, Caleb looked into Washington's eyes. He saw regret there. Understanding. He also saw necessity. It did not wear Stallworth's Yankee snarl.

But it was no less imperative. He had tried to defend Flora from its iron grip. It was no longer possible.

"I'll write the letter," he said.

twenty-four

At Great Rock Farm, Hannah Stapleton awoke to find sunshine streaming in her window for the second day in a row. Was the Great Cold ending at last? She lay there, listening to the drawled, sibilant call of a snow lark, wondering why she felt so contented. Then she remembered: Paul was returning from New York today.

At first, after Paul had told her that he was a spy, his trips to New York had been a source of new anguish for her. Although he had laughed at her fears, there was always the possibility that one of Walter Beckford's agents might betray him. It was clear, from what he had told her, that most spies lived in a shifting, shadowy world of loyalty to the cause they served and regret for the cause they were betraying.

Hannah sensed that Paul himself was not much different in this respect. His loyalty to America was a fragile thread, consisting largely of his failed, suppressed longing for his father's love. His midnight revelation of his spying implied another thread—equally fragile, she was sure—Paul's love for her. Looking back over the two and a half years of their life together at Great Rock Farm, she realized that she had wanted, needed this love. It was a need that had grown more acute as the collapse of her love for Hugh and his repugnance for her became visible.

Odd how loyalty to America, to the revolution, had become so entangled in both her loves. Hugh's increasing disgust with the war had paralleled the decline of her affection for him. Paul's revelation of loyalty had confirmed, even exalted, her love for him. Why? It was not simply the memory of that harrowing encounter with John Nelson and Wiert Bogert in Hackensack. It was Malcolm Stapleton, something he embodied that gave meaning to the word "American." All the brutal, bloody stories he had told her about his warrior days in the north woods. His memories, which reached back through his father to the first comers, the Stapletons who had built this house and more than once fought attacking Indians from its windows and doors. The old man spoke for the long struggle to build a nation in the wilderness, the pride in that achievement, the strength it had required. In spite of all the sermons on humility she had heard in her Quaker youth, Hannah wanted that pride, that strength, for her sons.

Daughter, the old man had called her, in the style of his day. Daughter this and daughter that. At first she had disliked it. But now the memory pleased her. She wanted to be his daughter. She had ceased to be the daughter of that meek, pious Quaker in Burlington who carped at the rebels and prated about everyone's longing for peace. Damn peace without honor, without pride!

Downstairs, Hannah repeated a morning ritual. She took Paul's latest portrait of her and set it by the window, where it caught the morning light. He said it was going to be the best painting he had ever done. At first glance it was a repetition of the "history" painting he had completed a year ago. She was wearing the same faded housedress; her hair was ribbonless, undressed. Again, it was winter. She stood by a window, looking out at a snowbound landscape. But Paul had transformed the winter light. He had found an inner radiance, a silvery-dark gleam that reminded her of the reflection in a running brook in December. The eyes of the woman of the portrait echoed the same subtle radiance. A ghost of a smile was on her lips. On second glance, the woman was as transformed as the winter light. She was no longer the weary, fading creature he had painted in similar workaday clothes.

Was it vision or reality? Hannah was not sure. But she wanted to be the woman of the second glance.

It was Sunday. Hannah decided to go to church. Dominie Freylingheusen was preaching in Hackensack. Like the rest of New Jersey, the Dutch Reformed Church was divided between rebels and loyalists. Rebellious Dominie Freylingheusen rode a circuit, preaching to like-minded churchgoers at Hackensack, Schraalenberg, and several other towns on successive weeks. Hannah asked Pompey to get out the sleigh and horses while she had breakfast.

The dominie proved to be his usual militant self, denouncing loyalists as depraved sinners and calling on his fellow rebels to stop backsliding, to turn out for militia duty and quit selling their corn and beef to the enemy. With vivid effect he compared losing the war to going to hell and implied that if they were defeated, the Americans, like all sinners, had no one but themselves to blame.

Coming out of church, she smiled and nodded to several neighbors. Dr. James Beattie, who had gone to Kings College with Hugh, fell into step beside her. "How is the rising politician?" he asked.

"Rising to what? He never writes me a line," Hannah said.

"He's been appointed to a very important committee that's in Morristown at this moment conferring with General Washington. According to the *New Jersey Journal*, Hugh made a speech in Congress proposing emergency measures."

"Thank you for the news," she said.

"I'm going to write him a letter warning him of the dangers of neglecting a pretty wife," Beattie said.

On the trip back to Great Rock Farm, Hannah's spirits dwindled in spite of the brilliant sunshine on the white fields. How could her husband come so close—Morristown was little more than an hour's ride away—and not even tell her? She began composing an angry letter to him. Perhaps she could make more of an impression by putting her grievances on paper, where he could not interrupt her. The only consolation she could find was Dr. Beattie's report that Hugh was taking a more active part in Congress. Could her exhortations have had something to do with it?

Coming up the path to the farmhouse, Hannah noticed a strange sleigh at the front door. A soldier in uniform lounged beside it, chatting with her son Malcolm. In the house, Pompey greeted her with a worried expression. "An officer from Morristown is in master's study. He says master's got trouble."

A short young man with a leonine head and an erect martial bearing emerged from Hugh's study. "Mrs. Stapleton?" he said. "I'm Colonel Alexander Hamilton. I'm here at General Washington's orders. May I speak with you?"

Hannah threw her cloak on a chair in the hall and followed Colonel Hamilton into the study. "I'll come to the point at once, madam," he said. "Your husband has apparently been captured by the British. He's in their hands in New York."

"What do you mean—apparently been captured?"

"It distresses me to be the bearer of such news," Colonel Hamilton said. "Congressman Stapleton was visiting a woman in Bergen. A woman we know to be a British agent. From what our people tell us—we have men watching her house—he seems to have gone willingly with his captors. There's a grave possibility that he's deserted to their side."

Hannah sat down on the edge of a wing chair. God was turning Dominie Freylingheusen's sermon, her early-morning meditation about pride and strength, into cruel comedy. "I—I don't know what to say," she murmured.

"I must ask your permission to search Mr. Stapleton's papers for anything that may shed some light on his—capture. General Washington feels we should continue to call it that until we have solid proof to the contrary."

"Yes," Hannah said, certain that no documentary proof was necessary. The proof was in her memory of Hugh's self-pity, his boredom, his disillusion with Congress, his antipathy to contumacious Yankees.

"I'd like to take the papers back to Morristown so I can examine them in detail."

"Of course."

She ordered Pompey and his son Isaac to bring a trunk down from the attic. As they filled it with Hugh's letter books and ledgers from the West Indies and records of his privateering and mercantile ventures in Philadelphia, Hannah glanced hurriedly at them and was amazed at the profits. Hugh was incredibly richer than he had ever intimated to her. Another example of the distance that had grown between them.

Colonel Hamilton departed, his sleigh sinking into the softening snow under the weight of the trunk full of papers. As the rest of the day drifted listlessly into dusk, Hannah realized that Paul had not returned from New York. Had he deserted her, too? Had he joined his brother in a joint decision to "improve some moneys"? That would be unbearable. God would not permit it. He would not allow her to be humiliated twice by these devious, hardhearted Stapletons. Her misery multiplied as she remembered her morning thoughts about becoming part of the family. She was trapped here, with no retreat, no refuge. She could not go home to beg crumbs from her father's table, to accept his condescending affection.

She got out Paul's unfinished portrait of her and set it on an easel. Was that woman a fool? Was that radiance in her eyes, on her face, a clever lie? She could not believe it. But where was Paul? Drinking with his former lover, Beckford, and his traitorous brother, Hugh, and the mysterious woman from Bergen, laughing at love and loyalty?

Little Malcolm came in to say good night. "When will Father come home again?" he asked.

"I don't know," Hannah said.

"He promised me a sleigh ride. Now the snow's melting."

"I'll ask Pompey to give you one tomorrow."

"I want it from Father."

She tousled his blond head and hugged him, whispering, "I hope he'll come soon."

She would accept Hugh, she would try to love him in spite of the woman in Bergen, Hannah told herself. If only he had not deserted to the British. That was all she wanted now. His loyalty.

About an hour after Malcolm went to bed, Pompey came into the parlor, where Hannah still sat staring disconsolately at Paul's unfinished portrait. "Mistress," he said, "they in the barns again."

"There's nothing we can do about it. Lock the front and back doors. Tie Achilles on the porch."

"I'd like to fight them just once, mistress."

"No. They'd kill us all, Pompey."

Before Hugh left, he had apparently commissioned Pompey to guard the house, without bothering to consult her or Paul. Tonight, as usual, she insisted on limiting the old soldier to defensive measures. A half-hour later, Achilles began barking. Suddenly his deep bass became a strangled yelp. With a tremendous crash the front door splintered around the lock and burst open. Wiert Bogert lunged into the hall, seeming to fill it from floor to ceiling. He was dragging Achilles by the tail. Blood oozed from the dog's slashed throat. "Hello, liddle lady," he said. "Here's your mutt."

Behind Bogert came John Nelson, herding the farm's half-dozen male blacks, including a very disgruntled Pompey, into the kitchen. Returning to the parlor, Nelson gave Hannah his shark's smile. In the firelight the scars of his tarring and feathering writhed up his throat. "We're here with marching orders from your husband," Nelson said. "He's joined the King's side and expects you to cooperate with us. We're going to collect twenty or thirty horses from loyalists hereabouts and put them in your barn for use later tonight. Until then this house will be under guard. Anyone, black or white, who tries to sneak off will be shot. Is your brotherly protector, Mr. Stapleton, here?"

Hannah shook her head.

"Maybe Beckford's put him to work, too. About time, I'd say."

"You understand all that, liddle lady?" Bogert said.

Hannah nodded, still unable to speak. She sat there for another hour while Pompey disposed of Achilles's corpse and wiped the blood from the hall floor. Something very important was obviously about to happen. Hugh's desertion, Paul's disappearance, were connected to it. But what could she do about it? She found herself despising her helplessness, almost hating her womanhood.

A light rain pattered against the windows. A pathetic, dismal sound. As it began to penetrate, almost absorb her mind, the front door crashed open again. Wiert Bogert loomed in the hall. "Get in here and stay," he ordered. "You don't go near d'barn again. John in command here."

Bogert shoved Paul into the parlor and returned to the barn. With a violent shiver, Paul threw off his hat and cloak; both were drenched. His breeches were equally soaked; his stockings were matted with wet snow from the road. Hannah threw her arms around him. "I've been praying and praying for you to come," she said.

"That explains why I'm here," he said in his wryest, coolest voice. "I'm in the grip of omnipotence."

She noticed he was not returning her embrace. She stepped back, puzzled. "Where have you been?"

"This morning I was on the outskirts of Elizabethtown," he said, "where I was supposed to leave some papers with a certain Colonel Dayton. Papers that would set the Americans running to defend the place. To no purpose—the attack is coming from the opposite direction. All the way down there I kept thinking about Hugh going over to them. I suppose you've heard about that."

Hannah nodded mournfully.

"It was proof—if I needed it—that the British were going to win. I stopped in a tavern and began getting drunk. I couldn't stand the idea of Hugh outsmarting me. I found myself wanting to be on the winning side, too. I wanted to show my bastard of a brother I could be as shrewd and despicable as he is."

"Paul, dearest," Hannah said, almost weeping. "Such hatred can only wound thee, not him."

Paul strolled over to the half-finished portrait and adjusted it on the easel. "That isn't the message I got on the wings of your prayers. When I came out of the tavern, I buried the papers in a snowbank. I went into Elizabethtown to tell Dayton the truth. I couldn't find him, so I left a message with one of his aides and came back here because I thought you might need me."

"I love thee for it," Hannah said.

Paul tossed his head, denying, as usual, the possibility that anyone could love him. Simultaneously, Hannah realized he was right—her words were not entirely true. She could never love Paul the way she had loved Hugh. She loved Paul's love for her, she loved his muted wish to be his father's son, she loved his artist's gift. When she said *I love thee* she added: *for it*. For this final act of courage and affection. There was something even worse in those words. She was saying them because she knew they were what Paul wanted and needed to hear. She was using that sacred word, "love," to bolster this man's fragile commitment to his country.

"Only when I got here did I realize that the farm was part of the plan. No doubt Hugh volunteered it. Becky's very thorough."

"What are they going to do?"

"Seize General Washington. Becky's coming out with the cavalry tonight."

"We can't get a message to Morristown without a horse," Hannah said. "What can we do to stop them?"

Paul walked over to the window. "Set fire to the barn. Destroy all the fresh horses."

"Yes," Hannah said. *"Yes."*

"One small drawback," Paul said. "Nelson has a half-dozen men out there besides Bogert. They'll kill us if we try it."

"We'll fight them," Hannah said. "Pompey, Isaac, the others will help us. We've still got your father's guns."

"I've never shot one in my life."

"Pompey knows how. He'll teach us."

"You're insane," Paul said.

"It's for my sons as much as for me. Your father's grandsons. No matter what happens, they'll know they had a mother, and an uncle, who weren't traitors."

"Insanity," Paul said. "Let's get the guns. Who'll set fire to the barn?"

"I will," Hannah said.

twenty-five

In her dreams Flora Kuyper heard the church bells of London once more. Or was it the single bell of the Ursuline convent on Chartres Street in New Orleans? She seemed to stand with her face pressed to the glass front of a shop. On the display counters were silver bowls and pitchers, sea-green and sky-blue china, gold bracelets studded with diamonds, silk shawls with cloth of gold woven through them. She heard her mother's voice saying, *Do you want these things? Then do as I tell you.*

The dream dissolved and she was alone in a nun's cell, wearing a dress of coarse cloth, tied at the waist with a crude rope. Somewhere the bell continued to toll. She had fled the temptations of the world. But the rope ran out the door and someone was pulling on it, dragging her like a fish on a line down a dark corridor to another room, overlooking a courtyard of the barracks beside the Place d'Armes. A heavy man with a sad, bruised face stood against the red-brick wall. Guns boomed and blood fell like a curtain down his forehead. *Father, Father.* She flung aside her nun's robe and ran naked down the corridor again to the shop window. She pressed her whole body against the glass, weeping. She looked down and there were hands on her breasts. The hands grew arms. She turned and saw William Coleman, smiling. She reached up to touch the curve of his cheek, to trace the memory of his smile with her fingers. She awoke weeping.

Wrapping herself in a blanket against the cold, Flora sat by the window, watching the world take shape. The huge old oak on the east lawn was the first thing to appear. Then the road beyond it, then the stone fence that marked the boundary of her property. Then the graves beneath the oak. Caesar lay there beside Henry Kuyper. Were they watching her now? Or was death an utter forgetting, an absolute blankness? She did not want to believe that. She wanted to believe that her father still existed somewhere, somehow, in the darkness, still caring for her. He alone had been content to wish her happiness. All the others—until Caleb—had insisted on owning, using Flora.

If William had permitted her to have the child in London, perhaps their life—or at least her life—would have changed. She would have had a purpose, a meaning beyond the world's traffic of use and abuse.

Perhaps Caleb was her child. There was something about him that awakened maternal feelings in her. But he was also a man. She remembered the baritone voice, turning her tentative French love song into an affirmation, vibrating with praise of New England's warrior God.

Perhaps Caleb was simply new. He made the world new. This sewer of a world, where one's worst expectations invariably proved correct, where the worst motives invariably prevailed. Caleb resisted such things; he defied them with a promise of unspoiled hope, of faith in himself, in her. He made her new again. He made her almost believe she could unlive the other memories, the degrading nights in London, the furtive afternoons in the barn with Caesar. Wounds in her womanhood, in her soul.

But William Coleman was more than a wound. He was more than acts, postures, degradations. William was birth and death. He was fundamental. She had known it for a long time. Even before their London world collapsed, every time she had asked the cards about their future, the Queen of Spades had confronted her. It was this sense of fate that had paralyzed her as much as her love for him.

William had taught her the power of love even when it was corrupted. He had murdered her heart and resurrected it by lacerating his own icy heart, in the end sacrificing it before her eyes like some weird God. It was impossible to forget his anguished reaffirmation of his love for her in Newgate Prison on the day they thought they were going to die.

Yet she had permitted Caleb to take her token, the bearded Queen of Hearts, and set out for Morristown to destroy William. Perhaps her dream had been trying to tell her that this decision was inevitable, that there was no way to escape his corrupted love except by killing him. Until she heard the truth about Caesar's murder, she had not believed William deserved death. Suffering, but not death. Now she believed it, wanted it, with only one reservation. She would not inflict the blow. In memory of that day in Newgate, she would not condemn him. She would simply turn her face away.

The cards had told her that Caleb would succeed. Last night she had turned up a Queen of Spades and a Queen of Hearts. Death and love in swift succession. She wanted him to succeed. She wanted to stop dreaming about William Coleman.

The red sun was rising into a cloudless sky. The glow tinted the brown spires, the gray roofs of New York. The city, image of the real world, was taking shape in the dawn. Major Walter Beckford waited there with his men and guns. Hugh Stapleton was there, too, locked in a prison cell.

She hoped Caleb would forgive her for Stapleton. She had sensed in their last conversation Caleb's yearning to return to his devotion to America. He wanted to bring her with him. But his attempt to invoke her father's love of freedom only confused her. England and its liberty were what her father had loved. How could the slaveowning Americans with their liberty slogans revolt against their mother country without convicting themselves of hypocrisy? They had thought their distance from England would make it easy for them to revolt. Now that it was proving to be a difficult, dangerous business, only a handful of the most stubborn rebels clung to the cause because for them, defeat would mean death. Flora did not want Caleb to be one of this remnant. His mind had already accepted the hypocrisy of the rebellion. She would not permit his heart to seduce him again. She would see that it remained loyal to her, a woman without a country. She told herself her own disloyalty was a virtue, not a flaw; it reinforced, purified their love.

Out on the road Flora saw a horseman riding hard, outlined against the red dawn sky. He slowed as he came to her gate, and trotted up the path to the house. He was wearing an American army uniform. Flora heard the crack of the brass knocker on the front door, Cato answering it. She rushed to the head of the stairs, where the word "letter" drove her back to the bedroom. She remembered the last letter that had been delivered by a man in an army uniform. It had told her that Caesar was dead.

Caleb? God would not permit it. The cards had forbidden it. Cato slowly ascended the stairs and knocked on her door. She told him to come in. "A soldier left this, mistress. Turned and rode away, though I offered him breakfast," Cato said.

The letter was addressed to her. She tore it open. It was a hasty scrawl, written on a piece of dirty paper. But it was Caleb's handwriting.

My dearest: This will be brought to you by one of Coleman's men. He has me prisoner in Red Peggy's grog shop. I've told him that I'm a servant of the King. He does not believe me. Only you can save me.

CALEB

"Bad news, mistress?" Cato asked.

"Yes," Flora said. "Get out the horses and sleigh. We're going to Morristown. As fast as possible."

411

"It'll be slow on the road, with the snow melting," Cato said. "Hard work for the horses."

"I don't care if it kills the horses. I want to go at a gallop."

Ignoring Nancy's plea to eat some breakfast, Flora was on the road in a half-hour. In spite of her demands, Cato refused to hurry the horses. "They'd be dead before we got to Newark, mistress," he said. "Then what?" She settled for a steady trot.

As they advanced into the countryside beyond Newark, they began passing other sleighs on the road. The distant clang of church bells explained them. It was Sunday. Flora looked into the solemn faces of farmers and their wives and wondered if God listened to their prayers. He had so long, so persistently refused to answer hers. Perhaps it was because she had never truly renounced William Coleman in her heart. She had never asked God to forgive her for that morning in New Orleans when she had crept out of her mother's house to meet William in the dawn.

If that was what God required for forgiveness, she was ready to surrender. She would willingly amputate whatever part of her heart or soul William Coleman still possessed. She would not only offer it to God as a mute sacrifice, she would renounce William to his face. She would threaten to expose him to the rebels if he refused to spare Caleb. She would confess—no, declare—her love for Caleb and her detestation of the very name William Coleman.

By the time Flora's sleigh reached Morristown the bright sun had vanished behind squadrons of scudding gray clouds. It would snow tonight or rain, depending on how far the temperature dropped. Cato asked directions at O'Hara's Tavern and soon found the

Vealtown Road. In a half-hour the sleigh stopped before Red Peggy's nondescript frame house. Flora went up the steps into a dim hall. From the left came the sound of voices. She opened a door and stepped into an equally dim taproom. A half-dozen men were sitting at tables. There was no one at the bar except a woman who was obviously Red Peggy. Her fiery hair glistened in the half-light. The bar, tucked into a corner of the room with no window near it, was especially dim. Flora could see little of the woman's face except her red lips and rouged cheeks.

Before she could take a step, Red Peggy said, "Down the hall, miss. The second door on the left. You'll find the gentleman you're looking for."

The drinkers stared at her. They were all rough, bulky men in homespun. They looked vaguely menacing. Flora backed into the hall and found the second door on the left. It was unlocked. She stepped inside and confronted an incredible sight. There, wearing Red Peggy's gingham dress, his lips, his cheeks still caked with rouge, his red wig tossed on a nearby table, was William Coleman, agent Twenty-six.

"What are you doing here?" he snarled in an unmistakably male voice.

"I came—to help—to save—Caleb."

"We killed him last night. He was a double agent."

"No! He wasn't!"

Tears streamed down Flora's cheeks. William ignored them. "Did you give him the bearded queen? Or did he steal it?"

"I gave it to him. I loved him. I'll always love him."

"No you won't. I'm still your lover, your fate. You

believed me when I told you that in Newgate. You'll believe it again."

Flora's will wavered, crumpled, in the ferocity of his purpose. It was true, what she had always suspected. William was more than corrupt ambition, he was evil, he had the kind of power that lived in curses and spells. That was how he had possessed her life. But how could she resist him without Caleb's strength, his goodness?

"Go back to Bergen immediately," William said. "The roads around here won't be safe tonight. The war is almost over. We'll be in London by summer, rich and famous. Forever beyond the reach of judges and bailiffs."

"Never," Flora said. "Never."

But she did not believe her own words. William smiled condescendingly at her defiance. "Go now, before they discover you're in Morristown and ask embarrassing questions."

Flora stumbled into the hall, obeying him, proving her defiance was worthless.

"Flora!"

The front door was open. A figure from the land of the dead stood there: Caleb. He ran toward her. Behind him strode a tall, uniformed man with a face that had once been handsome but had been ravaged into ugliness by anger or grief. Behind him came a half-dozen blank-eyed soldiers with fixed bayonets. It was madness. They were all ghosts. Next would come Caesar with his raging mouth and murderous hands.

"Did you see Coleman?" Caleb gasped. "Where is he?"

The hand on her arm was solid flesh. This was no ghost.

"Consider yourself under arrest," rasped the tall man in the officer's uniform.

"Shut up, for God's sake, Major," Caleb said. He seized Flora's hands. "My dearest, I can explain. I'll explain everything. But we've got to find him first. Where is he?"

Flora heard William Coleman's words: *He was a double agent.* She saw guilt in Caleb's eyes.

"There was never a word of truth to any of it, was there?" she said. "Let me congratulate you on being the cleverest liar I've ever met."

"There was more truth in it than I've ever spoken in my life," Caleb said. "Even when I lied, it was for—for your sake. For your future happiness."

"Jesus Christ," the major roared. "We haven't got time to worry about her happiness." He wrenched Flora out of Caleb's grasp and pushed her against the wall. "Where is he? Coleman. Twenty-six."

A reincarnated Red Peggy, her wig in place, rushed into the hall from the taproom. "Major," she cried in her gushy nasal voice, "is something wrong?"

"What is this woman doing here?" the major thundered.

"I have no idea," Red Peggy said. "A gentleman said she'd be coming. He gave me some money to see that they had a room to themselves. I suppose I shouldn't allow such things but a body's got to live, Major. What with the price of everything out of sight I can't make much serving liquor here—"

"Shut up," said the major. He turned to his squad of soldiers. "Search every room, from the cellar to the attic. Look in barrels, chests. He's got to be in here."

"Let me go with them, Major, to make sure nothing's stolen. You know how soldiers are," Red Peggy said.

"You get back in that taproom and tell me the name of each man in it," the major snapped. He strode down the hall, leaving Flora and Caleb alone.

"Please tell me the truth," Caleb begged her. "Prove to Major Stallworth that you're on our side. The side your father would have wanted you to be on. Liberty's side, Flora."

"You must think I'm the greatest fool that ever existed," Flora said.

"You've seen him. I knew it, the moment I saw you in the hall. You had death on your face. You looked as if someone had just condemned you to die."

"I'd like to see you condemned to die. And him, too. I despise you both."

The soldiers clattered up and down the stairs as they stood there. Major Stallworth emerged from the taproom looking baffled. Red Peggy followed him.

"All local farmers in there," Stallworth said. "I know every one of them."

The major stood there fuming until the soldiers returned from the cellar and the upper floors of the house to report that they had found no trace of the fugitive.

Stallworth muttered a curse. "Does she admit she saw him?"

"Not quite," Caleb said. "But I'm sure she did."

The major turned to Red Peggy. "What did the gentleman who met this woman look like?"

"He was as tall as you but much more handsome, Major," Red Peggy said. "He wore a maroon coat and buff breeches, a violet waistcoat. His boots were dark red—"

The major waved her into silence. "This gets us nowhere."

Flora glared at William Coleman alias Red Peggy. He was going to get away with it. His voice, his mannerisms, were perfect if slightly gross imitations of femininity.

"Flora," Caleb said, "William Coleman tried to murder me last night. This man, Major Stallworth, rescued me. Did Coleman tell you that when you saw him?"

"I wish he had killed you. I wish you'd killed each other."

"He tried to kill me for the same reason he killed Caesar. To keep you as his slave, his possession. Is that what you want?"

Flora glared at Red Peggy. She remembered Caleb asking her about Caesar's death: *Did you think it was pleasant—left to die in the snow?* She remembered the British officers looking forward to the pleasure of owning slaves. She had thought love was the only defense against William's evil spell. That had been her mistake. Hatred was the answer. Hatred even annihilated Newgate. Hatred was all she felt now for that hideous moment in their death caps with William babbling about love. Hatred, hatred, hatred would be her guide, her God, from now on.

"You're all vile—and stupid. He could be standing next to you right now and you wouldn't know it," Flora said.

Caleb and Stallworth stared at her, baffled. Stallworth

thought she was mocking them and began working himself into a fury. But Caleb saw that her hatred included William now. The Yankee hypocrite had learned to read her eyes, her voice. Flora watched exultation flare on his deceitful face as he made the crucial connection.

William was watching too. Before Caleb could move or speak, he pulled off the red wig, revealing his ugly shaved head. "All these years I thought I was your fate, Flora," he said. "Instead you're mine."

twenty-six

"To the Queen."

"The Queen."

Everyone rose to drink the solemn toast. Opposite Beckford, beside Lieutenant General Knyphausen, sat Major General James Robertson, the royal governor of New York. Robertson's head wagged like a signal flag on his shrunken neck. He was almost seventy. Beside him sat one of his "wards," as he called them—a redheaded American girl with strumpet written all over her. She and several friends provided entertainment at Robertson's all-night parties. When he was in liquor, Robertson acted the fool. Sober, he was one of the shrewdest politicians in the British army. He was drawing the double salary of general and royal governor of New York as a reward for his testimony before Parliament in 1778, when the politicians decided an investigation of the conduct of the war was necessary to assuage public opinion. Robertson had carefully defended certain reputations and shredded others.

Having performed the essential toasts to the King and Queen, General Knyphausen rose to depart. His normally severe manner always grew more frigid when he was exposed to the casual morality of the British officer corps in America. Knyphausen was another reason why Beckford had selected Alice Fowler as a female escort. Pietistic to the core like most of his men (the German infantry went into battle singing hymns, the British shouting blasphemies), Knyphausen would never have tolerated any moral irregularities in his aide.

"All right, Beckford, now that Attila the Hun has gone off to say his prayers, what's this bold stroke that you've been concocting?" Governor General Robertson said.

"I have no idea what you're talking about, General," Beckford said.

"You've got a New Jersey congressman in the Provost," said Major General James Pattison, taking Knyphausen's empty chair. "Is he part of it?" Pattison was Robertson's creature; as commandant of police he had a network of informers throughout New York.

"A piece of good luck, nothing more," Beckford said.

"Let me tell you something, Major," Robertson said. "Something I've learned from forty years in the army. The man who does not share the glory with his fellow officers may discover in time that he has no one with whom to share shame."

"I hope I'll never be accused on either side, General," Beckford said.

Black Sam Francis, the mulatto proprietor of the Queen's Head Tavern, mustered his waiters and began serving another round of port. It was time to depart. With a smile and a bow, Beckford led Alice to the door and put her in a hack. "Can we expect you for dinner some night soon?" she asked in her plaintive way.

"Perhaps tomorrow," Beckford said.

In the twilight, Major Beckford strolled across the city to the Provost Prison. Gray clouds were massing in the northeast, and the wind had an edge to it. The temperature hovered just above freezing. It would snow or rain tonight; neither would be unwelcome. Bad weather would help keep the New Jersey militia indoors.

The orders, signed by General Knyphausen, had gone to Brigadier Birch at noon. Another set of orders had been handed to Lieutenant Colonel Simcoe, directing him to stage an attack on the New Jersey shore, opposite Staten Island at midnight. "This will lend useful support to an operation of the cavalry under Brigadier Birch and Major Beckford, the details of which secrecy prevents me from describing," read the etched-in-acid final sentence.

At the Provost Prison, a guard rushed to inform the provost marshal, William Cunningham, of Major Beckford's presence. A massive, florid-faced man, who carried a club at his waist as a symbol of his authority, Cunningham was probably the richest jailer in the British empire. For every prisoner on his rolls he received a stipend from the army budget. Most of the money went into Cunningham's pocket. Very little went into filling his prisoners' bellies.

"How is our congressman today?" Beckford asked.

"Difficult. He refuses to touch the food we give him," Cunningham said. "It's better fare, let me tell you, than many a poor loyalist is eating in this city."

"I'm sure it is," Beckford said. "I want to talk with him."

The provost marshal escorted Beckford up the twisting stairs to the second floor. The chill emanating from the walls caused the major to draw his cloak around him. "I took it upon myself to deprive the congressman of his greatcoat," Cunningham said. "Your orders were to make him less than comfortable. It's outrageous for a rebel to own a coat that a British officer can't afford."

"I agree completely, Provost Marshal," Beckford said, certain that Cunningham had already found a British officer who was prepared to pay a bargain price for the coat.

Congressman Stapleton rose as they entered his cell. The only furnishings were a slop bucket and a pile of straw for a bed. Stapleton needed a shave. His expensive clothes were wrinkled and dirty. Although the congressman struggled to control it, he was trembling from the cold.

"Mr. Stapleton," Major Beckford said, "compassion impels me to make this visit. I fear for your health in this place."

"As well you should, sir," Stapleton replied.

"Having deprived me of my only article of warm clothing."

"All I need hear from you is a promise to be reasonable and you shall be escorted to my residence, where food and warmth await you."

"As I tried to sleep in this icebox, all the while listening to this son of a bitch beating other prisoners," Stapleton said, pointing to Cunningham, "my reason as well as my feelings told me only one thing: don't surrender."

"You'll have your friend General Washington for company later tonight."

"I'm sure you'll find him no more happy about his accommodations than I am."

"Nevertheless, I think his presence will make you a more reasonable man."

Going downstairs, Cunningham was growling like a bear. "You heard what he called me, Major? I'd like your permission to treat him with more severity."

"Not yet."

"Is it true, what you said about Washington?"

"If you mention it to anyone, I'll have you court-martialed, Provost Marshal."

"It will never pass my lips, Major."

Cunningham's venal face was aglow with admiration for Walter Beckford, the man who was about to make him George Washington's jailer.

At five o'clock, as dusk gathered, Brigadier Samuel Birch sent his aide to report that the last of the cavalry's horses had arrived from Long Island. He mustered 384 dragoons and 36 officers. Beckford rode to Birch's headquarters, out on the Bloomingdale Road. In the brigadier's stable, with the wooden training horses behind them like skeletal reminders of death and duty, Beckford stood on bales of hay and described their mission to the assembled officers.

"We're about to attempt something which, if it succeeds, will end the war: the capture of Mr. Washington. My spies at Morristown have penetrated his Life Guard. All the men on duty tonight will be in the King's service. We should therefore have no difficulty in achieving total surprise.

"To break down the door of Washington's headquarters, should anyone have time—or the presence of mind—to barricade it, we have a mine constructed by Major Whittlesey of the engineers." Beckford gestured to his batman and was handed the cask of powder, with the protruding spear that Henry Whittlesey had devised. "The insertion of this metal tip in the front door will activate a clock mechanism inside this barrel which will cause it to explode in sixty seconds."

Awed exclamations of delight. Beckford could see and hear similar adulation as he told the story to His Majesty and his court at Windsor. A triumph of British daring, scientific genius. He could see his memoirs being sold by the thousands in bookshops across England. *An Account of the Capture of George Washington and the Effective Ending of the Rebellion in America,* by the Right Honorable Major Sir Walter Beckford.

The major stepped down and let Brigadier Birch discuss the tactics of the mission. That done, the companies were paraded in the fields west of the Bloomingdale Road and formed into a column of fours. In a half-hour they were across the frozen Hudson conferring with the commander of the British fort at

Powles Hook. He reported that his latest patrols had found the countryside quiet.

As they came out of the commander's quarters a drizzle began to fall from the night sky. "A good omen," Beckford said. "Rain will wet their powder and leave Washington's Life Guard helpless. Your troopers can cut them down at their leisure."

"A pleasant prospect," Birch said. "Are you sure you want to risk yourself to plant the mine?"

"Quite sure," Beckford said.

Brigadier Birch had finally realized that this operation was going to succeed. He was casting about for a way to put himself at the head of the list of its heroes. But no one was going to thrust the spear trigger into the door of Washington's headquarters except Walter Beckford.

They set out, a long line of men with heads bowed against the weather, silent except for the jangle of bridles, the squishy thud of their horses' hooves in the wet snow. The advance guard rode a half-mile ahead of them and regularly sent back troopers to report. The road was clear for the first ten miles. Just beyond New Bridge the advance encountered two farmers coming home from a tavern, drunk and singing Dutch songs. Both were cut down, their horses seized. A mile farther on, they met a loyalist farmer on his way to New York with a sleighload of provisions. He cried out, "God save the King," seconds before a saber split his skull.

Behind Beckford and Birch there was an abrupt crash, an eruption of curses, the whinny of a horse in pain. Birch called a halt. They galloped back to find a fallen horse, a badly injured man. "General," said one of the officers to Birch, "the men tell me the horses are getting hard to manage. I think they're breaking through the crust of snow and it's cutting their fetlocks to the bone. Another ten miles and they'll be completely crippled."

"We'll slow our pace and see if that improves matters," Birch said.

They plodded forward to Hackensack, where the advance guard waited for them on the green. They told the same story. At least ten horses so badly crippled they could barely hobble. Officers reported at least fifty other horses in the main column in the same condition. They found a candle in one of the deserted houses near the town green and examined the legs of another twenty or thirty horses. On almost every animal the fetlock, the lump of flesh and sinew just above the hoof, was sliced raw.

"Are you sure of those reserve horses?" Birch asked. "We're going to need them."

"They're waiting in the barns of Great Rock Farm, just twenty miles away."

Birch ordered the advance guard forward again. The drizzling rain continued. Soon Beckford's horse was in trouble. Twice the animal stumbled and the major hauled him erect with a savage pull on the bridle. Beside him, Brigadier Birch's horse crashed to his knees and collapsed. Birch commandeered a horse from a dragoon in the next rank and ordered him to double up. "We may have to fight on foot," Birch said. "What a goddamn bloody mess."

"You read your orders, Brigadier. They explicitly stated that you were to make this attack at all hazards," Beckford said.

"Make it we shall," Birch replied. "But I may have a few words with you when we get back to New York."

Three horsemen loomed out of the night. "Where's Major Beckford?" bawled a captain. "We have a man here who says he's one of his agents. He claims our plan is discovered and we should turn back. The Bergen County militia is gathering behind us and Harry Lee's cavalry is coming at us from Morristown."

"Where is the fellow?" Beckford said. "Let me see him before you cut his throat."

"It's Caleb Chandler, Major," said a familiar voice. "So help me God I've risked my life to save you. The woods along the Warwick Road are thick with cannon and infantry for two miles north of Morristown. I saw Lee's cavalry parade at Jockey Hollow."

"Look, sir," called a dragoon, "is that a signal?"

Off the road about a mile away a gush of flame leaped against the night. "That's Great Rock Farm. Where our fresh horses are waiting," Beckford said numbly.

"*Were* waiting, Major," Birch said.

Beckford dug his spurs into his crippled horse and sent the animal hobbling down the road to Great Rock Farm. By the time he reached the barn it was a huge tower of flame. John Nelson came running up to him, screaming, "Your friend the painter ratted. They fired the barn and turned the bloody house into a fortress. I've lost three men trying to break down the door."

"Are you sure?" Beckford said dazedly. Was it possible? Paul?

"He left this on the porch. He called to us to use it for target practice."

427

By the leaping flames of the barn Beckford saw Paul's portrait of him—the same resolute expression on his face, the background precisely as he had described it, the cavalry charging, the Ford mansion in flames. But a dunce cap had been added to his head.

Beckford cut away the ropes holding the mine on his saddle. "Take this," he said. "Shove the spear in the front door and the charge will knock it down in sixty seconds. Go in there and kill every man, woman, and child in the house."

"With pleasure," Nelson said.

Beckford swung his horse around and tried to goad him back to the main road. The anguished animal refused to take another step. The major leaped from the saddle and tried to shoot him. The rain had dampened his powder and his pistol clicked uselessly. He labored back toward the main road on foot. Halfway there, he was confronted by Brigadier Birch and a dozen of his officers.

"Damn it, Major," roared Birch, "we have no time to waste. That fellow—your agent—tells me your whole network is uncovered. Your chief agent caught, disguised as a woman. It's the talk of Morristown."

"And will soon be the talk of New York, I fear," said one of the officers in a distinctly mocking voice.

Beckford laughed bitterly. "I begin to think Mr. Washington is a genius, after all."

"I begin to think you're a fool," snarled Birch. "Get up behind one of these fellows and—"

A terrific explosion raced across the snowy darkness from Great Rock Farm. Birch's horse skittered wildly. "What in hell was that?" he said.

"The mine," Beckford said.

"God damn all," Birch said. "We've risked four hundred men and ruined four hundred horses to blow up a bloody farmhouse."

twenty-seven

Inside the house at Great Rock Farm, they had wedged beams, cut from the underpinnings in the cellar, against the front door. Elsewhere they had erected barriers in hallways and doorways, jumbles of furniture and mattresses. These obstacles were Pompey's idea. It was the way they had fought the Indians in the north woods in his youth. Malcolm Stapleton had ordered his men to pile branches and bushes in front of their bivouacs to trap the Indians when they charged. Would it work against the savages they were about to challenge? Hannah wondered.

Pompey and the other blacks were amused by the dunce cap Paul had added to his portrait of Walter Beckford before he propped it up outside the front door. Paul said that he hoped it would convince Nelson that the plan was blown. He might retreat without attacking them. Hannah saw the caricature's deeper significance. Paul was abandoning once and for all the double agent's ambiguity.

While they were turning the house into a fortress Hannah had obeyed Nelson's arrogant orders to give food and rum to his men. She met him at the kitchen door with whatever he demanded, truckling to his boastful humor, humbly nodding to his reiterated threat to kill anyone who tried to leave the house. He talked freely about the trouble he was having with local loyalists, who were reluctant to volunteer their horses. To speed the roundup, he withdrew the sentries from the front and back doors. Hannah's cringing obedience, his contempt for the blacks, and his assumption that Paul was in Beckford's pay had convinced Nelson that there was no need to worry about them.

When Nelson withdrew the sentries, Hannah ordered fifteen-year-old Lewis, the youngest of the blacks, to take little Malcolm through the woods to the Van Damm farm a mile away. Then she and Paul rehearsed the plan to burn the barn. She practiced with the pistol-shaped fire lighter until she was able to get a flame three tries out of four. She went over the story she would use if she encountered one of Nelson's men: she wanted to say good-bye to her favorite horse.

At 2 A.M. Hannah crept out through the cold rain and reached the barn unchallenged. She opened the back door and threw herself into the dank winter hay. Beyond her, in the darkness, the horses stamped and snuffled. *Poor beasts*, she prayed. *Forgive me for this terrible act. I wish there were a way to tell you why I am doing it.*

She took the pistol tinder from the inner pocket of her skirt. It had the trigger and flintlock mechanism of a gun, without the barrel. Inserting a candle in the metal loop beside the flintlock, she added some grains of gunpowder to the tinder in the pan. She pulled the trigger. The flint clicked against the metal. There was a spark but no flame. Her heart almost stopped beating; the click had seemed so loud. She tried again. This time the candle became a finger of flame. She thrust it into the hay. At first it only ran thinly across the dank outer fibers. Then it burrowed like a voracious snake into the dry inner stuff.

Whuff! In seconds the whole interior of the barn was blazing light. It reminded Hannah of the illumination she had once imagined her soul would receive when she ascended to the God of Glory. Now it was earthly salvation she sought as she crawled backward toward the door in the ferocious heat and stumbled into the rainy, half-white darkness. She pulled her skirts above her knees and ran for the house while behind her a voice howled, "She burning them!" It was the monster, Bogert. Once, she fell and thought she was doomed. She imagined Hugh learning of it in New York and wondered if he would feel any grief or guilt.

As the wet snow struck her face, guns roared in the house; she heard the bullets hissing through the darkness above her head. The battle had begun. They needed her in the house. Paul, Pompey, needed her. To hell with Hugh! She scrambled to her feet and lunged toward safety while muskets boomed behind her and more bullets hurtled above her to smash into the old timbers.

Paul flung open the kitchen door and she crashed

into his arms. "Welcome home," he said. They helped Pompey and his son Isaac wedge a beam against the door. They piled chairs on the kitchen table and placed them behind the beam to create more obstacles for the attackers. Isaac was left to guard this position. In the front hall, Paul picked up his father's favorite gun, the huge double-barreled musket. Pompey handed Hannah a lighter musket called a fusil. They waited behind another barricade of chairs and tables. The other blacks, four of them, guarded side windows.

Pompey had given them all lessons in loading and firing the clumsy guns. He had made them repeat at least two dozen times the basic routine of ramming home the bullet and powder charge, sprinkling powder in the firing pan, then squeezing, not jerking, the trigger. As they waited Pompey shouted one more reminder: "Aim low!"

Two more volleys from Nelson and his men smashed out windows and thudded into the timbers. Then they rushed the house. Wiert Bogert crashed his huge shoulder against the front door. But the reinforcing beams held. Paul and Pompey forced him to retreat with blasts from the front windows. Other guns thundered on the right and left flanks. From the back of the house came a cry of agony. Isaac, Pompey's son, came staggering into the hall, blood gushing from his mouth. Pompey steadied his musket on a chair and killed the man who came charging at them from the kitchen.

The blacks at the side windows shouted that they had hit at least two other attackers. That eliminated almost half of Nelson's force. Pompey ordered two of the blacks to guard the kitchen door. They waited for a few minutes while the light from the burning barn flickered wildly on the shattered windows and the screams of the dying horses filled the house.

A blast of musketry blew the last shards of glass from the front windows. Footsteps thudded on the front porch. A strange pause. Then a blinding, head-splitting explosion. Fragments of the front door flew past them like bullets. A huge billow of smoke gushed into the hall. Out of the murk came Wiert Bogert and two other men. They thrashed against the barrier of furniture and mattresses, roaring curses and firing their guns. Paul's gun boomed and Pompey fired a second later, toppling the two lesser men. Hannah pressed her fusil against her shoulder and aimed it at Bogert. She pulled the trigger and felt a jolt of pain as the gun recoiled. Bogert fired back at point-blank range. Pompey shoved her aside and the bullet struck him in the chest. Dropping his musket, Bogert flung chairs and chests right and left to get at them. As he burst through the barrier the mortally wounded Pompey tried to club him with the butt of his empty musket. Bogert brushed the gun aside and drove his fist into the old man's face.

"Get up the stairs," Paul shouted. Hannah obeyed him, scrambling on her hands and knees. Behind her, Paul backed up crabwise, reloading his gun. Bogert drew a pistol and shot Paul above the heart as he reached the top of the stairs. Gasping in agony, Paul pulled both triggers of his father's old gun. The blast struck Bogert in the chest. It would have sent an ordinary man hurtling backward down the stairs. But the monster continued to stumble upward until his hand clutched Paul's dangling foot. Weeping, Hannah kicked the hand away and dragged Paul into the bedroom.

"Load the gun," Paul said as she propped him against the wall. "Load—the—gun."

She obeyed him like a child, mechanically ramming home the cartridges and the balls, sprinkling the powder in the pan, while more blasts of gunfire, screams of rage and pain, echoed downstairs. Then terrible silence.

Then footsteps on the stairs. John Nelson's cry: "Oh, lad, lad, the bastards have done you, they've done you. Why didn't you wait for me?"

Then a scream of madness. "But we shall have revenge, lad!"

John Nelson, in his filthy regular's red coat, rose from the stairwell. His face was streaked with powder and blood, his musket leveled. "We would have sailed home," he shouted. "We would have sailed home together from this murdering country."

Hannah clutched Malcolm Stapleton's gun to her breast, its barrel pointed to the ceiling. Nelson paused at the door. Paul lay against the wall, helpless, dying, his shirt soaked with blood.

Nelson glared contemptuously at her. He assumed she was incapable of using the gun. Her grief, her dazed horror, made her look like a female parody of a soldier. Then he recognized Paul. "There you are, you buggering little doublecrosser," he said. Ignoring Hannah, he strode across the room, raising his musket to bring the butt down on Paul's head.

All in one motion, one moment of mingled love and despair, Hannah leveled and fired the old gun. The two bullets struck Nelson in the back, flinging him against the wall. The recoil of the gun flung Hannah in the opposite direction. A dense cloud of white gunsmoke swirled into the center of the room. Nelson writhed along the wall for a moment, then managed to turn, still gripping his gun.

"Bitch," he said. He tried to raise his gun to a firing position. Paralyzed, Hannah watched him through the haze of gunsmoke. "Bitch," Nelson choked again, and slid sideways down the wall into oblivion.

Hannah did not know how long she leaned against the bed, clutching the gun. Voices downstairs aroused her. She listened indifferently, not caring whether they were British or American. Then more footsteps on the stairs.

A blond-haired, remarkably handsome young man wearing a green coat and a leather cavalryman's helmet appeared in the doorway. "Mrs. Stapleton?" he said. "Thank God you're alive. I'm Major Henry Lee. We saw your barn burning—"

"It's part of a plan to seize General Washington. The British cavalry—"

"—are hobbling back to New York as fast as their crippled horses can carry them. One of our spies fortunately penetrated their plan."

Hannah stared numbly at another spy. Paul's eyes were closed, his face peaceful. She found herself yearning for the power to proclaim his courage throughout America. The prodigal son had returned to his father's house in time to rescue it from disgrace. His heroism would never be recorded in a history book. Their murderous little skirmish would probably not even be mentioned in the newspapers. She alone would have to keep Paul's memory alive in her ruined heart.

Major Henry Lee, her rescuer, only made the ruin of that treacherous organ more complete. He was so young, so handsome. His flowing blond hair, his confident smile, reminded her of Hugh ten years ago. Hugh, her traitor husband.

Hannah asked Major Lee if there were any survivors downstairs. He said three of her blacks were wounded but alive. His men would rush them to Morristown to be treated by the army's doctors. "It might be best if you came, too, madam," Lee said. "The loyalty of this countryside is too uncertain to leave you here alone."

In the morning, Major Lee's troopers buried Paul and Pompey and Isaac beside Malcolm and Catalyntie Stapleton in the shadow of the great hump of rock that had given the farm its name. They stopped at the Van Damm farm to pick up little Malcolm, then rode on to Morristown.

At headquarters, General Washington received Hannah with grave courtesy. He shook hands with Malcolm, then sat him on his lap while Major Lee described the battle at Great Rock Farm. Washington listened with fascination, his eyes, his whole face, coming alive. As Lee finished the story the general reached across the desk and took Hannah's hand. "I grieve for your losses, madam. For your brother-in-law and your brave blacks. But let me say what comes irresistibly to my lips. Malcolm Stapleton would have been proud to call you his daughter."

"I find it embarrassing, Your Excellency," Lee said. "We had four hundred British within reach of our sabers and only this lady struck a blow at them."

"There were strong and sufficient reasons for our tactics, Major," Washington said. "I'll explain them to you at another time. Now, would you take this young man on a tour of our camp while I talk for a few moments with his mother?"

Major Lee, knowing a reprimand when he heard one, obeyed. As he left, Malcolm informed him that he wanted to see a cannon.

Washington smiled briefly. "There are times when Major Lee makes me wonder if he and your son are the same age," he said. "What he tells me of you, however, is more important than his disappointment at my not letting him cross sabers with the British. Your courage, madam, makes me hope you can bear a frank discussion of a matter that must be very painful to you."

"My husband."

"Yes. He's been unfaithful to you. But there's no proof that he's been disloyal to his country. Flora Kuyper, the woman he was visiting, is here at Morristown. We've questioned her rather closely. She tells us that Mr. Stapleton didn't leave willingly with his captors."

Hannah remembered her halfhearted prayer, asking only for Hugh's patriotism. Did she still mean it? Did she really care what happened to him now? "I'm—I'm glad," she said.

"I'm afraid, now that the enemy's plans have miscarried, they may abuse him. Would you be willing to go to New York to help your husband?"

"How could I help?" Hannah asked.

She stared absently away from Washington at the titles of books on a shelf: *General Essay on Tactics*. *The King of Prussia's Instruction to his Generals*.

"Two ways. You could bolster his courage. We suspect the British will try to get—either by persuasion or abuse—a statement from him, calling for a

439

negotiated peace. It could do us a good deal of harm."

Hannah nodded, signifying only her agreement that such a statement could be harmful. "What else?" she asked.

"You may also embarrass the British into giving Mr. Stapleton better treatment. The British are always anxious to appear humane, no matter how inhumane they may be in private. They can hardly refuse a wife's request to visit her husband in prison. If you succeed in getting the congressman moved to better quarters, we can begin to think about rescuing him."

"How?" Hannah said. She could not imagine that anything less than a British surrender would free Hugh from their cordon of men and guns.

"We're sending one of our ablest spies to New York with orders to make the attempt the moment it appears possible."

Hannah nodded numbly, not really believing George Washington, again not really sure she wanted to go to New York. She was incapable of any gesture of love or support for Hugh at this moment.

"I hope you'll consider yourself my guest while you recuperate from last night's ordeal," Washington said. "Mrs. Washington is upstairs, eager to do everything in her power to make you comfortable. As soon as you feel ready to go to New York, let me know."

Hannah realized, as she nodded again, that as far as this man was concerned, the matter was decided. She would go to New York. She would try to rescue her unfaithful, more or less traitorous husband. She would do it for Paul, for Pompey, for Isaac, as much as for Hugh. In spite of death and desolation, what had happened last night at Great Rock Farm was not an ending but a beginning. She had joined a mysterious fraternity, to which this man belonged. Like him, she owed a debt to men who had died for her and for an idea of a country—the United States of America. Her personal feelings were no longer important. *Malcolm Stapleton would have been proud to call you his daughter.* She understood what those words meant.

twenty-eight

Uhhhhhh, moaned the March wind. The gray sky seemed low enough to touch the treetops. Cato sat on the coachman's box like a black statue. The horses were plodding past the place on Morristown's green where Caleb Chandler had found Caesar Muzzey's body. Some of the same snow, beaten into pocks and hollows by last night's rain, was still there.

Beside Caleb in the sleigh sat Flora Kuyper in a purple dress and traveling cloak. She had spent the night at O'Hara's Tavern. She stared straight ahead, her eyes rigidly averted from his forlorn gaze. They stopped in front of the Ford mansion. Caleb tried to help her out of the sleigh. "Cato will do it," Flora said, withdrawing her hand. "I don't want to touch you if I can avoid it."

Yesterday afternoon, they had driven here in the

same sleigh with William Coleman and Major Benjamin Stallworth beside them. Coleman had persuaded Stallworth to let him change to male clothes. Red Peggy's fluttery mannerisms and voice had vanished with her rouge and skirts. The man who had seduced Flora confronted them, a compound of willful sensuality and domineering pride. When they brought him to General Washington, agent Twenty-six had at first arrogantly refused to confess or reveal anything. But Stallworth had trumped the bearded queen with predictable savagery. "Tell us what you know or Mrs. Kuyper hangs tomorrow morning," he had said.

Caleb, his eyes on Flora, had almost protested. But he remained a prisoner of necessity. "Does this proposal have your approval, General Washington?" Coleman had asked.

"Yes," Washington said. His voice had been as hard as Stallworth's, without the iron rasp.

The threat had worked. William Coleman had begun to bargain with them. In return for Flora's safe conduct to New York, he had agreed to reveal Beckford's route and plan of attack. Once Flora was in New York, he said that he might, under certain conditions, agree to provide the names of the men in his network in Morristown.

After locking Coleman in the town jail and leaving Flora under guard at O'Hara's Tavern, Stallworth had proposed putting a brigade of infantry and a dozen cannon in the woods along the Warwick Road to annihilate Beckford and the British cavalry. Washington had demurred. He wanted to defeat and disgrace Beckford as an intelligence director. "It will blind

444

them for a few months and give us the time we need to revive this army," he said.

He pointed out that it would also give Caleb unshakable credit with the British. How could they distrust a spy who had saved four hundred dragoons from slaughter? "You may be able to use this good faith to free Congressman Stapleton," the general added in his casual way.

Now, the morning after Major Beckford had stumbled back to New York in mortified disarray, Flora Kuyper was about to join him. Stallworth had cryptically ordered Caleb to bring her to headquarters first. An aide escorted them to George Washington's office. The general closed the door and studied Flora for a moment.

"You think ill of us, madam?" he said.

"Why shouldn't I?" she said

"You think we set this young man to snare your affections, out of malice?"

"What else can I think?"

"There was, from your point of view, some malice in our policy. We prefer to call it patriotism—or necessity. But as far as Mr. Chandler was concerned, he had no choice but to obey our orders. I saw how difficult this was for him, Mrs. Kuyper. It was clear that his heart belonged to you before we put it under the orders of his country. Now that we've met, I can understand why."

"You're too late with your explanations—and your compliments, General," Flora said.

"You alone can be the judge of that," Washington said. "But if you'll let an older, if not wiser, man advise you, the heart eventually heals its wounds—

445

especially if there's another heart to which it can turn for honest sympathy."

"I've never had honest sympathy from any man in my life—except my father."

"Not true, not true. I've seen with my own eyes Mr. Chandler's sympathy. Let me assure you, madam, you also have mine. I hope you don't see our sending you to New York as banishment."

"Are you trying to turn me into a spy for you?" Flora asked.

"No. I'm trying to tell you that as far as the government of the United States is concerned, you have nothing to fear."

"I despise your forgiveness—as much as I despise Mr. Chandler," Flora said. "I'll take advantage of it in only one way. Let me bring my slaves with me. I assume that my farm will be confiscated. I don't want them sold at auction like cattle."

"Confiscation can be prevented," Washington said. "I have some influence with the civil government of New Jersey."

Flora shook her head, all willful passion. "I don't trust you. I want them with me."

"How will you support them and yourself in New York, madam?"

"I intend to free them."

"I look forward to the day when a free country will permit me to do the same thing for my blacks. But how will you support yourself without their labor?"

"I intend to pursue the profession for which you and Mr. Chandler have trained me, General—whore."

Washington lowered his head for a moment. "Madam," he said in a mournful voice, "I accept the rebuke in the name of the United States." He raised his head and became the commander in chief again. "Mr. Chandler, take Mrs. Kuyper to the jail to say good-bye to the prisoner, William Coleman. He insists on it as one of the conditions for giving us further information. Do you have any objection to seeing Mr. Coleman, madam?"

"Not in the least," Flora said. "I find him no more—or less—despicable than Mr. Chandler—or you."

At the Morristown jail, William Coleman's wrists and ankles were manacled and leg chains wound in heaps around his feet. He looked ghostly. The shadowy cell seemed to have sapped some of the defiant vitality he had displayed when he was captured.

"Flora, dearest," he said. "I was afraid you wouldn't come."

"He brought me," Flora said with a contemptuous nod toward Caleb. "He's my keeper—for the moment."

Coleman tried to take her hands. Flora stepped back, refusing to let him touch her. He accepted the rejection and dropped his weighted arms to his sides.

"This is the last time we'll meet," he said in a sad, steady voice. "You have good reason to hate me, I know. But in these ten years past I've done nothing but out of love for you. We shared the same hard fate—to have been born too low for our dreams and desires."

"For your dreams. Your mad, grandiose dreams," Flora said.

"A gambler's dreams. But my last card can still recoup most of your losses. Tell Beckford I'll die a loyal servant of the King, confident that His Majesty's generosity will protect you. Assure him I've betrayed no one and a mutiny is still possible."

For a moment Caleb was confused. This did not sound like a man who was going to negotiate for his freedom by revealing all the members of his network once Flora was safe in New York. Studying that arrogant, sensual face, stamped now with mourning, but also suffused with a remarkable resignation, Caleb realized that William Coleman did not want freedom. In London he was a convicted felon who could offer Flora nothing but a life of poverty and disgrace. By dying in Morristown he could finally prove the truth of his love for her, the love that he had avowed and betrayed too often. Caleb saw that William Coleman had made Flora his faith, his hope, his charity. From the moment of his capture he had done nothing, said nothing, that was not connected to his obsessed, corrupted love.

"I don't want your king's protection, William," Flora said. "I won't accept it even if it's offered."

"Yes, you will," Coleman said with a blaze of his extraordinary gray eyes.

Flora shook her head. "I'm going to practice the profession you taught me in London, William. But I won't gamble the money away."

"No," he said, stumbling toward her over his chains. "No. I forbid it."

Flora stepped back again and the chains caught Coleman. He swayed on them, groping helplessly toward her.

"Good-bye, William," Flora said.

She turned and walked out of the jail. Caleb followed her. Behind them, William Coleman roared: *"I forbid it. I forbid it. Flora!"*

Outside, Caleb tried to help Flora into the sleigh. Again she asked for Cato's hand. As they repeated this ritual of detestation Benjamin Stallworth rode up. Caleb wondered if he should tell the major what he had just heard from Coleman. He decided to say nothing. He did not really think that Coleman's mutineers, shorn of their leader, could wreck the army. Perhaps he also owed something as a human being to William Coleman. Who else but Caleb Chandler understood the nature, the power of the love that had destroyed him, its unique compound of pity and beauty, sadness and desire?

Major Stallworth handed Flora an order, signed by General Washington, permitting her to take her blacks and any other movable property she chose to New York. A half-dozen of Major Henry Lee's green-coated cavalrymen waited to escort her. Caleb gripped the side of the sleigh, staring at Flora's face in frozen profile. "I won't let you do it," he said. "I'll come to New York and stop you."

"If I ever see your lying face in that city, I'll tell Beckford the truth about you. I'd enjoy seeing you hanged."

Caleb saw that she was beyond his reach, beyond the reach of them all, in a world of loss that she was determined to explore to its depths. It was a glimpse of damnation as the theologians described it—the rejection of even the possibility of faith or hope or love. Where, to whom, could he turn to save her? Washington had tried, with his worldly common sense. Stallworth, the minister manqué in the service of Mars, did not think she was worth the trouble. Every other minister Caleb knew would declare her beyond the mercy of New England's God.

He did not know how long he clung to the sleigh,

staring at that beautiful, hatred-suffused face. "Will you stand free, Mr. Chandler?" Cato finally called.

Caleb withdrew his hands and the sleigh surged up the road toward New York. Would she turn her head, give even a hint of regret, irresolution? She never moved. The sleigh rounded the bend in the road about a quarter of a mile beyond Washington's headquarters and disappeared.

"Listen to me, Chandler," rasped Benjamin Stallworth. "You'll be on your way to New York tomorrow. Under no circumstances are you to go near that woman. You're there to get Stapleton out of the Provost, remember that. Remember you're the one—with her help—who put him there. Are you listening to me, Chandler?"

"I'm listening," Caleb said, his eyes still on the empty road.

But in his mind roared a voice that echoed William Coleman's farewell: *I forbid it.*

twenty-nine

In his cell in the Provost Prison, Hugh Stapleton crouched in a corner on his pile of straw, trying to escape the chilling current of night air that the March wind swept through the glassless window. His head ached, his nose ran; he had the worst cold of his life. After three days of prison food, his stomach alternated between hunger and nausea. The meat was foul, the soup rancid with grease, the bread as hard as stone.

Footsteps ascended the stairs. He placed his eye to the small, barred opening in the cell door. Were they bringing George Washington to share this misery? If Beckford's plan had succeeded, the general would have been captured yesterday. But the British would probably try persuasion first; only if Washington was defiant would they consign him to the Provost.

One part of the congressman's mind dreaded Washington's appearance. His capture would mean the end of the rebellion. Another part of his mind almost welcomed it. He needed an ally, an example, if his own defiance was going to last much longer. On the other hand, perhaps a captured Washington would counsel negotiation, a qualified surrender. The congressman's ordeal would be over.

Stapleton got a glimpse of Walter Beckford's fat face in the flickering lantern light of the passageway. Then the lock turned, the door swung open, and the director of British intelligence walked into the cell. He was accompanied by the chaplain from Connecticut, Caleb Chandler, wearing the same threadbare cloak and old-fashioned suit he had worn the night they had met on Morristown green.

"Mr. Stapleton," Chandler said, extending his hand, "how nice to see you again, sir. I wish it were in better surroundings."

"So do I," Stapleton said, ignoring his hand. "And I wish you were in better company."

"How are you this evening?" Major Beckford asked.

"As cold—and as much an American—as I was two nights ago. Have you captured General Washington?"

"Our plan worked perfectly," Beckford said. "Now all we need is your signature on this statement calling on Congress to negotiate peace."

He drew a piece of paper from his pocket and thrust it at Stapleton.

"I couldn't possibly sign such a statement without conferring with General Washington," the congressman said.

"That's out of the question," Beckford shrilled.

"He'll soon be on his way to the gallows. But you can still save your neck if you cooperate."

The congressman began to look closely at Major Beckford. His tone was much too strident for a man who had just executed the most daring coup of the war. He was not exuding the sort of confidence he had displayed at Flora Kuyper's house. There was something wrong with the expression on Caleb Chandler's face, too, something fraudulent about his supercilious smile.

"I begin to suspect you're a liar, sir," Stapleton said to Beckford. "I wouldn't be surprised if General Washington is sitting down to supper in Morristown at this very moment. Would to God I were with him."

"No matter where Mr. Washington is," Beckford said, "you are here, sir, in our power. If you want to get out of here alive, if you don't want your reputation ruined, you will sign this statement."

"If I have to choose between being known as a fool or a traitor, I prefer the fool. It has the merit of honesty. I have been a fool. I was never a traitor and nothing you say or do to me can make me one."

"Flora Kuyper is here in New York. She's prepared to describe your meetings with her in detail."

"The *Royal Gazette* will sell out that edition," Stapleton said. "I hope the editor makes it clear that you set her to the business. If the world knows me as a fool, it should also know you as a swine."

For a moment Major Beckford looked as if he might burst into tears. "Talk some sense to him," he all but wailed to Caleb Chandler.

The chaplain replaced his supercilious smile with a sanctimonious manner. "Let me first admit that Mr.

Washington has not been captured," Chandler said in an infuriatingly unctuous tone. "That was merely a stratagem of Major Beckford's, to speed your persuasion. The plan to seize the great man miscarried, but I was fortunately able to warn the major and the British cavalry in time and they returned to New York without the loss of a man."

"You've been in this bastard's pay from the start?" Stapleton shouted. "You goddamn Yankee hypocrite."

"I became a servant of His Majesty out of a conviction that only his goodness can restore peace and prosperity to America," Chandler said.

"Piss on His Majesty and His Majesty's servants," the congressman roared.

"Sir, your language shocks me," Chandler said. "I'm trying to save you from unnecessary pain and suffering."

"Thus far," Beckford added, "I've protected you from Provost Marshal Cunningham. If I walk out of here without your signature, that protection will be withdrawn."

"The more I hear, the more I think you're trying to save your own neck, Major," Hugh Stapleton said. "As for this contemptible man of God, I'm sure he's like every Yankee I've ever known—ready to sell his soul for the right price."

The turncoat chaplain's eyes squinted with indignation. "Your blasphemous reference to my calling is bad enough, sir. But to heap contumely on the place of my birth—"

"Don't waste any more breath on him, Mr. Chandler," Beckford snapped. "We'll see how patriotic he feels after a week or two in a dungeon belowstairs."

"May God have mercy on you, Mr. Stapleton," Chandler said.

"Go to hell," the congressman said.

The frustrated persuaders departed. For a few minutes Hugh Stapleton felt good. The argument had been almost as invigorating as a warm fire in his cell. But a *whoosh* of the March wind through his window reminded him of how chilled he was, how isolated. He lay down on his bed of straw and realized that the failure to seize George Washington would only make the British more determined to wring some profit out of capturing him. While the circumstances of his capture, the motive that had brought him to Flora Kuyper's house in Bergen, would incline the Americans to abandon him.

A half-hour later, Stapleton heard the familiar stomp of Provost Marshal Cunningham's boots on the stairs. He opened the cell door and gave the congressman a grim smile. "We've got orders to escort you to the accommodations you deserve, you rebel bastard," he said. An Irish sergeant almost as big and mean-looking as Cunningham gestured with a musket. They led the congressman down the winding stairs to the prison's dungeons, fifty feet below the ground. Here the cold had a harsher, more abusive power. The below-zero days of January and February still lurked in this subterranean world.

Cunningham opened an iron door and pointed into a cell not much wider than a grave. There was an inch of water on the floor. The walls oozed slime. "I won't go in there," Hugh Stapleton said.

Cunningham punched the congressman in the face, sending him flying into the watery muck on his back.

"Sweet dreams, rebel," the provost marshal said, and slammed the door.

Congressman Stapleton stumbled to his feet, his coat and breeches soaked. He was in almost total darkness. Only a faint light entered the cell through a slit in the door. There was no furniture, only a slop bucket; not even straw for a bed. For the first day, or what he thought was the first day—it was hard to judge the passage of time—he received neither food nor water. The cold was unrelenting, voracious. It seemed to emanate from the walls in a brutal parody of heat. Refusing to lie down in the muck, the congressman tried to sleep standing up and found it impossible. He finally collapsed into a huddled fetal ball, searching for warmth in his congealing flesh.

He awoke desperately hungry and thirsty. He pounded on the cell door and shouted for food and water. Another Irish soldier eventually responded. He threw a piece of bread in the muck and handed him a cup of water. "Eat up, rebel," he said. "That's breakfast, dinner, and supper."

Much later, as Hugh Stapleton crouched in a corner shivering convulsively, Provost Marshal Cunningham opened the door. "Ready to sign that statement, rebel?"

"No," the congressman said.

"You're a fool, rebel," the provost marshal said, and slammed the door.

Was he right? Hugh Stapleton wondered. If he died in this inhuman icehouse, who would know? The British would publish a lie: Congressman Stapleton hanged himself in his cell. Something like that. His letter to Flora Kuyper would be flourished to substantiate the story. The turncoat Yankee chaplain,

Chandler, would vouch for it. Hannah, his sons, George Washington, his fellow congressmen, would see no reason to doubt it.

Worse, the war might well end in a negotiated peace two or three months after his death. Was there any other alternative to the present stalemate? He had read enough history to know that the advantage in such negotiations lay with the side that held out longest. The supplicant was always the loser. Was that diplomatic difference worth his life? Didn't it make his death even more meaningless? Wasn't there a very good chance that someone else in Congress, captured or free, would issue the call for reconciliation Beckford was demanding?

For a while Hugh Stapleton clung to his personal resentment of Walter Beckford. The fat sodomite, probably with the connivance of his brother, Paul, had selected him for plucking. He would not give the Williamite bastard the satisfaction of breaking him!

As the cold began to bite into the congressman's bones, the cell door opened again. The Reverend Chandler, his supercilious smirk intact, introduced a middle-aged, scholarly-looking officer, Major Henry Whittlesey of the engineers. Whittlesey said the Reverend Chandler had persuaded him to make this visit. "I want you to know that many officers in the garrison sympathize with your situation and sincerely hope you'll see the wisdom of a call for negotiations. Personally, I've long been hoping for a peace of reconciliation."

"You have an odd way of reconciling people, sir," Stapleton said. "So far I've become reconciled to only one thing—an early death."

"I'm sure Major Beckford had no idea that conditions in these dungeons were so harsh," Chandler said, drawing his cloak around him to ward off the cold.

"Would you be so kind as to tell him about them?" Stapleton said.

"I'd be happy to do so—but he's indisposed," Chandler said, missing the sarcasm. "Some of the cavalry officers have made a most unjust attack on him for the failure of the attempt to seize Mr. Washington. There's even talk of a court-martial."

"That's the best news I've heard in days."

"But it won't alter your situation, sir," Whittlesey said. "Unless you change your mind."

The visit deepened Hugh Stapleton's moral confusion. The cold soon evaporated the small satisfaction of Walter Beckford's disgrace. Major Whittlesey was right. It did not alter his situation. Others besides Beckford wanted his signature on a call for peace. Why not sign it? Hugh Stapleton was a businessman, not a politician. All his life he had lived in comfort, ease. Who could expect him to endure this kind of torture?

Alone in the icy darkness, the congressman groped for the answer to this question. Certainly not Congressman Samuel Chase of Maryland or Robert R. Livingston of New York. They were men of the world, they knew there were limits to a gentleman's endurance. But the voices, the faces, of these acquaintances had no resonance. Neither did his mother's voice: *You have gotten yourself into a bad bargain, Hugh,* she would say. *You must cut your losses and buy your way out of it.*

Only one voice gave him a different answer—a voice that came out of the grave: *Tell those limey*

458

bastards to go fuck themselves. That was what his father would do, say. But he had had the physique and endurance of a Hercules. He had marched and fought through two Canadian winters. Scraps of the journal he had published in the 1760s drifted through the congressman's mind: *With the temperature 20 below zero every man knew that even a bullet in the arm or leg meant death unless the limb was immediately amputated. The Indians and French came at us through the snow like howling ghosts.* A hero. But he was dead. What did voices from the grave matter to the living?

Wait. Another voice. General Washington: *This army is America's only protection from defeat and disgrace.* He knew. He had soldiered with the British, like Malcolm Stapleton. He knew their peculiar capacity for arrogance; no different, perhaps, from other warrior nations. The price of defeat was disgrace, humiliation, no matter where or when it happened. Did Hugh Stapleton want that for his country, his sons?

Another voice swirled out of the darkness. With it came the memory of his wife's weary country face, glaring at him across the dining-room table at Great Rock Farm: *If you care about your country, your sons, you should be urging them to resist, resist to the last bullet.*

His country? He had never had much faith in the shaky confederation called the United States, mingling hotheaded Southerners, pacifist Philadelphia Quakers, liberal New Yorkers, and self-righteous Yankees. He had never given much thought to the meaning of the word "American." He wore it as a label, using it to his advantage in London, where it

459

often charmed curious English ladies, abandoning it the moment it seemed inconvenient, when the word inspired unpleasant associations, such as crude provincialism.

His sons? He barely knew them, after three years in England and the West Indies, another year and a half in Philadelphia. Hugh Stapleton remembered with a twist of forlorn regret his resolution to improve on his father's performance. Malcolm Stapleton had been away, fighting in Canada, in Cuba, for years at a time during Hugh's boyhood. He had come home to stranger sons.

If you care about your country, your sons, his wife had said. She suspected the truth. He did not care about either of them very much. He had been ready to abandon both for Flora Kuyper. Now, in this icy coffin in which his indifference had cast him, Hugh Stapleton tried to find some residue, some inheritance of his father's, his wife's caring, beneath his businessman's philosophy of maximizing profits and cutting losses, beneath his city cynicism and sophistication.

What had he cared about in his life, beyond "improving some moneys"? Beautiful furniture, silver, good food, fine wine. None of them traveled to this freezing hell. Friendship? But it was almost always the friendship of the good fellow. Fellowship did not provide much warmth in the dungeon of the Provost. What had he *loved*?

Another face: framed by hair as yellow as a fresh-cut rose, skin as smooth, glowing as one of Gainsborough's duchesses. Hannah's face, Hannah's voice whispering on their wedding night: *Husband, I love thee so*. She had been so beautiful! How could he have forgotten the joy, the ardor, of those first years of his marriage? How had three years of piling up money, of visits to expensive whores in Amsterdam, the West Indies, so eroded his memory? Was it because Hugh Stapleton, collector of beautiful things, had simply seen Hannah as one more trophy, one more tribute to his impeccable taste? Yes, there was no question that his egotism had helped him lose the real value, the real meaning, of those years. Now, stripped of his pride, his possessions, that memory became the one thing that gave him the strength to endure his agony.

Although they would never know it, he would prove to himself that he cared about the sons created by that love. He would accept this punishment as just, as something he deserved, for betraying that love. Through that love he would somehow manage to care about his country, that dubious proposition called the United States. He would summon caring for his sons' sake, for Hannah's sake.

More days—or were they hours?—passed. A cup of water, a crust of bread in the muck, then Cunningham's taunt: "Are you ready to sign, rebel?" Once, he did not answer. Cunningham charged into the cell and kicked him in the stomach. "I asked you a question, rebel," he shouted.

"No," Hugh Stapleton gasped.

His breathing was labored now. The cold had filled his lungs with mucus. Jolts of icy pain ran along his bones, gnawed the joints of his fingers, shoulders, knees. He could no longer bend his legs or move his fingers. Most of the time he was too weak to stand. He found it difficult to swallow, his throat was so raw. He ignored the bread and water shoved at him by

461

the indifferent guards. His mind began to wander. He thought he was in London, Philadelphia. He excoriated the King. He addressed Congress, weeping, begging their forgiveness. When he awoke from these semi-nightmares, he forced himself to remember New York, Hannah in her green paduasoy gown at the end of the dining-room table, with the smiling faces of friends between them.

Gradually the memory changed to the other face, his tired country wife at the end of the dining-room table in Great Rock Farm. He loved both faces. Now he understood what Paul meant about living in terror. Now he understood what British gentlemen were prepared to do to win this war. *"You limey bastards can go fuck yourselves,"* he roared. *"Do you hear me? Go fuck yourselves."*

No one answered. He was buried alive down here. In Morristown, in Philadelphia, they were saying, *Good riddance to the whoremaster.* Samuel Chase and those other hypocrites were denouncing him as a traitor. Washington was shaking his head in his mournful, disappointed way. Hannah, his sons, were hanging their heads, weeping. If there were some way of telling them, he could accept this miserable death. "Oh, God," Hugh Stapleton whispered, praying for the first time in decades, "tell them somehow. Let them find out how I died, why."

Plop, the bread, *splash,* the water. "Ready to sign, rebel?"

"No," the congressman croaked.

Much, much later, the cell door opened again. Hugh Stapleton raised his head to answer the usual question. He did not want another kick in the stomach. A woman was standing in the doorway, her bonnet and skirt outlined against the dim lantern light. "Oh, my God," Hannah said.

He was sure it was one of those hallucinations men have on the edge of death. God was taunting him, sending him a vision of the one person in the world he wanted to see.

"Oh, Hugh. Husband," Hannah said, dropping to her knees in the muck. She hugged his slimy, bearded face to her breast.

It was the touch, the reality, of a genuine woman. "Is it—you?"

"Yes."

"How did you—get here? Is the war over?"

"No. But it shall be over for some people if you're not treated better. I'll blow out their brains!"

She began berating Provost Marshal Cunningham, who stood outside the cell. "How can you treat any human being this way, much less a member of the American Congress? I demand that you remove my husband from this—this sewer immediately."

"He shan't be moved without an order from my superiors, madam," Cunningham growled. "He's been treated no worse than other disobedient, stiff-necked rebels."

"In that case I weep for all your prisoners, sir," Hannah said.

"If—If I'm dead when you come back," Hugh Stapleton whispered, "tell the boys, Washington, I—I wouldn't sign anything. I never signed anything."

"You won't die," Hannah said, holding him against her again, this time with ferocity. "You *won't* die."

The door clanged shut; the cold and darkness engulfed the congressman again. He began to doubt the visit. He was still dying. His breath still bubbled in his chest. It had been a wish after all, the realistic details embroidered by his failing brain. Then he believed it again. *I won't die*, he told himself. *I won't die*. He crawled around in the muck until he found a piece of bread. He was too weak to chew it. The crust stuck in his throat and he almost choked before he spat it out.

Hours, or days, later, the cell door opened. Hannah knelt beside him again. By this time Hugh Stapleton was too weak to raise his head. He heard Hannah ordering someone to be careful. Hands lifted him onto a stretcher and carried him up the stairs. In a cell on an upper floor of the prison, he was lifted onto a bed, and warm blankets were drawn over him. A half-hour later, Richard Bayley, the Stapletons' family doctor before the war, arrived to examine him. Bayley had stayed in New York, a loyalist. But he was a humane man. "It's enough to make me change my allegiance," he muttered as he peered down Hugh Stapleton's raw throat, then checked his laboring pulse.

Two orderlies from the British hospital stripped off the congressman's filthy clothes, shaved and bathed him, and put him into a flannel nightgown. Hot flannel soaked in oil of wintergreen was wrapped around his swollen joints. Dr. Bayley ordered braziers of charcoal placed at the head and foot of the prisoner's bed. For the first few days he permitted only hot beef or chicken broth in the congressman's starved stomach.

Those first days were disconnected and delirious. Hannah was often there, urging him to take more broth. She told him a story about fighting British partisans in the old farmhouse. Paul was dead, a hero. He had been an American spy. Several times he asked her if it was true, or had he dreamed it? She said it was true. On the fifth night Congressman Stapleton had a dream. He was laboring through deep snow in the north woods beside his father. Some enemy was pursuing them. The old man became exhausted. "This is as far as I can go," he said. "You go on." He sank down behind a tree and raised his huge double-barreled gun to his shoulder, waiting for the enemy. Hugh swayed there, tormented. Shouldn't he stay and fight? he wondered. "Go *on*," Malcolm Stapleton roared, glaring over his shoulder at him. Hugh floundered through the trees. When he looked back, he could no longer see the old man.

In a week the congressman was sitting up in bed, listening to Hannah tell how she had gone straight from her first visit to the prison to the residence of the royal governor, General James Robertson. He had been stationed in New York for many years before the war and had several times been a guest at their dinner table. "I remembered you considered him an egregious ass in those days," she said. "Dr. Bayley assured me he's a bigger fool than ever, still fancying himself the very model of a modern courtier at the age of sixty-nine."

The congressman nodded, enjoying every word. He remembered Robertson well—a pompous, elongated, spindle-shanked character, who looked more like a minister or a college professor than a soldier.

"I stormed into his parlor," Hannah continued, "where he was tête-à-tête with two girls young enough to be his granddaughters! When he heard my story, he denied everything. He summoned General Pattison, head of the military police, and the two of them denied even knowing you were a prisoner. I told them their performance was worthy of the Drury Lane, and threatened to notify General Washington of your condition. There would soon be several captured British colonels wearing irons and living on bread and water in our prison camps."

"Washington promised you that?"

Hannah nodded. "He never deserted you for a moment once he learned from Mrs. Kuyper that you hadn't gone willingly with the British."

The mention of Mrs. Kuyper made the congressman uneasy. "A remarkable man, Washington," he said.

"Yes," Hannah said. "His mind is seldom clouded by sentiment. He urged me to come here for two reasons. First, a call for peace from a congressman could have disastrous consequences. Second, there are only a handful of merchants with as much hard money as you can contribute to the bank Robert Morris is forming, to fund the army."

Hannah's voice was as cool and unsentimental as Washington's mind.

"Even for those reasons I'm sure it wasn't easy for you to come," the congressman said.

"It wasn't," Hannah said. "It became even more difficult when General Robertson said there was a letter he could show me that you had written to Mrs. Kuyper. Major Beckford wanted to publish it, but Robertson has been delaying permission in the hope that you can still be persuaded to call for a reconciliation—or at the very least abandon the rebellion."

"Say what you feel about Mrs. Kuyper," the congressman said, studying his still-swollen fingers. "I deserve every word."

"I'll say nothing now," Hannah said. "I hope we'll have years together to understand what happened between us. Let's concentrate on getting you out of this place."

"How?" Hugh Stapleton said. "It's obviously going to be a long contest of wills."

"Dr. Bayley says you won't survive a long contest. You need exercise, fresh air."

"You can put every cent I have in Holland into Morris's bank now. I'll give you power of attorney."

"Don't—"

She placed her hand over his mouth. He saw tears in her eyes. "My feelings are so complicated—I don't know whether to—to kiss you—or damn you—or cry."

"I love you," he said. "That's one of the few things I discovered downstairs."

Hannah dried her eyes and sat down beside him on the bed so she could speak in a confidential voice. "George Washington told me he was sending one of his most dependable spies into the city with orders to help you escape. He declined to tell me his name. He said the motto for success in espionage was as much secrecy as humanly possible. He said I—or you—would recognize the fellow by a token—a miniature of George the Third—which he'd pretend to give you to encourage you to turn your coat."

Footsteps on the stairs. Provost Marshal Cunningham's growling voice: "I tell you, Parson, it's the wrong policy. Another day in the dungeon and the bastard would have signed anything we put in front of him. This mollycoddling will get us nowhere."

Another voice, in the corridor now: "I disagree, Provost Marshal, and I'm not alone. Remember, the

Bible tells us a soft answer turneth away wrath. Kindness, a reminder of His Majesty's benevolence, is the best way to melt a rebel's hard heart. It was what changed my allegiance."

"Shit," rumbled Cunningham. "Your allegiance was changed by a few hundred golden guineas. Everyone knows that, Parson."

The cell door swung open and there stood the Reverend Caleb Chandler, the same supercilious smile on his long Yankee face. "What the hell do you want, you damned hypocrite?" Hugh Stapleton said.

"Mrs. Stapleton, how do you do," Chandler said, doffing his frayed tricorn hat. "All the Americans in New York admire the courage with which you procured better treatment for the congressman."

"I forbid my wife even to speak to you," Hugh Stapleton said.

"What is the purpose of your visit, sir?" Hannah said, coolly ignoring her husband's show of authority.

"I'm here, madam, to bring you whatever help religion may offer to rescue the congressman from his unfortunate situation. Surely a merciful God abhors war. So does a merciful king. Both beings urge Mr. Stapleton to issue a call for peace, to reconcile our divided country."

"If I were in better health, sir, I'd get up from this bed and kick you out of here," Stapleton said.

In the doorway, Provost Marshal Cunningham shook his head in disgust. "You're wasting your time and mine, Parson."

"Give me a half-hour alone with them. I promise you that you'll be amazed by their change of heart."

Cunningham grunted contemptuously and slammed the cell door. "This is outrageous," Hugh Stapleton fumed. "Who else but a Yankee would have the gall—"

Caleb Chandler took a gold case from his pocket. In the same unctuous voice, loud enough for Provost Marshal Cunningham to hear as he descended the stairs, Chandler said, "I've dipped into my dwindling funds to purchase this gift for you. A lovely portrait of His Majesty, painted by your late brother in happier days. Major Beckford sold it shortly before he was transferred to Canada."

Caleb Chandler opened the gold case. Hugh Stapleton stared in bewilderment from the familiar image of royalty to the Yankee face above it. The supercilious smile had vanished. It had been replaced by a bitter grin.

"It's beautiful," Hannah exclaimed. "You're so kind, Mr. Chandler."

"Yes," Congressman Stapleton murmured. "So kind."

thirty

Caleb Chandler stalked down Broadway through the slush and mud of early April. It was twilight. The ruined hulk of Trinity Church loomed on his right, surrounded by charred foundations of other buildings destroyed in the fire of 1776.

At Bowling Green, he turned down Marketfield Street. "Good evening, sir," called a female voice from a doorway. "Would you like to come home with me?"

"No, thank you," he said.

Since the end of the Great Cold, a man could not walk a block without getting one of these invitations. The women were all Americans, daughters of penniless loyalists stranded in New York by the endless war. As usual, the encounter reminded Caleb of Flora Kuyper. She was only a few blocks away in the

Holy Ground, practicing the same profession in a style and for a price that was beyond the reach of these pathetic streetwalkers.

"Good evening, sir. A shilling for an hour, two for a night," whispered another voice from another doorway.

"No, thank you," Caleb said, and kept walking.

"My mother needs the money, sir."

Caleb kept walking. There was nothing he could do to help these women. There was nothing he could do to stop the way the machinery of war devoured individual lives. There was nothing he could do to change the way the world worked. It made no sense from the perspective of the tormented present. He could only hope that in a hundred or a thousand years, others would look back on the brutality and cruelty and stupidity, and see a thread of purpose in it all.

At the moment, he was on his way to risk his life to save a man he disliked while the woman he loved destroyed herself. In spite of this absurdity, a kind of exultance bounded in his chest. He was sure he could extract Congressman Stapleton from the Provost Prison. He was equally certain he could save Flora Kuyper. Not for a long time had that demoralizing voice whispered *fool* in the corner of his mind. Caleb Chandler the spy had proven that he was cool enough, steady enough, to outwit Walter Beckford and the rest of the officers of the British garrison in New York.

Day after day he had lived on the edge of extinction, never knowing when one of agent Twenty-six's Morristown network might arrive in New York with the truth about him. Most of the time he enjoyed the danger; it made him feel more alive, more powerful, than the pious, prating chaplain Caleb Chandler had ever felt.

For almost a month now, Caleb had sat at the bar in the Queen's Head Tavern, which was run by a husky West Indian mulatto named Black Sam Francis, one of Washington's most trusted spies. Caleb cadged drinks from Brigadier Samuel Birch and other cavalry officers, and applauded their profane condemnations of Major Walter Beckford.

Playing the unctuous toady, Caleb had switched his allegiance from the discredited intelligence director to Birch and his cavalrymen. They could not forgive Beckford for making them look foolish and—even more heinous to cavalrymen—disabling half their horses. The brigadier had demanded a court-martial. Outraged, Lieutenant Colonel John Graves Simcoe wanted both Birch and Beckford court-martialed. Lieutenant General Knyphausen had resolved the squabble by transferring Beckford to Canada.

That left the cavalrymen with nothing to discuss but the latest favorite of the Holy Ground, Flora Kuyper. She had chosen for her residence a Negro house run by a black woman who called herself Madam Plaisir. Madam made the amorous quadroon her star attraction and set a price of ten guineas for a night. The customers were more than satisfied. Each was the center of attention at the Queen's Head the following night as he told his friends the remarkable things Flora was ready to do after a few drinks and a little laudanum. Caleb hung on the fringe of listeners, growing more and more enraged.

Nothing could be done about Flora until Congressman Stapleton was strong enough to walk out of the Provost. Those were Benjamin Stallworth's orders. For two weeks after Caleb displayed the token, the Jerseyman was barely able to hobble on his swollen ankles and knees. Two days ago, Stapleton had walked across his cell with a reasonably normal stride. That night, Caleb had told Black Sam Francis to notify Stallworth. Before dawn, a messenger was across the no-longer-frozen Hudson with the word that the plan was in motion.

Caleb made no secret of his visits to Stapleton. He announced each one at the bar of the Queen's Head. He said he had helped to capture Stapleton and was vexed at Beckford's clumsy failure to persuade him to change sides. Caleb was soon reporting that the congressman was becoming much more amenable. He described him clutching the miniature of George III and almost weeping with regret for rebelling against such a good king. What was needed now, Caleb told all and sundry, was a visit from a distinguished officer, who could convince the wavering politician that genuine reconciliation was possible—but if it were refused, the consequences for America would be terrible.

Who was better qualified to communicate such a message than Brigadier Samuel Birch, commander of the only undefeated arm of His Majesty's royal army? Caleb poured this suggestion into the ear of the brigadier himself. Birch found his cringing, fawning manner amusing. He was also inclined to look on the turncoat chaplain with a certain superstitious fondness. As Caleb frequently reminded him, he had saved Birch's life. Riding at the head of the column, the brigadier would have gotten the first blast of those cannon that had been waiting in the woods outside Morristown on that rainy night a month ago.

So the brigadier, urged by his aide, Captain Arthur Quimby, to whom Caleb had retailed the proposition at even greater length, had agreed to join Caleb for a late-night supper in Congressman Stapleton's cell.

At the Queen's Head, the brigadier was entertaining a sizable audience with the story of his visit to Flora Kuyper. It was now a week old, but he could not stop talking about it. "'Madam,' I asked her as we fucked away, 'is there anything you won't do?' 'Yes,' she replied, 'but you have to keep *asking* to find out what it is.' I didn't find out, so I'm down for another ten guineas tomorrow night."

"Perhaps she'll draw the line when you wear your spurs, sir," crowed Arthur Quimby.

"Brigadier," Caleb said, "our appointment with the congressman. Have you forgotten?"

He had both heard and not heard those obscenities. They were talking about Flora but he told himself it was not the woman he loved. At the same time, he knew it was the woman he loved. But Caleb now believed in his personal, purely human power to restore, heal, forgive, without help from God or anyone else. He was sure he could outwit Satan himself, if that shadowy figure had anything to do with this nightmare.

By the time Caleb got the brigadier out of the Queens Head and into a hackney coach, Birch was somewhat drunk. This was all to the good and part of the plan. Brigadier Birch got drunk every night. As the coach lumbered across the city to the Provost he threw a convivial arm around Caleb's shoulders.

"Have you tried fabulous Flora, Parson?"

"Too expensive for me."

"She's worth every penny."

"I'm sure she is. But we poor Americans must settle for humbler satisfactions."

"God damn it, Chandler, don't you loyalist buggers ever stop sounding the poor mouth?"

"Perhaps it's simply a wish to remind gentlemen like yourself, who have influence with government, of our sacrifices for His Majesty."

"Ah, fuck off, Chandler. I told you I'd get you a living from my cousin the bishop, didn't I?"

"I'm deeply grateful for it. A chance to preach the gospel to loyal subjects for the rest of my life is all I wish. In the meantime I must survive. I hope you'll recommend me to whoever has charge of the secret-service fund now if we succeed in getting a signed statement from Congressman Stapleton."

"Nobody's in charge of intelligence as far as I know. Not that it matters. The bloody business just wastes money on buggers like Beckford's asshole friend Coleman. I knew that prick in London. He'd stick it into anything, male or female, animal, vegetable, or mineral."

"But a loyal subject. A pity the Americans hanged him."

"Good riddance, I say. I wish we could have hanged Beckford, too. If there's anything lower than a whore, it's a spy. I'm in favor of hanging all of them instead of *turning* them, the way Beckford claimed to do. I bet I know how the bugger turned them and why."

The coach stopped. They were in front of the dark stone bulk of the Provost. The East River rushed to the sea a few hundred feet away, white chunks of ice whirling on its dark surface.

"Now, what am I supposed to say to this rebel

bastard?" Birch said as the guard unlocked the gate and saluted the brigadier.

"Reconciliation, how much all the officers want it. On fair and equitable terms. And the growing impatience, the hunger for vengeance, among the troops."

"That's true enough," Birch said.

In Hugh Stapleton's cell a waiter from the Queen's Head Tavern had already laid out their dinner. There were hot meat pies and a sea bass and a haunch of that symbol of English hospitality, roast beef. The congressman rose to greet them with a warm smile. "I was wondering to whom I owed this feast," he said as Caleb introduced Brigadier Birch.

"When I heard from the Reverend Chandler how Major Beckford had mistreated you, Congressman, my breast swelled with indignation and shame that such a thing could be done to an American gentleman," Brigadier Birch said. "I was doubly mortified when Chandler told me that some people thought I was associated in your abuse. I resolved to prove it otherwise—and show you that generosity is the hallmark of Britain's attitude toward America."

"I'm deeply grateful," Stapleton said.

"Too bad Mrs. Stapleton couldn't join us," Caleb said.

"Yes. She sends her regrets. She had to hurry home to nurse our younger son through the measles."

In the center of the improvised table were a half-dozen bottles of claret and port. Caleb played the jovial majordomo, pouring claret into Birch's glass at twice the rate he served himself and Stapleton.

"Chandler tells me he's managed to change your mind somewhat, Mr. Stapleton," Birch said as he chomped on veal pie.

"He's revived some of my respect for old England."

"Then I'm here to revive your affection, sir," Birch said, raising his glass and draining it. Caleb promptly refilled it.

"I wouldn't be surprised if we share some London friends," Stapleton said.

Birch began mentioning names of politicians and officers. Stapleton managed to claim a knowledge of about half.

"Not one, not one, I assure you, sir, bears any *serious* enmity to America," Birch said. "Not one who wouldn't open his purse to the man who helped end this quarrel."

"Ah, you remind me of British generosity, sir," Stapleton said. "I recall the time I was in London and unfortunately lost every cent gambling at Boodles. Not for a moment did I have to worry about becoming a pauper. My British friends rushed to supply me with money."

"And not a cent of interest charged, I'll wager," Birch said.

"Of course not," Stapleton said.

"To English generosity," Caleb said, raising his glass.

By the time they reached the dessert—a brimming bowl of syllabub—Brigadier Birch had drunk enough wine to stop noticing when his glass was being filled or from which bottle. This permitted Caleb to select his port from a bottle marked by a dab of red ink on the label; it had in it a mixture of laudanum and other narcotics guaranteed to immobilize the brigadier.

"Reconciliation," Birch said, clutching the table. "Certainly—every gentleman. But the troops. Ver' impatient, sir. Cut a swath if we don't restrain'm. Believe me, don't let resentment of Beckford—goddamn buggering—say, Chandler, that wine is the damnedest—"

The brigadier's head crashed onto the table. Quickly, Caleb and Hugh Stapleton hoisted him onto the cell's cot and threw a blanket over him. From beneath the cot the congressman pulled an exact duplicate of the brigadier's uniform, cut to his larger physique by another Washington spy, the New York tailor Hercules Mulligan. The congressman added a wig and a tricorn hat trimmed with silver lace, and posed for a moment. Caleb nodded.

He draped Stapleton's arm around his shoulder and they practiced walking together. Stapleton let his knees buckle, making him look as if he were the same height as Birch.

"Remember, you're drunk," Caleb said.

Caleb kicked the door and roared, "Sergeant of the guard. Turn out."

The sergeant came running and hastily opened the door. "Our prisoner's drunk himself to bed," Caleb said. "The brigadier's in the same condition. Leave these dishes and silver here until tomorrow. If there's as much as a spoon missing, you'll pay for it."

"Yes, sir," the sergeant said as Caleb lurched past him, Stapleton-Birch clinging to his shoulder.

"Here's for your trouble," Caleb said, and thrust a guinea into the soldier's hand.

"Many thanks, sir. I'll run ahead and make sure the carriage is ready."

Caleb and Stapleton-Birch reeled down the prison stairs singing a royal army song, "Britons Strike Home." At the gate they could hear the sergeant saying, "Driver, the brigadier's comin'. Look lively."

"The British Coffee House," Caleb called as they climbed into the carriage.

They continued their singing until the carriage bounced onto Broadway. There Caleb ordered the driver to turn north. "There's the sweetest little bit of American fluff out on the Bloomingdale Road that I want you to meet, Brigadier," he said loud enough for the coachman to hear them.

"I'm just in the mood for it," bellowed Stapleton-Birch.

They sloshed through the mud of this country road for a half-hour. When they began to ascend Harlem Heights, Caleb called to the coachman to stop. "We must have missed the house in the dark," he said, climbing up on the box. He put a pistol to the driver's head and added, "Don't make a sound, my friend, and you won't get hurt."

Stapleton drove the carriage into a nearby field and helped Caleb bind and gag the coachman. They left him sitting upright in the passenger compartment. Caleb slipped a guinea into his pocket—twice as much money as he would have earned from an ordinary night's work.

They labored through fields and over fences to the Hudson shore. The congressman found the walk exhausting. Twice he had to sit down on a rock to regain his strength. Peering into the black night on the river, they could see nothing but floes of ice drifting past them. At last they heard the faint lap of oars, the occasional *chunk* of a floe against a hull. A whaleboat with a half-dozen oarsmen emerged from the darkness. From its prow, Major Benjamin Stallworth growled, "Mercury."

"Mars," Caleb replied.

Caleb helped the congressman into the boat, but he did not follow him. He stood there for a moment, wondering how he could resist it. One step and he would be on his way back to Morristown, where George Washton would shake his hand and call him a patriot. The same single step and he would be chaplain of the 2nd Connecticut Brigade again, watching men being lashed five hundred times for robbing a henhouse, kneeling beside dying youngsters in the hospital, trying to give them faith when he had none. Maybe that was why he was able to resist taking the step. But the other reason was there, too. Flora's voice, between a chime and a sigh, singing *"Plaire à celui que j'aime."* He needed her to help him remember with a certain affection—perhaps even with love—that other man, the fool who believed in moral meanings and spiritual purpose. Besides, he had promised Flora that he would rescue her. He needed to keep that promise to sustain the man he had become, the spy with the steady nerves who enjoyed danger.

"Hurry up, Chandler," Benjamin Stallworth snapped. "They have sentries patrolling this shore."

"I'm going back for Flora Kuyper."

"Don't be an idiot, Chandler."

"What do you care? You've got the congressman."

"She hates you, Chandler. She'll hang you."

"No, she won't."

Stallworth made a strangling sound. Caleb could not see his face, but it was easy to imagine his expression. "I'll come back for you," the major said. "I'll wait until an hour before dawn."

"God bless you, Stallworth," Caleb said in the mocking tone that had become a code between them.

"You're the one who needs His blessing, you damned fool."

thirty-one

At Madame Plaisir's, Flora put one, two, three, four, five drops of laudanum in the glass of wine and drank it all down. Would Caleb come tonight? she wondered. She wanted to keep her nerves very calm and steady so she would be ready for him. She was sure that he would come eventually. His stupid New England conscience would force him to keep his promise. Then she would keep hers. She would inform the British officer who happened to be enjoying her when Caleb appeared that this long-nosed creature was an American spy and should be arrested and hanged without delay.

"I say," called the infantry captain who stood beside her bed in his shirt, "what the devil are you drinking there?"

"Something to make me happy," Flora said. "So I can make you happy."

"Well, let's get on with it," the captain said. "Ten guineas is a deuced lot of money."

She took off her night robe and lay down beside him in the bed and let him get on with it. She did not think about what he was doing to her. Only when he kissed her did his foul breath penetrate the glaze of laudanum that protected her. Most of the time the positions that he ordered her to assume did not require her to touch his lips.

"Not very bloody enthusiastic, are you?" the captain said. His teeth were yellow. Without his wig he was almost bald.

"You were wonderful," she said.

Downstairs a fiddle began scraping. Madam Plaisir provided other amusements for her customers besides this fundamental entertainment. "Let's go down for a drink and a bit of a dance," the captain said, pulling on his buff breeches. "It might wake you up."

Flora smiled dreamily and let him help her into her night robe. Down the stairs they went to the parlor, where a half-dozen black, brown, and tan girls and their customers were doing a drunken gavotte. The girls' night robes were tied loosely at the waist; they might as well have been dancing naked. Madam Plaisir, enormously fat and as black as Flora's grandmother, sat in a corner keeping time with her fan. Her red wig was tipped over her right ear. It was well past midnight and Madam, like everyone else, was drunk.

In New Orleans the ghost of Flora was at a different dance, although many of the dancers were the same color. It was a splendid affair, in the ballroom on Condé Street, and she was wearing the white silk gown with ruchings of intricate lace that her mother had sewed for her. Handsome creoles waited breathlessly for an opportunity to put their arms around her while her mother watched sternly from the balcony.

The front door bell jangled. Madam Plaisir hurried to answer it. A late customer. There would be an argument when Madam Plaisir insisted one of the girls had to take him. Madam was proud of her motto: no one is ever turned away. Most of the girls complained when they had to take more than five men a night. From the start Flora had said her motto was the more, the better. But Madam Plaisir had decided they could both make more money if she limited herself to one a night for the first few months. When the wealthier British officers got tired of her, she could begin to take as many customers as she wanted.

"That's her," Madam Plaisir said above the music. "But all you can do is talk. She's taken for the night. Flora, come here for a minute."

Flora turned, leaving the infantry captain drunkenly gavotting by himself. Caleb stood in the parlor doorway. His expression was so sad, so tormented, she wondered if she had already betrayed him. Had she met him yesterday and called the watch? Were the watchmen outside now, leading him to the place of execution? Was that why he had stopped? So she could tell him once more how much she hated him?

He said nothing. He looked at her as if she were the one who was being executed. Grief, mourning, were stamped on his face. Maybe she was dead. Maybe Beckford had killed her for betraying William. Maybe this evil dream was hell.

"Go upstairs and put your clothes on," Caleb said. "You're not going to stay here another night."

Caleb turned to the startled dancers. "Ladies and gentlemen, forgive this intrusion by a man of God. I'm a minister, concerned with the salvation of this woman's soul. She persuaded me to declare my loyalty to the King. But through a misunderstanding, we quarreled and she thought I no longer cared about her. That's why—"

"Come back in the morning, Parson," the infantry captain said. "I paid ten guineas for her. She's mine for the night."

"I can't come back in the morning. I'm sailing for London on the mail packet. I want to take her with me."

Sailing for London. The lying words awakened memories of William Coleman, the original liar. "He's an American spy," Flora said. "Arrest him and hang him."

"My dear girl is drunk," Caleb said, taking her hand. "I'll be happy to give you my note for ten guineas. I'll remit it the moment I get to London. His Majesty has promised me a most generous reward for some information I brought with me when I deserted the American army. I saved four hundred dragoons from slaughter. Brigadier Birch will be happy to attest to what I'm saying. In fact, he's promised to stand for any debts I contract before I sail—"

"He's a liar, he's a spy," Flora screamed. "He wants to take me back to the Americans."

The infantry captain and several other officers began moving toward them. "I don't like the smell of you, Parson," the captain said. "I think we'll call the

486

watch and see if this drunken bitch is telling the truth. Meanwhile, I'll get my ten guineas' worth."

The captain grabbed Flora's arm and tried to drag her toward him. Suddenly there was a pistol in Caleb's hand. It boomed and the captain sprawled on the floor, blood gushing from his chest.

"Murder!" Madam Plaisir screamed, and Caleb dragged Flora into the street. "Now do you believe me?" he shouted in her face. "There's a boat waiting. Come, please."

He dragged her toward a carriage. "No," she cried. "Never." She kicked at him and slashed his face with her nails. "I love you," Caleb said. "Please."

"Murder!" screamed Madam Plaisir in the doorway of the house. Two officers squeezed past her and rushed at Caleb. He drew another pistol and shot one of them. He clubbed the other man in the face with the empty gun and carried Flora as far as the carriage. Men ran toward them from other houses. The shrill whistle of the city watch cut the night. "He's a spy," Flora screamed.

Caleb tried to lift Flora into the carriage. He had her in his arms when a shot rang out, then a second and a third. Flora felt the bullets thud into his back. "Oh—God," Caleb groaned.

He stumbled away from her. "Gentlemen, I surrender," he said. "Please don't hurt this lady."

Two more pistols crashed. The bullets flung Caleb on his back in the mud. Flora clung to the carriage, staring dazedly at him while Madam Plaisir screamed, "Shoot him again, the goddamn spy."

The carriage was commandeered to rush the infantry captain and the other wounded officers to the army hospital. The watchmen took a statement from

Madam Plaisir. The rest of the crowd returned to the other houses in the Holy Ground to resume their pleasures. Flora knelt beside Caleb and touched his dead face. "I'm sorry," she whispered.

Madam Plaisir loomed over her. "What the hell you doin' there in the mud? You gonna catch your death. I ain't wastin' my time and money nursin' sick whores. Come on, now. Let's go back to work."

She pulled Flora to her feet and led her into the house. "A little laudanum and you'll be good as new," Madam Plaisir said. "You got Brigadier Birch comin' tomorrow night. Repeat business. That's important, Flora."

"Yes," Flora said.

She looked over her shoulder at Caleb lying in the mud. For a moment she wanted to weep. But Madam Plaisir was right. A few drops of laudanum and she would feel as good as new.

——————— *thirty-two* ———————

Hugh Stapleton spent the night dozing in a carriage on the New Jersey side of the Hudson. He awoke in the dawn as Major Benjamin Stallworth pulled open the door and dropped into the seat opposite him. The major's face was a strange combination of grief and rage. "They killed him," he said. "The goddamn whore called for the watch and they killed him."

"I—I wish I'd had a chance to thank him," Stapleton said.

Stallworth glared at him. For a moment the congressman thought he was going to say something insulting. Instead the major drew his cloak around him and said nothing for the next two hours as the coach jolted and rocked along the road to Morristown.

Beyond Hackensack, the noon sun proclaimed a

beautiful April day. Stallworth glared at the greening pastures and orchards as if he somehow disapproved of them. "Land of milk and honey," he said.

"I beg your pardon," Congressman Stapleton said.

"That's what a friend of mine called this country in the last letter he wrote to me."

"Was he killed in battle?"

Stallworth shook his head. "The British hanged him as a spy in '76."

They were silent for another mile. Stallworth continued to glare out the window at the bountiful landscape. Then he spoke again in the same snarling voice. "Why do bastards like you and me survive this business and the best—the best—die?"

"I'm afraid only God can answer that question," Congressman Stapleton said.

"It'll be the first thing I ask Him if we ever meet," Stallworth said.

They rode on toward Morristown to renew the struggle for that scarifying prize, victory.

Afterword

This book was written under a grant from the Principia Foundation. It continues a series of personal histories drawn from the diaries, journals, letters, and memoirs of the Stapleton family. The author wishes to thank James Kilpatrick, director of the foundation, for his support and encouragement.

After the war Hugh Stapleton served two terms as a senator from New Jersey. He continued to flourish as a merchant, becoming one of the pioneers in the China trade. Hannah Stapleton had two more sons by her husband. She died a month after celebrating their fiftieth wedding anniversary, in 1819.

Among the other principals, George Washington's later life needs no summary. Colonel John Graves Simcoe, whose published journal corroborates the plot to kidnap Washington, became governor of Upper Canada, where he did his best to make life miserable for Walter Beckford. Resigning his army commission, Beckford drifted from Canada to the West Indies in minor civil service jobs obtained for him by his mother's family. He died of yellow fever in Jamaica in 1790. Benjamin Stallworth became a congressman from Connecticut and in his old age wrote a book arguing that American independence was won through the intervention of divine providence. Brigadier Birch died in London, a full general. Repeated searches of New York newspapers, police records, and burial reports failed to produce any mention of Flora Kuyper.

Best Of Bestsellers
from WARNER BOOKS

___**PALOVERDE**   *(A30-345, $3.95)*
   by Jacqueline Briskin   *(In Canada*
                                    30-670, $4.95)

The love story of Amelie—the sensitive, ardent, young girl whose uncompromising code of honor leads her to choices that will reverberate for generations, plus the chronicle of a unique city, Los Angeles, wrestling with the power of railroads, discovery of oil, and growing into the fabulous capital of filmdom, makes this one of the most talked-about novels of the year.

___**SCRUPLES**
   by Judith Krantz   *(A30-531, $3.95)*

The ultimate romance! The spellbinding story of the rise of a fascinating woman from fat, unhappy "poor relative" of an aristocratic Boston family to a unique position among the super-beautiful and super-rich, a woman who got everything she wanted—fame, wealth, power and love.

ESPECIALLY FOR YOU
FROM WARNER

__THE OFFICERS' WIVES
by Thomas Fleming   *(A90-920, $3.95)*
This is a book you will never forget. It is about the U.S. Army, the huge unwieldy organism on which much of the nation's survival depends. It is about Americans trying to live personal lives, to cling to touchstones of faith and hope in the grip of the blind, blunderous history of the last 25 years. It is about marriage, the illusions and hopes that people bring to it, the struggle to maintain and renew commitment.

__ANGEL OF LIGHT
by Joyce Carol Oates   *(A30-189, $3.95)*
In this book, Joyce Carol Oates explores our political heritage and gives us a novel of mounting drama with all the import of Greek tragedy. It is a story of loyalty, betrayal, revenge, and finally, forgiveness. Oates weaves a strand of history throughout—the quest for justice against those in power begins with America's founding—but dominating the novel is the story of this highly placed family whose private lives are played out in a public arena.

__BELLEFLEUR
by Joyce Carol Oates   *(A30-732, $4.50)*
A swirl of fantasy, history, family feuds, love affairs and dreams, this is the saga of the Bellefleurs who live like feudal barons in a mythical place that might perhaps be the Adirondacks. A strange curse, it is said, hovers over the family, causing magical and horrible events to occur. Past and present appear to live side-by-side, as the fantastic reality of the Belle-fleurs unfolds.

__ADULT EDUCATION   *(A37-192, $6.95)*
by Annette Williams Jaffee   *(In Canada A37-352, $7.95)*
Adult Education introduces a writer of uncommon promise. This ruthlessly comic look at marriage is also a warm portrayal of friendship between two women. Rebecca Schuman, one of the freshest literary creations of recent years, achieves adulthood through her friendship with a beautiful Swedish woman who gives Becca a sense of her own worth and complexity.

BEST OF BESTSELLERS FROM *WARNER BOOKS*

___**THE CARDINAL SINS**
by Andrew Greeley (A90-913, $3.95)
From the humblest parish to the inner councils of the Vatican, Father Greeley reveals the hierarchy of the Catholic Church as it really is, and its priests as the men they really are.

THE CARDINAL SINS follows the lives of two Irish boys who grow up on the West Side of Chicago and enter the priesthood. We share their triumphs as well as their tragedies and temptations.

___**THY BROTHER'S WIFE** (A30-055, $3.95 U.S.A./
by Andrew Greeley A30-650, $4.95 Canada)
A gripping novel of political intrigue does with politics what THE CARDINAL SINS has done with the church. .

This is the story of a complex, clever Irish politician whose occasional affairs cause him much guilt and worry. The story weaves together the strands of power and ambition in an informed and clear-eyed insider's novel of contemporary politics.
DON'T MISS IT!!!

___**THE EXECUTIONER'S SONG** (A36-353, $4.95 U.S.A./
by Norman Mailer A30-646, $5.95 Canada)
The execution is what the public remembers: on January 17, 1977, a firing squad at Utah State Prison put an end to the life of convicted murderer Gary Gilmore. But by then the real story was over—the true tale of violence and fear, jealousy and loss, of a love that was defiant even in death. Winner of the Pulitzer Prize. "The big book no one but Mailer could have dared...an absolutely astonishing book."—Joan Didion, *New York Times Book Review*.